Eternal Empire

~The Final Court of Mystery Novel~

Book Fourteen

Sarah E. Burr

Other books by Sarah E. Burr

The Court of Mystery series

The Ducal Detective
A Feast Most Foul
A Voyage of Vengeance
A Summit in Shadow
Throne of Threats
Paradise Plagued
Burdened Bloodline
Sovereign Sieged
Crown of Chaos
Harrowed Heir
Ravaged Reign
Innocence Imprisoned
Ardent Ascension
Eternal Empire

More Cozy Mysteries by Sarah

Trending Topic Mysteries
Glenmyre Whim Mysteries
Book Blogger Mysteries

www.saraheburr.com

Welcome to the Realm of Virtues…

Centuries ago, priests of the Ancient Faith lorded over the continent, building their empires on fear and greed. Poverty and sickness ravaged the world, forcing a faction of rebels to rise and overthrow these tyrants preaching in the name of silent gods. The leaders of this movement, known in the annals of history as the Rebirth, proclaimed the realm would no longer answer to nameless demons and gods, but to the virtues of bravery, humility, kindness, and intelligence. Sealing their pact, these newly anointed leaders drank the dew of the fabled kingsleaf flower, marking them and their offspring forever as destined rulers of the realm with their royal eyes. Under their care and guidance, the dukedoms flourished for over five hundred years.

Yet, inequality and injustice persist. Malevolent foes plot their next move. It is up to Duchess Jacqueline Arienta Xavier and her loyal companions to root out the evils that haunt the Realm of Virtues.

The
Realm
of
Virtues
The
Brave Sea
Lysandeir
Cetachi
Pettraud
Kwatalar
Nensina
Crepsta
Saphire
The
Sea of
Intelligence
The
Sea of
Humility
Zaltor
Beautraud
Tandora
Hestes
Savant
The
Kind Sea
Isla
Delacqua

Chapter One

Duchess Jacqueline Arienta Xavier studied the slip of weathered parchment in her hand.

We aim to cross the southeast border within the coming day, where the herbalist was last seen. Will write when able. No sign of our shadow, either.

G

The woefully short message brought a frown to her lips. Yet, she knew it was for the best that their communications remain brief. Someone else might be reading them.

"Is that an update from George?" Perry's concern wiggled its way into her whirling mind.

Jax glanced across her desk, her amethyst gaze resting on her beloved husband. He sat at his own workspace, a fixture she'd recently installed in her study. Without it, Jax feared she would barely see the man, due to her busy schedule.

"It is." She rose from her chair and closed the distance between them. "Unfortunately, it's not very insightful."

Perry accepted the letter, his brow furrowing as he skimmed its meager contents. "Virtues, it's been over a fortnight since George last wrote. But it looks like he and Serafina have finally picked up the trail and found a safe way out of Savant." He kissed her palm before placing the note back into her hand. "No doubt thanks to your skillful intervention."

She twisted one of his dark, wild curls with her finger. "You give me too much credit, dearest. After learning about Savant's dire circumstances, it only made sense to try and cease the terrible power struggle afflicting the nation."

"Yet, no one else in the realm saw fit to take action." Perry held her gaze, his lavender eyes burning bright with pride.

Because they all look to Saphire. The thought both pleased and overwhelmed her. She glanced away from his handsome face, guilt beginning to claw at her throat. "I should have intervened sooner."

"If you had done that, there's a very real chance your assistance wouldn't have been as well-received." Perry stretched his toned arms above his head, stifling a yawn. "If things in Savant hadn't been so dire, the warring factions may have declined your offer to facilitate a meeting on neutral ground."

Jax abhorred the notion that innocent people had to suffer for such a realization to come to fruition. "Things are *still* dire." She wrung her hands as she considered the current circumstances. "Yes, there's been a ceasefire, but violence isn't the only enemy of peace. We have hunger and homelessness to combat as well. Vice-Admiral Hightower has already requested *five* additional caravans of supplies." She'd sent the trusted officer and her fastest horses to Savant with a humanitarian delegation. A demonstration of her commitment to helping the war-torn land.

Perry winced. "I'm going to have a hard time being chivalrous to our guests after hearing such news."

"Me too." Jax returned to her chair, her focus narrowing on the stack of papers before her. "Honestly, I'd rather neither lot take up the seat of power after all the pain they've inflicted these past weeks. But we must start somewhere." She selected the scribbled reply she'd received from Finral Lothaine, the leader of Heartsworn. His faction was the least funded, but it had support from more of Savant's citizens. Whereas Corentin Allard's group, Lion's Bane, had several wealthy benefactors yet less backing from the people.

When Duke Qylvard Savant's untimely death was announced little more than a month ago, his duchy had dissolved into civil war, with different citizen groups vying to claim his empty throne. Two strong contenders emerged after weeks of fighting. However, battles and riots continued to rage with no signs of ending.

Upon receiving word from her friend, George Solomon, that the citizens' rebellion had driven many Savantians to acts of desperation, Jax understood the time for waiting things out had passed. Alarming reports indicated that food and medical supplies were running dangerously low in the duchy, so she had written to Lothaine and Allard, offering her aid. In return, Jax asked that the men travel to a neutral meeting ground in her homeland of Saphire. *I wish for there to be a peaceful resolution between* Savantians *in this conflict,* she'd emphasized. *You have my word that your claims to its throne will be protected as long as civility is upheld during this summit. Should either of you break this agreement, rest assured, the might of Saphire and her allies will descend upon your nation, and order shall be restored.*

Jax didn't like threatening either man with claiming Savant for herself should they undermine the peace of this upcoming gathering. She may have been the ruler of many nations throughout the Realm of Virtues, but none had come to her through the use of force. Her ideals and leadership had earned her these thrones, and unless the Savantians offered the duchy to her, she had no desire to take it. Well, perhaps that wasn't entirely true. Jax *had* once dreamed of ruling all the nations within the Realm of Virtues, if only to ensure the democratic ideals her current lands practiced were implemented and upheld by all. Yet, with the recent ascension of new leaders who promoted these same values, other duchies were following in her footsteps, intent on bringing a better future to their citizens. She didn't have to bear the burden herself anymore.

The only nation in turmoil, still chained by the old ways of the realm, was Savant.

"Do you think Lothaine and Allard will adhere to the summit guidelines you've set?" Perry cocked a dubious eyebrow.

Jax studied the curt response Corentin Allard had sent, in which he begrudgingly accepted her invitation to Saphire due to his soldiers needing the medicine she offered. "While I'd like to think so, the fact of the matter is, neither party trusts my intentions. They believe I plan to take Savant as another jewel in my already weighty crown." A sad smile spread across her lips. "And after being under Qylvard's tyrannical rule for so long, I cannot blame them." Jax rubbed at the pressure building behind her right temple. Out of habit, her fingers traced the subtle scar that disappeared up under her hairline.

"Qylvard may have been a terror, but history is on your side, Jax. Every nation under the United Duchies came to you honestly."

She appreciated her husband's unwavering support. "Still, I must be on my best behavior." A light giggle floated over her lips. "The only role I intend to play during this gathering is peacemaker. An expeditious one, too, if I'm to resolve this nightmare before Carriena's wedding in little more than three weeks' time."

Perry didn't join in her laughter—her words only deepened his growing frown. "I worry about what trouble this might bring you, my love. Both Lothaine and Allard have proven they will do whatever it takes to claim Savant for themselves. They've put thousands of lives at risk, the very people they wish to rule. Who's to say they won't try to take down someone they believe to be just like Qylvard?"

The thought of losing her life terrified her. There was still much she wished to accomplish in the realm to guarantee its security going forward. But Jax kept her head held high and her determination resolute. "Then I will prove to them I am nothing like that vile man."

Perry rose with fluid grace and came to her side. "Of course you're not. I just hope these men are willing to see it." He pressed his lips against her aching temple, lingering on the old battle wound she had earned from going head-to-head with the late Duke of Savant.

She leaned into his warmth before replying. "Your concern has been noted, Lord Percival. Besides, Aizen and Ziri are doing their best to ensure our safety." Jax pointed to the detailed schematic Captain Rami Aizen of the Ducal Guard had provided her during a recent briefing.

"What's this?" Perry studied the sketch with interest.

"*This* is where we shall all convene for the Savantian Summit." She gestured to the large map of Saphire hanging nearby from a wall. "Glennfeld Manor. One of the Crown's largest estates. It's near the southern border. Very stately and obscenely grand." Jax rolled her eyes in a teasing manner. "If I'd had a younger sibling, it would have been their permanent residence once they married."

Perry hunched over her desk to examine the interior layout Aizen had drawn. "It looks like a fortress."

"That's the whole point." Jax folded her arms. "*I* wanted to host the delegations here at the palace, but Aizen was adamant the risk would be far too great. He didn't think it wise to allow Savantian forces to roam through Saphire's southern lands on their way here."

"He has a point, my love." Perry shifted on the balls of his feet. "There'd be little to stop them from scattering and assaulting your southern villages."

"Yes, I realize that now." Jax's brow wrinkled with annoyance. Not at Perry, but at the fact she hadn't originally foreseen such dangers herself. Luckily, she was humble enough to listen to wise counsel and accept that when it came to strategic maneuvers, there were better, more experienced minds than hers. "Aizen wanted the summit to take place in a controlled makeshift encampment near the southwest border, but I persuaded him that we needed to be a little more…diplomatic with our setting."

Perry chuckled. "You wish to welcome these men as if they were a royal delegation."

"What I *wish* is for us to treat them like respected leaders," Jax said with a slight sniff. "Not the thugs Aizen seems to think they are."

"So, why Glennfeld Manor, of all places?" Perry perched on the edge of her desk.

Jax's throat tightened with sudden emotion. "Well, I think it would be nice to visit it one more time before…" Her words trailed off.

Anxiety danced in Perry's eyes. "Before what?"

"Sit down, won't you, dearest?" Jax beckoned him to take a more comfortable seat. "I have something to discuss with you."

"You're not planning to ship me off to Glennfeld permanently, are you? You haven't grown tired of me already?" While Perry's words were said in jest, there was a glimmer of apprehension in his gaze.

Jax shook her head in hurried reassurance. "You're stuck here at my side forever, I'm afraid. You see, I have plans for Glennfeld." Her hands dropped to cradle her belly—her sadly empty belly. "While Master Charles has encouraged me to hold on to hope that we may yet conceive a child, I must begin thinking about Saphire's future—the *realm's* future."

Perry's pale skin lost all its natural color. "I see."

With the amazing alchemical and medical advances across the continent over the last decade, women had been carrying babies safely and successfully to term well into their forties. Having recently celebrated her thirty-first birthday, Jax was still in the prime of her life, yet for all their efforts, she and Perry had not succeeded in conceiving a child.

An *heir*.

Virtues, how she'd grown to hate that word. And not only because every other question she fielded from her advisors these days was when she would produce an heir. No, she hated the sense of destiny it forced upon someone. Her whole life, she had been labeled as the Saphirian heir, shackling her to the duchy's throne. She loved her nation with every fiber of her being, but only because she had accepted her fate at a very young age. Had she not, perhaps she would have turned out as greedy and corrupt as the late Qylvard Savant.

In recent months, Jax had been thinking even more about what it meant to be an heir. Her uncle, Darian Fangard, had ceded the Duchy of Cetachi to her after learning his wife was pregnant. His tender, thoughtful words floated through her mind often. *"I do not want my son or daughter to be the heir apparent to Cetachi's throne. I want them to be able to choose whatever life they see fit. I don't want them to feel tied to a crushing duty, forced to push their personal feelings aside for the sake of their duchy."*

At the time, Jax hadn't agreed with her uncle's actions but held her tongue. Yet, as the weeks passed, those words had wormed their way deep into her mind and heart. Shouldn't every parent want such a thing for their child? Could she really ask of her offspring what her father asked of her? Jax knew beyond a shadow of a doubt that her parents loved her and had only made her the heir because that was how things in the realm had been done for hundreds of years. But things were changing now. People held greater power over themselves and had the chance to forge their own destinies. Could Jax deny such a decision to her own flesh and blood?

"I need to ensure the Unified Duchies are left in capable, just hands," she explained, not quite meeting her husband's intense gaze.

"Do you intend to pick a successor and install them at Glennfeld?" Perry's kind voice held no judgment.

"No." She willed herself to share her plan out loud. She had been stewing on the notion ever since they'd returned from Lady Uma's eventful engagement party three weeks ago. "I'd like to turn Glennfeld into a school."

Perry did a double take. "A school? For what? Whom?"

She grinned at the sudden enthusiasm brimming from him. He didn't think her idea absurd. In fact, he sounded rather excited. "For people who wish to become leaders. Future village premiers. Governor Royales. Right now, our elected officials are learning by doing and by what I have taught them. But I won't be around forever. This school can see that young and old minds alike are molded."

Perry bobbed his head. "I like the idea, Jax. Truly, I do."

She sensed his rebuttal. "But?"

He winced. "Won't this lead to another disparity among the masses, with only the wealthy being able to afford this special education?"

"Ah, perhaps." She smiled. "*If* I didn't intend for the school to be free to those who are accepted."

"Free?"

Jax selected one of the documents she had been working on for the past hour. "I'm in the process of setting up a grant to fund the school, its teachers, and staff. With Glennfeld being Crown property, the estate costs would be minimal, save for upkeep and staff, much of which I already maintain now. With tuition no longer an issue, students would be admitted based on an entrance exam and interview. We'd accept anyone over the age of eighteen who displays an earnest desire to promote and better our democratic ways."

"I must say," Perry mused, his smile growing wide, "this sounds like an incredible opportunity for higher education in the realm." He paused. "What do you think the Academy will have to say about it?"

Jax rolled her eyes. "Headmaster Daghir doesn't own the right to teach people." The Academy had been the lone source of higher education on the continent for as long as Jax could remember. As much as she championed the school and its progressive ideals, the Academy was still in a state of transition after the former headmaster's sudden passing. She couldn't rely on them to help her bring her goals to fruition.

"Have you spoken with your advisors about this?" Perry steepled his fingers together.

She reached across the desk and took his hand. "No. I wanted your opinion on the matter first. Do you think I'd make a fool of myself announcing that I planned to open a school? Would anyone come?"

Perry threw his head back and laughed, the hearty sound shaking his entire being. "Would anyone come? Darling, I think you'll have more applicants than you'll know what to do with."

The thought was daunting but heartening. "I'll have a hard time turning away anyone interested in learning how to govern."

"Then I shall help," Perry reassured her, "for I think this is a fine idea. But what, may I ask, does this have to do with our situation?" His gaze darted to her belly.

Jax glanced longingly out the window, admiring the beautiful castle grounds covered in summer wildflowers. "Our people already elect their village leaders and each duchy's Governor Royale. What if..." Was she really going to suggest it? "What if they elected the High Throne as well?"

As the reigning Duchess of seven nations, Jax had recently united her holdings under the Unified Duchies banner. While each nation had a Governor Royale to oversee its administration, all the governors reported to her, the High Throne, to ensure no corruption took root. She also managed the Unity Fund, from which the nations were financed.

Perry's jaw dropped to the floor. He blinked several times before he was able to respond. "Y-you want to give up your Crown?"

"Not give it up, per se." She rose from her chair and glided to the window overlooking the sweeping meadows between her castle and the capital city, Sephretta. "But I do not wish to burden our child with its heavy weight. I want them to find their passions in life, discover what makes their heart beat faster, and follow that love to the ends of the realm."

Perry was at her side in an instant, his arms encircling her waist. "But what about everything you've built, Jax? Everything you've worked toward?"

She considered her deep-seated dreams of ruling the realm and bringing democracy to all. A year ago, she believed it to be a feat only she could accomplish. But the human spirit had proven her wrong. She didn't need to hold dominion over every nation to see democratic ideals flourish. That was already happening beyond her borders, with other sovereigns changing their ways. The duchies of Tandora, Lysandeir, Mensina…Virtues, even Beautraud and Zaltor were working toward giving their people a voice.

Yes, it was time to let go of her lingering desire for power and fully embrace what she had long been preaching.

"What I've worked toward is for our people to be happy. To be able to live a life where they can choose their own fate." Jax turned to face her husband, threading her fingers through Perry's hair. "I wish that for our child as well, should we ever be blessed by the Virtues."

He cupped her cheek in his warm, calming palm. "I shall support whatever decision you make, my love."

"Thank you." She kissed him deeply, wishing they could return to bed. "You might be the only person to do so once I bring forth this proposal to my advisors."

He chuckled. "While your courtiers might give you a hard time, I'm sure Uma and the others will at least agree."

Jax pictured the faces of her loyal companions and smiled. "If only everyone else could so readily take my side as you all do." Savoring one last kiss, she broke their embrace and returned to her desk. "While my plans for the school will have to wait until after the summit has concluded, I shall use our excursion at Glennfeld to assess what updates the estate needs in order to function properly as an educational institution."

"Two birds, one stone." Perry smirked as he reclaimed the chair at his workspace. "I shall reschedule my museum opening until after Carriena's wedding, then, so that I can be at your disposal."

"Thank you, dearest."

Jax sincerely appreciated his dedication to her cause, even at the expense of his own endeavors. Since he'd become her consort, he'd opened a grand theater in Saphire, and now there was this new museum to look forward to. She was very proud of Perry's achievements in the cultural world.

"It will be a lovely event to attend once all this unpleasantness with Savant is behind us."

Perry nodded at the scrap of parchment discarded on her desk. "What do you make of George's missive? Can we hope to see him and Serafina at Carriena's wedding?"

Her gaze dropped to the scribbled writing once more. *We aim to cross the southeast border within the coming day, where the herbalist was last seen.*

"We can always hope, but Serafina's mission takes precedence, I'm afraid."

George's cryptic words were meant to be nearly indecipherable should this letter fall into the wrong hands. The *herbalist* no doubt alluded to Elias Pettraud, Perry's brother and a traitor to them all. His proclivity for using poisons to carry out his dastardly deeds had earned him the moniker "the herbalist" in George's secret communications. "I just hope Elias is found and the Intelligeye sigil is recovered before it falls into the hands of his mysterious new master."

Perry stilled at the mention of his eldest living brother. "I cannot believe what he did to the Solis twins," he seethed through gritted teeth. "To poison Lenora's siblings so savagely, after all that woman has done for our family."

Jax's hand tightened into a fist. For many years, Lenora Solis had served as the Pettraud court physician and helped raise Perry and his brothers after their mother's death. To learn Elias had poisoned Lenora's younger brother and sister all in pursuit of some ancient artifact was yet another reason he must be stopped. The man had no issue harming others if it meant his own gain.

As she stewed over her brother-in-law's numerous misdeeds, Jax traced George's words *No sign of our shadow* with a finger. "And luckily, there's been no sighting of Emeraude Odaire, either."

"Let's pray it stays that way." Perry reached for his quill and returned to his work.

Jax did not share his optimism. During their recent visit with Uma's future in-laws, Jax and her companions encountered the Grandmaster of the Shadow Brethren, the realm's criminal guild. The meeting had been…enlightening, to say the least. Emeraude had declared her intent to hunt down George and Serafina as they seemingly shared the same quest: to locate the Virtuous Favors.

Jax still didn't understand what the Virtuous Favors truly were. From what she'd gleaned from Serafina, they were fabled relics created around the time of the realm's founding. Whether they really contained mystical powers bestowed by the Virtues had yet to be seen. But dark forces were at play in the struggle to find them. Not just Emeraude Odaire. No, someone who troubled Jax even more: an unknown foe who had already caused a great deal of misfortune across the continent.

A nightmare by the name of the Dark Magus.

Chapter Two

A fervent knock on the door interrupted Jax and Perry's work. "Duquessa? Might I have a moment?"

As the powerful, lithe figure of General Ziri Axesinger strode into the study, Jax gave the woman a welcoming smile. "Always."

Ziri acknowledged Perry with a dip of her chin before clasping her hands behind her back. "I've just received word from my sources that the Savantian delegations are nearing the southwest border. They're about a day out from arriving at Glennfeld."

"They're traveling together?" Perry raised his eyebrows in surprise.

Ziri shook her head, her raven braids sweeping across her shoulders. "Not exactly. Heartsworn's caravan is about two leagues behind Lion's Bane. They seem to be purposely keeping their distance from one another."

"A wise move," Jax murmured. "It would be just our luck for one of them to be assassinated during their journey here."

Perry grimaced at her morbid joke. "Please, don't even put the scenario out there, Jax."

"Yes," Ziri agreed with a smirk. "May we have one gathering that isn't beset by a dead body?"

Jax held up her hands in defense. "It's not like I orchestrate such terrible things."

"We're only teasing you, darling," Perry reassured her.

The sting of truth still brought heat to Jax's cheeks. "If our guests are nearing the border, we should set out for Glennfeld before dawn tomorrow. With our carriages, it will take a few hours to make the journey. I want to ensure we're there to greet both delegations." She pushed her chair away from her desk, content with the work she had accomplished.

"Aizen figured as much," Ziri said. "He's already assembling your escort."

"By escort, I'm assuming you mean ten *thousand* soldiers?" Jax rolled her eyes at the exaggeration.

Ziri chuckled, the sound like the low, melodic strings of a cello. "No, he's followed your orders and only selected seventy of his best Ducal Guard officers. Anything more, and he agreed it might be seen as an act of aggression on Saphire's part."

"Quite sensible." Rami Aizen had only been Captain of the Ducal Guard for a short while, but he had proven his merit numerous times over.

"We're prepared for a week-long stay." Ziri shifted on the balls of her feet. "Do you think the negotiations will take longer than that?"

Jax shuddered. "Virtues, I hope not. If these men can't agree within a few days, I don't see much hope for success." She gathered the correspondences she needed to send and tucked them under the crook of her arm.

Perry collected his letters and followed suit. "Are any of your courtiers joining us for this mission?" he asked Jax as the three departed the study.

"No. The only one whom I'd like to attend is Jaquobie, but he and Lysette aren't departing Cetachi until tomorrow."

Jax thought fondly of the High Courtier, a man who had once felt like a vexing opponent when she first began her reign. He'd been in Cetachi these past few weeks working alongside Governor Darian Fangard to oversee Cetachi's admission into the United Duchies. "At least they'll be home for Carriena and Bernard's wedding." She beamed, anticipating the happy event glimmering on the horizon.

"Uma and Sabine are ready to leave at your command." Ziri then glanced toward Perry as the trio strolled toward the correspondence tower containing Saphire's prized crowned falcons. "Will Hendrie be in attendance?"

Perry shook his head. "I won't need his assistance. I'd rather he oversee any issues with the museum opening that may pop up in my absence." Hendrie Dumont, Perry's former valet and current private secretary, was also a dear friend who'd accompanied them on many adventures.

"I hope you've instructed him to keep sweet Hilde company." Jax wiggled her eyebrows with a coy grin.

Perry chuckled. "Trust me, the man needs no instructing."

Hilde Croxford, Uma's future sister-in-law, was a guest at the palace, having recently been freed of a dreadful, abusive relationship. While she wasn't quite ready to court anyone yet, the moment she'd been introduced to Hendrie, sparks had flown. It made for a glorious sight, especially knowing all the pain Hilde had endured at the hands of her late husband.

"Then we will only need to take two carriages." Ziri halted at the base of the tower. "That makes security measures much simpler."

"I do try, you know."

Ziri's lips curled at Jax's jest. "I shall return to Aizen and finalize arrangements."

"I hope we'll see you at dinner!" Jax called down the long, white-stone corridor as her archspymaster disappeared with a wave.

Perry held the heavy door open for her, the sounds of flapping wings floating down from the spiral stairs. "It seems like everything is falling into place for this summit."

Jax gathered her skirts for the ascent up the tower and took a fortifying breath. "Let's hope it all *stays* in place."

‡

"Those weapons don't look like a tentative peace agreement is in effect."

George Solomon cast a sidelong glance at his frowning companion. "No, they do not." With a grim chuckle, he returned his attention to the rocky chasm fifty feet below. Ten men, each armed with a sharp polearm and a gleaming great sword, stood between them and the Hestian border.

Serafina Braeknoch tightened her grip on his forearm. "We should cross the ridge under the cover of night. The moonlight will be bright enough to guide our way yet cloak us in shadow from the eyes below."

George debated their woodland surroundings. From their perch atop a tree-lined cliff, they'd monitored the heavily-armed men to gauge a plan. The border guards hadn't allowed anyone to pass through the canyon all day. Not even those who offered hefty sums of gold. And even with his skills of evasion, there'd be no way to make the crossing without being seen. The towering walls of the chasm cinched too tightly together—even in darkness, he'd be spotted.

Serafina was right. Cresting the mountain ridge into Hestes was the only viable option. His heart clenched with sudden aching. The decision meant leaving behind a dear friend.

With tender murmurs, George scurried toward the beautiful white mare munching quietly on the green vegetation peppering the mountainside. His treasured companion would not be able to follow him into battle this time.

He reached out a hand and stroked Merida's silky mane. The Crepstian horse, a breathtaking creature known for its bountiful reserves of stamina, had followed him into many dangers without hesitation. But he could not risk Merida losing her footing on the treacherous, rocky passage and hurting herself. "I'm sorry, girl, but I'm afraid our time together has come to an end."

Serafina leaned against a tree, studying George with compassionate understanding. "We could try to cross the northern border, like we did before," she proposed. "We'd be able to take the animals with us then." She reached out a hand and ran her fingers over her mare, Emma's, back.

George sighed. "We're already days behind Elias, and all we

know for certain is that his trail brought him here. To turn around and head north…"

She came to his side and placed a gentle palm on his shoulder. "Merida and Emma will make their way back to the nearby village. They'll find a loving family, I'm sure of it."

He tried not to picture the beautiful creatures wandering the woods alone. Instead, as he undid Merida's tack, he mapped out a plan of attack. "Once we make it into Hestes, we'll have to find new mounts, and quickly. We won't get anywhere on foot." As he dropped the leather bridle to the ground, George uttered a silent curse. He'd make Elias Pettraud pay for all the suffering he'd wrought with his selfish actions.

They'd been hunting the traitor for more than a month now, and the rogue always seemed to be one infuriating step ahead of them. After discovering what Elias had done to Veritas and Verdine Solis, leaving the siblings for dead, George felt ready to strike him down at first sight. Unfortunately for his bloodlust, they needed him alive. Not only did Serafina need to recover the Intelligeye sigil he'd stolen, but they also wanted answers as to why Elias had done such a thing to begin with. Why had he apparently sided with this mysterious figure who called himself the Dark Magus?

At least they'd been able to pick up Elias's trail after he'd fled the Solis estate. George hated how long it had taken them to unearth the information, but the civil war raging throughout Savant had slowed their travels. Town squares had become battlefields, and it was hard to get people to talk. Everyone they spoke to seemed so frightened. But it appeared the war had also forced Elias to move slowly across the duchy or risk being found out. Because of this, luck was somewhat on George and Serafina's side.

A week after the couple departed the Solis estate in search of Elias, they'd stopped by a rundown tavern to inquire whether there were any sightings of nobles or royals fleeing the area. While the proprietor wasn't all that helpful, George overheard a group of weary citizens chatting excitedly about finding a man with lavender eyes hiding out in a cavern near a local fishing hole. He'd run off into the brush before they could capture him, but from their unflattering descriptions, George knew this wandering vagrant had to be Elias. Even though they were a day or so behind him, Serafina asked the patrons where this fishing hole was located, and from there, they'd been able to pick up the lavender-eyed man's trail trampling through the woods. Elias, while a skilled Pettraudian knight, did not appear to be a seasoned outdoorsman, for George was easily able to follow in his wake through the dense forest.

They'd pursued the trail for several days, causing George to question Elias's ultimate goal. He'd assumed the man would try and deliver the Intelligeye sigil to his supposed new master. If that were the case, why had he chosen to go so far south when the northern borders were much easier to cross? Why had he dared trek so close to the capital, where the heart of a civil war raged? Had they made a mistake concluding that Elias and the Dark Magus were in league with each other? Or had the Dark Magus left the wilds of Beautraud and taken up residence in Savant?

Truth be told, George didn't even know if the Dark Magus had ever been in Beautraud to begin with. He'd never met the man. He only knew that the Dark Magus wanted the Virtuous Favors, ancient relics Serafina was sworn to protect. The Dark Magus had manipulated Qylvard Savant into doing his bidding, and now, seemingly, Elias Pettraud. Why? What did he want with these fabled artifacts? It was one of the many questions that kept George up at night as they slept under the stars.

Elias's woodland trail had eventually stopped on the outskirts of a small border village. According to a chatty barmaid, Elias had spent a night at the local inn, putting out feelers for someone to smuggle him into Hestes. She'd said that a less-than-scrupulous merchant gang offered to help in exchange for gold. They'd left the village two days ago and hadn't been seen since.

George eyed the mountain pass overhead. The barmaid told them Monsaut Chasm was the nearest crossing for five leagues. The Noirceur Mountains dominated the southern landscape, and there were very few paths safe enough to travel, whether by foot, horse, or carriage. The men Elias hired would have needed to take him through here. How had they managed such a feat if the passage was blocked by unyielding guards?

As he placed Merida's saddle on the soft earth next to the discarded bridle, Serafina's hand snaked up his arm and cupped the back of his neck. "George, why don't we try and get some sleep before the sun goes down?" Her gaze was laden with concern. He knew she was worried they were walking into a trap. So was he.

He reached for her hand and pulled her fingers to his chapped lips, pressing a tender kiss against her warm skin in answer. Sleep would do them both good.

Chapter Three

A burst of hot air warmed his neck, and George's eyes flew open. A slim dagger was already in his hand as he prepared to spring into action to ward off any threat.

Instead, a large pair of glowing eyes stared down at him, catching the light from the rising moon. Merida's soft nose nudged his shoulder, as if telling him it was time to make his move.

Emma, however, was nowhere in sight, and George wondered if she had already ambled down the mountain.

"Aye, girl. I'm up." He scrambled to his feet and gave the horse an affectionate pat. "You best be off after Emma. Try and stick together, all right?"

Merida cocked her head, and George prayed to the Virtues that she understood him. He wasn't abandoning her out of spite. He simply didn't wish danger to befall her.

Ignoring the writhing guilt in his gut, George knelt down beside Serafina and gently gripped her shoulders.

"Is it time?" she murmured as she wiped sleep from her eyes.

He nodded as he peered over the ledge to gauge the scene below. Ten different men stood at attention at the mouth of the chasm crossing. Ten imposing men who looked well-rested and fed.

"I wonder which faction they belong to?" George whispered as he studied them. Whoever they were, they were much better organized than the rebels in the north.

Serafina tugged on a thin summer cloak now that the night had given way to cooler temperatures. "I suspect these sentries are from Lion's Bane. While you loosened the barmaid's tongue back in the village, I overheard a few of the inn's patrons talking about them. Lion's Bane controls most of the southern border, whereas Heartsworn controls the seas and the north."

"And they're all that's left?"

She nodded. "The citizen factions have been gobbling each other up. It will be interesting to see who emerges the victor."

"Jax will make sure the most deserving ascends the throne." George's confidence in his oldest friend burned brightly. She was the reason for the tentative peace agreement between the Lion's Bane and Heartsworn factions. He and Serafina had learned about Jax's recent involvement during their trek across the nation. The Duchess of the Unified Duchies had invited the leaders of both Savantian factions to a summit, hence the ceasefire currently in place.

Serafina's lips curled downward. "I don't know if any of them are deserving after what we've seen since arriving in this nation."

George agreed with her. Once they'd left the Solis estate, the further east they rode, the more ruins of war they encountered. Burned, empty husks of towns that had been ravaged. Looted manors, the bodies of their noble inhabitants left behind to rot. All done in the name of "liberation." What the Savantians didn't understand was that they were already free. With Qylvard's demise and no one to take up his mantle, the people of Savant were free to choose their own future. But they had chosen to go to war with one another, eager to wield authority over their countrymen.

Yet, even with the terrible circumstances surrounding him, George thought—and not for the first time—how glad he was to be away from Saphire at the moment. He did not envy Jax having to deal with the power-hungry individuals who'd put their people's lives at risk all for the chance to sit on the empty Savantian throne. Despite the fact they were about to scale a dangerous mountain ridge in the dark, George was content to be by Serafina's side.

"Ready?" he asked once he secured Merida's saddlebags to his back. They contained only two days' worth of food and water. Once they crested the mountain, they would need to find a village and restock.

Serafina tied her long auburn hair in a braid and adjusted her boots. "Ready." She hiked Emma's saddlebags over her shoulder and set off toward the mountaintop.

George ran his hand through Merida's mane once more. "May the Virtues guide you, ol' gal." With a final pat goodbye, he straightened his shoulders and took off into the night.

‡

They didn't get far.

George and Serafina were only twenty paces from their campsite when a cry went up from down below.

"Oy, you drags! Here's your spoils."

The gruff call froze George in his tracks. With a quick glance at Serafina, he noted her wide eyes, eerily prismatic in color.

She tilted her head toward the edge of the cliff. "What's going on?" she mouthed.

George inched along the ledge, trying to position himself so he could hear better. All day, they'd listened to muffled conversations muted by the dense landscape around them. The excited announcement was the first clear statement they'd heard.

As George peered over the cliffside and down into the chasm, he spotted a new man standing among the ranks. While the bow strapped to his back wasn't as imposing as the sentries' weapons, his gleaming armor was much more formidable. He appeared to be someone of high rank.

The others clamored around him, clapping as the newcomer reached into a leather sack and extracted two green glass bottles.

More cheers went up.

"Wine?" Serafina murmured as she crouched beside him.

George frowned. Why would these guards imbibe alcohol while

on watch?

"It appears to be a celebration of some kind." Serafina continued to study the scene with her sharp gaze.

The thought troubled him greatly. "What could they be celebrating?" Had Jax already been successful in her mission to broker peace? He counted the days on his fingers since he'd last had word from her. No, the summit wasn't set to begin yet. When she'd written to him about her plans for peace, she'd told him the date of the Savantians' arrival in Saphire. The leaders weren't due until tomorrow.

But if it wasn't peace they were celebrating, what was it? Had the Lion's Bane carried out a successful attack despite the ceasefire?

They watched in confused silence as the men below poured their wooden cups full of wine. The newcomer raised his above his head. "May that royal swine reap what he deserves," he roared with a laugh.

The guards all cheered and threw back the contents of their cups like they hadn't drunk anything in days.

Serafina's hand found his in the shadowy darkness, her fingers as cold as new-fallen snow, despite the humid, summer heat.

Ice ran through George's veins, too. Royal swine? It could only mean one thing…

"Imagine," the newcomer below bellowed, "trusting one of the Dundainee crew."

George had never heard of the Dundainee before, but if these men were indeed reveling in the capture of Elias Pettraud, the Dundainee must be the merchant gang the barmaid had told him about. "We should get closer," he urged his companion.

Serafina agreed without hesitance. "If we double back toward our campsite, we should be able to slip down to the chasm path from there."

With silent yet hurried footsteps, the couple retraced their path along the cliffside. Merida still stood at their abandoned camp, a white beacon in the moonlight.

Her ears twitched when she spotted George. *Back so soon?* He swore he heard the mare ask.

George willed her to flee. If they slipped up and were spotted near the chasm crossing, they would need to make a quick escape, and the thought of Merida being taken in by these men made him heartsick.

Serafina led the way down the cliffside, her adept grace reminding George of a phantom. He noted how her path expertly kept them from just beyond the reach of the flickering torches that lit the chasm passage. Such skill was a sign of the intense training her father had put Serafina through as a young woman, preparing her to protect the Virtuous Favors with her life.

Despite what seemed like hours, only a few breathless moments passed before they arrived at the chasm floor. Inching closer to the cluster of sentries, George's heart thrummed as their voices grew clearer. "What does Commander Crowe plan to do with the lout?" one of the men asked.

Serafina tugged on George's elbow, pulling him behind the protection of a moss-covered boulder shaded by a large elderberry bush.

"Forced to stare at his sorry mug for the interim, I'm afraid." The newcomer poured himself another cup of wine. "What with this ceasefire and all, we're not allowed to move between regimens until word comes from Lord General Allard himself."

"What?" another guard spat out the question.

The higher-ranking man shrugged. "I know it sounds ridiculous, but breaking the ceasefire's rules is tantamount to declaring war against Duchess Saphire. We should be counting our blessings she hasn't interfered any more than she already has."

"Ah, come on now, Sergeant Tautou," a soldier with a youthful voice said, "surely we could best her on our own turf."

Sergeant Tautou, the wine bearer, grew still. "Don't tell me the alcohol has already gone to your head, boy. Lion's Bane may be mighty, but even if we joined ranks with those Heartsworn delinquents, we'd have no hope against Saphire. She's too powerful."

Another young sentry scoffed. "What nonsense are you speaking, sir? We are Savant. We are fire!" He was joined by several others in the war chant.

Tautou hissed for them all to be silent. "You fools. Have you not heard the tales? The Duchess of Saphire has ended men far greater than you with a single word. Just look what happened to our late Duke! No, it is by her grace and her grace alone that Savant as we know continues to exist."

"Then why don't we do something about it?" the young man Tautou had first reprimanded snapped. "Just like we did with that royal dog who tried to cross our border."

Angry shadows danced across Tautou's dark-skinned face. "We are doing something about it, you dolt. Lord General Allard is set to arrive in Saphire by sundown tomorrow. He has gone there to earn the Duchess's respect and secure the throne of Savant so that we can live our lives as we see fit. But until then, we will abide by the rules of the ceasefire and wait."

"So, I'm not getting the new posting promised to me?" an older-sounding man grunted.

Tautou shook his head. "Not yet. But rest assured, you'll be with the group to escort our prized pig to the capital when the time comes."

George heard Serafina's sharp intake of breath like a shriek in the night. He knew his senses were playing tricks on him, but he prayed to the Virtues nonetheless that the men up ahead hadn't heard her. Inwardly, he, too, was screaming. Elias was *here*. Or at least, he was nearby at whatever camp Sergeant Tautou had come from.

"Since you all will be on border watch for the foreseeable future, I'll make sure to bring a few more bottles the next time I check in," Tautou told the grumbling group. "Have faith in the Lord General. He and the Vice Lord Admiral are two of Savant's greatest minds when it comes to outwitting an opponent. They'll have that Heartsworn pup eating out of their hands in no time." He rose from his rock perch. "Now, I need to get some rest. I return to South Haven in the morning."

The sentries mumbled their goodnights as the sergeant retreated into a small tent near the mouth of the crossing.

Silence settled over the men as they continued sipping their wine, and George realized they shouldn't linger in their hiding spot any longer.

Serafina must have read his mind, for she was already inching back into the dark shadows of the mountainside. Noiselessly, they traipsed through the forest and underbrush, their footsteps taking them along a familiar path.

The moonlight shimmered on Merida's creamy white pelt as she stood guarding their campsite with regal grace. Almost as if she'd been expecting them to return.

"Thank the Virtues you stayed, old friend." A crooked smile stretched across his face as George ran a hand through his shaggy hair. Once inky black, it was now streaked with threads of silver, revealing the thirty-eight years his bones did not yet feel. "For I think we're in need of a horse." He glanced at Serafina to determine their next move.

"We won't be putting Savant behind us just yet." Her eyes sparkled with the thrill of the hunt.

The Virtues had indeed smiled upon them this night, for the traitor Elias hadn't escaped the duchy after all. He'd been captured by the rebels and was currently being held somewhere called South Haven. And with the ceasefire in place, there was a sliver of hope that George and Serafina just might be able to catch up to him.

Chapter Four

"Looks like the gang's back together."

Serafina tossed her hair over her shoulder, the long auburn strands shimmering in the early morning light. A laugh trilled quietly over her lips at George's cheerful remark. "I found her eating toad moss only a few hundred feet down the mountain." She patted Emma on the neck before buckling her tack in place.

George checked Merida's saddle before offering the majestic animal an apple from his pack. "I'm glad they stayed close." He didn't want to think about the outcome if they hadn't overheard what they did last night. Why, the two of them would probably be wandering around Hestes right now, aimless and untethered.

Serafina's palm rested on his tense shoulder, her touch putting him at immediate ease. "Sergeant Tautou looks like he's almost ready to head out."

He nodded his understanding. It was time for them to make their way toward the main road. With any luck, they could follow Tautou at a distance under the guise of travelers seeking asylum from the war. It was the ruse they'd used during their trek across the duchy, and it had worked for the most part. As long as Serafina kept her eyes averted. Their mesmerizing color, a mixture of gold and periwinkle, revealed her noble and ducal bloodlines to anyone looking at her too closely.

The morning air was already humid and warm. Sweat dripped down George's chest as he climbed atop Merida. He'd yet to adjust to the steamy Savantian climate and prayed the road to South Haven would be shaded.

Murmurs bubbled up from the chasm, signaling that Tautou was preparing to ride out. George leaned slightly over the cliffside, urging Merida to keep steady. He watched the Lion's Bane sergeant clap the sentries on their shoulders as they exchanged shifts with the day guard. With so many men shuffling about in the canyon, George and Serafina would need to be more careful with their movements. Someone might spot them hovering above.

Once Tautou mounted his horse, George nudged Merida into action, navigating the surefooted mare swiftly down the mountain pass. Emma and Serafina kept close behind, and within the hour, they arrived at the main road running parallel to the Noirceur Mountain ridge.

George squinted, trying to assess their surroundings. "I don't see Tautou." He halted Merida's steps to properly get his bearings.

"I doubt he pushed his mount as hard as we did." Serafina rode to George's side, her body swaying gracefully atop her saddle.

She made an astute point. Their quarry wouldn't have the speed and endless stamina of the legendary Crepstian horses at his disposal.

George hopped off Merida's back and handed her reins to his companion. "I'm going to comb the canyon path for any recent tracks, just to be sure."

Serafina nodded her understanding and urged the horses into the shadow of a nearby poplar tree.

George hurried along the dirt road, locating the spot where it intercepted with a worn pathway leading to the chasm pass. Kneeling to the ground, he ran a hand over the dusty trail. It didn't look like it had been recently disturbed, meaning Tautou hadn't yet passed by this way since his arrival.

George quieted his breath, listening to the symphony of natural sounds around him. Birds chirped in the light of a new day, and every so often, he heard the growl, grunt, or squeak of some woodland creature. He continued to soak in the world, the minutes passing as he waited for signs of human activity. He was just about to give in and return to Serafina when a faint, rhythmic *clop-clop-clop* finally reached his ears.

Someone was approaching.

His heart hammering, George sprinted down the road to rejoin Serafina and the horses. "Incoming," he hissed as he jumped onto Merida's back and clicked his tongue.

At his command, the horse began to stroll at a slow pace. If it was Tautou, George didn't want the man to think they'd been standing around waiting for him.

Merida and Emma were about twenty paces out from the canyon pathway when the Lion's Bane officer trotted onto the scene with his big bay stallion.

The sergeant's attention was on them immediately, but his expression was one of curiosity rather than suspicion.

George merely tipped his chin in the man's direction. "Morning, sir." He'd managed to somewhat mimic a Savantian accent after immersing himself in the dialect while staying with the Solis twins.

Tautou slowed his horse to a halt. "Awful early to be out on the roads, isn't it?"

"Our home was destroyed by Heartsworn vermin earlier this week." George summoned his best acting ability to play the role of an aggrieved villager. "We're trying to find sanctuary. Even with the ceasefire in place, I don't trust those warmongers to hold to their oath."

Tautou's chest swelled at the mention of the Heartsworn faction. "Sounds about right. No respect for the common folk."

Ah, yes. Your men showed so *much more respect by turning away asylum seekers at the border all while alleviating them of their gold.* George wisely kept his sardonic thoughts to himself. "Any suggestions where we might find shelter, good sir?"

At the deference in George's question, Tautou straightened in his saddle. "There's a Lion's Bane settlement about three leagues from here for displaced common-born. As if Heartsworn would ever do that," he added with a snort.

George hoped he'd kept his expression neutral at the man's use of the term "common-born." He hated the word and the oppression it stood for. That Savantians still used it so freely to describe themselves both angered and aggrieved him.

"Thank you," he managed. "Are you perhaps heading that way? My wife and I would feel much better if we were under the protection of an armed officer." He motioned to Serafina's hunched form.

Tautou studied her as if seeing Serafina for the first time. The corner of his lip curled in a sneer, and George could almost hear the man saying, "Poor sod," to himself.

George kept a smile of his own at bay. Before leaving their mountainside camp, Serafina had rubbed dirt across her arms and face in an effort to disguise her regal beauty. With her bent posture, she'd clearly repelled Tautou's potential interest in her. It seemed George and his "wife" were safe for the time being.

"I'm headed to South Haven, so seeing you to the settlement is on my way." Tautou gave a tug of his reins and spurred his horse into motion.

George guided Merida in step with the Lion's Bane sergeant, while Serafina kept pace behind him. "We're not much familiar with these parts. What's in South Haven?" He spoke slowly to avoid tripping over his fake Savantian accent.

Tautou gave him a sideways glance and raised his eyebrows. "One of our main war camps," he enunciated, as if he believed George did not have the mental capacity to understand.

George didn't dare correct the sergeant's assumptions. It provided the perfect cover for fact-finding. "You lot have made good work with your conquests."

"Our Lord General does not lead us astray."

George fought to keep from rolling his eyes at the grandiose title of the Lion's Bane leader. To him, it meant this Lord General fellow cared more about power and notoriety than the people he was supposed to be fighting to liberate. Instead, he continued to stroke the sergeant's ego. "I bet the nobles run cowering from their estates when they see Lion's Bane coming."

A vicious grin broke out across Tautou's face. "Oh, we don't let them get away." The cold lethalness in his tone made George shiver.

"That's good. That's good." The words tasted sour on George's tongue as he feigned agreement. "They should suffer like we have. The lot of them. Would like to give our local lord a swift kick in the you-know-where."

Tautou chuckled at the brutish candor. "Get in line, fella. We've got men protecting some royal pig around the clock because most of our soldiers feel the same as you."

George clenched Merida's leather reins in veiled triumph. "Royal pig? You've taken someone with ducal blood prisoner?" He plastered on a slack-jawed expression.

Tautou nodded. "The cad thought the Dundainee would offer him safe passage across the border." He barked out a laugh. "Just ended up paying them to deliver him to us."

"What's a royal doing around these parts?" George asked. "He's not from Savant's bloodline, is he?"

The officer shrugged. "He gave us some foreign name, but we can't find any connection to a ducal family. Probably thinks he can pull the wool over our eyes. But have no fear, we'll get him to talk."

"I have no doubt." George pressed his lips in a thin line. "You say he's being watched day and night for his protection? Why not let your men have their fun?"

Tautou snickered. "Because our commander thinks someone will pay through the nose for him to be returned. Best he be in one piece."

"I thought Lion's Bane was well-funded?" George knew he was taking a risk with such a probing question, but since Tautou was traveling alone, he felt emboldened. Even if the officer turned on them, Tautou stood no chance against a former Captain of the Saphire Ducal Guard and a combat-trained archivist.

To his surprise, Tautou gave him a wide grin. "Can never have enough gold, can we? Every piece makes it much easier to squash those filthy Heartsworn lurkers."

George broke away from the man's hardened gaze, unnerved by the hatred pulsating in Tautou's eyes. Mere weeks ago, Lion's Bane and Heartsworn had been countrymen, living alongside one another without issue. It astounded George how quickly the duchy had become divided in the wake of Qylvard Savant's death.

A sudden lump bulged in his throat. A death *he* had delivered. All the destruction George had witnessed across the nation…*his* sword had been the catalyst. While he knew it foolish to hold himself accountable for the actions of others, he couldn't quiet the feelings of guilt and shame roiling within him.

Silence eventually fell across their group, and George was content to pass the time admiring the beautiful scenery around them. Despite its current political climate, Savant offered a tranquil, luscious landscape. Leafy trees arched overhead, speckled with bright yellow and pink flora. Small critters skittered along twisting branches and birds darted across the blue skies hovering above them. Had his mind not been filled with racing questions about warring factions and intercepting Elias, he might have found their ride along the countryside road enjoyable.

Chapter Five

"Oh my," Sabine Arceneaux cooed at the massive, elegant structure rising before them. "This might be even more architecturally impressive than the palace. Will wonders never cease?" She threaded her arm through Ziri's, smiling excitedly at her sweetheart.

"It is quite beautiful," Ziri purred in agreement before turning her bronze gaze on Jax. "If the delegates feel slighted at being received here, well, then there's no pleasing them."

On Jax's other side, Uma Dorrow sucked in a breath. "I can't remember the last time we came to Glennfeld, Jax, but it looks even more striking than in my memories." Before she and Sabine had been named Shieldmaidens of the Iris, Uma had served as Jax's lady's maid and lady-in-waiting, back when the antiquated roles were still relevant within Jax's court. Now, she stood beside Jax as her friend and confidante, and fiancée to the dashing young man on her arm.

Yanis Croxford adjusted his Ducal Guard uniform, the only one among their group looking wary. "Is seventy men really enough to protect this place?"

"I would have liked a hundred more," Rami Aizen admitted, his golden Captain's armor glittering in the morning sun. "Even so, with our current numbers, we have enough men to cover the estate border so that no one gets in or out. The manor, per the Duchess's request, will only have men posted at the entrances and inside the wings to give our guests a sense that they are trusted to roam as they please."

"Can so few interior sentries keep the Savantians in line?" Yanis raised a critical brow.

Aizen nodded. "According to the terms our Duchess laid out, Heartsworn and Lion's Bane were permitted ten guards to escort them on their travels, and only two companions will be allowed to accompany the faction leaders once they reach the Glennfeld barracks."

Sabine looked taken aback. "And these men agreed to such stringent restrictions?"

"I implored them that it was for their own safety," Jax explained. "Besides, with the turmoil in Savant, neither faction has many men to spare in the first place."

"A wise move on your part, my love." Perry's hand rubbed the small of her back. "With fewer guests, we'll be able to keep an eye on them all."

Glad he agreed with her, Jax turned her attention to the stately matron standing at the foot of the grand marble steps. "Madame Rosalyn, how good it is to see you."

"Welcome to Glennfeld, Your Grace." The estate manager's unlined dark skin gave no sign that she had aged in the ten years since Jax last visited. "We are delighted to host you once more."

Jax closed the distance between them and clasped Rosalyn's hands. "I'm happy to see you looking so well. Thank you for getting the house ready in such short notice."

"Of course, Duchess." The commanding woman waved forth a horde of maids and footmen to collect the bags from the two carriages in which Jax and her companions had arrived. "We are honored to play a role in resolving the current conflict vexing Savant."

"*Hopefully* resolving," Jax countered with a slight wince.

Rosalyn smiled warmly. "You always seem to achieve what you put your mind to, Your Grace. Have faith that the Virtues will guide you."

Jax thanked her for the vote of confidence before ushering her companions forward. "I'd like to get our group settled into our rooms before our guests arrive."

"This way, then." Rosalyn quickly introduced herself to everyone before leading the Saphirians up the stairs toward the gilded, two-story entrance. "As you requested, Duchess, your party will be lodged in the west wing." She glanced over her shoulder at Aizen. "Captain, the men you sent ahead have already combed through the west and north wings."

Aizen straightened his shoulders. "I shall meet them for a formal briefing." He arched an eyebrow at Ziri. "Do you have everything under control here?"

Ziri chuckled at his unnecessary question. "Go. We'll defend the Duquessa if the need arises."

For added measure, both Sabine and Uma flashed the ornate daggers strapped to their traveling boots.

"Oh my." Madame Rosalyn's brown eyes widened at the shock. She clearly wasn't used to seeing beautiful, delicately dressed women armed.

Jax grinned at the estate manager's reaction. Not only were Ziri, Sabine, and Uma her dear friends, but they were also her fierce bodyguards.

As Sabine and Uma hid their daggers under the hems of their gowns, Jax noticed Perry's happiness dimming slightly, and he absently massaged his abdomen. Little more than six months ago, he'd received a near-fatal bolt to the stomach. The wound had since healed, but his ability to fight with strength had been permanently disabled. Due to his injury, Perry still grappled with his inability to physically protect his wife, and Jax knew it pained him to see others take his place. Nevertheless, she tightened her grip on his forearm, leaning against him to let him know she needed him at her side. His support and love were all the protection she required.

Satisfied his charge would be watched after, Aizen departed for the soldiers' quarters with murmured assurances that he would alert them of the Savantians' arrival when the time came.

"I hope you'll find the estate to your satisfaction," Madame

Rosalyn said as she welcomed the remaining Saphirians inside the cavernous three-story marble entrance hall. Five chandeliers dangled from the ceiling, their candles casting a golden glow across the shiny white stone floor.

As Sabine and Uma marveled at the opulent sight, Jax made a mental note to sell the gaudy decorations. The gold they brought in could be used to fund her school or give aid to a charitable organization.

The idea entered Jax's mind more than once as Madame Rosalyn led them up a red-carpeted staircase. *In fact, I should take inventory of all the Crown's properties.* What she couldn't sell, she would donate, perhaps to Perry's new museum. She visited these properties so rarely—the art that hung from their walls would do more good in a place where the public could enjoy it.

"I doubt our guests will have ever seen such magnificence in their entire lives," Uma observed as her russet gaze took in the sight.

I'm betting on it.

While Jax had done away with oppressive classist labels in her own lands, Duke Savant had long fought to keep his citizens separated by common, noble, and ducal bloodlines. Heartsworn's Finral Lothaine and Lion's Bane's Corentin Allard were members of the Savantian common-born class, made to work and serve the nation's nobles for little pay in return. Even though Allard's rebellion was well-funded by merchant backers, his amassed wealth paled to the might of Saphire. Jax wanted to both tempt and intimidate the men by bringing them here.

"Rosalyn, are the guest suites in the north wing outfitted with the silk linens?"

"And the Kwatalarian cotton towels, per your note," the estate manager assured her. "I also had a bottle of 1287 Houlton Bordeau placed in each room."

Jax's mouth watered at the excellent vintage. Its dry sweetness was one of her favorite wines. "Wonderful, thank you. I'm glad you had enough time to arrange it. I thought a welcome gift would be a nice touch."

"Aren't you afraid all this wealth might pit them against you,

Jax?" Sabine's lower lip quivered as she assessed a dazzling portrait of some distant Xavier relative framed by jewels.

"That's all part of the plan, my dear." Jax chuckled. "Once they see the gold Saphire has at her disposal, the Savantian factions will realize a fight against us is futile, should they not resolve their differences. I'd like to see both sides band together to build the future they long for."

Sabine twirled a strand of her white-blond hair. "I should have known there was a reason."

They arrived at their rooms in the west wing a few minutes later. "Duchess, you and Lord Percival will be situated here." Madame Rosalyn pointed to the suite door at the end of the hall. "Lady Sabine and Lady Uma will be on either side of you, with General Axesinger and Sir Yanis buffering them."

With assignments doled out, Rosalyn excused herself to see to meal preparations.

"We'll also have four Ducal Guards stationed along the hallway." Ziri counted off where they would stand watch.

Jax frowned. "I'd rather they be stationed around our guests to protect them."

"Aizen has six guards overseeing the north wing," Ziri replied confidently. "That will be more than enough. The others on duty will be assigned around the manor to watch for any trouble at the estate border."

A sigh of relief passed over Jax's lips. With only five delegates scheduled to join them in the main house for the peace summit, it seemed like more than enough security.

Sabine wrung her hands, her nervousness evident. "Well, I suppose all that's left is to trust in the Virtues."

"Best we do not leave things *entirely* up to them." Perry's arm tightened protectively around Jax's middle, but an easy smile spread across his lips. "Let's keep our wits about us, shall we?"

Chapter Six

"We've been on the road for hours. How much longer are we to go on, dear? I'm getting tired."

The raspy, grumbling voice that came from Serafina's hunched figure startled George from his daydreams. Sergeant Tautou, too, was taken aback by the harsh delivery of her question, and a cringing scowl settled across his sun-worn face.

George did his best to bury his laughter. Serafina really couldn't have sounded more unappealing. "Are we nearing the settlement?" he asked the Lion's Bane officer.

Tautou slowed their pacing. "The turn-off will be coming up shortly." He narrowed his gaze as he scanned the road. "Our men patrol this road intermittently, so you shouldn't run into any bandits. As for the opposition, we're supposed to immediately send word to the Lord General in Saphire if a breach in peace has been made."

"We'll be safe then?" Serafina's voice crackled.

"Yes, ma'am."

A few more minutes of traveling passed before Tautou pointed to a secluded forest path branching off the main road. "This will take you to where you need to go."

"Thank you." George bowed his head. "You have my gratitude,

good sir."

Tautou clicked his tongue, and his horse took off down the road, a cloud of dust lingering in his wake.

Serafina pulled Emma alongside Merida. "Should we follow him?" she whispered in her normal, lilting voice. The familiar sound soothed his soul.

"It's too risky." George stared after the retreating officer. "We need to find a more covert way into the war camp to speak with Elias."

Serafina cursed under her breath. "What's the point in speaking with him? If Elias is being held at South Haven, then the Intelligeye sigil will have already been confiscated from his person."

"We need to understand his involvement—if any—with the Dark Magus. Besides, if the sigil looks anything like your medallion," George began, his gaze flicking to the shimmering gold chain peeking out from under Serafina's tunic collar, "I'm sure it's been placed in the camp's treasury. Or it's in the care of its ranking officer."

Fear and uncertainty marred Serafina's elegant features. "Then what do we do? I cannot abandon my duty to protect the Virtuous Favors, George. Not when I've been tasked by prophecy to safeguard them."

Memories floated through his mind of the eerie verse Veritas and Verdine Solis had shared and the strange future the warrior twins foretold.

In our care, the sigil will sleep,
until the Kindhearted sage
thwarts a cunning dark mage,
proving it theirs to keep.

It was by these cryptic words that the Solis twins had transferred guardianship of the Intelligeye sigil to Serafina. The Kindhearted sage.

He reached across the space between their horses, his hand seeking hers. "We'll find a way—together. I promise." Her warm skin was soft against his.

The tension in her shoulders visibly loosened. "I'm sorry. I don't mean to be frustrated with you." She paused to trace a finger over his strong jawline. "It's just…we've lost so much time trying to catch up to Elias."

As her finger flitted across his lips, he kissed it. "Let's not waste anymore, then. We'll head to the settlement and make a plan from there."

Determination flared in her eyes as she nodded her agreement. Wordlessly, they urged their horses into motion and trotted down the shaded forest path.

Chapter Seven

"If the weight of the world wasn't on your shoulders, this would be a lovely spot to vacation." Perry rested his chin atop Jax's head as they enjoyed the afternoon view from their bedroom balcony.

Jax savored the fresh air laced with the aroma of wildflowers. Unlike the palace, which neighbored the bustling northern city of Sephretta, Glennfeld was located in a remote southern valley where Saphire's natural beauty was on full display. "Who knows? Perhaps we shall reach a peace accord by dinnertime."

A chuckle rumbled within Perry's chest. "If anyone can do it, it's you, darling."

Jax turned her body to press her lips against his when a shrill cry from a heralding horn caused her to stiffen. "Our guests have arrived." She craned her neck and leaned over the balcony railing as much as she could, hoping to glimpse the procession on the road. However, due to their location in the west wing, the side of the manor blocked her view.

Perry tugged her back, pulling her against his chest. "Just one more moment of this." He squeezed her tightly, his yearning and love for her radiating from his slender frame.

When they parted, her husband's normally calm lavender gaze

was calculating and cool.

He's getting better at donning the mask of a ruler, even though he no longer has a Crown of his own.

Jax smiled proudly at him before similarly arranging her features. *If this is to be a success, we must have the respect of our guests.*

Otherwise, Heartsworn and Lion's Bane would consider her to be just as useless as Qylvard.

They met Sabine and Ziri in the corridor, both women looking ready for the figurative battle ahead.

"We told Uma and Yanis to enjoy themselves out in the gardens," Sabine hurriedly explained the absence of their other party members. "Although I think they both opted to visit the border to assess the arrival of our guests from a distance. They'll welcome the Savantians at dinner."

Jax nodded her approval. It was honestly for the best, so as not to overwhelm her visitors with new faces. Besides, hearing that Uma and Yanis could enjoy some romantic time to themselves brought her great joy. "Then let the games begin."

Aizen was already waiting for them in the grand entrance hall, a scowl seared deep into his walnut skin. "I've sent escorts to guide the delegations from the estate border. The Savantian soldiers have been relieved of their weapons, and everyone's bags have been inspected. Based on the initial report from my officers," Aizen grumbled as he reached into the small pouch belted to his waist and pulled free a folded piece of parchment, "the Lion's Bane deputy carried a longbow with him but willingly released it into our care. On the contrary, the Heartsworn deputy had a knife hidden on his person. He claimed it was just a whittling knife, but it's been confiscated nonetheless."

Perry clapped the Captain on the shoulder. "No one is getting away with anything under your watch, are they, mate?"

Aizen did not crack a smile. "If it were up to me, we wouldn't even allow butter knives at dinner."

"Come now." Jax shushed the crotchety Captain. "These men accepted my terms in good faith. Give them some credit."

He lanced her with a severe stare. "I'll give them credit when they have earned it, Duchess."

She sighed. There would be no reasoning with the overly protective man. "Who have the faction leaders brought to accompany them?"

"Finral Lothaine—the Heartsworn lad—opted to bring only his deputy, Pierre Yves." Aizen's sharp gaze continued to scan the parchment for details.

"What do we know about him?" Jax asked.

Aizen grunted. "My men didn't get much. Yves seems the strong and silent type. He let Lothaine do all the talking."

"What about Lion's Bane?" Jax asked. "Tell me about their party."

Aizen handed her the report marked with the seal of the Ducal Guard. "Corentin Allard is accompanied by his second-in-command, Nanteuil Dvorak, and his daughter, Vivienne."

Jax's eyebrow rose with surprise. "His daughter, you say? In his letter, Allard didn't give me the impression he much valued the opinions of women."

Her dry humor elicited chuckles from Sabine, Ziri, and Perry.

Aizen, however, was all business. "I think you'd be right, Duchess." He pointed to a note scribbled at the bottom of the report. "All he seems to do is berate the poor girl."

Jax studied the looping script. *The dynamic between father and daughter is strained. The lady does not appear happy to be here.* "Then why bring her?" Jax wondered aloud.

The peal of a horn burst outside.

"I suppose we're about to find out," Aizen muttered before giving a curt nod at the two officers guarding the door.

The men nodded and reached for the handles in unison, pulling the double doors open with a grand, sweeping flourish.

"Oh my," a feminine voice cooed from the threshold.

It took Jax's eyes a moment to adjust to the afternoon light pouring into the hall, but soon the figures of her guests came into focus.

Five strangers stood before her, their wary stances the only thing similar about them.

"Greetings, my dear gentlemen and lady." Jax stepped away from

Perry's side, positioning herself at the forefront of her companions. "I am Duchess Jacqueline Xavier, and I am honored to welcome you to my home." As a sign of respect, she dipped her chin in acknowledgment of each visitor.

The tallest and most handsome of the group cleared his throat and took a tentative step toward her. "Thank you for the warm reception, Duchess Xavier." He bowed stiffly at the waist, his bronze cheeks darkening with some unknown emotion. "I am Finral Lothaine, governor of Heartsworn."

Jax noted his use of the title "governor" with interest, as it was a position implemented throughout her lands. Perhaps this meant she could find some common ground with the man.

"May I introduce my companion?" Lothaine swept back a large hand, beckoning forward the stockier, pale man to his right. "My deputy governor, Pierre Yves."

Yves was Lothaine's opposite in every way. Where Lothaine's brown eyes were warm and welcoming, Yves's were harsh and cold. Lothaine stood tall, with Yves only coming up to his shoulder. Their state of dress was also vastly different. Lothaine looked to be in his traveling clothes, while Yves wore a fine silk suit.

"Your Grace." Yves merely nodded in her direction, his lips barely moving as he mumbled her title.

Quite the charmer, that one, Jax mused. To Yves, she returned his cool greeting with a slight tilt of her head. "I hope you had pleasant travels?" she asked, her kind gaze returning to Lothaine.

A momentary flash of panic darted across Lothaine's chiseled features. "Uh, yes, Your Grace. Thank you for asking."

Jax noticed Lothaine send a spooked glance toward Yves. It made her wonder if an individual of her station had ever acknowledged them kindly.

She quickly switched her focus to the other three guests. "And who else do I have the pleasure of receiving?" Her tone, while light, commanded them into action.

A middle-aged, tan-skinned man of medium build hurried forward. Much like Yves, he wore a fine silk suit, but his expression was significantly more friendly. "Greetings, Duchess Xavier. I am

Nanteuil Dvorak, Vice Lord Admiral of the Lion's Bane faction." He held out a cautious hand, and when Jax did not hesitate to shake it, he couldn't hide his surprise. "May I introduce Corentin Allard, our fearless Lord General?"

As Dvorak motioned to the older, bearded man in their party, Jax marveled at the contrast in introductions between the two Savantian factions. Lothaine had led the charge all on his own, while Allard required his second to announce his fancy, self-imposed title.

Allard strode to Dvorak's side, his powerful, heavy steps echoing in the entrance hall. His mane of gray hair reminded Jax of a large, wild cat, and she wondered briefly if that was how Lion's Bane had come to have its name.

"Duchess. We've heard many tales about your valor and fairness." Allard's voice was low and deep, like the beginnings of a far-off avalanche. "I look forward to deciphering fact from fiction."

Jax couldn't resist a smile at the older gentleman. While he was not nearly as dashing or charismatic as Lothaine, he clearly had his own type of charm. "I hope I don't disappoint." Her gaze flicked to the pretty young woman toying nervously with the lace on her fine mauve gown. "I understand we are joined by your daughter, Lord General Allard?"

The man's eyes reflexively brightened at the use of his title. The sight of such a joyous spark made Jax's heart ache. She didn't want to think about the disrespect and oppression these poor people had been subjected to under Savant's rule.

"Yes, Your Grace. My little singing lark, Vivienne."

Under the stern gaze of her father, Vivienne shuffled forward. She was indeed very beautiful, with shimmering brunette ringlets that fell well past her slender shoulders. Her peachy skin grew red as she arrived at her father's side. "It's an honor to meet you, Duchess Xavier." Her melodic voice was a mere whisper.

"Please, call me Jacqueline." Jax reached for the young woman's hand and squeezed. "I'd like for you *all* to call me Jacqueline."

She swept her regal gaze around the group. "As I stated before, you are welcome here within the walls of Glennfeld under the terms of our summit agreement," Jax reminded her guests with a careful smile. "I do hope we can work together to aid the Savantian people." She swiftly turned to her own companions and made the appropriate introductions. Jax swelled with pride as she spoke the names of her treasured loved ones.

"Now, my estate manager, Madame Rosalyn, will lead you to your suites so you can settle in." Jax folded her hands gracefully in front of her. "Please take some time to rest. I know you all rode hard to get here. We shall reconvene at dinner, which will be served at six."

As they had been since Jax presented Ziri as her archspymaster, the Savantian visitors continued to stare at her with dumbfounded expressions.

"Y-you're not making us camp outside with our guards?" Lothaine's nose wrinkled, confusion running rampant across his face.

Jax shook her head. "Of course not, Governor Lothaine."

Aizen cleared his throat. "Your guards have been escorted to the estate barracks, where they will stay under the care of my men. Now that your bags have been inspected, I've had them placed in your suites."

Vivienne brought a hand to her mouth to cover a whispered gasp.

Her father shot a silencing glare her way before saying, "Well, consider me surprised that we're allowed to lay our heads down within this grand manor."

Jax met his challenging gaze. "And why is that surprising, Lord General?" She assumed she already knew the answer, but she wanted confirmation regardless.

"Forgive my candor, Duchess, but enough of this song and dance," Yves snapped, drawing everyone's attention to his quivering frame. "*We* are common-born. *You* are of royal blood. Don't pretend you don't see us as beneath you."

His accusation hung in the air like a sharpened guillotine, but Jax didn't flinch. It was just as she feared. Her heart clenched with compassion as she responded to his accusation. "My dear sir, in my lands, you are *people*. People capable of achieving anything you set your minds to." Her whole body thrummed with conviction as her tone grew firm. "My *current* opinion of this group is only soured by the fact that you have let innocent citizens suffer while you wage your power games."

Yves shrank at her condemning words, his skin paling even further. She'd clearly hit a sore spot.

"I hope," Jax continued, her attention turning to rest on both Lothaine and Allard, "that your two factions can find a way to end their needless suffering. Then we shall all part as allies and friends."

Lothaine looked like he wanted to throttle Yves for speaking so rudely, but instead, he swallowed his rage. "That is my hope as well, Duch—Jacqueline."

"Agreed." Although Allard didn't quite sound like he meant it.

With a tight smile, Jax dusted her hands over a job well done. "Excellent. Now, please feel free to enjoy the comforts of your suites. The estate is open for you to explore as well." She motioned for Madame Rosalyn to take control of the delegation.

At her wordless bidding, the estate manager whisked their guests away, and murmured exclamations over Glennfeld's opulent beauty echoed through the halls as the Savantians were escorted to the north wing.

Chapter Eight

"My, my," Perry *tsked* once the Saphire group was alone in the foyer. "What a curious bunch."

Jax practically collapsed against him. She was relieved to have made it through their first encounter relatively unscathed. She was honestly surprised Yves's sharp remark was the only moment of discomfort during the ordeal.

"I'll say," Sabine chimed in. "These factions make no sense to me. It's like the deputies are assigned to the wrong leaders."

Jax agreed that Lothaine and Dvorak appeared more likeminded, and Allard and Yves certainly had the same pompous air about them. "Balance is important when it comes to leadership."

"Opposites attract, so they say." Perry kissed her temple, the simple act relieving the stress building behind her eyes.

Aizen folded his arms as a scowl contorted across his features. "How exactly do you plan to have Lothaine and Allard reach an accord, Jax?"

She appreciated him using her more familiar name, now that the formalities surrounding their guests' arrival had passed. "If Heartsworn and Lion's Bane truly wish for the people of Savant to be treated equally and have their best interests at heart, I will recommend they implement the democratic systems we've put into place. It is not for Lothaine or Allard to decide who shall lead, but their people."

Her Captain cocked an eyebrow. "And if these men merely wish to lord over others as they have been lorded over in the past?"

Jax cringed at the very real possibility. "As long as the bloodshed ceases, I will honor my agreement." The admission tasted sour on her tongue. She hated the thought of oppressed people living within the realm, but Savant was not hers to claim.

Sabine tugged a strand of her white-blond hair. "With the guests settled, is there anything we need to do before dinner?" She shot a quick glance at Ziri, her cheeks growing pink.

Jax smiled. "No, my dear. Please, spend the time as you see fit." She reached for Perry's arm. "I'd enjoy a walk around the estate grounds."

Perry's eyes twinkled, as he likely knew she wanted to assess the state of things for her school project. "Sounds lovely."

Sabine threaded her fingers through Ziri's with a growing grin. "I spotted a ballroom while exploring earlier. Care for a dance?"

"A dance? We have no music." Ziri's eyebrow arched with a tease.

Sabine stuck out her tongue. "We can make some of our own."

Happy laughter bubbled within Jax as her friends dashed off. She was glad to see them making the best out of a tense situation.

Aizen ran a hand over his close-cropped dark hair. "I suppose that leaves me as your escort." He looked somewhat embarrassed that he had to intrude on Jax and Perry's romantic stroll.

"You said so yourself," Jax reminded, "that the borders are well guarded, Rami. Take this time to rest. Tonight will be when the real battle begins."

Aizen's gaze narrowed. "You know I can't allow that, Duchess."

And we're back to formalities. She sighed inwardly. There'd be no use trying to dissuade him from being their shadow as they strolled the estate.

The Captain did maintain a respectful distance as she and Perry took in all Glennfeld had to offer, allowing Jax to pretend for a fleeting moment that she and her beloved had the world to themselves.

"I'm afraid you might put the Academy out of business, Jax," Perry murmured as they stood at the edge of a small pond on the property. "The grounds here are absolutely breathtaking. You'll have people clamoring to attend."

"I hope so." She admired the hulking willow tree before them and stroked its vines with a delicate touch. "I can already visualize outdoor lessons in that gorgeous gazebo. The sweeping design was inspired, letting in so much natural sunlight."

Perry put his hands on his hips. "I wish I had brought my paints. This view would have made for a lovely scene."

"There's a small merchant village nearby." She ambled to his side and threaded her arm through his. "Perhaps they have a craft shop?"

"I'll survive a few days without a brush in my hand." Perry then grimaced. "I only hope we're not here long enough to require a visit."

‡

George and Serafina rode for another mile before the trees began to thin out around them. Sunlight pierced through the leafy canopy overhead, and George guessed it had to be nearly noontime. He noted coils of smoke curling up into the sky, a sign of campfires nearby.

"We're getting close," he murmured, his alert gaze scanning the tree line. He hadn't asked the Lion's Bane sergeant what kind of security this settlement had in place—such a probing question would likely make the officer suspect him a spy.

Serafina's right hand dropped to her side and disappeared under her travel cloak. She was undoubtedly reaching for her crossbow, should it be needed.

Inwardly, he huffed with agitation. All he had for protection was a slim dagger in his boot. He wished he hadn't needed to wrap and tuck his sword under Merida's saddlebags, but if Sergeant Tautou had caught sight of such a glorious weapon strapped to George's horse or person, he would have immediately known George was no mere displaced villager.

The couple slowed their horses and continued along the trail until the woods gave way to a vast clearing. In the distance, a horde of tents and makeshift huts peppered the swaying fields of golden grasses. George counted at least sixty structures.

"Virtues, I didn't expect so many people." Serafina's eyes pinched with sorrow. "So many seeking refuge from war."

The sight angered George. All these poor people, forced from their homes. It wasn't fair. "At least no one should question our appearance."

"They will if *you* continue to do the talking."

George whipped his head in the direction of her giggles. "What's that supposed to mean?"

Serafina's lips cracked into a wide smile. "Your Savantian accent is absolutely dreadful. I can only assume the Virtues were lending their protection whilst you chatted with Tautou. Or perhaps the Lion's Bane soldiers are more brawn than brain."

He playfully swatted at her. "Everyone's a critic, huh? Fine, you can take the lead among these people." He stared into her prismatic eyes. "And if anyone asks about your lineage—"

"I'll say my mother was a common-born servant preyed upon by some duke's younger brother." It was an explanation they had come to rely upon during their travels to explain her odd eye color. George could tell Serafina hated the lie. Her noble-born father had been a great man, and the two had forged a deep bond after the death of her royal mother.

She straightened her shoulders, her features set with resolve. "Leave it to me."

The sun's full strength bore down on them as soon as the horses trotted away from the shade of the tree line. George fanned himself as the path turned into trampled grass, snaking through the field toward the bustling camp. As they drew closer, he spotted children running about while men and women washed clothes and stirred massive cauldrons over fires. Everyone appeared to be working. He didn't detect a single soldier watching over them.

They'd reached the edge of the settlement when someone finally noticed them approaching. A young child pulled at a man's tunic while he plucked feathers from a bird carcass and pointed their way. The man stared at them warily from his perch atop a barrel. "Oye, you from Jairdant?"

George wished he had taken out the map Verdine Solis had given them so as to refresh his memory about the village names throughout the nation.

"We're from Proviencia," Serafina answered in a flawless Savantian tongue.

The man raised his eyebrows, his skin red from the sun. "Bit far from home, aren't you?"

"We could not find shelter where we felt safe." Her reply was both cool and full of sorrow. "We hope we are at the end of our journey."

The man jumped to his feet and shuffled forward. "Well, we should be able to accommodate you as long as you aren't expecting a four-course meal." He half-smiled at his joke. "The name's Gunther."

"Hello, Gunther. I'm Sera, and this is my husband, Gio." She motioned George and his horse forward under the guise of the assumed identities they'd been using throughout their travels. "Our horses have been riding hard. May we feed and water them first?"

Gunther studied the two beautiful beasts, momentarily dazzled by their calm grace. "Where did you come across such jewels?"

Serafina smiled at his admiration for the animals. "We...rescued them from an earl's stable." Her cheeks colored at the lie as she and George slid off their mounts.

Gunther barked out a hearty laugh. "Ha! *Rescued* them, did you? Aye, I understand." He winked elaborately. "Yes, let's get them fed. We've got a stable of sorts on the north side of the camp." He glanced over his shoulder and shouted, "Marie! We've got two new faces. Ready a tent in quadrant three, will you? My back is feeling a bit sore."

A stout, dark-skinned woman with gray hair emerged from a nearby hut. "Gunther, you git. *You* ready the tent." She used the damp towel in her hands to slap the man's backside.

He cringed and rubbed the spot. "Virtues, woman. No need to be rough."

She shooed him away with the threat of another smack. "Sorry about that." Marie wiped her forearm across the perspiration on her brow. "His 'bad back' complaints always resurface whenever there's physical labor to be done." She rolled her brown eyes with a huff. "I'm Marie, the camp's matron. Let's get your horses settled."

Serafina reiterated their false identities in introduction before asking, "How did you come to be matron?"

"Well, someone had to step up and help all these poor, struggling souls." Marie wiped her hands on her apron. "And Commander Crowe surely wasn't going to do it, even though he's the leader of the Lion's Bane battalion 'overseeing' these parts." Her sarcasm evident, she waved the couple forward and began leading them through the camp.

"Are we to be protected by them?" Serafina tugged Emma along while George walked silently beside her with Merida. "Will Lion's Bane protect us from the Heartsworn soldiers?"

Marie cast a sidelong glance her way. "I wouldn't be counting on it, lass. Lion's Bane may have provided us with bedding, but that's all those brutes are good for."

At her sardonic response, George raised an eyebrow.

Marie must have noted his reaction. "Where did you say you were from?"

"Proviencia," Serafina answered.

"Ah, I see." The older woman sighed as a group of happy, if dirty, children ran past. "Then you probably don't even know how this settlement came about. Commander Crowe and his men burned down my village, searching for the four-year-old son of a neighboring estate's earl." Her voice grew heavy with emotion. "He was the only member of the household they couldn't account for. But instead of letting it go, they hunted him, believing my people had taken in the little lad."

Serafina placed a comforting hand on the matron's shoulder. "I take it you hadn't?"

"No." Marie wiped a tear from her dark eyes. "The poor child drowned while trying to cross the stream that ran through the earl's estate. But of course, no one knew until after our homes had been razed to the ground." Her sadness was suddenly overshadowed by anger.

"So, in an effort to clean up his mistake, Crowe relocated my village here, to show how 'sorry' he was. Sorry my arse. As if he could apologize away for the innocent lives lost." Emotion pooled once again in her eyes. "Soon, Lion's Bane started calling it a refuge and began sending other people who'd been displaced by the war, too. Of course, they only sent people who'd been left destitute by Heartsworn soldiers. That's who you'll find here, mostly. But no, not me and my kin."

Serafina shot George an unreadable look before she spoke again. "Forgive me, Marie, but I find it quite surprising that the people from your village are still alive to tell such a story."

Marie chortled. "You and me both, child. But it helps Commander Crowe is my nephew-in-law." She winced. "My poor niece. Always thought she deserved better. But I wager her devotion to me is the only thing keeping me and my people safe."

"How many people does this settlement serve?" Serafina continued to probe for information.

Marie stewed on the question momentarily. "I'd say we're now at two hundred souls. Maybe more. I've lost track."

By now, they'd arrived at a haphazard-looking stable area. While there were plenty of chickens and goats running about, George could only spot two cows and one horse. He frowned—Merida and Emma would stick out like sore thumbs here. He prayed they'd be safe.

He and Serafina quickly situated the animals under Marie's watchful gaze. "You both have a noble air about you. Did you spend time working in an estate?"

George merely grunted while Serafina replied, "Yes, my mother was the head maid for a baron, and I worked under her for much of my life." She motioned to George. "My husband was a valet."

Marie studied her intently. "I take it your mother had…uh…relations with this baron?"

Serafina's cheeks flushed. "N-no. I don't know much about my father, other than he was some foreign Duke's brother."

Marie's expression melted into soft sympathy. "Virtues, what a fine mess. Well, you won't find any lecherous royals here, my dear. Come. Let's get you a bed for the night."

As they left the horses to their grain, George nudged Serafina to continue her questions.

Marie must have noticed the action. "Is your husband mute?" She stopped, her hands on her hips.

George cursed under his breath. *She's one sharp woman.*

Serafina shook her head, scrambling for a reasonable response. "No. He…he inhaled a bit too much soot when a Heartsworn mob burned our house down, and his throat has been seared." She placed a comforting hand on George's cheek. "The healer who treated him said he needs to rest his vocals, or he won't heal properly."

"Oh my. That sounds terrible." Marie shuddered as she resumed leading the way.

"He can still work, though," Serafina hurriedly added. "We're both looking for work, in fact. An officer we met on the road told us about a war camp not far from here. Do they need skilled labor?"

Marie's scowl returned. "Aye, they need it. Not sure, though, if they're willing to pay anything for it."

Serafina's expression grew pleading. "If there's even a small chance, we'll take it. We've got to rebuild our lives somehow."

"I understand." The matron nodded her sympathy. "Although, until this blasted war is finished, I'm not sure that's even possible. It's ridiculous," she huffed. "I don't know what these bloody men were thinking. We suffered under Duke Savant long enough, and now this? Thank the Virtues Duchess Jacqueline got wind of our plight and was able to knock some sense into their empty heads."

George smiled at the fond way Marie spoke about his dear friend.

"We heard news about the peace summit during our trek here," Serafina offered. "Has there really been a ceasefire at the Saphirian Duchess's order?"

Marie bobbed her head. "I've even heard whispers that she sent medical supplies and food to the cities. Not nearly enough to go around, mind you, but it's a start." Her worried gaze surveyed the bustling camp all around them. "I hope we won't be forgotten."

Before Serafina could prod for more information, the matron stopped in front of a patch of dry, yellowing grass. "We'll set you up here. Gunther is likely taking his sweet old time bringing you a tent." Her face twisted with consternation.

George held up the saddlebags he'd slung over his shoulder. "We have gear of our own we can use," Serafina explained. "We don't need to take it from someone else who might be in need."

"Very well." Marie dusted off her hands. "I'll leave you two to get situated."

"Marie," Serafina called out as the matron turned to leave, "You mentioned the Lion's Bane camp might be in need of workers?"

"Ah, yes. We have a group that treks over there daily to see what tasks need doing." Marie shaded her eyes in the afternoon sun. "They head out around dawn." She didn't offer any other insight.

"Thank you." Serafina smiled and bid the woman goodbye.

When Marie was out of earshot, George dropped their bags to the ground, a plume of dust rising. "Well, I guess we have some time to kill." As much as he wanted to make for the war camp now, he knew it would be too conspicuous for them to do so. If they were to infiltrate the camp and figure out the whereabouts of Elias and the Intelligeye sigil, they would have to do so under the cover of the other laborers.

Serafina raised an eyebrow at his phrasing. "Then let's get that tent up, dear *husband,* for I have an idea how we can pass the time." Her expression turned flirtatiously coy.

Despite the intensity of their mission, an easy, eager smile spread across his face in anticipation of her touch.

Chapter Nine

The hours exploring the Glennfeld estate danced by quickly, as they always did when Jax spent time alone with Perry. The couple was back in their suite preparing for dinner much sooner than Jax would have liked.

She studied her reflection as she nestled a simple yet stately gold crown among her honey-colored tresses. "How do I look?" she asked her husband. She wore a plum-colored gown with a neckline much lower than she was used to. Sabine had assured her when the dress was ordered that it was the latest fashion across the realm.

Perry removed the white glove adorning his right hand and traced his fingers over her exposed collarbone. "Regal and ravishing. Your beauty may prove too much of a distraction for any peace talks to occur."

She laughed at his glowing compliment. "Your beauty is always distracting, yet somehow, I manage." She kissed his cheek. Perry looked painfully dashing in a dark blue suit with cream trim. The fabric made his lavender eyes glow brightly in the candlelight.

Their friends had all gone ahead to the banquet hall to allow the couple to make a grand entrance as the hosts of the fete. When Jax and Perry arrived outside the massive doors, Madame Rosalyn greeted them with a deep bow. "Everyone is seated, Your Grace. Lady Uma and your companions have had an...*interesting* time keeping things civil."

"Oh, dear." Jax's brow furrowed at the estate manager's delicate phrasing. "Are our guests already at each other's throats?"

Madame Rosalyn shook her head, her lips pursed with bemusement. "Not quite. It seems some of them took offense to your hospitable offering."

Jax grew even more confused. "The wine? What's so egregious about a simple gift?"

Madame Rosalyn folded her arms with a sigh. "Apparently, the grapes come from a vineyard where Master Yves's childhood rival works, and Master Allard abstains from the drink altogether. His deputy is quite worried about the...temptation it presents."

Perry scoffed. "Virtues forbid. How will we ever recover from such a flagrant affront?"

Even though his words were in jest, Jax's frown deepened. "I should have been more thoughtful with my selection."

How careless of me, she cursed inwardly. The misstep was a rude reminder that Jax was dealing with individuals she knew hardly anything about. It wasn't a position she was used to being in or liked.

Perry sobered at her unnerved expression. "We will find a way to calm the waters, my love. Come. Time to dazzle."

She gave him a grateful smile, although inwardly, she continued to berate herself for making such a foolish error. Jax needed this summit to go smoothly if there were any hopes for success. It did not bode well that her guests were already annoyed with her. "Madame Rosalyn, if you'll announce us."

"Of course." The svelte woman disappeared through a side door, likely on her way to the crier's pulpit. Moments later, her silky voice rang out, "Announcing Her Royal Highness, Duchess Jacqueline Arienta Xavier, and His Royal Highness, Lord Percival Pettraud."

The heavy doors swung inward, opened by two of the ornately dressed banquet hall attendants. Jax held her chin high and kept her gaze focused on her chair at the head of the long dining table. From her peripheral vision, she noted how Dvorak and Yves gaped at her figure. Governor Lothaine acknowledged her entrance, but his attention seemed more drawn to Lord General Allard and Vivienne, who were seated across from him.

Jax briefly assessed her dear friends, who had strategically positioned themselves around the table. Yanis sat at the end by Dvorak, while Ziri was situated between Lothaine and Yves. Sabine was next to Yves, and Aizen between Dvorak and Vivienne. Uma watched over the scene from her place to the right of Jax's chair, next to Allard, leaving Perry to claim the seat to Jax's left beside Lothaine.

"Good evening, everyone." Jax smiled warmly as she arrived at her dining chair. "I hope we haven't kept you waiting."

"Not at all, Duch—Jacqueline." Lothaine spoke up with a wide grin as she sank into the silk-cushioned seat. "We were just getting acquainted with Lady Uma and her fiancé." He motioned across the table.

Uma dipped her chin at the recognition. "Governor Lothaine was telling us that he has a cousin who works on the Croxfordshire estate."

"What a small world." Jax spread her napkin across her lap, prompting everyone else to hastily do the same. "Do you have plans to visit them while you're in Saphire?"

"No, ma'am." Lothaine shook his head. "While I am very much enjoying the accommodations you've so generously provided, I am eager to return home."

"Generously?" Yves broke out in a snort. "More like thoughtlessly." His mumbled words echoed around the table.

Lothaine shot him an annoyed glare. "Pierre, I highly doubt—"

Jax cut the red-faced young man off. "Please, Governor Lothaine, allow me. It seems I have offended Master Yves with my wine selection." She placed a hand on her heart, doing her best to portray the picture of humble contrition. "I offer my sincerest apologies, dear sir. It was not my intention to make you feel inferior over grapes."

Her sly, stinging words hit their intended target. Yves swelled with indignation. "I do not feel *inferior*—"

"Oh, wonderful. I'm so glad the matter is resolved, then." Jax struggled to keep her smile demure rather than triumphant. She did not appreciate Yves's petulant actions, especially at the cost of Lothaine's dignity. She'd already taken a liking to the earnest young governor, and she did not enjoy seeing him bullied by his seemingly wealthier subordinate when he'd been chosen as his faction's leader.

Before Yves could recover from her veiled rebuke, Jax turned to the Lion's Bane representatives. "And I hear apologies are also due to you, Lord General Allard. I did not realize you abstained from alcohol."

"No apologies needed, Duchess," his deputy, Dvorak, began with a wince, "for there has been no harm done."

"No harm done?" Allard bellowed. "There *will* be harm if you don't let me have a bloody drink at this blasted dinner, Nanteuil."

Jax's eyes widened at the sudden outburst. All around the table, her dining companions reacted with muffled giggles and snorts. Nanteuil Dvorak, however, grew pale.

"Now, my dear Lord General—"

Allard batted the man's protests away and reached for his goblet. "You worry far too much. One drink won't kill me."

Based on how loose Allard's tongue was, Jax wagered he'd already had more than *one* drink.

"Health troubles?" Yves sneered. Evident glee over learning such a fact shone brightly in his gleaming gaze.

"N-nothing of the sort." Dvorak didn't sound too confident.

"I'm fit as a fiddle," Allard snapped as he downed the contents of his goblet and signaled a nearby attendant for more.

Vivienne reached out a hand and delicately pulled back her father's arm. "Papa, perhaps we should wait for our host?" Her pinched gaze darted to Jax, and she could almost hear the young woman's pleas for help.

"Miss Vivienne is right. We're behaving like animals." Lothaine gave her a crooked grin before turning to his hostess. "Apologies for our abominable manners, Jacqueline."

On the contrary, this has been most illuminating.

Jax was sorry to put an end to the enlightening conversation, for it had provided her with invaluable information about the two factions. Allard obviously couldn't handle his liquor, and Lothaine was too generous to act upon such knowledge.

Instead of voicing her inner thoughts, she merely smiled and raised her own glass. "It is with hope in our hearts that we gather around this table. Please, let us enjoy breaking bread together as we work toward Savant's radiant future."

Everyone murmured their agreement over the toast, and the brief silence that eclipsed the room was broken by Madame Rosalyn instructing for a tomato puree soup to be served.

"Were you all able to take some time to enjoy the estate?" Jax asked her guests once everyone had steaming bowls in front of them.

Allard barked out a laugh. "I took some time to enjoy the comforts of my room. After the hard ride north, it felt nice to put my feet up." A scowl spread across his features. "I would have enjoyed it more, had Nanteuil not confiscated the lovely gift you gave me. A fine vintage, if I do say so myself."

At the mention of his name, Dvorak dabbed at his brow. "My good sir, please."

Lothaine cleared his throat. "Well, I'd be happy to share a glass or two with you, Allard, should it pave the way for civil discourse about the state of Savant's affairs." An easy smile curled on his lips.

Ah, perhaps Lothaine isn't as generous as I originally thought, Jax mused. He was clearly using Allard's proclivity for drink as a bargaining chip.

The older man scoffed. "As if I'd be *that* desperate to drink with my enemy."

Vivienne rolled her eyes at her father's slurred response. "I spent some time out in your beautiful gardens, Duchess. They are simply stunning."

"Thank you. I shall pass your compliments along to the Glennfeld groundskeeper." Jax lowered her head bashfully. "I'm afraid any plant I've ever tried cultivating myself ends up wilted and beyond saving."

Her attempt at self-deprecation brought about a round of light chuckles.

"Well, Duchess, you have many other admirable traits to be immensely proud of," Dvorak offered before spooning his soup into his mouth. After he swallowed, he added, "Your recent lumber deal with Tandora was quite something. Clever, and beneficial to both nations to boot."

Jax was taken aback by such praise. "It certainly makes it easier when the benefits of a new trade agreement are evident." Dvorak had to be incredibly well-connected to know of her arrangement with Duke Tsade. It had only been finalized last week.

A low snarl came from Yves. "Is that how you view us, Duchess." He gripped his spoon. "Elements of a trade?"

As Ziri eyed the dull utensil as if it were a weapon, Lothaine growled at his deputy. "Enough, man. Save your fervor for negotiations."

"Negotiations?" Yves snapped. "You're far too naive for your own good, Lothaine. It will be your downfall."

"From the way I see it," Lothaine replied coolly with folded arms, "my open mind is what convinced Heartsworn to rally behind *me*, not you. Maybe you need to be reminded of that."

At those tense words, Yves looked like he might explode with anger.

"So, you were elected the leader of Heartsworn, Governor Lothaine?" Perry's effortless smile cut through the waves of fury radiating off the two men. "How did it all come about?"

Lothaine looked somewhat hesitant to answer.

"It was the Duchess's influence, wasn't it?" Vivienne asked. "You looked to how she's been managing her nations?" Yet, instead of sounding snide, the young lady appeared captivated.

Lothaine's cheeks grew dark under her admiration. "Why, yes, Miss Vivienne. Duchess Jacqueline did serve as inspiration." He paused before forging ahead. "Most of us figured that if Duke Savant opposed whatever she was doing so strongly, it must've had some merits."

At this, Allard chuckled. "I have to say, I'm impressed with your logic, boy."

Lothaine's lip twitched at the slight condescension layering Allard's use of the word "boy," but before he could comment, Dvorak inquired, "You said *most* figured. Was the decision not unanimous?"

Jax wished to know the answer to this astute question as well.

Lothaine glanced down at his soup bowl, swirling its contents with his spoon. "No, but when is democracy ever unanimous? At least everyone's voice was heard, and roles were assigned accordingly."

Jax shared piqued glances with Perry and Uma. From the leering expression on Yves's face, Jax wondered if his assignment as deputy governor had been the result of the dissenters' votes.

"And there is the error of your ways." Allard rumbled with deep laughter. "Now you find yourself saddled with a deputy who would sooner stab you in the back than help you."

"Papa!" Vivienne's cries were nearly drowned out by the protests of the offended men erupting all around her.

"Lord General, I beg you," Dvorak implored, "please refrain from such comments at a social gathering."

Lothaine bellowed, "At least I didn't have to *buy* my way into power."

"How dare you suggest such a thing." Beyond a sneer, Yves was the least expressive with his reply.

"Gentlemen, please," Jax called for calm. Her silencing gaze quickly found Madame Rosalyn standing in the shadows and wordlessly begged her to cease providing Allard with alcohol. "I realize there is a great deal on the line for all of you, but I must remind everyone that our ultimate goal is to help the *people* of Savant prosper. Such a task will not be achieved if you cannot maintain civil discourse."

She steeled herself as she delivered the following warning, "Qylvard could not see beyond his own self-interests, a trait entirely unbecoming of a good, just leader. Do not follow in his footsteps. Think of your people. Not your lust for power."

Resentment reared in the heated gazes staring back at her. She knew Allard and Lothaine would detest being compared to the likes of Duke Savant. Jax prayed such a move would incur self-reflection rather than continued bickering.

Her words hung in the air, finally broken by Lothaine's calm resolve. "Quite right, Jacqueline. We have the ability to shape Savant for the better. A blank canvas to build a world where we can all thrive."

"An admirable vision, Governor Lothaine." Vivienne took the words right out of Jax's mouth.

Dvorak glanced nervously at Allard, as if worried how the Lion's Bane leader might retaliate. Allard glared at his daughter but said nothing further.

Chapter Ten

With the soup course completed, Jax motioned for their dishes to be removed and the main course to be served. She hoped getting more food in Allard's stomach would assist with his recovery.

Uma and Sabine took turns facilitating lighthearted conversation, their bubbly enthusiasm giving Jax a welcomed reprieve while she enjoyed her smoked venison. Her spirits were lifted by Dvorak's and Lothaine's gallant attempts to engage in topics such as Savantian wildlife and flora. With his words, Dvorak painted an eloquent picture of the southern shores near the capital, where many of the Lion's Bane camps were located.

Lothaine's descriptions of northern Savant were layered with similar warmth, revealing his deep love for the land. Vivienne seemed enraptured as the young governor shared tales of roaming the valleys surrounding the Bosquet estate where he worked. An estate that he now oversaw, as it served as Heartsworn's main war camp.

Throughout the entire discussion, Allard kept his head down, casting mournful glances at his empty wineglass, while Yves sent resentful stares around the table, not contributing anything other than the occasional grunt.

By the time honey-glazed fig pudding was presented, the atmosphere had relaxed into something almost akin to being enjoyable. Allard's state of mind seemed clearer, and he readily began to participate in the conversation. Over dessert, he regaled Jax and her companions with tales about his time in the Ducal Guard when Qylvard's father had been Duke of Savant.

"It was always the one place where the color of my eyes didn't matter," Allard murmured, his demeanor growing wistful. "I traveled far and wide, witnessing sights I'd only been able to dream until then. I made many friends, both common-born and noble. It showed me life wasn't as restrictive as we'd been led to believe."

His expression suddenly darkened. "But then Qylvard ascended the throne and demoted any common-born who'd made it past Corporal rank. We were divided by blood and sent to bunk inside thatched huts that barely kept out the wind. All around me, men grew sick from malnourishment while the nobles dined like kings in the insulated barracks."

Jax's chest pinched with outrage. "An unacceptable way to treat anyone, let alone those whom Qylvard depended on to defend him."

Allard nodded. "When my contract ran out later that year, I did not return."

Lothaine placed a balled fist gently beside his empty platter. "Then you know firsthand how vital it is that our *people* be the ones to make the decisions about the duchy's future, not the elite few."

"I would never act as the Duke did." Allard's nostrils flared. "I would never place one people above the other."

Yves arched an eyebrow. "What about the crusade Lion's Bane led *against* the nobles? Was it not your faction calling for their heads in retribution?"

Jax stilled at the serious charges being leveled.

Dvorak spoke up. "Malicious propaganda. That was Heathcliff's group, not our doing. In fact, Allard put a stop to those calls several weeks ago once Heathcliff peacefully surrendered to us."

Perry's hand found Jax's under the table. She risked a quick glance his way, noting he appeared just as concerned as she felt. In his brief communications since departing Saphire, George had informed them that Savantian nobles were being commanded to relinquish their wealth or forgo their lives in order to fund the citizens' rebellion.

"Peacefully surrendered?" Yves folded his arms. "I heard it was because Heathcliff's four top councilors were found dead in their tents, and Heathcliff couldn't manage without them."

Allard rose from his seat in a fluid motion. "You heard wrong, boy. We negotiated an agreement, and Heathcliff agreed to fall in line under *my* command."

Yves merely smirked in response as Allard reclaimed his seat.

"Miss Vivienne," Jax interrupted, eager to settle the simmering tempers. They were so close to making it through this first evening unscathed. "When your father introduced you this afternoon, he called you his little singing lark. Do I take that to mean you have been gifted with vocal talent?"

Vivienne's pale cheeks blossomed pink. "It's merely a play on my middle name. Lark, in honor of my mother's family."

"Come now. Even we lowly men of Heartsworn have heard about Miss Vivienne's glorious songs." Lothaine's charming words deepened the flush spreading across the young woman's face and down her neck.

She met Jax's inquiring gaze. "I-I do enjoy singing, Your Gr— Jacqueline. Though I cannot be so bold as to say I am gifted."

"Well, as your father, I most certainly can." Allard beamed with obvious pride. "Come, my sweet lark. Sing us all a song."

Vivienne shot a panicked glance across the table, and Jax caught Lothaine giving her a nod of encouragement.

Interesting…

"What shall I sing for the Duchess of Saphire that she hasn't already heard performed by someone of far greater skill?" Vivienne's question trembled across her quivering lips.

Jax hoped the warm smile she gave would soothe Vivienne's evident nerves. "Something from your homeland would be lovely."

Vivienne rose and hurried to stand beside Jax at the head of the table. She pointed to the domed ceiling above them. "The sound will carry better here."

A singing lark, indeed. The young woman clearly understood how to use her surroundings to enhance her performance.

With a deep breath, Vivienne opened her mouth, and melodic words floated out from deep within her petite frame:

Oh, how I yearn
For the days long ago.
When we wandered together
Through fields of fresh snow.

Your desire was strong
And your will ever true.
To throw off the chains
And begin the world anew.

Guided we were
And bestowed with a win.
Yet what once seemed good
Turned quickly to sin.

And now here I stand,
So alone do I feel
With only your sigil
To prove it was real.

The hauntingly deep melody continued to echo all around as Vivienne pressed her lips together at the conclusion of her song, her hands shaky as she gripped the skirts of her gown.

Jax didn't realize she was clapping—it felt like she was looking down on the strangely moving scene from above, taking in the mesmerizing tune.

"Oh, my!" Sabine cried in awe, her eyes teary. "That was simply stunning."

Perry rose to his feet and applauded. "A breathtaking performance."

Vivienne's cheeks looked like they might melt off right into Jax's lap, so she reached for one of the singer's trembling hands. "You have a voice like none I've ever heard before, my dear. That was truly an unforgettable experience." Jax wasn't exaggerating. The words still rolled around inside her head, vivid and strong. "Is that piece something you wrote yourself? As a tribute to the rebellion?"

Vivienne shook her head, her brown ringlets fanning out all around her. "O-oh, no. This little ballad is one of the oldest folk songs I know." Her bright gaze traveled to her father. "Virtues, it's been passed down by our people for so long, I hardly even know who or what it was originally about."

"I see." Jax had to tamp down her budding curiosity about the lyrics, since Vivienne didn't seem to have the answers. "Regardless of its origins, it was extremely moving. Thank you for that exceptional performance."

Vivienne dropped into a clumsy curtsy and hurried toward her seat.

Jax pushed herself back from the table before she troubled the woman with getting settled. "And I believe such a performance is the perfect way to end our evening. Masters Lothaine and Allard, I invite you to join me tomorrow at nine in the council room to begin our discussion."

"And what are *we* supposed to do, Duchess?" Yves's question dripped with malice.

Jax leveled him with a matching glare. "Per our agreement, Masters Lothaine and Allard may bring whomever from their party should they wish to have their efforts assisted."

Her gaze broke away from Yves and hovered over both Allard and Lothaine. She prayed both leaders might be willing to face her alone—she did not wish to concern herself with Yves's troublesome ego during their negotiations.

"Thank you, Jacqueline," Allard grumbled as he wiped his beard clean of lingering dessert crumbs. "My party and I shall retire and see you in the morning."

Lothaine stood before Allard had even set down his napkin. "As shall we." He gave a curt nod to Yves to follow his directive.

Allard snorted and rose from the table, his gait somewhat

unsteady as he shuffled toward the exit.

"Good evening, Your Grace." Vivienne smiled at her hostess before following in her father's wake. "And to you, good sirs." She threw a quick glance over her shoulder, her bright gaze sweeping over Lothaine and Yves.

While Dvorak offered his thanks, he didn't immediately chase after the Lion's Bane duo. "Duchess, if I may," he began, wringing his hands, "could you please have the kitchen send up a few extra water pitchers to the Lord General's suite? I…wouldn't want him to grow parched in the nighttime."

Lothaine and Yves both shared a smirk at Dvorak's delicate attempt to dance around Allard's drinking problem. "Oh, I doubt the Lion will allow himself to grow 'parched.'" Yves laughed unkindly.

Dvorak ignored the man's dig and kept his pleading gaze on Jax.

"Of course, sir. Madame Rosalyn will send someone up right away." As she said this, Jax could see the estate manager already issuing instructions to one of the banquet hall attendants.

Dvorak bowed his head. "Many thanks, Your Grace. Good night." He then turned and departed.

Yves followed suit with only a stiff nod toward Jax and her companions.

Now alone with the Saphire group, Lothaine rocked on his heels, looking like he had something more to say.

"Did you require anything further, Governor?" Jax raised an eyebrow.

He chewed on his lower lip before asking, "Might there be a library here within the manor, Jacqueline? I find reading before bed helps calm my mind."

"Of course. Sabine, Ziri, would you show him the way?" While her request was made lightly, she stared down her friends, hoping they'd read her mind. *Please, use your charms to get whatever information you can out of this lad.*

Sabine's lip curled as she shot Ziri a knowing glance. "We'd be happy to."

Jax nearly chuckled aloud at the apparent glee on Sabine's pretty face. Her dear friend loved nothing more than being given a covert mission alongside her sweetheart.

"Right this way, Governor Lothaine." Ziri stretched out a toned arm and escorted the man out of the room with Sabine.

Once the echoes of the closing doors had finally faded, Jax released a breath. "Well, we survived one encounter."

"Barely." Uma scoffed as she tossed her brunette hair over her shoulder. "That Yves fellow is just about as unpleasant as they come."

Yanis agreed. "What are the members of Heartsworn thinking, putting that man in a position of power?"

"You heard what Lothaine said." Jax dusted off her skirts as she wordlessly motioned for her friends to join her and Perry for a nightcap. "Yves must have been selected to speak for those who don't yet believe in democracy."

"Why? Because of his wealth?" Perry asked. "It can't be because of his winning personality."

Jax giggled. "Lion's Bane is backed by several wealthy patrons. It makes sense that Heartsworn would need to find support among those with deep coffers."

"A tragic decision on their part," Aizen muttered as they all moved into a small salon off the banquet hall. "Lothaine would be a given to back in this matter if he didn't have Yves as his shadow."

Jax sighed as she claimed an inviting cushion on a silk-upholstered loveseat. "I agree." She liked Governor Lothaine, not just because of his affable nature but due to his ideals closely mirroring her own. It was encouraging to see other leaders in the realm wishing to fight for equality and opportunity for all.

"If only Dvorak had been his right-hand man instead," Uma said as she settled on another loveseat next to Yanis. "He seems like a decent chap."

"Too bad he's forced to act more as a chaperone than a deputy." Yanis patted her knee. "I would've liked to hear more about his views rather than his concerns about Allard drinking too much."

Jax frowned as she replayed the Lord General's behavior in her mind. "Such a vice does not bode well for Allard's longevity as a leader."

"Or a living human being," Aizen added. "He'd already put back two drinks before you and Perry arrived in the banquet hall."

Uma nodded. "And based on his unsteady steps when he entered, he must have been enjoying your gift before he even came down to dinner."

"I guess Dvorak didn't abscond with it fast enough." Jax winced. "I had no idea Allard had such a problem. I never would have placed such a temptation in his room had I known."

"It must be one of Lion's Bane's best-kept scandals," Aizen grunted in consolation. "Ziri's spies provided nothing about this habit."

"Well, if that's the case," Perry said as he poured everyone a glass of honeyed mead, "then Lion's Bane should be commended on their ability to keep state secrets."

"A mark in their favor, I suppose." Jax accepted the drink from her husband with a sardonic smile.

Uma inched to the edge of her seat cushion. "Do you have a hope as to how all this works out, Jax? Is there a faction you're personally backing?"

Jax mimed sewing her lips shut. "Even if I wanted to share, dear one, it would be far too dangerous to do so." She glanced around the room. It was empty, save for her treasured companions. "Should anyone—even one of Glennfeld's staff members—overhear my thoughts, it could risk the sanctity of this peace summit." As much as it pained Jax to keep secrets from her friends, there was too much on the line for the Realm of Virtues at the moment.

Uma's cheeks colored, but she nodded. "Understood."

The conversation then turned to Vivienne's spellbinding performance. "I don't think I've ever heard such a beautiful song in my life," Perry admitted. "It gave me chills."

"No wonder she travels with her father." Uma swirled around the contents of her drink glass. "Hearing such music would lift anyone's spirits."

"It certainly held Governor Lothaine's attention," Aizen murmured.

Jax couldn't hide a small snicker. "You noticed it, too?"

"Noticed what?" Yanis's brow wrinkled.

"That Vivienne and Lothaine seem quite taken with one another." Jax's smile grew. "I must say, it's nice to see such obvious affection amid all the tension."

Uma's eyes widened. "You really think so?"

"Between her batting lashes and his focus barely leaving her face, I'd say so." Jax chortled.

"I have to agree," Perry added. "I haven't seen such longing gazes since the palace chef began caramelizing the pecans on your morning sweet buns." He leaned closer to her, his teasing words whispering against her ear.

A scowl stretched across Aizen's lips. "Do you think Allard is aware his daughter is infatuated with his greatest rival?"

"I doubt that man was aware of much until we reached dessert," Perry joked.

Jax was inclined to agree with him when muffled noises outside the salon preceded the arrival of Ziri and Sabine. "That was quick, my dears. Did you get Lothaine situated?"

Sabine hugged herself, her expression miffed. "Well, we showed him the library."

At her curt response, Ziri stifled a little giggle. "Pay no mind to her. Sabine is a bit put out that our feminine wiles had no effect on the man."

Jax shook her head with a *tsk*. "If you ladies couldn't loosen his tongue, I suppose that all but confirms our suspicions."

"That he's completely besotted with Vivienne?" Sabine countered. "Yes, we were able to garner *that* much."

Ziri shushed her sweetheart before adding, "He was quite chatty about her illustrious performance. Although, I got the sense this isn't the first time Lothaine has heard her sing."

The observation piqued Jax's interest. "Really? I didn't think Heartsworn and Lion's Bane had met with one another prior to this gathering—except on the battlefield."

"Well, that's just it." Ziri stroked her chin. "Lothaine mentioned that Vivienne often serenades her father's troops to rally their spirits. How Lothaine knows this, being in a rival camp, I'm not sure."

"He has no love lost for Allard, however." Sabine perched on the arm of the sofa Yanis and Uma occupied. "He's disgusted that the poor girl is left caring for such a drunkard."

"The dynamic between Allard and Lothaine *is* quite strange." Jax puzzled over the scene at dinner and her takeaways from the evening. "Nothing like two warring leaders, if I'm honest. Lothaine holds an almost personal animosity toward Allard, and the 'Lion' seems to view Lothaine as if he were a mere gnat."

Perry nodded. "I get what you mean. Not so much as an adversary, but an annoyance."

"Right." Jax sighed. "It will make for interesting discussions tomorrow. Of that, I'm sure."

"Do you think Yves and Dvorak will be included?" Aizen arched an eyebrow.

Jax shuddered. "While the thought of being trapped in a room with Yves all day is highly unappealing, they brought their deputies for a reason." It was foolishly naive of her to wish otherwise.

"Then you need your rest." Uma rose and motioned around the room. "We all do."

As much as Jax would have liked to forget her troubles and enjoy the company of those around her, she knew Uma was right. Savant stood on the edge of a knife, and one wrong move from her could send the entire duchy plunging into the abyss. Despite these peace talks taking place on her soil, Jax couldn't let her guard down in the slightest. The fate of the realm depended on it.

Chapter Eleven

George stretched his arms over his head as he climbed out of their tent, his muscles still warm from Serafina's touch. His entire body hummed with contentment as he admired the crimson sunset on the western horizon. While he hadn't gotten much rest after erecting their tent, he certainly felt energized, his hope in their mission renewed.

Serafina soon joined him, lacing her tunic back into place before pressing herself against his broad back and wrapping her arms around his chest.

He covered her hands with his, treasuring the feel of her, of having her love all to himself. For so long, he had yearned for someone to love him, only him, and all of him. Her being there at his side made the chaotic hubbub of the refugee settlement fade away for a time.

But a tantalizing smell quickly brought his mind into focus. "What's that?"

Serafina sniffed the air. "Oh my." Her eyes glittered with enthusiasm. "Venison?"

"Smoked venison, I think." George remembered a similar aroma from palace banquets. "With some sort of sweet glaze." They hadn't had a meal made up of more than dried fruit and bread in days.

Hand in hand, they followed the scent on the breeze, delighted to find a clearing at the center of the camp containing several smoldering fires cooking racks of juicy-looking meat. People sat on the ground and at makeshift tables, chatting away as they waited for dinner to be ready. George noted that while they looked tired and dirty, smiles and laughter were shared. It was a welcoming sight.

"Ah, I see you found your way to our grand dining hall," Marie joked as she emerged from the gathered crowd. She patted George on the back. "All settled?"

He gave her a wry smile. This was like no dining hall he'd ever experienced.

"Yes, thank you, Marie." Serafina beamed. "Where did all this meat come from?"

Marie gave her a wink. "Commander Crowe sent it back with the labor group. Looks like someone's guilty conscience got the better of him tonight."

Serafina and George both chuckled lightly.

"You're in luck. We don't normally eat this well. Here, let me help you find a spot." Marie beckoned them to follow her down a row of makeshift tables and eating circles. "I'll introduce you to another new face who showed up not long after you did. She's a bit surly. Probably could use a dining companion or two."

Happy to engage with the locals about the goings-on in Savant, Serafina and George trailed behind Marie through the boisterous crowd. She stopped near the opposite outskirts of the dining area beside a worn burlap square laid out on the grass.

"Jacqueline, was it?" Marie put her hands on her hips, addressing the shadowy figure sitting cross-legged on the ground. "I'd like you to meet Sera and Gio. They're new to the camp, too."

George's heart skipped at the familiar name, but as his gaze rested on the copper-skinned woman and the strands of burgundy-colored hair peeking out from underneath her hood, his blood froze in his veins. *Virtues.* It was as if she'd stepped off the pages of Jax's letters.

Even from her seated position, George could tell the woman was stunningly beautiful and powerfully built. Her dark eyes sparkled as she stared back at him without fear. The corner of her lip curled upward as she held out her arm. "What a pleasure to meet you, *Gio.*"

George reluctantly shook her hand, his gaze darting to her exposed forearm. He swallowed at the sight of the inky X-shaped tattoo, crowned by a half-moon. Jax had hand-drawn that very same symbol in one of her recent notes, warning him about the person who bore it.

"*Jacqueline,*" he growled through gritted teeth.

Serafina's wide eyes revealed she, too, knew the true, terrifying identity of the woman on the ground before them.

Marie didn't seem to notice the tension layering the air. "Excellent. Well, I must be off to make sure the unattended children are fed." She left them with a friendly wave.

Once the matron was out of earshot, George glared at the newcomer. "What are you doing here, Odaire?"

Her lips curled even more, exposing a gleaming, white smile. "Oh, goodie. Jacqueline's written about me, then? My, I feel so honored to be included within the Duchess of Saphire's official correspondence."

George hated how she spoke about Jax as if she were a dear friend. "What do you want?" he hissed.

Emeraude Odaire, the elusive Grandmaster of the Shadow Brethren, raised an eyebrow. "If Jacqueline has written to you, I'm sure you already know."

Serafina's hand instinctively went to her chest, the Kindheart medallion nestled underneath the fabric of her tunic, hidden from view.

Emeraude noted the action, her dark eyes sparkling with intrigue. "May I see it?"

George and Serafina exchanged resigned looks. It was as they feared after reading Jax's letters. The Grandmaster of the Shadow Brethren was hunting the Virtuous Favors for herself.

Emeraude's expression grew shrewd at their shared reaction. "There's no need for alarm. We're all friends here." An impish grin broke out across her lips.

"I think you and I have a different definition of *friend*." George's hand twitched, yearning to reach for the wrapped bundle strapped to his back, which contained his prized sword. He hadn't wanted to leave it at their campsite for fear of thieves, but Serafina scolded him that he couldn't very well have the magnificent weapon on display without raising questions they didn't wish to answer. Therefore, he'd swaddled it in his cloak and carried it discreetly.

Emeraude chuckled as she held up her hands in a defensive gesture. "Come, now. I promise I'm not here to cause trouble." In an instant, her face contorted into hard, cold rage. "Unless you have what is mine."

George, a seasoned soldier and former Captain of the Saphire Ducal Guard, had to resist shrinking back at her lethal tone. *Jax was right. This is not a woman to be trifled with.*

"I take it you've been following us?" Serafina studied Emeraude with a cool, calm gaze. "For how long?"

The Grandmaster shrugged. "Since you left that little village inn for the mountain pass. The Virtues certainly smiled upon me. It was quite fortuitous to catch wind of your trail while I was in the area."

George cursed under his breath. For days, he hadn't remotely been aware of Emeraude's presence, watching them from the shadows. She was a force to be reckoned with, indeed.

"What do you want from us, then?" Serafina stood by George's side, united against this dangerous threat.

Emeraude batted her long lashes, the picture of feigned innocence. "I'm merely here to claim what's rightfully mine." She pointed a finger at Serafina's chest.

Serafina shielded the spot with her hand. "If you believe this to be yours, then you are sorely misinformed."

Instead of anger, Emeraude's expression flickered with the smallest shadow of doubt. "You carry an ancient relic called a Virtuous Favor, do you not?"

George waited for Serafina's answer, unsure whether the truth or a lie would be more damning for them. Without his sword in hand, he knew they both were at Emeraude's mercy. She was that formidable an assassin.

"I do." Serafina's words were measured. "It is a relic my family has protected for centuries."

As the words floated across Serafina's lips, Emeraude's eyes widened, and she leapt to her feet. "*What? Centuries?*" she seethed through gritted teeth. "That's impossible."

George was surprised by the fury radiating from her, but strangely, he didn't feel as if it were directed toward them.

"I do not lie." Serafina emulated an eerie calm as she spoke. "My family has been part of the Forgotten—*Favored* Ones since Allonious Xavier ordered his companions to spirit the relics away. I am a descendant of the great Gwendolyn Dawnbourne."

George stilled at the poignant title his beloved used. Serafina's father had long called members of their covenant the Forgotten Ones—people destined to spend their lives in the shadows, protecting the Virtuous Favors. What had brought about this new term, George did not know. Perhaps it was their time spent with the Solis twins, where they learned about ancient prophecies now in play. Whatever the case, he approved. It suited Serafina's noble mission.

Emeraude staggered back a few steps before collapsing onto the burlap blanket. "No. That can't be true." This time, she didn't sound accusatory. She seemed defeated.

When Serafina made no comment, Emeraude balled her fists and punched the earthy ground. "He said *you* had stolen it," she whispered, almost to herself. "That it had been hidden away in *your* fancy archives."

"Stolen what?" Serafina lifted her chin, clearly affronted by the accusation. "Who said this?"

Emeraude ignored the questions, glancing up at her. George was surprised to see that her eyes seemed…sad. "Which one do you carry then?"

"You haven't earned that knowledge. Yet." Serafina pressed her lips together.

The Grandmaster raked the ground with her fingers, watching as the loose dirt fell from her hand. "It seems I've been deceived."

"By whom?" George knelt beside her, his curiosity outweighing his mistrust.

Emeraude met his gaze, and George's surprise grew at the sight of tears glimmering in her eyes. "By the one who gave me this," she spat as she slapped something cool and smooth into George's palm.

He studied what appeared to be a small stone. In the camp's firelight, it was hard to make out all its features, but it appeared to be either black or midnight blue. As he turned it over, he caught sight of some imperfections in the rock, perhaps a carving or scuff mark.

Serafina crouched on the burlap blanket beside him and leaned close to examine the item herself. "What is this? Some type of gem?"

Emeraude now sat hugging her knees to her chest. "It's a nightmare stone."

The name meant nothing to George, but from the way Serafina went rigid and knocked it out of his hand, he knew there was more to the story.

Emeraude picked it up with a little snort. "It's harmless, lady archivist. Its bark is much worse than its bite."

George raised an inquiring eyebrow in Serafina's direction, silently asking her to explain her knee-jerk reaction.

Her apprehensive gaze never left the stone.

Emeraude smirked at her wary countenance. "Lord Pettraud merely believed the nightmare stone to be a legend, but clearly, you do not. Let me reassure you—I have not been plagued by hallucinations since it came into my possession two months ago."

"Hallucinations?" George parroted, confused.

Emeraude held the stone flat in her palm, its polished surface capturing the dying sun and glow from the camp. "The legends say when nightmare stone was first discovered in the heart of the Azure Mountains, it decimated the mining expedition team that found the ore deposit. It caused great chaos—so much so, the Duke of Beautraud at the time ordered the mine to be filled in to prevent anyone from accessing the stone and using it as a weapon."

"You really haven't been affected?" Serafina's lower lip quivered.

Emeraude shook her head. "I won't lie, receiving it gave me goosebumps and left me unnerved, but it was my own mind playing tricks." She closed her fingers around the stone, her anger flaring.

"Tricks upon tricks."

"Who gave it to you?" George was still waiting for an answer to his original question.

Emeraude's muscles relaxed slightly. "I don't know his name. I hoped your Duchess could help me."

George wished he knew all the details about how their meeting had gone. He couldn't quite believe Ziri had allowed Jax to face off with the Grandmaster of the Shadow Brethren, but then he realized that if Jax had wanted to speak with Emeraude, nothing short of death would have stopped her. "Why did you think Jax would know?"

Her lip twitched into a small smile. Why, he wasn't sure. "I thought she would recognize the family crest. She's seen enough of them in her time."

"Family crest?" Serafina tilted her head.

Emeraude rose from the burlap blanket and motioned them to follow her. They made their way to a nearby fire, the smell of the venison juices dripping into the flames making George's stomach grumble with hunger.

Emeraude held the stone out toward the firelight, banishing the shadows that had obscured it before. "I wanted to know whose crest this was."

Together, George and Serafina leaned forward to examine the strange symbol etched into the inky midnight-blue rock. A crescent moon set within a blazing sun stared back at them, the icon sending strange shivers up George's spine. His gaze flicked to Serafina's neck, remembering the other necklace that hung alongside the Kindheart medallion. But it wasn't only the familiarity of the etching that gave him pause. The very nature of the design emitted a sinister feeling.

Emeraude cocked her head, astutely studying them for any sign of recognition. "Have you seen this before?"

"No." Serafina's reply was small and fragile. "But we *have* seen something similar." Taking a deep breath, she pulled forth the thinner chain hiding underneath her tunic, dangling the Dawnbourne family crest over the fire for Emeraude to see. As the surname suggested, the gold crest reflected a dawning sun molded behind a pair of rolling hills. The artistic style was nearly identical to the one carved into Emeraude's nightmare stone, down to each sun's rays.

Emeraude's shaking fingers reached for Serafina's pendant, stroking the image set in gold. She quickly yanked them back, as if the metal had seared her fingertips. With the same hand, she ran a finger along the tattoo inked into her skin, tracing the crescent moon that looked like a crown over the Shadow Brethren's X. The mark declaring her the guild's Grandmaster.

George noted the similarities between the moon in her tattoo and the one on the nightmare stone. What was going on here?

"Why do you have a crescent moon above your guild brand?"

Both Emeraude and Serafina looked at him with perplexed expressions at his sudden change in topic. "It's my Grandmaster marking. It symbolizes my rank."

"But why a crescent moon?" George pressed.

She shrugged. "Because it means something to me. My father used a wax seal bearing a moon to sign his correspondence. I chose it for my Grandmaster mark so I would never forget the promise I made to myself."

Serafina's prismatic gaze had also been drawn to the eerie tattoo. "What is your connection to the Virtuous Favors, Emeraude? Please, tell us."

George expected a fiery retort from the young woman, but she released a heavy sigh instead. "Let's get ourselves some food first, shall we? It's quite a long tale."

Chapter Twelve

The trio settled onto the burlap blanket that was to be their dining table for the evening, each bearing a small platter containing glistening, glazed meat and a few mouthfuls of potatoes. While George eyed the meager feast hungrily, the apprehension he felt in Emeraude's presence made his stomach queasy.

The Grandmaster of the Shadow Brethren sat with crossed legs and took a few bites of venison. She chewed in silence for several minutes, but eventually cleared her throat. "Before I fell in with the guild, I was the daughter of a respected merchant." Her dark eyes filled with haunted regret. "I lived with my father and brothers in a comfortable cottage on a Hestian viscount's estate. Every day, I worked alongside my father to help care for my younger brothers in the absence of our late mother. We were happy for a time. Until everything changed."

George listened intently to her tale, his food still untouched.

"In the middle of a summer's night, the Viscount's estate was attacked. I woke to the screams of the household carrying across the fields and my father desperately trying to hide us all." Emeraude's lilting words were filled with pain. "He hurried us into a small crawlspace under the floorboards, begging for us to be quiet. I tried to calm my three brothers as best as I could, and together, we crouched under the floor of our home for what felt like hours." Her gaze dropped to the earth beside the burlap blanket, tracing an unknown symbol in the dirt with the hilt of her knife.

"The cries from the estate faded, and we thought whoever had attacked the Viscount had finally retreated. But then we heard footsteps outside our cottage." She took a fortifying breath before continuing, as if she were reliving the memory.

"It all happened so fast. The men were through the front door in an instant, tearing apart our home. They found us hiding under the floorboards just as quickly. My father tried to defend against them, but he was no match for these brutes. They had him pinned to the floor with a sword to his throat, and my brothers and I were quickly bound with ropes. We were helpless as they ripped apart our home, taking whatever items of value they could. I thought them terrible barbarians, but the worst was yet to come."

Emeraude blinked back the emotion in her faraway gaze. "One of the men called that they had found something hidden in the walls of the crawlspace, and I never saw my father look more devastated in my entire life—not even when my mother died giving birth to my youngest brother. The man climbed out of our hiding place, holding a small, flame-shaped medal in his palm. I'd never seen it before, and I couldn't understand why my father sobbed uncontrollably at the sight of it. It was small, around the size of a plum."

Emeraude's fingers tightened around her knife as she stabbed at a piece of meat. "My father begged the men to leave the gold medal. He offered my brothers and me in exchange. He told them we would grow to be good, strong workers. The man who found the piece—he seemed to be in charge—laughed at my father's offer before driving a sword through his chin. He pocketed the treasure my father was willing to sell his children for and led my brothers and me away as our house burned to the ground. We were tossed into a wagon and traveled with our captors for weeks before arriving at our new home—the Zaltorian enclave of the Shadow Brethren. I was eight at the time."

Beside George, Serafina let loose a small gasp of astonishment.

Emeraude chewed on another piece of venison. "During the first months of our captivity, I couldn't rid that gold medal from my mind. How could my father, a man I thought loved me more than life, be willing to trade me and my brothers for such a small, unremarkable trinket? It didn't make sense." She shook her head.

"But then my brother Edward died. While the Brethren kept me in the kitchens as a maid, they began training my brothers to serve the guild. Edward, only seven, had been on his first scouting mission when he slipped and fell into a gorge." Emeraude briefly closed her eyes. "His death forced me to focus on staying alive. I wouldn't be able to find any answers if I died at the hands of my kidnappers. So, instead of sulking, I started listening and watching. Learning how the Brethren trained for combat. How they used the shadows to move silently about. How they became revered assassins across the realm." Her grip tightened once more around her knife.

"When I was twelve, I asked for my first contract. The Zaltorian enclave leader, Prelate Adnan, the man who had killed my father and ripped me from my home, laughed at my gumption, but gave me a writ. I was to kill a local financier who'd lost many people a great deal of money. I brought Prelate Adnan the man's head before nightfall, much to the enclave's surprise. Neither of my two remaining brothers had ever managed such a feat, and they'd been in training since our capture. It was then I was formally welcomed to serve the Brethren."

George bristled at her brutal story. "Why serve the people who imprisoned you?"

She met his gaze, her expression unreadable. "Because at the time, I believed it the only way to find the answers I sought. As a working member of the Brethren, I was given certain freedoms, like the ability to come and go as I pleased. And I needed to find out *why* my beloved father had been willing to sell his children to murderers and thieves in exchange for a mere trinket." Her fingers balled into a fist. By now, the sun had set, and the long shadows from nearby campfires washed over her.

"And did you?" Serafina asked quietly.

Emeraude shrugged. "It took me years before I located a collector living in Hestes. A collector who had combed through the ruins of the Hestian Viscount's estate after the Brethren ransacked it. While the guild may have robbed the land of all its gold, they left behind some fairly valuable documents in the Viscount's archives. This collector…allowed me to peruse them."

George shuddered at her pregnant pause. He highly doubted "allowed" was the right word to describe what had happened.

"It was in these documents that I found the Viscount's lineage, harking back centuries, around the time of the realm's founding. The original family name, Nightguard, could be traced back hundreds of years. To my surprise, I discovered that my father's family had once been linked to the Nightguard house. A young lord had married a commoner and was forced out of the manor, but not the estate. His family would continue to live in a small cottage on the estate's border for years to come. The home *I* had grown up in," Emeraude whispered, almost in disbelief at her own story.

"What I found even more intriguing is that while the Viscount adopted a different family name, this man continued using the Nightguard moniker, as did his heirs, until my great-grandmother decided to take her husband's name." Firelight shimmered in Emeraude's eyes. "From there, I began researching more and more about the Nightguard family, visiting every archive in the realm. Even Saphire's." A small, knowing smile curled on her lips.

"But it wasn't until my twenty-third birthday that I found something worthwhile. In Isla DeLacqua, of all places, while I was on a contract for the guild. I learned that an old estate had fallen into ruin, abandoned by its residents. On a whim, I decided to visit their library and have a look at what was left behind. To my amazement, I found it filled with old documents, dating back to before the Realm of Virtues was established. Letters home from someone named Corporal Lunara, a man who fought alongside the rebellion in an effort to overthrow the Ancient Faith and its corrupt Supreme Priest. In his letters, Lunara described a man in his unit, one he greatly admired. His name was Solmaud, and he was widely considered one of the greatest fighters within the resistance."

George had been in the process of finally bringing a piece of venison to his lips when Emeraude's words almost made his heart stop. *Solmaud*? This was a name he knew from Serafina's tales about the origins of the Virtuous Favors.

Solmaud the Victor was the man to whom four ceremonial gold relics had been gifted before the final duel against the Ancient Faith's champion. When he emerged victorious from the fight, Solmaud told the rebellion's leaders how his hand had been guided by bravery, intelligence, humbleness, and kindness during the clash. The leaders, in turn, believed each of these virtues came to Solmaud through the special gifts *they* had crafted for the warrior to wear into battle. Using this as the base of their power, their divine right to rule was established, and that was how the Realm of Virtues was born.

"What?" Serafina had put aside her platter altogether, sitting in rapt attention in front of Emeraude. "You found letters that spoke of Solmaud?"

"That and much, much more." Emeraude grinned. "But one note nearly took my breath away. Corporal Lunara wrote to his wife about the epic duel he witnessed, when Solmaud battled the Ancient Faith's strongest warrior and emerged the victor, effectively putting an end to the war. Accompanying the letter was a portrait he'd drawn of the man, believing Solmaud to be a god among mere mortals. This portrait changed everything for me."

She placed her half-eaten plate on the ground and wiped her hands on her pants before reaching for the travel pack strapped to her side. As Emeraude rummaged around, George and Serafina seized on the brief lull in excitement to scarf down some of their meal.

George tried to savor the meat, but the sweet glaze turned to ash on his tongue as Emeraude extracted an old piece of parchment from her bag.

"Is that the letter?" Serafina choked on her bite.

Mindful of her surroundings, Emeraude laid the brittle paper on the burlap. An instant later, she had a candle in her other hand and lit the wick for more focused light.

George set his dinner aside, making sure his hands were clean as he scooted forward to examine the detailed charcoal drawing of a chiseled, rugged warrior. His square jaw and sharp cheekbones nearly jutted off the page, his hair cut close to his head. Paired with dark brows and wide eyes, he was a formidable-looking figure. But it wasn't the man's features that fascinated him the most. It was the strangely familiar item pinned to the man's breast pocket. A large, round setting that held what looked to be a massive gemstone.

Beside him, Serafina stifled a quiet whimper. She'd seen the resemblance, too.

The Kindheart medallion.

But that wasn't all he wore. No, Solmaud the Victor was decorated in many fine accessories, with several items displayed on his chest and arm. George stopped counting after eight. But if the Kindheart medallion was pinned to this man's chest, that had to mean the other Favors were on his person, too.

"Do you recognize any of these items?" There was a current of desperation in Emeraude's voice. George almost felt sorry for her.

Serafina was silent for a time before she finally bobbed her head. "I do. I see the relic my family has long protected."

"Which one?" Emeraude's tone was surprisingly gentle. "Please. I have to know."

With a shaking hand, Serafina reached for the other chain around her neck, carefully shifting her body so as to shield them from prying eyes. From underneath her tunic collar, she withdrew the gold disc, a glimmering aquamarine stone set in its center. "The Kindheart medallion." Serafina let the relic sway in the air before hurriedly stowing it away.

Emeraude continued to stare at the vacant space the Kindheart medallion had occupied, her trance-like gaze unblinking. George was about to wave his hand in front of her when Emeraude pointed to the drawing of the medallion pinned to Solmaud's chest. "She holds the Kindheart." Again, the dazed woman sounded as if she were speaking to herself.

When she straightened, her stare turned hard. "Then I would like to ask for your help, lady archivist."

"My help?" Serafina looked puzzled by the sudden request.

"I have never forgotten the item my father was willing to place above my own life." Emeraude's finger pointed to the ancient portrait, to a small, flame-shaped medal pinned to the breast of Solmaud's uniform. "I need your help to find it."

Chapter Thirteen

Serafina's lips drew into a thin line, her brow wrinkled with worry.

"What makes you think that medal is one of the Virtuous Favors?" Her hand swept over the drawing. "This portrait shows Solmaud decorated in many fine pieces."

Annoyance flickered in Emeraude's eyes. "Corporal Lunara had much more to say about the matter. He chronicled the aftermath of Solmaud's duel with the dedication of a scholar. In his diaries, he wrote about how the four crafted items Solmaud wore to battle had become revered by the newly established world order. They were deemed the 'Virtuous Favors,' said to be imbued by the Virtues of Humility, Kindness, Bravery, and Intelligence. They were soon put on display in Saphire's capital city, the center of the realm, and celebrated as holy relics."

Emeraude's expression clouded over. "But Lunara soon noted how tension began brewing between the nations' rulers, each wanting to hide the Favors away from the public, to bask in their glory all for themselves. Things got so bad, Corporal Lunara worried he'd be called to war again. But then, the Favors were stolen from Saphire, never to be seen again."

George stroked the stubble on his chin as he considered

Emeraude's words. Corporal Lunara's account of the relics' origins sounded nearly identical to the story Serafina's father had passed down to her.

Serafina, however, looked dubious. "Be that as it may, what makes you think that tiny medal is one of the favors?" She pointed to several other larger pieces pinned to the warrior's uniform. "Why not any of these?"

Emeraude *tsk*-ed at the question. "Because Corporal Lunara visited Saphire to pay homage to the Virtuous Favors alongside many of his comrades." She reached again for her pack. "And as he seemed to have a habit of doing, he made a sketch of what he saw." She unfurled another roll of parchment, this one larger and made of thicker fiber.

The illustration showcased the same detailed strokes as Solmaud's portrait. The artist had captured a large, ornate display case with four tiers, each supporting a different item. George immediately noticed the Kindheart medallion on the bottom level, followed by a shield-shaped piece and an eight-pointed star artifact. On the top tier rested a small flame-shaped medal that looked just like the one pinned to Solmaud's breast pocket in the portrait.

"I can't believe it." George felt Serafina's cold fingers encircle his wrist, her grip almost unbearably tight. "Four relics bestowed by the very Virtues themselves." Tears ran down her cheeks. "The Virtuous Favors."

Emeraude raised a bemused eyebrow at Serafina's emotional reaction.

"Sorry." Serafina smiled bashfully, trying to collect herself. "My entire life has been in service of these relics, yet this—this is the first time I've seen them all together."

Any trace of amusement vanished from Emeraude. "What do you mean, all together?"

"My childhood was steeped in stories about the Favors." Serafina rubbed her temples. "But they were separated for a reason. My family's responsibility was only to the Kindheart medallion. We knew nothing of what happened to the others, and I only know them by name, not sight."

"She speaks the truth," George added. While they hunted for the Intelligeye sigil, they did not know what the relic looked like. The Solis twins had not shared a description of the item with them. Not because they wouldn't, no, but strangely, because they *couldn't*. Whether it was Elias's poison or—as the twins believed—the effects of prophecy at work, neither could recall details of a treasured relic they'd guarded for years. George's apprehensive gaze moved to the sketched image, wondering which of the three remaining artifacts the sigil was.

Emeraude's hand balled into a fist. "Then I am no closer to finding this blasted piece than I was yesterday." She flicked her wrist dismissively at the hand-drawn flame-shaped medal atop the display case.

The action exposed her forearm, and George again caught sight of her Shadow Brethren tattoo. She'd said she used her father's seal as her Grandmaster marking so that she would never forget the promise she made to herself. How had an eight-year-old girl seeking answers about her father's betrayal become the leader of the Brethren?

"I didn't think you'd admit defeat so easily."

Emeraude's head whipped in his smirking direction. "What do you mean? If *she* doesn't know anything more," she pouted, jutting a finger toward Serafina, "what else can I do? I've spent over fifteen years scouring this continent for clues, and this is all I have." She indicated the two documents lying on the burlap blanket, her expression surly.

George folded his arms. "Were you aware that Duke Savant embarked on the very same mission after the Shadow Brethren colluded with the Coalition of Right?"

Emeraude's eyes widened so quickly, he feared they might pop from her skull. "*What?*" The question was a low hiss. "I never bowed to the Coalition."

"Oh, we know you didn't *bow* to them." George thought back on his most recent trip to the Academy, where he, Jax, and their friends had foiled a devious Brethren plot to find long-lost treasure. "But we know Qylvard issued a contract to the guild. And we know he sought refuge among you for a time."

Emeraude composed herself, donning a calm façade. "What does the guild's business dealings have to do with anything?"

"Well," George began with a toss of his shoulder, "while you and your kind were sheltering Qylvard, did the two of you ever discuss the Favors? He was of ducal blood. Perhaps their stories had been passed down to him."

Emeraude scowled. "I did no such thing. I could barely stand to be in that odious man's presence."

Serafina tilted her head. "Then why offer him sanctuary?"

"Because I had no problem with his gold," Emeraude snapped.

"Did you know that once your enclave was raided, Qylvard set out to find Serafina and take the Kindheart medallion from her?" George thought he might get a rise out of the assassin by mentioning the Shadow Brethren stronghold being stormed, but she barely batted an eye at the barbed remark. It was Qylvard's deceitful actions that made her nostrils flare.

Emeraude turned to Serafina. "Is this true?"

"Yes," Serafina said. "It's how George and I met."

He couldn't resist sending a tender smile her way at the fated memory. "So tell us, Emeraude, when did this mysterious man come to you with information about Serafina having *your* family relic?"

Her brow furrowed as she tapped her chin. "Several weeks after our main enclave was raided. I'd ordered the Brethren to scatter into the wind. We'd rebuild when the time was right." Her determined dark eyes glittered in the firelight. "I thought I'd use the time to revisit Isla DeLacqua to see if I could track down anything more about Corporal Lunara. But before I got my affairs in order and departed Beautraud, I was summoned to a meeting."

"Where?" Serafina asked, breathless. "How?"

"It was at a rundown tavern in some little-known corner of the duchy." Emeraude's lips pressed together. "As to how I was invited, I received a letter containing the tavern's address and a drawing." She pointed to the flame-shaped artifact in Corporal Lunara's sketch. "Of my father's special relic."

George and Serafina shared stunned looks.

"When I arrived at the tavern, a man in a hooded cloak approached me and asked me to sit down." Emeraude took the nightmare stone in her hands and began to turn it over. "He didn't introduce himself—he jumped right into a proposal. He said, 'Countess Braeknoch has stolen what you seek.'"

Serafina stiffened with indignation.

"At the time, I had no idea who Countess Braeknoch even was," Emeraude admitted. "And when I asked how this man knew what I was looking for, he chided me, saying that he didn't think it the Brethren's place to question their clients." She scoffed. "How he knew I was with the Brethren, I don't know. I am known only as 'Grandmaster' among the guild and its associates, yet his invitation was addressed to my birth name." Her expression hardened. "When I pressed him again on how he came across this information, he said he had his ways. When I asked him what he wanted in return, he merely slid this across the table."

She held the nightmare stone up with two fingers. "He wanted nothing, other than for me to carry this as a token of our contract."

George's arm instinctively wrapped around Serafina's shoulders.

"I picked up the stone to examine the carving, and when my gaze broke away, the stranger had vanished." Emeraude's jaw clenched. "Never before has anyone ever been able to slip through my grasp undetected. To say I was unsettled would be an understatement." She studied the nightmare stone with wary eyes.

"While I was intrigued by his claims, I also was extremely distrustful. I spent some time searching for information about this strange ore. When I realized it was nightmare stone, I knew I was up against a formidable force. I began looking into Countess Braeknoch, and once I learned of her recent ties to Jacqueline, I decided a reunion was in order." A sudden smile curled on her lips. "Since the Duchess and I have history."

Apprehension roiled in George's stomach as her haunting account ended.

"No one knows I hold a Virtuous Favor beyond our circle of friends," Serafina murmured, her troubled gaze meeting George. "Except..."

George turned to Emeraude, his entire body rigid. "Have you heard of a man who calls himself the Dark Magus?"

The Grandmaster's scoffing laughter quickly quieted at the couple's tense expressions. "Well, anyone who's spent time in Beautraud has heard of him. He's a myth, a fable to scare young children into behaving."

Serafina's hand rested on her chest, the Kindheart medallion hidden beneath her tunic. "I'm afraid he is very, very real."

"Or at least, someone has recently adopted the moniker," George pointed out. "This Dark Magus character issued Qylvard with the task of stealing the Kindheart medallion from Serafina. And I'd be willing to bet"—he pointed to the nightmare stone—"he's the one who propositioned you."

Emeraude swelled with indignation. "What makes you think that?"

"Jax couldn't tell you of any house whom such a crest belongs to, could she?" George scooted to the edge of the burlap blanket and began tracing images in the dirt. "But the sight of it unnerved her, right? As much as she tried to bury it, you could see it in her face."

Emeraude's expression was an unreadable mask.

George continued with his hunch. "Think about all the imagery we've seen at play surrounding the Virtuous Favors." His elbow jutted in Serafina's direction. "The Dawnbourne crest." He quickly drew the scene of the rising dawn on Serafina's family emblem in the dirt. "The seal your father used." George drew Emeraude's crescent moon tattoo. "And then there's the insignia of the Solis family, a clan with confirmed ties to the Favors." Deciding not to elaborate more about the Intelligeye sigil in front of the Grandmaster just yet, he copied down the image of the blazing sun, high in the sky.

Emeraude's quick intake of breath validated George's suspicion.

He studied her intently. "The Dawnbourne and Solis crests…you've seen them before today, haven't you?" While he knew the answer, he wanted confirmation from her.

She slowly nodded. "A few years ago. I found them carved into the bedrock underneath an old Ancient Faith temple in Saphire. Five crests in all. I recognized two. The one my father used, and…" Her gaze took on a faraway look. "The emblem of House Xavier."

George forced a calming breath. Jax had spoken of finding an altar when she and Perry had ventured into the old tunnels near Favored Crossing. "Jax said only a few runes were discernible. The others had been vandalized."

Even in the shadowy firelight, he noticed Emeraude's cheeks reddening. "When I saw my father's seal etched into stone, I feared for the secret he'd guarded. I wanted to destroy the entire altar so as to protect whatever covenant he had with the Virtuous Favors, but Jacqueline and her husband interrupted my work before I could complete it."

"How did you find out about the altar beneath Favored Crossing?" Serafina shifted so she could hug her knees to her chest. "I'd never heard of such a place until Jax told us about her adventure."

"I came across the information five or six years ago, through some skilled detective work on my part, if I do say so myself." The corner of Emeraude's lip curled upward. "You see, I thought it curious that the Virtuous Favors were stolen right from under Allonious Xavier's nose and that, ultimately, very little was done to retrieve them. It made me wonder if Allonious was somehow involved in their disappearance. I decided I needed to learn more about him, so I spent a summer in Saphire conducting research in the ducal archives."

George straightened. "The ducal archives? That's not possible."

"And why not?" Emeraude raised a taunting eyebrow.

"Those archives are not open to the public. Even scholars aren't allowed to visit." A growing sense of dread filled him. "It's for the ducal family only."

"Is that so?" Emeraude blew on her fingernails, as if she'd been buffing them.

George felt the venison flip in his digesting stomach. "H-how did you gain entry?"

"I'm the Grandmaster of the Shadow Brethren, my dear boy." Despite having to be nearly a decade younger, Emeraude scolded him as if he were a small child. "There is no place in this realm that is off limits to me. Now, shall I continue my story?"

George bit back his heated questions. The information she had was more valuable than his wounded ego.

"Within the Saphirian ducal archives, I came across some travel logs made by the Ducal Guard during Allonious's reign. It took me a while, but I eventually noticed a pattern. After the Favors were stolen, every year, during the summer solstice, the Duke would leave the capital attended only by a small party of guards. In these records, it was noted each time as a 'nature retreat.' Wondering why a grand Duke would embark on such a journey, I did some more digging, this time in Allonious's journals."

George shuddered at what he was hearing. If Jax learned that the Grandmaster of the Shadow Brethren had broken into her family's private archives and read her ancestor's personal thoughts…Virtues, he was glad he was no longer the Captain of the Ducal Guard with the sworn duty to report such a grievance.

"While Allonious mentioned nothing about the relics other than dismay over them being stolen," Emeraude continued, "he *did* make mention about this nature retreat and how he valued taking time away from the throne to enjoy the simple pleasures of life. He included a small sketch of the campsite, and above the tree line, I could just make out the outline of a building in the distance."

Emeraude rubbed the back of her hand across her eyelids. "At first, I thought I was seeing things because I recognized the domed tower of an Ancient Faith temple. I'd seen them throughout Zaltor after I was captured by the Brethren. But I'd been led to believe that the temples were destroyed in other nations, following the great war. Intrigued by what the Duke of Saphire was doing near an Ancient Faith temple, I redirected my search, looking for old records mapping out where the Ancient Faith temples in Saphire had been located. It took some time, but I eventually found a map in a Zaltorian library.

"One by one, I visited each, finding that most had been completely decimated, with villages and towns built atop their foundation. But the last temple I came upon still stood, despite being in utter ruin. And once I learned of a hamlet nearby called Favored Crossing…well, I knew something was afoot."

George pointed to the Dawnbourne, Nightguard, and Solis seals.

"Do you remember the fourth crest you found carved into the altar beneath the temple?"

Before you destroyed it, he wanted to add, but thought better of it.

With a nod, Emeraude ran a long finger through the dirt. "It's very similar in design to that of the Dawnbourne emblem," she explained as she drew a sphere nestled between two rolling hills. "But notice how Serafina's emphasizes the sun's rays? This one did not. It was merely a half-circle with no other detail."

Serafina pulled out the necklace with her family's insignia and studied it. "The imagery reveals the sun turning to night. We have dawn," she said, holding up her own crest. "Midday belongs to the Solises, this unknown house must be linked to dusk, and Emeraude, you own the night."

"And there's this." George traced the nightmare stone etching into the earth. "A moon within a blazing sun. The Virtuous Favors as one."

Serafina shivered. "The Dark Magus has styled himself his own sigil, showing his dominion over the Favors."

"How are you so sure the man I spoke with was the Dark Magus?" Emeraude raised a skeptical brow.

George placed a hand on Serafina's open palm. "Because he sent you after her. When Qylvard failed to bring him the Kindheart medallion, the Dark Magus gave the task to you."

"That's a lie." Emeraude swelled with indignation. "The hooded stranger sent me after a woman who supposedly stole my family relic. If this man really was the Dark Magus, he would have already known Serafina didn't have my father's treasure."

George realized he had offended her honor. "I didn't mean to suggest you'd made such a contract with him. I'm saying you've been *used.* The Dark Magus sent you after Serafina, knowing you were searching for your family's relic." He snapped his fingers as his theory continued to develop. "For some reason, he wanted you two to meet. And all he asked for in return is for you to carry this." He reached for the discarded nightmare stone and held it up against the flickering light of the nearby campfires.

Serafina gnawed on her lower lip. "Well, it's quite possible he expected Emeraude to kill me before I even had the chance to prove that I didn't have her relic. Then, she would've been left with the Kindheart medallion."

"Which he'd be more than willing to take off her hands," George suggested.

Emeraude scoffed. "Please. After finding out Serafina didn't have my father's treasure, I would've realized I'd been duped by the contract-giver, and I would've kept the medallion for myself."

George frowned at the plausible scenario as he studied the nightmare stone. As night blanketed their campsite, the intensity of the stone's color seemed to deepen, and he was beginning to feel as if he held an endless void in his palm. He tore his wary gaze away, and his attention moved instinctively to the night sky. Clouds shifted overhead, and the newborn moon appeared, its light shining brightly.

A heartbeat later, he felt a strange warmth radiating from the stone, growing uncomfortable against his skin. A warning? Or something else?

"We need to get rid of this. Now." He jumped to his feet, frantically scanning the campsite. "We need to get this stone away from all these people."

"What? Why?" Both Serafina and Emeraude pressed as they rose from the burlap blanket.

George absently massaged his thigh. His muscles had grown tight sitting down for so long, but fear spurred him onward. "I know this might sound absurd, but something tells me he's *watching* us through this." With wide eyes, George begged his companions to believe him. He didn't entirely understand how a simple stone could be used as a type of looking glass, but deep in his heart, he knew the Dark Magus capable of such otherworldly power. After all George had experienced during his adventures, he'd come to believe in such mysterious abilities.

Serafina's face drained of color at his accusation. "He knew you'd track me down, Emeraude," she hissed in a terrified whisper. "He knew you'd lead him to the Kindheart medallion. Virtues, he may even think we'd help you find the Favor *you're* searching for."

"Collecting them all in one place," George concluded grimly. "Prime for the taking."

Emeraude glanced uneasily from Serafina to George. "Have you both gone mad? How in the Virtues can some man be *watching* us through a stone? What you're talking about, it—it isn't real. It isn't *possible*."

George balled his fist around the stone, hoping that by doing so, he was suffocating whatever mysterious power it possessed. "In all my years serving Saphire and the Ducal Guard, I have encountered many strange things. Things that couldn't be explained within the limits of our understanding."

He held Emeraude's dubious gaze. "You said so yourself, the nightmare stone was buried away long ago due to the chaotic influence it had on those it encountered. What's to say this Dark Magus cad hasn't harnessed its bizarre effects to do his bidding? He must have the ability to do so. He clearly wants the Virtuous Favors so he can control whatever divine power they wield."

George shot a desperate glance at Serafina, asking for her support in this. She knew firsthand the Favors were imbued with some unknown esoteric force. She'd told him how the Kindheart medallion spoke to her from time to time. Everyday pieces of jewelry didn't *talk* to their wearers.

"He's right, Emeraude. Think about it." Serafina placed a tender palm on the Grandmaster's forearm—the gentle touch made the young woman flinch. "Why else would this hooded man give you a mythical stone to carry on your person during this contract? He meant to use it to *track* you."

Emeraude shifted warily on the balls of her feet. "So, how do we get rid of it?"

Relief flooded through George that they'd somehow convinced her of the danger. "We first need to put some distance between ourselves and this camp. Then, we can bury the stone in the jungle and be done with it."

Serafina tugged at his shirtsleeve, her eyes narrowed. He knew she wouldn't like this plan—it meant putting distance between Elias and information about the Intelligeye sigil.

"If this Dark Magus is as demonic as you believe him to be," Emeraude began, her words calculated and drawn out, "if he arrives to find the stone buried and us gone, he might look for answers at this camp and unleash his disappointment on these refugees." She motioned to the people milling all around, oblivious to the threat lingering over them.

George suppressed a smile. He hadn't expected the Grandmaster of the Shadow Brethren to care about innocent bystanders.

"Then what do we do?" Serafina gave a nervous tug of her braided hair. "It's not like we can toss it into a fire and destroy it."

Emeraude took the stone from George. "We're, what, three or four leagues from the coast? I'll ride out tonight, cast it into the sea, and be done with it."

"Really? You'd do that?" Serafina asked, seeming genuinely surprised.

"Of course." Emeraude folded her arms, her expression murderous. "I will *not* let someone use me as a pawn in their power games. I am the Grandmaster of the Shadow Brethren. *I* do the using."

George almost laughed at her petulant remark but thought better of it.

"You could just kill us, take the Kindheart medallion, and give the Dark Magus what he wants."

George whipped his head in Serafina's direction, about to ask why she would ever put such an idea in Emeraude's mind, but the Grandmaster responded first.

"I could, yes." Her tone was cool and commanding. "But this is about what *I* want, lady archivist. If the Dark Magus is collecting the Virtuous Favors for himself, I doubt he would play nicely when it comes to locating my father's treasure." In the blink of an eye, Emeraude had a long dagger in her hand, its tip bouncing back and forth from George to Serafina. "Whereas I believe you two would be much more willing to assist in my search."

George held up his hands. "There's no need for threats, now. I thought we were all friends here."

She smiled devilishly at him for using her own words against her.

"Emeraude, we don't know anything about the Virtuous Favor your father protected." Serafina's plea rang with conviction. "I wish we did because then we could help ensure it didn't fall into the hands of the Dark Magus." She wisely didn't share that she and George shared a larger goal—to locate *all* the Virtuous Favors and bring them home to Saphire, away from the Dark Magus's reach.

"Really?" Emeraude drew out the word. "I heard from a pretty little barmaid that you two have been asking questions about a royal-eyed man. Why?"

George had an answer for her that didn't involve the Favors. "Elias Pettraud is a traitor to Saphire, and I've been tasked with bringing him back for punishment."

"Is that so? A traitor to Saphire, you say? Why, you'd think Jacqueline would send more than two people after him if that were the case."

From her tone, George could tell Emeraude was stringing them along. "It's a delicate matter, given the civil war plaguing Savant. She didn't think it wise to send a horde of Saphirian soldiers to accomplish the task."

"She didn't even send an active member of the Ducal Guard." Emeraude's expression grew shrewd. "An odd decision, indeed."

George shifted his gaze to Serafina. *What do we do?*

Serafina took a deep breath and held her head high. "We believe Elias stole a Virtuous Favor on behalf of the Dark Magus. That Favor has since been entrusted to my care by the Solis clan we mentioned earlier." She threaded her fingers through George's calloused hand. "George and I plan to get it back."

"I see." If Emeraude was surprised by her declaration, she didn't show it. "Then I'm coming with you."

Serafina raised her palm. "It would be a waste of your time. The Favor we seek has been guarded for centuries by the Solis family. It couldn't be the one that belonged to your father."

Emeraude spun her dagger in the air before sliding it into her boot. "I realize that. But if this Elias fellow is working with the Dark Magus on his quest to find the Favors, he might have information about where mine might be."

George gave Serafina a covert shrug. *She has a point,* he thought. His beloved still looked unnerved.

"If you are worried that I will steal this Favor from you," Emeraude began, clearly noticing Serafina's hesitance, "why don't you enter into a contract with me?"

Serafina stiffened. "The last thing I want is the Brethren getting involved with this."

"Considering I *am* the Brethren, we already are." Emeraude's smirk turned slightly threatening. "But by entering a contract, I am bound to fulfill my end of the agreement, or I forfeit my life."

George raised an eyebrow. "Sounds extreme."

"And hard to enforce," Serafina added with a scoff.

Emeraude placed a hand on her hip. "Am I to take it that neither of you knows about the Grand Covenant?"

She took their silence as an affirmation and paced around them in a small circle. "When a formal contract is drafted within the guild, the Brethren's seal is stamped on the document. There is…a *bond* within that seal, wherein if the one who is contracted should fail or break the contract, death befalls them before they can draw another breath."

George's mouth dropped open. "That can't be possible."

"It's how many a member has died throughout the centuries." Emeraude's response was strangely unreadable.

Serafina shook her head. "What you're talking about…it's almost like—"

"Magic?" Shadows slid across Emeraude's sharp features. "I must agree, for I have no other explanation for how the seal forges such a deadly bond."

George's grip tightened on Serafina's hand. Now he knew why Emeraude so readily accepted his theory that the Dark Magus held the power to track them through the nightmare stone. He'd come across some inexplicable things throughout his life, but this Grand Covenant surely rated as one of the most unbelievable. Yet, if the Kindheart medallion spoke to Serafina, and prophecies from long ago were coming to pass, what was to say that deadly magic couldn't be imbued within a simple wax seal?

"What do you propose this contract entail?" George asked, wondering what tricks Emeraude had up her sleeves.

She reached for the pack strapped at her side, rummaged around, and pulled out a blank sheet of parchment. "That you're hiring me to help you find this Elias Pettraud and locate whatever relic it is you seek. Once the relic is found, it is to be delivered and left with the client."

"For eternity," Serafina interjected. "Just to ensure you can't try and steal it from me at a later date."

Emeraude chuckled. "You archivists do love your fine print. All right, I'll accept those terms with a stipulation of my own." The laughter vanished from her glittering eyes. "I shall be allowed to extract whatever information Elias Pettraud has about my father's Favor through any means necessary."

George flinched, understanding the torture she likely intended to inflict. Even though Elias had caused his friends immeasurable suffering, George didn't approve of such cruel methods. He had also intended to bring Perry's brother back to Saphire to be tried for his crimes. But if Elias were the prisoner of the Lion's Bane rebel faction, George doubted such a feat would be possible.

"Doesn't this Grand Covenant conflict with the contract issued by the man who gave you the nightmare stone?" Serafina countered.

Emeraude shook her head. "I never entered into a formal agreement with him. He vanished before I could make such an offer."

George could feel Serafina's gaze on him, waiting for his answer. Her commitment was to the Virtuous Favors, whereas his was to seeking justice for all his companions.

"As long as you don't harm either Serafina or myself during this mission, we have an agreement." He held out his free hand to shake on it.

Instead, Emeraude whipped out a quill from her bag and hastily scribbled across the parchment. "Is this satisfactory?" She held the document out for them to read.

George squinted to read her handwriting in the dim light. "Yes."

Serafina nodded her acknowledgment.

Emeraude again reached for her pack and when she withdrew

her hand, she clutched something in her fist. With graceful movements, she darted over to a nearby campfire and held the object close to the flames for a time. It looked like an old branding stamp. When she returned, she jabbed her fingertip with the point of her quill, allowing a few drops of her blood to drip onto the page. She then pressed the hot brand at the bottom of the contract, and when she removed it, a blood-red seal shimmered in its place.

"Then a Grand Covenant is forged between us. Upon my life, I will help you find Elias Pettraud and locate your lost Favor."

George and Serafina shared a wary look, and George thought with a jolt of panic, *Have we just made a deal with a devil?*

Chapter Fourteen

The sunlight tickled her cheeks, encouraging Jax to wake from her fading dreams. Disentangling herself from the comfort of Perry's slumbering arms, she admired the beautiful morning blossoming outside her window. The sight of the lush green meadow filled her with hope. *Perhaps, by tonight, we shall have peace.*

Jax inwardly reprimanded herself for such wishful thinking. Today would undoubtedly be trying. Allard and Lothaine would each want their say, believing themselves to be in the right when it came to ruling the Savantian people.

"I must be wise about this," she murmured as she climbed out of bed and meandered into the suite's luxurious washroom. "Letting them speak too freely may end this summit before it's even started."

She studied her reflection in the washroom mirror, noting the faint lines in the skin around her eyes. *Those weren't there a year ago.* And she'd probably gain a few more before all was said and done with this summit.

As Jax washed her face and returned to the bedchamber to select a comfortable gown, she mulled over her strategy for the day. In order to make any progress, she needed to understand what these men truly wanted. What fueled their desire to lead Savant? Simply the lust for power, or was something greater guiding them toward this future?

She remained deep in thought as she secured the golden clasps of her violet gown.

"At least the weather seems to be cooperating." Perry's arms encircled her waist as he pulled her against him, away from her concerns.

She kissed him good morning, wordlessly asking for his assistance with the remaining clasps on her dress. "Indeed, especially if a walk is required to cool down heated tempers."

His brow furrowed with worry. "Are you sure I cannot attend the meeting with you? I'd be more than happy to sit mute at your side."

Jax placed a tender palm on his chest, her fingers sliding under the neck of his tunic to caress his skin. "I want the Savantians to feel as though they outnumber me. If any inkling of threat is perceived, it could spell disaster."

Perry gave her a crooked smile. "It's been a long time since I've been considered a threat to anyone."

She sensed heartache layered beneath his joking words. She knew how greatly her husband missed his days of being an adept fighter. "Since we've had no reports otherwise, I assume all is quiet down in the estate barracks, but perhaps you can see how the Savantian guards are faring? They can't be too pleased to be separated from their charges."

Perry stepped back and gave her a formal bow. "I shall return with a full report for you this evening, Duchess."

She giggled at his grandiose delivery. "I will eagerly await your assessment." Jax then reached for her crown and secured it among her honey-colored tresses. "I'm off to the council chamber to prepare. Wish me luck."

"Are you not going to have breakfast?" Her husband's eyebrows inched upward in obvious disbelief.

Jax chuckled. "I'll ask Madame Rosalyn to bring me something. Don't worry. I won't try to negotiate peace on an empty stomach." She gave him a parting kiss. "Do take some time to enjoy the day, darling. Perhaps you could sketch some ideas for the school renovations, too?"

He brightened at the challenge.

‡

Jax glanced up at the door, surprised to find that Madame Rosalyn had returned not only with a mouth-watering glazed pastry but with Lord General Allard, as well.

"Jacqueline. Good morning." The older man dipped his head in salutation once Madame Rosalyn had delivered breakfast and excused herself.

"A good morning to you. I hope you had a restful night?" Jax studied the man. After seeing him drink so heavily, she wondered if he'd be able to function today. Surprisingly, he looked none the worse for wear.

Allard shuffled inside the intimate quarters of the council room and took a seat on the opposite side of the rounded table. "Yes. Quite peaceful, thank you." His dark gaze went to the map of Savant Jax had laid out across the polished tabletop. "Drawing battle lines, are we?"

Jax acknowledged his barb with a sharp grin. "I always value a bit of perspective when puzzling out the solution to a problem."

"There's no need to 'puzzle' anything out, Duchess." Allard folded his arms with a scoff. "The answer is simple. My experience and financial backing make me the ideal leader to bring a new age about for Savant."

Jax matched his gruff stance. "Convince me, Lord General."

"Well, I, er…" Allard floundered momentarily. Evidently, he hadn't been expecting her to put him on the spot in such a direct manner. "Not only do I have the military training from my days in the Savant Ducal Guard, but my career as a merchant has grown my network of connections. I know how to give the people what they want."

"When it comes to material matters, yes," Jax admitted. "But being a leader is more than securing goods for your people. You have to create growth and opportunity for them to thrive."

"And that's where my financial backers come in. With their coffers, I can rebuild Savant without any help from other nations." He eyed her warily.

Jax shook her head. "My dear sir, Saphire would not have become the nation she is today without relying on the aid of allies. Isolating yourself as you build anew will not bring you the prosperity you seek."

Allard, his cheeks red, opened his mouth to protest when Lothaine strode into the room. "Apologies, Jacqueline, am I late?" He paused and cautiously assessed her face-off with the Lion's Bane leader.

"No. Not at all, Governor." She motioned for him to take a seat at the table.

An impish grin spread across his handsome features as he sat in the high-backed chair. "If we are to call you Jacqueline, I must insist you call me Finral. It seems only fair."

She smiled her gratitude at his claims to value fairness.

Allard, however, made no such offer.

"Your opponent here was just telling me why he has what it takes to be Savant's leader," Jax explained, not wanting Finral to feel like he'd been slighted. "The Lord General declares his military experience, merchant career, and financial backers make him ideal for the position."

Finral's gaze flashed with indignation. "I believe there are a great many more things that define a good leader, and those who have joined Heartsworn believe so also, or I would not be sitting here as their *elected* governor."

Allard snorted. "You make it sound as though you have a whole nation behind you. Your numbers rank, what, three hundred? Four hundred?"

The young governor bristled. "With Guillaume's group joining Heartsworn, we are now over eight hundred soldiers. But we have many more civilian supporters on our side. A majority of the Savantian people champion *us*."

"Oh, I'm positively quivering in my boots." Allard mocked. "Look, I only agreed to this summit because I don't wish for any more bloodshed. I'd like to see an end to the fighting. But my men number over a thousand, and they *will* fight until Lion's Bane secures the throne. So, you can either peaceably surrender now, Lothaine, or we can continue this out on the battlefield."

"I won't be threatened into cowering to your demands," Finral growled.

Jax cleared her throat. "Nor will I allow such terms to be reached. I made *my* view clear. Either a strategic, viable agreement is reached, or Saphire will be the one to end the fighting once and for all."

Allard's nostrils flared. "Then Lothaine will need to decide whether he'd rather see Savant in the hands of a fellow countryman or a foreign duchess." He spat the final words out as if they tasted sour.

"Why do you want Savant's throne so badly, Allard?" Finral's voice grew quiet. "What future do you want for our nation?"

The older man stilled at his opponent's change in tone. "I…" He seemed at a sudden loss for words. "I want our people to walk with their heads held high. I want them to know they are worth just as much as someone from a noble or ducal bloodline."

"And how do you plan to do that?" Finral challenged. "How do you plan to instill that sense of worth into our people?"

"Well—"

"Face it," Finral snapped as he jabbed his finger in the air. "Neither of us knows the first thing about leading a nation."

Allard swelled with anger. "So, what? We're supposed to just *give* our homeland to *her*?"

While Jax didn't entirely appreciate being spoken about like she wasn't sitting across the table from the arguing men, she held her tongue. Finral's humble admission intrigued her. Not many aspiring leaders would make such a bold, self-deprecating statement.

"No! Of course not. But don't you see the opportunity we have today?" Finral's eyes sparkled as he motioned to Jax. "You and I are in the presence of arguably the most powerful person in the realm. Jacqueline has *seven* nations under her control, yet she somehow has the time to sit here and listen to our incessant bickering. Don't you want to know how she does it? How she leads? How she has given the common-born across her lands a new lease on life?"

He sat back, his ardent passion beginning to wane. "I, for one, would like to know. I want to understand what it means to *be* a leader. I want to know what I'm in for, because I, too, will not cede my claim to you. I know your wealth has bought you well-armed soldiers and advanced weaponry, but our men have a fire in their souls that will not be doused so easily." The governor of Heartsworn then rested his gaze on Jax, his expression hopeful and pleading. "Jacqueline, will you teach us? How have you taken so many nations and rebuilt them from rubble?"

When Allard didn't immediately protest, Jax assumed this meant he'd been hooked by Finral's rather brilliant proposition. While he hadn't admitted anything out loud, Jax suspected there was more to Finral's request than merely gaining knowledge. Perhaps he believed that once Allard heard the never-ending work and sacrifice that went into ruling and protecting a duchy, the Lord General would rethink his desires.

The corner of her lip curled. "Where to begin?" Jax rose from her chair and retreated to one of the bureaus behind her, its drawers filled with maps. She extracted a chart of the entire realm and rolled it out across the table, covering the Savant one.

She spent the next several hours detailing her ascension to each of her seven thrones and the challenges that had come with every new acquisition. Not only did she have to deal with nobles unwilling to part with their prejudiced ways, but she also had to supply malnourished villages with food and water and figure out how to enable growth in areas that had fallen into ruin. She had to accomplish all this while ensuring the standard of living didn't falter in her existing holdings or risk the sting of rebellion.

"People do not appreciate change when it negatively impacts them, even in the slightest. Even when it is change for the greater good," she counseled her rapt audience.

Finral's eyebrows rose. "Sounds a bit cynical, Jacqueline."

She shrugged. "It is an unfortunate side effect of humanity. We've grown to inherently care more about ourselves than our neighbor."

Allard simply responded with a snort. "How do you enact

sweeping change then?"

Jax detailed the struggles she'd gone through trying to convince those of former nobility to join her in this new future. "Of course, I had to make concessions, such as the continued use of their titles. But their titles don't actually *mean* anything anymore. I doubt they'll be around in a few generations."

She noted how both Finral and Allard had started rubbing their eyes. "Why don't we break for the day? I realize I've given you a great deal to think about." She studied them both with keen interest, doing her best to gauge their thoughts about all she had shared. "Take what we've discussed and return to your advisors. We shall reconvene talks tomorrow morning."

Finral nodded and rose from his chair to stretch. "I appreciate your candidness with us, Jacqueline. It's certainly been illuminating."

"Yes, agreed," Allard grumbled as he followed suit. He took his leave from the room, murmuring something about needing to confer with his man, Dvorak.

Finral stared after him, even once Allard had disappeared from the council chamber.

Jax worried she'd overwhelmed the young man with the magnitude of the role for which he was fighting. "Is there something on your mind, Finral?"

Her question seemed to startle him from his thoughts. "Oh, a great many things, but we've troubled you enough for now. Will we all dine together this evening?"

She gathered the maps she had used during her presentation and returned them to their places. "Dinner will be served at six for anyone who would like to join."

"Wonderful. I shall see you and your companions, then." With a bow of his head, Finral left the chamber.

Jax's shoulders dropped with heavy relief. *Thank the Virtues.* She'd managed to keep an open dialogue between the two sides, thanks to Finral's perceptive request. The fact that Allard had stayed and listened to her account was encouraging. It showed a willingness to learn, and she could never fault anyone for that.

A roaring pang of hunger pierced her stomach, interrupting her reflections on the session. Grateful the unflattering sound hadn't embarrassed her in front of her guests, Jax went in search of sustenance. Lunch had long since passed, and she'd been too engrossed in discussions with Allard and Finral to eat the finger sandwiches Madame Rosalyn had delivered earlier in the day.

It took her a few tries to make her way to Glennfeld's kitchen, as she hadn't ventured these fine halls since she was a child. The manor's kitchen was located on the ground floor of the east wing and was a beautiful, bright open space humming with activity. She counted at least seven people already hard at work on dinner preparations, and the smoky, sweet smells of grilled meats made her mouth water.

"Your Grace!" A tall, gangly man with a Kwatalarian accent jumped at the sight of her. Despite the confusion on his face, he merely asked, "How may I assist you?"

She smiled reassuringly at him. Given his robes and hat, she assumed him to be her head chef. "Hello, good sir. Might there be anything left over from lunch I could snack on?"

Within seconds, she had a plate of cured ham, grapes, and cheese bread in front of her.

"Would you like us to make you a salad or soup, Your Grace?" The chef rocked on his heels, ready to spring into action.

Jax shook her head. "This is more than enough to keep me satisfied until that delectable-smelling dinner is served." She eyed the large pot on the stove with anticipation. "Thank you."

She munched contentedly at the savory platter as she took the passage toward Madame Rosalyn's office. Perhaps the estate manager would know where her companions had dispersed to while she'd been in session with the Savantian leaders.

"What do you mean, having second thoughts?" A familiar voice hissed, catching Jax's attention.

She stopped in her tracks, trying to figure out from where its owner was speaking. She realized the voice was coming from an alcove up ahead.

"We're better than this, Pierre," Finral answered in a low growl. "We don't need to resort to such underhanded tactics."

Yves cursed at the young governor's response. "Are you mad? This is war. You said yourself he has no plans to back down."

"Well, that was before the Duchess made Allard's head spin with everything she manages," Finral snapped. "You should have seen the old fool. He looked like he might lose his breakfast at the thought of having to work so hard."

Yves scoffed. "Do you think she knew what you were trying to do? She seems to have taken a liking to you. Could she have embellished her duties to dissuade Allard from wanting the throne?"

"I don't know. I wouldn't put it past her to figure out my true intentions. She's sharper than that wretched Qylvard ever gave her credit for."

Why am I not surprised? Jax mused to herself as she inched closer to the alcove. She didn't want to alert them of her presence, but their whispers had dropped even lower.

"And the only reason she favors me is due to Heartsworn adopting her democratic values. I *told* you that electing our leadership would pay off in the long run."

"Yes, yes," Yves said with an exaggerated sigh. "Her believing *I* am the horrid villain who hates equality has endeared you to her. Our ruse seems to have spread to Allard's camp, too, as he believes there is dissension brewing between us."

"He doesn't think you'll support me as our influence grows," Finral seethed. "He sees us as divided and weak."

"Just as we planned." For the first time since she'd met the man, Yves sounded happy. "Then, all we need is for him to approach me and offer an alliance. Once he thinks I'm in his pocket and willing to betray Heartsworn, he'll give the throne to you without hesitation, believing I will literally stab you in the back and hand power over to him."

Jax pressed her free hand against her chest, willing her heart to stop beating so loudly. What a diabolical scheme she'd just happened upon!

"We have only to wait, my friend." Finral's words hummed with excitement. "Come, I saw the others outside. We must join them and continue to play our parts."

"What would you have me insult this time?" Yves joked.

Jax hurriedly glanced around the hall for a hiding spot and quickly pushed herself against the wall in the shadow of an alabaster statue, the only place that offered shelter. She waited with wide eyes as Yves and Finral strolled in the direction of the foyer, clapping each other on the back. No wonder they had been so free with their words—from what their conversation suggested, everyone else was outside, enjoying the afternoon sun.

She waited several minutes before extracting herself from her makeshift hiding spot. She didn't want to give Finral or Yves any sense that she'd come from the same direction.

As she finished eating her snack, Jax mulled over what she'd heard. It was an ingenious act of deception, really, and Yves had perfectly played his part of the aggrieved dissenter. Allard had even commented as much at last night's dinner. His remark about Yves stabbing Lothaine in the back took on a new light. Was Allard already planning to make such an offer to Yves? Time would tell, she supposed.

As her appreciation for such inventive thinking faded, a troubling notion settled on her shoulders as she arrived at the manor's entrance. She recalled Finral speaking about how Heartsworn's adoption of democratic views had been his idea. Had that merely been done to manipulate her into supporting their side? Did Governor Lothaine not actually believe in the ideology he currently practiced? If his faction did take the Crown, would those values be tossed out and another tyrant be installed on the throne?

Chapter Fifteen

"All right, you lot!" a broad-shouldered man in gleaming red armor called with gruff irritation. "Get in line and wait your assignments."

George, Serafina, and Emeraude shuffled to the back of the weary labor group, allowing those in true need of work to the forefront of the line. The trek from the refugee settlement to the war camp had been more arduous than George expected, and he'd had to help someone to their feet more than once along the way. When Marie had mentioned the labor group, he'd foolishly assumed it consisted of only strong, able-bodied men and women. However, the people rushing ahead of them in line to secure work were of all ages, even young children. It made George's chest tighten for their dire situation. As he stood at the back of the worker line, he let his gaze drift upward, toward the midday sun. If he'd been keeping track of the days correctly, Jax's peace summit was set to begin today. He prayed his friend helped Savant reach a solution soon. He didn't envy the grave challenge she faced.

"Virtues. These poor people." Serafina wiped at the perspiration on her brow with the back of her hand. "Having to trek all this way in this heat, only to then be thrust into manual labor." Her troubled gaze rested on an elderly man who'd been one of the first to receive a paid assignment: carrying grain bags toward the outer stables. From where they stood, his struggle was evident.

Emeraude glowered at the scene, kicking the dirt up with her leather boots. "These people have already suffered enough at the hands of these brutes, and yet, they continue to be exploited."

"I wouldn't think the Grandmaster of the Shadow Brethren would have such compassion," George muttered, somewhat bemused by the severeness of her scowl.

She lanced him with a disapproving glare. "And I wouldn't expect the former Captain of the Saphire Ducal Guard to understand what it truly means to survive in this world, even if he is common-born."

It wasn't her biting delivery that gave him pause, but rather, the undercurrent of pain shimmering in her eyes.

Eager to keep focus on their mission, Serafina rested a hand on George's arm as she stood on her tiptoes and assessed the war camp. "Where do you think Elias is being kept?"

George shifted his attention to the perimeter. "Sergeant Tautou said he was under the supervision of several guards. I imagine we'll have to survey the site to pinpoint his location."

Serafina eyed the long line of laborers. "What if they turn us away because they're out of work?"

"There's always something that needs doing in a place like this," Emeraude commented with a subtle shrug.

"We just have to make sure we have the freedom to move around." George studied Emeraude's sharp face, which showed no signs of fatigue, even though she'd been up much longer than either he or Serafina, having ridden to the coast to toss the nightmare stone into the sea. "Any ideas on how we go about getting some alone time with Elias?"

Emeraude buffed her fingernails against her linen tunic. "Well, I know I can slip in undetected without anyone being none the wiser. Skill of the trade and all." She smirked before adding, "But if you two want to be there with me, we'll have to get creative."

There was no way George was letting Emeraude speak with Elias alone. Despite the so-called "Grand Covenant" between them, he didn't entirely believe her. It could all be a grand act of deception in an effort to make off with both the Intelligeye sigil and information about where the flame-shaped relic might be.

And then we'd be even further behind than where we started. Picking up Elias's trail had been difficult enough. If Emeraude absconded with the Intelligeye sigil, he doubted they'd be able to find the Grandmaster ever again. He was smart enough to know when he was outmatched, and humble enough, despite the glory he'd achieved as the Ducal Guard's highest-ranking officer, to admit Emeraude was his superior in almost every way.

Humbleness, huh…

A flash of inspiration hit him. He and Serafina had been too tired to discuss everything Emeraude had revealed last night, instead opting to focus on their plan for today. But now, as he stood in line thinking about Corporal Lunara's drawings of the four relics, he felt fairly confident he could identify each Favor. Obviously, the Kindheart medallion was the large, round piece on the bottom tier of the Saphirian display case. Then, there was the Humblemind crest. It seemed most sensible that it would be the relic with a shield-like appearance, in the same vein as many house crests. And where Emeraude recognized the flame-shaped piece on the top, it indicated that the remaining eight-pointed star was the Intelligeye sigil, leaving the Bravesoul pendant to be Emeraude's family treasure. Of course, his theory fell apart if the Humblemind crest wasn't the shield piece…

"Did you have an idea as to how we can cause a distraction?" Serafina seemed to have noticed his spinning mind.

George scrambled for a response, now that Emeraude was staring him down too. He, of course, wanted to share his theory with Serafina, but he didn't trust Emeraude to hold up her end of the deal. If she learned her father's treasure was the Bravesoul pendant, she could very well abandon their plan to strike out on her own. As much as it pained him to admit, they needed her expertise getting to Elias and making him talk.

"It looks like there's a stable in the middle of the camp." George tossed his chin in that direction. "Those are probably the officer's horses, to ensure the ranking leaders can flee quickly should the camp be raided."

Emeraude's lips curled into a devious grin. "It would be a shame if someone were to let those animals loose, then."

Serafina twisted the hem of her shirt with worry. "What about the laborers? We can't risk innocent people getting trampled by a panicked horse."

George realized she'd made an astute point. "We'll bide our time until the laborers are called to leave." He wrapped an arm around her in reassurance. "Once we're inside the camp, it will be harder for them to keep tabs on us."

"Agreed." Emeraude's jawline grew firm. "We should reconvene at the outer stables, where the pack horses are housed. I doubt many soldiers will be milling about in that section. Do either of you know the sparrow's chirp?"

George furrowed his brow, confused by her question. "You mean, the bird call?"

She nodded. "It's always good to have a signal should we need to catch each other's attention."

"I can mimic it." Serafina raised an eyebrow at George, waiting for his answer.

He pursed his lips in response and blew out a low, cheeping whistle.

Emeraude grinned her approval. "All right, we're almost up."

The line of workers had dwindled quickly, and soon, George and his two female companions stood in front of the burly man in red armor.

"Marie sent a message saying she had some new faces for us." The big man, who was even taller than George, glared down at them as if they were ants. "I'm the camp's warden, Major Foix. You look fit enough to help with the blacksmith at the armory." He pointed George in the direction of billowing smoke. "And these pretty ladies"—his glare turned into a leering smile—"will have the task of cleaning out our officers' tents."

George's stomach clenched. He prayed Serafina stuck with

Emeraude. He didn't want to think about an officer cornering her alone in his quarters. And though he knew she could take care of herself, he hated her being in a position where she had to.

"I'll be fine." Serafina seemed to sense his distress and gave his hand a quick squeeze. "Might even find something good," she whispered with a smile before she and Emeraude took off in the direction the warden had indicated.

"Oy, you! Get moving!" Major Foix pushed George into action, sending him stumbling a few steps before he regained his balance. Straightening and letting the warden's bellowing laughter roll off his shoulders, George headed for the armory to begin his workday.

Chapter Sixteen

"Duchess!" Madame Rosalyn's appearance in the manor's foyer distracted Jax from her thoughts. "Have you completed your dealings for the day?"

"Yes." She smiled at the estate manager. "And survived, no less."

Madame Rosalyn's pinched gaze dropped to the empty plate—save a few crumbs—in Jax's hands. "Were the sandwiches not enough, Your Grace? Will you require more sustenance during tomorrow's conference?"

"Oh, no. It's my fault." Jax chuckled. "I merely wasn't fast enough, and Lord General Allard took it as a sign I didn't want my share."

Rosalyn snorted. "Given how I just caught the sly devil trying to sneak off with a bottle of mead from the salon, I can't say I'm surprised." She held out her palm, wordlessly offering to take Jax's empty plate.

Jax winced as she gave the dish to the estate manager. "You didn't happen to stop him, did you?" The last thing Jax wanted was a repeat of the previous night's dinner.

"Of course I did," Rosalyn jokingly bristled. "I wouldn't wish his drunken antics on anyone, let alone you, Your Grace." She shuddered. "I convinced the Lord General that the mead he planned to pilfer was a special bottle only you and Lord Pettraud are allowed to drink. That sent him on his way."

"Excellent." While Jax was grateful for the woman's quick thinking, she couldn't help but worry that Allard would believe her hypocritical because of it. "I'd appreciate it if everyone in the household did their part to keep alcohol away from the Lord General for the remainder of the summit."

"I'll alert the staff and guards immediately, ma'am."

"Thank you." Jax sighed with relief. "Did you see where Allard went?"

"I directed him outside to join the rest of your guests." Rosalyn pointed beyond the front doors. "Lady Uma arranged a picnic and games for the others to enjoy."

"Wonderful. I shall go find them." Jax thanked the estate manager and waited while one of the two sentries opened the door for her.

She shielded her eyes against the searing sun as she stepped out onto the veranda. Her keen gaze spied several familiar figures dashing around the manicured southeast lawn. From the looks of her friends' movements, a game of badminton was underway.

As she hurried toward the action, Jax plastered on a carefree smile. She didn't want Perry and the others to get wind of the Heartsworn secret she'd overheard just moments ago. She'd tell them in due time. For now, she would let Lothaine and Yves continue to play out their little war game, and she wouldn't interfere unless they gave her serious concern to do so.

"Darling!" Perry noticed her approaching first. He stood off to the side of the makeshift badminton court, his tunic loose and rolled up past his elbows.

Her other friends were in the grips of the game and merely called out their greetings before returning their attention to the competition.

Worry seized her chest as she neared her husband. Perry didn't make any moves to walk toward her, and from the way his left hand clutched at his abdomen, she wondered whether he'd strained himself playing.

"How did everything go?" he asked in a low murmur once she

arrived at his side.

She gave him a searching smile. "As good as I could have realistically expected, I suppose."

"So, no peace agreement, but still open for discussion?" He tilted his head, hope glittering in his eyes.

She laughed. "An excellent summation, my love." Jax surveyed the intense game unfolding before them. Yanis, Uma, and Vivienne rivaled Ziri and Sabine in the match. "How has the day gone out here?" She tried to ignore Perry massaging his old wound. If he wanted to share his pain, he would tell her.

"Uneventful, beyond the fact that that Yves fellow threw a bit of a tantrum in the banquet hall during breakfast," Perry muttered as the couple watched Yanis dive in an attempt to smash the shuttlecock over the net.

"About?" Jax asked as Ziri skillfully leapt to return the hit.

"Lothaine not allowing him to join your discussions," Perry replied. "He was quite enraged."

Jax clapped when Sabine secured a point for her team. "Was Dvorak in the banquet hall at the time, by any chance?"

"He was." Perry shot her a questioning look. "Why?"

Uma scored a point for her side a moment later.

I'm sure it was all for show, Jax mused inwardly, *with Yves hoping the Vice Lord Admiral would report his discontent to Lord General Allard when the time was right.*

To her husband, she replied, "I'll tell you when we're alone." Her gaze darted to Vivienne. "Where are our other guests?"

"The Heartsworn duo came by just before you did. I think they were heading toward the pond." Perry pointed over his shoulder at the shimmering water in the distance. "At lunch, Dvorak asked Aizen if he could speak with their guards in the barracks. Haven't seen him since."

Jax scanned the grounds, spying Finral and Yves walking near the tree line, about a hundred yards off. As she assessed the stately manor, she spotted Dvorak and Allard in animated discussion on the veranda.

Perry had followed her gaze, for he added, "Oh, there's Dvorak.

Hmm…those two seem rather pleased with themselves."

Indeed, the Vice Lord Admiral appeared almost gleeful as he spoke with Allard. *I'd be willing to bet he's recounting Yves's churlish outburst at breakfast.* Her attention moved to Yves and Finral, who also looked locked in a dynamic conversation. However, Yves's wild arm movements suggested severe displeasure. *Another performance for us all?* She had to admire his dedication.

"Jax! Would you like to join in?" Sabine hurried over to her, wiping sweat off her forehead.

Jax smiled as her friends crowded around her. "I'm having fun watching you all dash about like loons."

"You seem in good spirits, Duchess." Vivienne tucked a loose strand of her silky brown hair behind an ear. "I hope that means the summit was fruitful." She dropped her gaze, suddenly shy.

Jax appraised the young woman, realizing she should be careful with her words in the Savantian's presence. After all, Vivienne was here in service to her father and would undoubtedly relay to him anything Jax said.

"That is for Masters Allard and Lothaine to decide." Jax forced a tight smile across her lips. She didn't like making Vivienne feel that she was purposely being kept at arm's length, but it was necessary for the sanctity of the peace talks.

Yanis shielded his eyes against the sun. "The Heartsworn lot doesn't seem very pleased."

While everyone's attention darted to Yves and Finral arguing in the distance, Jax kept her gaze on Vivienne. The young woman's eyes widened and flicked toward her father's figure. She almost hummed with eagerness to speak with him.

"Actually," Jax spoke up, "I will join your game. Vivienne, may I take your place?"

Sabine's brow furrowed. "Why not join our team to make it even, Ja—"

Ziri nudged her sweetheart in the side. "I need the training, Duquessa, so please, let's keep the numbers as is."

Jax smirked, glad Ziri understood her true intentions for casually dismissing Vivienne from their group. As if Ziri needed any training.

Vivienne's shoulders dropped with sudden relief. "Of course, Jacqueline. I shall check in on my father in the meantime."

As I expected. Jax wiggled her fingers in a wave as the young woman dashed off. Vivienne was no doubt intent on sharing the observations Jax's group had made about the contentious Heartsworn duo.

"What's that triumphant look for?" Perry whispered in her ear. "You seem very pleased with yourself."

Jax released a light giggle. "Oh, just admiring all the political games at play here."

"Is this part of the whole 'I'll tell you later' thing?" Perry asked with a bemused grin.

She kissed his cheek. "Indeed. You can fill me in on your inspection of the barracks, then, too." Picking up the racket Vivienne had discarded on the ground, she joined Yanis and Uma on the makeshift court. As they played, she half-hoped her other guests would join them, but eventually came to terms with the fact that the Heartsworn and Lion's Bane factions would likely keep their distance from one another until dinner.

As the afternoon stretched on, it was easy for Jax, surrounded by her dear friends, to get swept up in their lighthearted game, forgetting for a time that the realm's peace weighed heavily on her shoulders. Well, not quite forgetting…George and Serafina were never far from her mind. She hoped the ceasefire in Savant had made it easier for her friends to cross into Hestes and continue their pursuit of Elias.

Nearing the end of their tie-breaking game, Jax dove for the shuttlecock to smash it toward Sabine when an urgent cry froze her in place.

"Oy! Fire!"

The call came from a member of the Ducal Guard running across the field, waving his hands in a frenzy.

Their game ended instantly, a sudden breeze bringing with it the terrifying smell of smoke.

Jax scanned the area, in search of the fire's origin. To her horror, dark tendrils rose up from behind Glennfeld.

"Is it the manor?" Uma rushed to Yanis's side, her gaze wide with concern.

Ziri was already sprinting toward the smoke.

Sabine bounced on her heels as her beau headed toward the danger. "It looks like it might be coming from the woods behind it."

Yanis kissed Uma's forehead and took off after Ziri. Jax spied several members of the Ducal Guard running from the barracks on the opposite side of the estate as well. Given the expansive distance separating them, it would take them several minutes to arrive on the scene.

Whoever was in charge of the manor's security must have realized the same, for the interior sentries spilled out of the house and raced toward the smoke. Jax sagged with relief at the onslaught of aid.

"Should we assist, too?" Uma chewed on her lower lip.

Jax weighed their options. The Ducal Guard were trained to deal with such situations. Amateur attempts to help would likely only hinder the professionals. "Let's get closer and assess the scene." Jax looped her arms through Uma's and Sabine's and indicated with a dip of her head that Perry should follow at his own pace.

Together, the anxious group hurried across several acres before they rounded the back of the manor. While Jax was relieved the building hadn't caught fire, the devastating sight of the bordering forest in flames left her breathless.

By now, forty or so of the Ducal Guard were on the scene, including Aizen. He ran the length of the line, issuing orders as his men heaved buckets of water onto the burning trees.

Jax spotted some of the kitchen staff and Madame Rosalyn lending their assistance by carrying buckets from a nearby well.

She turned to her companions. "Let's find some containers and bring water from the pond." Protocol be damned. Jax couldn't stand idly by while everyone else around them was fighting this blaze.

Neither Sabine nor Uma protested—the young women sprang into action and raced for some discarded buckets.

Perry, however, looked painfully aggrieved. He massaged his abdomen vigorously, his breathing having become alarmingly labored.

"Darling," Jax said fearfully, placing a comforting hand on his lower back. "Should I send for a physician? Are you —"

"I'm fine, Jax. Just a bit sore. Go help the others." Perry gave her a stressed smile as he pressed his hands against his knees. "I-I'm afraid I need to sit this one out."

She nodded. *Virtues, he must be in even more agony than I suspected.* She knew how much it hurt his pride to stay behind.

Gathering her skirts, Jax took off in a run toward the pond, where she helped Sabine and Uma pull buckets of water. The buckets were quite large, and once filled, Jax strained to lift them, but luckily, her dear friends were in much better shape than she. Barely breaking a sweat, Uma and Sabine took off toward the fire, ready to assist.

True Shieldmaidens of the Iris, Jax thought. She then looked around the banks of the pond, searching for anything else she could use to transport water to the forest.

Seeing nothing, she debated a moment. While the trees were engulfed in fire, so too was the underbrush. If they could smother the flames below, that would help prevent the fire from spreading along the ground. With a decisive tug, Jax ripped off the top lining from her dress skirt and plunged it into the lukewarm pond water. Once it was fully saturated, she ran back toward the tree line, dragging her wet, heavy skirt.

"Aizen! Here!" Before the Captain knew what was happening, she tossed the wet ream of fabric at him.

Instinctively, he understood her intention and threw the waterlogged skirt on a burning conifer shrub, suffocating the flame.

Heartened by her contribution, Jax began tearing off a second layer of fabric. At seeing Yves and Finral running from the manor and toward the commotion, Jax's propriety briefly caused her to blush, but she realized such thoughts were useless in the dire situation. She'd rather her guests see her in a state of undress than have her future school burned to the ground.

Uma and Sabine must have noticed her solution, for they, too, began tearing off the outer layer of their dress fabric. Together, they ran back and forth from the pond, giving wet swatches of cloth to the nearest Ducal Guard soldier.

By the time Jax was down to her petticoats, Dvorak had also joined in the fire-fighting efforts, with Vivienne arriving shortly behind him.

Allard was the last of her guests to arrive, huffing and puffing as he neared the tree line. After listening to him lauding his military prowess just this morning, Jax found it odd that he was so out of shape.

Under Aizen's steadfast direction, they managed to contain the fire's spread, and within thirty heart-pounding minutes, the raging flames had been thoroughly doused.

"Thank the Virtues the wind wasn't stronger, or we'd have been in a world of hurt." Yanis sagged against Uma as Jax and her companions assessed the chilling, charred scene.

Sabine rested with her arm around a soot-covered Ziri. "How did this happen?"

"Once things cool off, Aizen and I will examine the area." Ziri squinted as she glanced up at the sun beginning to dip near the western horizon. The sky around them was cloudless. "It's not as if a lightning strike caused this."

"Indeed." Jax folded her arms as she surveyed the blackened flora. It amounted to about thirty feet in diameter—relatively small and focused, due to the forest's immense size.

Beside her, Perry cleared his throat. "Now that the worst is over, perhaps it might be time to change." Despite the pain in his voice as he leaned against a broken branch for support, his gaze held a mischievous twinkle.

Jax realized she, Uma, and Sabine were standing amongst a horde of soldiers, almost in their knickers. "You're probably right." She smiled, letting out a weary chuckle. Due to the warm summer weather, no one had a cloak or coat to offer to help maintain their modesty.

"Darling," she said in a lowered voice, "are you sure you don't need me to send for a physician?"

Perry reached for her hand and gave her a reassuring squeeze. "I'm fine, my love. Just outdid myself, that's all. Perhaps a nice bath before dinner will help set me right."

She eyed him warily, hoping he wasn't putting on a brave face in an attempt to spare his pride. "I think we all could use a soak." Her gaze trailed over her tired, ash-laden companions before landing on her guests standing a distance away.

"I'll meet you back inside," she told Perry before summoning her courage and gliding over to the Savantians. She realized she must look an awful fright, but she wanted to reassure them that their peace summit was under control.

"Jacqueline!" Vivienne squeaked as she caught sight of her approaching. "Goodness, how brave you all were! And what quick thinking." She indicated to her own gown, of which she had ripped off the top layer in an effort to lend her aid.

"Thank you for your assistance, Vivienne." Jax took the young woman's hands in hers and squeezed. "Thank you all for your help," she added, directing her sincerity more toward Lothaine, Yves, and Dvorak. Allard, in his strange, out-of-breath state, had done little more than watch. "I apologize for such a frightening disruption."

"Please, Duchess, there's no need for apologies." Dvorak blotted his face with a handkerchief. "As if you could have thwarted Mother Nature."

"Yes, Jacqueline," Allard scoffed, "you may be a formidable force, but we know you're not *that* powerful."

"We're just glad things didn't escalate further." Finral ran a hand through his soot-streaked hair.

Yves merely nodded his agreement.

Jax appreciated that the delegates were giving her grace in this matter. They had every right to be angry that their security had been compromised whilst on her lands. "I realize you all must be quite exhausted after that taxing exertion. I shall ask Madame Rosalyn to have dinner sent to your rooms, so that you may bathe, eat, and retire early."

"Thank you, Duchess." Dvorak bowed at the waist. "Your dedication to our comfort is most appreciated."

The others murmured similar statements before starting the trek back to the manor.

Jax regarded the group as they trudged along, admiring how they'd come together in a moment of adversity. There hadn't been a barbed word between the two factions while they'd worked alongside the Ducal Guard to eradicate the threatening fire. Perhaps there was hope for a peaceful resolution yet.

Chapter Seventeen

George wiped at the sweat stinging his eyes as he pulled another red-hot blade from the forge. With deft hands, he brought it over to the master armorer for shaping.

"You're the best one Foix has sent my way," the blacksmith eyed him appreciatively before he slammed his hammer against the steel.

George stepped away from the workstation as sparks began to fly. He'd lost track of time since he'd arrived at the camp armory. His strained muscles suggested he'd been at it for several hours. He hoped Serafina was having an easier time with her assignment.

Even though there was a tentative ceasefire whilst the Heartsworn and Lion's Bane leaders were in Saphire, it was clear that these men were wasting no time preparing for the next battle. Shining swords, chest plates, and chainmail gleamed at the ready, fresh from the forge, and George spied several training drills taking place along the war camp's borders. He was surprised by their skill level and amazed at how well this battalion operated. It was almost as if they'd been fighting together for years, not weeks.

"Where'd you say you came from again?" the blacksmith asked once he set aside his hammer.

George grunted, "Proviencia," doing his best to mirror the man's

Savantian lilt.

"Beautiful this time of year." The blacksmith shook his head. "A shame it's all being razed to the ground."

While George would have liked to try and get more information out of the chatty artisan, he knew he couldn't risk his cover being blown by his poor accent. He merely nodded and resumed tending to the forge.

"Not much of a talker, huh?" The blacksmith laughed to himself before engaging a passing soldier in conversation.

George kept his back to the two men but listened to their exchange carefully in the hopes he'd learn something useful about the camp's inner workings or, even better, Elias Pettraud's whereabouts.

"I'll have Heathcliff's men outfitted by the end of the day, Lieutenant," the blacksmith reassured the soldier.

"Make it quick." The lieutenant didn't sound enthused. "The Vice Lord Admiral wanted them in our regalia two days ago."

"Still shocked Heathcliff handed over his sword," the blacksmith replied. "From what I heard about their last meeting, he didn't seem too fond of the Lord General's leadership."

"Well, things change," the lieutenant barked back. "Heathcliff knew he couldn't keep things running without his top councilors."

"Any idea how they all died so suddenly?" The blacksmith's hushed question didn't escape George's attention.

"Nothing finite has been determined," the lieutenant admitted, "but rumor has it that once Heathcliff submitted to our side, his head chef was put to death."

"Blimey, was he a spy working for Heartsworn?" the blacksmith gasped.

"That's what the Vice Lord Admiral mentioned when I spoke with him last," the lieutenant replied. "Those scoundrels are growing bolder with their schemes."

The blacksmith scoffed. "Growing desperate, more like it."

Clang, clang, clang!

Somewhere in the distance, a loud bell chimed, its peals resounding through the encampment.

"Ah, there's dinner." The blacksmith clapped his hands together.

George turned to see the lieutenant glaring at the man. "Heathcliff's men, *tonight*." The large, imposing warrior then stalked off.

The blacksmith sagged at the rebuke but turned to George with a grateful expression. "All right, fella. You're free. See Major Foix for your wages. And here—" He paused, casting a quick glance around to ensure no one was watching. He then selected a shiny steel dagger George had helped him forge earlier in the day. "A special token for your hard work. If anything, you can sell it back to another battalion for a pretty price." He winked.

George gruffly thanked him for the kind gesture but knew he wouldn't be selling this fine blade. He hadn't been able to bring his beloved sword into the war camp. Worried that he'd be searched upon entering, he hadn't placed a dagger in his boot, either. Now, he hid the thin blade under the leg of his trousers, the metal cool against his skin.

"Tell Foix to send you my way tomorrow," the blacksmith called out with a happy wave goodbye as George stalked off toward the camp's entrance.

However, once he'd put some distance between himself and the armory, George surveyed the scene, quickly calculating how to blend into the crowd of soldiers. He needed to meet up with Serafina and Emeraude at the outer stables, where they'd planned to use the pack horses for cover.

He spotted a laundry line of gray tunics and pants billowing in the breeze nearby. A quick assessment of the off-duty soldiers told him that these were their casual uniforms. Keeping to the growing shadows of the setting sun, George slinked toward the clothesline with his head down, so as not to draw attention. Empty wash bins sat abandoned, and George wagered that some of the settlement laborers had been assigned to this area.

With a sneaky hand, he yanked a dry uniform off the line and quickly threw the gray tunic over his dirtied white shirt. His traveling pants were dark enough to allow him to move to a more private spot behind a nearby tent before changing into the Lion's Bane attire.

Once he was dressed for the part, George maneuvered his way through the bustling camp toward their intended meeting place. The sun barely hovered above the horizon, and already, soldiers were celebrating the close of another day with food and spirits. George scowled at the ample rations being devoured while the poor refugees at the South Haven settlement were limited to meager portions. With the ceasefire in place, it wasn't as if these men needed the additional sustenance for fighting. They certainly weren't in the frame of mind for it, what with the copious amounts of alcohol being consumed. His earlier musings about the battalion's professionalism evaporated.

"Hey! Devlin, ain't it?" A hulking man with glassy eyes grabbed George around the neck and pulled him toward one of the many campfires.

George slid out from under his grip and sidestepped the staggering fellow as he tumbled gracelessly onto the ground.

"What am I doing down here?" The man blinked several times before laughing and striking up a conversation with the soldiers already gathered around the fire.

Shaking his head at the lack of discipline, George quickened his pace toward the outer stables. If wine and mead continued to flow freely into the night, it could aid their plans to infiltrate Elias's holding cell. It could also cause severe problems, especially if a drunkard caught sight of Serafina or Emeraude and tried getting handsy.

The stables where the pack horses were kept were much quieter, as he'd hoped. While George knew how important these animals were to a war camp's ability to move from place to place, he suspected the rebels would prioritize the officers' mounts over these creatures. After hearing the fancy titles the Lion's Bane leaders had fashioned for themselves, George suspected ego to be a driving force for this faction.

He said hello to the horses munching contentedly on some hay. As he stroked one of the sturdy beasts, he kept watch from the corner of his eye, on the lookout for his companions.

Groups of soldiers ambled past, hooting and hollering while they tossed back sloshing tankards, but other than two stable hands tending to the animals, George didn't see anyone.

Anxiety hardened at the base of his neck, and he straightened his shoulders so he could scan his surroundings more effectively. Spying a wood crate next to the stable structure, George leapt atop it, and the height advantage gave him a better view of the sprawling camp. It covered several acres, with easily over one hundred tents. The size of the army impressed him. Lion's Bane certainly had mobilized its forces expeditiously.

"'Cuse me, sir. Can I help ye?" a familiar, lilting voice called to him.

George's heart quickened at just hearing those melodic words, and he searched for Serafina, his gaze landing on the stable hand waving in his direction.

A grin spread across his face as he jumped down to the ground. "Well done, you."

From under the brim of a floppy hat, Serafina grinned. "Emeraude nicked the clothes for us." She motioned to the other figure, who leaned casually against the handle of a pitchfork.

With their hair tucked under their caps and dirt smeared across their cheeks, George marveled at their disguises. "I didn't even give you a second glance when I arrived here." They'd even stuffed their shirts at their stomach to hide their feminine curves.

"You and every other man here," Emeraude muttered with a snort.

Serafina cupped his face in her hand, her touch both calming his nerves and igniting a storm within him. "You look exhausted. They didn't work you too hard, did they?"

George tilted his head to kiss her palm. "I'm fine. I spent the day working alongside the blacksmith. Decent chap." He reached for the dagger in his boot. "He even gave me a parting gift."

Emeraude eyed the blade hungrily. "We'll make good use of that yet." She lifted her pant leg and revealed a hoof pick strapped to her calf. If anyone could turn a tool into a deadly weapon, George had no doubt it would be her.

"Did you learn anything useful from your smithy friend?" Serafina asked.

He shook his head. "Not about Elias. You?"

"I read a few reports while cleaning the warden's quarters." Serafina's lips pursed into a frown. "Mostly financial items. Lion's Bane is extremely well-funded. Foix writes they can last until the winter should the conflict drag on."

Emeraude propped her pitchfork against the stable wall. "I was assigned to the camp's top-ranking officers, and despite the merriment around us, they're intent on pushing their agenda whilst this ceasefire is in place. Commander Crowe—Marie's nephew— wants to send some of his men to Heartsworn as spies to undermine their efforts."

George bristled at the disturbing news. Should he write to inform Jax of this devious plot? If the opportunity presented itself, he would, but given the current state of their mission, he doubted such a missive would reach his friend in time. "If Lion's Bane is caught and the Heartsworn leaders are notified while under Jax's care in Saphire, she will not be pleased that her terms have been violated."

"A risk Commander Crowe is well aware of but willing to take." Emeraude's lips drew into a grim line. "According to the correspondence he's been sending to the other war camps."

Serafina wrung her hands as she surveyed the quiet stables. "So, nothing about transporting a prisoner to the capital?"

Emeraude shook her head.

"We'll have to use our wits to locate him then." George rubbed the back of his neck. "We have at least ten acres to cover." It seemed a daunting task.

"We should be able to move freely in these disguises." Serafina motioned to their clothes. "And seeing how plentiful the mead is here, it won't be long before the soldiers drink themselves to sleep. We have that in our favor."

"But we'll have to stick together until that happens," George pointed out. "Our whistling signal won't be able to cut through the din."

"I say we start at the center of the camp, near the officer's horses." Emeraude's shoulder rolled in the direction she mentioned. "Elias is a valuable commodity. So much so, they aren't even documenting his existence."

Serafina nodded her agreement. "Let's go. If anyone stops us along the way, George can say he's escorting us to take care of the animals."

With a plan in place, the trio took off toward the camp's center. As the minutes passed, the soldiers around them grew louder and rowdier, frequently stumbling into their path. George had to restrain himself from knocking some sense into them whenever they crashed into Serafina. While he wanted to rush to her aid, he knew Serafina was capable of taking care of herself—indeed, her quick footwork allowed her to avoid colliding head-on with the swaggering brutes.

There was no evening breeze, and the stagnant, humid air grew heavy with campfire smoke and sweat. As the trio navigated through the more congested sections of the camp, the reeking smells made George's stomach flip in disgust. He was glad he hadn't eaten anything since lunch, or nausea might have slowed him down.

It took them a good ten minutes to reach the heart of the camp. George tugged at his tunic collar, his skin slick with moisture. He eyed the soldiers nearest to him, wondering how they weren't overheating in this uncomfortable atmosphere. He supposed he wasn't accustomed to the intense Savantian heat, and the added warmth from the cookfires did nothing to alleviate his discomfort.

"There are the horses." Serafina's fingertips stroked his forearm, her gaze landing on a stable a few yards ahead.

George frowned at the sight. "Now what?"

"Take a look at that tent three rows over." Emeraude used her elbow to covertly signal the direction.

His gaze came to rest on a structure encased in dull, black fabric. George doubted he would have paid it any mind—if it hadn't been surrounded by nine guards. The guards stood at rapt attention, clutching sharp spears. They appeared to be the only people— besides George, Serafina, and Emeraude—who were not partaking in the free-flowing ale and mead.

"I think we've found our target." Serafina gnawed at her lower lip. "But how are we to get past *nine* armed guards?"

Emeraude, too, looked vexed. "I'd offer to go in alone, but they've got every inch of that perimeter covered. Even I would have a hard time."

George's head swiveled around the raucous scene. Men sang hearty shanties by the fireside while others attempted drunken jigs. Howling laughter echoed in the dusky twilight as soldiers stumbled from group to group. The powerfully built horses housed in the nearby stables tossed their manes nervously, clearly unsettled by the disorderly conduct. The sight made George realize these creatures had been selected for their regal appearance, not their comfort on the battlefield. *Another act of hubris that will likely come to bite Lion's Bane where it hurts.*

"Do you think it's always like this?" Serafina murmured, her unease evident.

He shook his head, unimpressed by the soldiers' antics. "They're reveling in the reprieve the peace summit has afforded them. Otherwise, I don't think this army would be able to function on a daily basis behaving like this."

"Yes, they hardly fit the part of battle-worn warriors." Emeraude offered a sardonic smirk. "Let's give them another hour or so of merriment. Then we can unlock the stables and spook the horses." She pointed to the nervous animals. "That should cause enough chaos to allow us to slip inside."

George didn't like the idea of involving the horses, who already seemed stressed enough.

"Okay, then. What do *you* suggest?" Emeraude stared at him, clearly picking up on his disapproval.

He sighed, as he didn't have an answer. His first immediate thought was to cause a distraction by setting an unoccupied tent ablaze. With all the campfires roaring away, it wouldn't be overtly suspicious for a wayward spark to catch on a tent flap. But a fire could quickly spread out of control, and given how far gone most of the camp's inhabitants were, it could spell disaster.

A satisfied smile twitched on Emeraude's lips. She knew her plan was the most effective.

"I doubt we'll even need to spook the poor dears," Serafina added, her eyes shimmering with the same concern George felt.

"They're anxious and clearly not bred for battle. All we need to do is unlatch their gates and they'll be off."

Emeraude held up a hand. "I'll unlatch the gates. You two wait near the black tent. In the event that the horses don't pull away all the guards, you'll need to seize whatever opening you can to get inside," she instructed. "Don't worry about me. I'll be able to follow."

George didn't quite appreciate her talking down to them, but at the end of the day, her evasion skills outmatched their own. Instead of becoming defensive, he reached for Serafina's arm. "Come on." To Emeraude, he said, "Good luck."

She vanished like a puff of smoke. George blinked, trying to pick up her trail, but she was somehow already crouching near the stables.

"Amazing. She'd give Ziri a run for her money," Serafina muttered, her expression somewhat slack-jawed.

George couldn't resist a chuckle at picturing his valued comrade's reaction to such a statement. "Don't *ever* let Ziri hear you say something like that."

Together, they crossed the aisles between them and the black tent, going over one more just in case they were being watched. Sticking to the shadows, they backtracked up the row, this one slightly less populated than the others they'd encountered. There were fewer campfires, too, and George surmised this might be where the higher-ranking officers were housed—away from the rabble-rousers.

Serafina motioned him behind a large water barrel that flanked an outhouse diagonal to their intended destination. It made for a good hiding spot while they waited for Emeraude to cause her chaos. The smell, though, he could do without.

George counted the seconds as they ticked by. From their crouched position, he had limited visibility, but he didn't hear anything indicative of something being amiss.

His thighs were just beginning to tire from squatting when a shrill cry rang out. His heartstrings tightened at the horses' braying wails, but the sound was soon replaced by a deep, penetrating rumble. George watched the men surrounding the black tent shoot bewildered looks at one another. The howling laughter from the merry celebrations turned to yells of confusion.

"They're not moving," Serafina hissed. She rested a white-knuckled fist on her knee. "What do we do?"

Before George could react, a horse barreled past the black tent, forcing four of the soldiers to leap aside to avoid being trampled. Another horse soon followed, and George swore he saw a shadowy figure atop its back, urging it onward.

She sure is gutsy, George mused to himself, admiring the opening Emeraude had given them.

With the four guards distracted by their near-death experience, one side of the tent was unmanned. Grabbing Serafina's hand, George dove out from behind the barrel and dashed across the aisle. A heartbeat later, he pulled the base of the tent up high enough for Serafina to roll under, and he quickly followed.

In an instant, the world around them vanished, and George found himself staring into endless darkness.

"W-who's there?" a pitiful, hoarse voice whimpered.

George blinked a few times, begging his eyes to adjust quicker to the change in light. As he did so, his breathing leveled, and soon, he was able to make out the shape of Serafina's profile next to him. Based on her fluttering eyelids, she was attempting the same.

"W-what's going on?" The panicked voice grew stronger. "Are we under attack?"

Outside, the sounds of hooves pounding the ground along with rushing footsteps made for a frightening symphony. Angry and disoriented cries rang out.

As his vision returned, George assessed the interior of the tent. Faint light seeped in from under the base of each wall, and there was a thin slit that ran down what he assumed to be the entrance. A small bucket sat in the opposite corner, and it appeared to be the only furnishing George could detect. A support beam stood erect in the center of the structure, and slumped at the bottom, was the figure of a man.

"P-please. Just let me go." The prisoner moaned. "My m-master. He'll pay you whatever you want."

George tensed as he finally recognized the familiar voice, despite the man's pathetic state. A surge of triumph spread through him now that their target was within reach.

"You wish to leave? But we only just got here." George couldn't help himself. This man had nearly ruined both Perry's and Jax's lives with his poisonous power games, not to mention the harm he'd done to the Solis siblings.

Elias Pettraud stiffened, twitching with confusion at George's taunt. "You're not Savantian. Is that—are you from Saphire? Has my brother sent you to rescue me?"

George almost felt sorry for the poor sod. "Oh, your brother sent us all right. Time for us to have a little talk."

Chapter Eighteen

"Ouch." Jax winced as her finger snagged in her damp tresses.

Perry limped toward her as he finished lacing his tunic. "Something the matter?"

She untangled her hand and sighed. "It's taking me longer than I would have liked to get my hair under control." She'd already spent half an hour in the bath trying to scrub away the smell of smoke, but it seemed to have buried itself within her skull.

Perry grabbed a discarded hairbrush and motioned for her to sit on the rug in front of the fireplace.

Wordlessly, she did as he instructed, her silky green skirts fanning out all around her.

With a gentle touch, Perry took a section of her hair in his hand and ran the brush through it, holding it near the heat radiating from the hearth. His rhythmic movements lulled Jax into a relaxing trance, her mind wandering from the shocking events of the afternoon.

"You're quite good at this, darling." She gave a contented sigh as she leaned against Perry's knees.

He chuckled. "I always enjoyed grooming my family's horses whenever the need arose. This doesn't seem all that different."

She cast an affronted look over her shoulder, her nostrils flaring in indignation. "Did you just compare your wife to a horse?"

"Well, that braying certainly makes you sound like one," he teased.

Shaking her head at his silliness, Jax sank back and let him work. "Are you feeling better?"

"I'm fine, darling." His soft tone held the slightest hint of irritation. Not necessarily aimed at her, but at the situation he often found himself in due to his wound. "The warm bathwater soothed my side quite nicely. Perhaps I'll take another before bed. I'll be right as rain in the morning."

His optimism helped loosen the knot of worry in her chest. She only hoped he was telling her the truth. Perry had a habit of swallowing his pain to avoid unwanted attention.

They were interrupted moments later by an impatient knock on the suite's outer door. "Duquessa? May we enter?" Ziri's distinct voice was muffled but clear.

Jax shot a worried look up at Perry, who helped her to her feet. "Come in."

The sitting room door opened, and Ziri and Aizen trudged into the suite, each haggard and unkempt.

Jax wilted at the sight of them. "Oh dear. I take it from your appearances that you don't bring good news."

Ziri managed a wry smile. "Astute as ever, Duquessa."

"The affected area is still too hot to investigate properly," Aizen said, launching into his report. "But from what Ziri and I can tell, none of the burned trees showed any signs of being struck by lightning."

Jax frowned. "Well, we already knew that, didn't we? The weather was gorgeous. There was barely a cloud in the sky."

"There have been instances of a phenomenon known as 'dry lightning,' Duchess." He clasped his hands behind his back, adopting a lecturing pose. "But our preliminary search has ruled that out. We'll have to wait until the ground has cooled before reexamining the scene further."

"And given that we were able to rule out such natural causes," Ziri added, her expression turning grim, "it's very likely this fire was set intentionally."

Jax felt her husband's hand press against the small of her back. "Why?" Perry asked. "What was there to be gained by such a thing?"

"*That* we don't know." Aizen gave a rueful shake of his head.

Ziri nodded. "Although we have our suspicions." Her bronze gaze met Jax's.

"Someone is trying to sabotage our peace summit." Jax's fingers balled into fists.

Perry frowned. "If that were the case, why light a fire in the woods *behind* the manor? It's not as if anyone was in any danger from it—except the poor forest life."

"Someone could simply be trying to cause trouble for Jax or the delegates," Ziri suggested. "And seeing how heavily the estate is guarded, perhaps this was the only way."

Jax stewed over the possibility. It didn't make any sense. Her people supported her decision to aid Savant during its time of upheaval. Why would anyone in Saphire cause trouble for their summit? And how would they infiltrate Glennfeld's fortified boundary? No, it was more likely that someone within the estate was to blame. *If* the fire had been set intentionally. "Have you spoken with the Savantian guards at the barracks?" she asked Aizen.

"Not personally, but two of my officers have," he replied. "From what my men have reported, none of the Savantian escorts were missing or even left the premises during the afternoon." He shifted on his feet. "Still, until we get to the bottom of this, I've doubled the watch down at the barracks. I'm also sending Yanis to take some men and scout the perimeter for any signs of activity before we lose the sun's light completely." He paused, a look of pain enveloping his face. "In order to conduct such searches, I've had to pull some sentries from the interior of the manor, Jax, so everyone needs to remain on guard."

Normally, Jax would revel in such a circumstance, but after the day's events, she worried the Ducal Guard were stretched too thin.

She could tell from his tense posture that Aizen felt the same. He had brought a smaller group of soldiers under *her* instruction, despite his own reluctance. At least he had the decency to refrain from saying

"I told you so."

"I understand." Jax brushed the wrinkles out of her gown. "I've instructed Madame Rosalyn to have our guests' dinners sent to their rooms for the evening, so the delegates should be contained for now."

Aizen raised an eyebrow. "Good. I would like to speak with them and understand their movements throughout the afternoon, but I realize that could put the peace summit in a precarious situation."

Jax couldn't resist a sardonic laugh. "Indeed. I doubt they would take kindly to me accusing them of starting a fire."

But it's a possibility we cannot ignore.

She sighed. "If we can hold off on questioning them until we're certain of the fire's origin, that would be preferred." After all, they didn't even really know what they were up against. There was no point in offending anyone—yet.

"I leave the diplomatic matters to you, Duchess." Aizen gave a grandiose bow, and Jax smiled at the flamboyant gesture.

She looped her arm through Perry's. "We were just getting ready to meet Sabine and Uma for dinner." Her unspoken invitation lingered.

"I'm going to clean myself up and chat with the staff." Ziri gestured to her dirty garb. "I want to see if anything unusual caught their attention before the fire started."

Aizen tugged at his collar. "I'm going to change as well and ride out to examine the roads surrounding the estate. See if there's been any recent activity on them. It's unlikely, but until we can investigate the fire's origins a bit more, I want to narrow our options."

Jax felt a hard lump congeal in her throat. The idea that some random passersby set the fire did seem far-fetched, but the alternative worried her even more. She was facing the very real possibility that someone among them was an arsonist.

"Be careful. Both of you." Jax wished her friends good luck, and they departed.

Perry ran a hand through his dark curls, his gaze lingering on the doorway. "Virtues, I'd hope this was all some sort of freak accident."

"Me, too." She leaned her head against his shoulder. "It may yet be. Perhaps the summer heat caused something to catch fire in the underbrush."

The sun's rays were intense, after all, she mused hopefully.

Once the couple finished dressing for dinner, Jax and Perry strolled down to the banquet hall. Sabine and Uma were already seated near the head of the long table in animated chatter, their freshly washed hair shimmering in the overhead chandelier.

Jax grinned at the sight of them. "I hope you two had an easier time than I did getting the soot out of every nook and crevice."

Her friends giggled as Perry and Jax joined them. Since they were not dining at a formal reception, Jax took a seat opposite Uma instead of at the head of the table while Perry sat by Sabine. "I gave up and decided to embrace the smell of smoke," Uma admitted with an elaborate shrug.

Jax sniffed her friend's hair and detected the faintest hint of the fumes. "How alluring."

Sabine's expression grew somber. "Have you heard anything from Ziri or Aizen about the matter?"

Jax nodded. "They stopped by our suite with a report." She paused and waited while the dining hall attendants plated a crisp salad topped with nuts and berries. She smiled her thanks at the staff before continuing, "While they can't yet be certain, it's looking like the fire was set intentionally and not as an act of nature."

Sabine stifled a gasp while Uma's brow furrowed with anger. "Who in the Virtues would do such a thing? And why?"

Jax stabbed a few lettuce leaves with her fork. "That is the mystery, dear one." She chewed thoughtfully before explaining, "The Savantian guards down at the barracks have already been cleared. Yanis is searching the grounds with most of our men for any signs of intruder activity. Aizen is scouting the roads surrounding the estate as well."

"You don't sound hopeful that they'll find answers." Uma raised an eyebrow as she dabbed her lips with a napkin.

Jax lowered her voice, despite the fact that they were currently alone in the hall. "I'm confident that the estate border is well guarded against trespassers. I don't think this issue arose from *outside* Glennfeld."

"Well, if the Savantian guards didn't have anything to do with it," Sabine said with a quivering chin, "doesn't that mean…"

"That one of our guests is involved?" Jax propped her elbow on the table with a frown. "Yes, I believe it does."

"But why?" Uma challenged. "What would any of them have to gain by setting a forest fire behind the manor?"

Perry took a sip of the mead in his goblet. "That's what troubles me most."

"But how could it be any one of them?" Sabine drummed her fingertips on the table. "We all saw them race out to assist with the fire from the manor."

Jax thought back to the chaotic scene. Yves and Finral had been the first to come dashing out of the house. Dvorak followed, and Vivienne wasn't far behind him. Allard was the last of her guests to arrive. Was it possible that one of them set the blaze, came inside, and then ran back out without being noticed?

"We need to speak with the manor guards to get a sense of everyone's movements." Unfortunately, it sounded like Aizen had most of them out helping Yanis with the ground search at the moment.

"Or we could just ask the delegates," Sabine countered as she chewed on her salad.

Jax winced at the suggestion. "I'd rather not make our guests feel like I'm accusing them of arson if I can help it. It wouldn't exactly foster the partnership I've been trying to forge with this summit."

Sabine blushed. "Oh. You're probably right." She tittered nervously.

"And we don't yet know for certain the blaze was set intentionally," Perry added with a knowing stare. "We could be dredging up a false mystery all for the sake of drama."

Jax felt her cheeks grow warm. "Well, it wouldn't be the first time, now, would it?"

"Too soon, Jax." Uma let loose a biting laugh at the inside joke.

With Perry's reminder that she could be making a mountain out of an anthill, Jax tried to relax and enjoy the meal the kitchen had prepared. Despite the setback from the fire, she felt confident that the peace discussions were moving in the right direction.

Just as the dining staff were serving braised quail with raspberry sauce, the doors to the banquet hall groaned open.

Hoping Aizen or Ziri were returning with a report, Jax plastered on an unaffected smile when Finral Lothaine and Nanteuil Dvorak slipped inside the room.

"Hello, Jacqueline." Finral dipped his chin in greeting. "I apologize if we're disturbing a private gathering."

"Yes, apologies, Duchess." Dvorak wrung his hands.

Jax waved away their regrets. "Nonsense. I just thought you'd be dining in your rooms this evening, given the trying events of the afternoon."

"We encountered Madame Rosalyn in the foyer and told her we wouldn't need trays." Finral's cheeks grew red. "I always find being around friends helps work through one's woes."

To Jax's surprise, Dvorak patted the young governor on the back. "As do I. Especially when in the company of one of the most fascinating figures in our realm's history." He glanced meaningfully at Jax.

"You flatter me too much, good sir." Jax motioned for the two men to join them. Neither needed additional encouragement. "I must say, your group continues to surprise me."

Dvorak chuckled, clearly understanding her meaning. "I find myself surprised, too, Your Grace. Governor Lothaine here has proven to be quite an extraordinary mind. If we weren't on opposite sides of the battlefield, why, I think I'd find myself calling him a friend."

Finral, for his part, answered cautiously. "I'd say the same. However, I can't quite reconcile how a man of your intellect and caliber has deemed it acceptable to follow ol' Allard." Although his expression was one of bemusement, there was a real question lurking in his troubled gaze.

Dvorak waited until after the dining hall attendants filled their goblets and brought them plates. "One thing I have learned with age is that we often have to make the best with what we are given."

"How can you say that? You *chose* to follow Allard." Finral kept his tone measured, but Jax sensed real frustration emanating from him.

Dvorak leveled him with a wizened stare. "*Was* there a choice for me? *You* were lifted into power by your peers, Lothaine. A leader among your men. Your rebellion happened very differently than the one I got caught up in."

A chastened Finral reached for his drink and took a long sip. While Jax dearly wished for Dvorak to speak more about the circumstances he alluded to, she kept her mouth shut.

"Well, should this summit resolve in my favor, let it be known that you would be welcomed into Heartsworn." Finral lifted his glass in acknowledgment.

Dvorak's expression turned sad. "I wish I could offer the same, my good fellow. Had we met in another life, perhaps."

Finral hesitated before taking a drink, but he still relished the liquid in his glass. "I haven't gotten the chance to properly thank you, Jacqueline, for the hospitality you've continued to show us all. Your taste in wine is really quite surprising. I'm looking forward to cracking open the bottle that was left in my room."

At the change in topic, Jax dabbed at her lips. "I would have thought you'd done so after last night's dinner."

Finral opened his mouth to reply when the banquet hall door creaked again, announcing the arrival of another guest. This time, Vivienne's pretty figure stood in the doorway.

"I hope I'm not too late to join you all." She dipped into a curtsy and hurried forward. "It took a bit longer than I expected to freshen up." Her hand went to her slightly damp hair, which she stroked nervously. "I-I know we were offered dinner in our rooms, but I'm rather wretched at being alone."

Jax noted the young woman's embarrassment and quickly came to her rescue. "Please, Vivienne, join us. I should be the one apologizing for assuming a private dinner would be preferred."

"Oh, goodness, there's no need, Duchess. Besides, that's probably what you and your companions are used to," Vivienne babbled as she sat down in the chair next to Finral. "I suppose sitting around commiserating one's woes is a symptom of being common-born."

Jax stilled at the offhanded comment, but before she could speak, Uma cleared her throat. "Rest assured, Miss Vivienne, we have been doing the same thing." She motioned to Jax and their friends. "It is a symptom of being human, not common-born. At least that's what we believe here in Saphire."

Vivienne's face drained of color at Uma's pointed words. "Oh, I didn't mean to suggest—"

"I know." Uma gave her a kind, if tight, smile. "I realize the gown you wore today is likely ruined beyond repair. If you should need an extra during your stay, Sabine and I would be happy to lend you one of ours."

Jax silently thanked Uma for her words of wisdom and for skillfully navigating the conversation into less murky waters. She yearned for the Savant group to understand the true meaning of equality and opportunity, and who better to show them the way than the accomplished Uma Dorrow.

Sabine eyed Vivienne's taller, lean figure. "Yes, I'm happy to donate one of mine if you don't mind your ankles on display."

"I've heard that's the style in Hestes these days." Vivienne's eyes widened with obvious delight at the notion of being so fashion-forward.

Jax observed Finral's eyes widening, too, but she suspected it for other reasons. "I must thank you all for your brave efforts to assist us with taming that dreadful fire," she added nonchalantly, hoping to gauge her guests' reactions to the frightful event.

"Of course, Jacqueline." Finral sliced into his quail. "I'm just glad the blaze was contained."

Dvorak nodded. "Any idea what started the terrible mess?"

"Captain Aizen and his men are currently investigating the matter." Jax gave her most reassuring smile to comfort her guests.

"I'm surprised you're not involved, Your Grace," Vivienne spoke up. She eyed both Dvorak and Finral. "I mean, your puzzle-solving exploits are well-known, even in Savant."

Jax forced a light chuckle, praying she appeared the picture of ease. "My attention is focused on much more important matters." She let a knowing look drift to Finral.

The Heartsworn governor's jaw tightened. "I appreciate your dedication to resolving Savant's issues."

Dvorak swallowed the bite in his mouth before adding, "You certainly gave the Lord General much to think about, Your Grace."

"Will he be joining us this evening?" Jax asked.

Vivienne shook her head. "No. Papa was grateful to take you up on the offer to have dinner in his room. After the day's events, he did not wish to be disturbed." She twirled a loose strand of her brunette hair. "I think the fire may have brought back some unwanted memories." As soon as the words were out of her mouth, Vivienne looked like she wished she could take them back.

Dvorak, too, cringed at her comment.

"Memories?" Sabine's voice bubbled with sympathetic concern.

Jax had to hide a sly smile with her napkin. No doubt Sabine had seen the curious reactions on their guests' faces, just as she had, and decided to feign innocence to pry further.

When Vivienne didn't immediately reply, Finral said softly, "Allard's wife died in a terrible barn fire several years ago. He tried to save her but couldn't. Ever since…he's had an aversion to flame."

Jax didn't know what was more shocking, the story or the fact the leader of Heartsworn was the person sharing it.

Finral must have sensed the Saphire group's bewilderment, for a panic look flickered across his face. "It's…something Heartsworn learned through reconnaissance." He shot a guilty glance toward Vivienne, although her melancholy gaze was focused on her lap.

Dvorak quivered, evidently irritated by Finral's oversharing, but he held his tongue on the matter.

"I'm terribly sorry for your loss, Vivienne," Jax murmured her condolences.

Sabine, Perry, and Uma offered comforting words as well.

The young woman finally looked up, her face a tight mask. "Thank you. I appreciate your kindness. However, losing Mama was one of the catalysts that brought my father and me closer together. So, I suppose I am grateful for that outcome."

Jax admired her ability to find the good in a tragic situation. "I'm also sorry to hear that the events of this afternoon have caused your father such distress."

As the words floated across her lips, she wondered if this had been the arsonist's goal in the first place. If Finral was aware of his opponent's aversion to fire, had either he or Yves started the blaze to give Allard a scare? "If he needs some time to recover, I'm sure Governor Lothaine won't object to delaying our negotiations tomorrow," Jax offered.

Vivienne shook her head. "I'm certain Papa will have forgotten it by the morning, Duchess."

Finral frowned at her answer. "I'd be happy to postpone, Miss Vivienne."

Vivienne seemed to squirm with guilt. "I don't think it will be necessary, Fin—Governor Lothaine. You see—" she paused, biting her lower lip with embarrassment—"I gave Papa the remainder of the wine that was gifted to me by Duchess Jacqueline. I figured it might help him through his pain."

Dvorak's eyes bulged at her confession. "Vivienne! You know we mustn't let him indulge—"

"I know, I know, but he was in such a sorry state." The young woman's eyes brimmed with unshed tears. "There was only a glass or two left in the bottle, so I figured it would just help him calm down and drift off to sleep."

Dvorak rubbed his temples as frustration rolled off his shoulders. "Virtues, let's hope so."

Jax felt sorry for Vivienne. She clearly wished to alleviate her father's pain, but medicating him with alcohol was not the wisest choice. "Would you like me to send for a physician to assist the Lord General? I'm sure he could prescribe a tonic or something."

"There's no need, Duchess," Dvorak replied with a defeated sigh. "As Vivienne said, I'm sure Allard will wake up right as rain tomorrow."

Jax nodded her understanding, although once her guests returned their focus to their food, she shot Perry, Uma, and Sabine a spooked look. Again, she regretted her decision to gift the Savantians wine, even though Finral seemed grateful for the gesture.

The rest of the meal passed by uneventfully. Dvorak did his best to engage in conversation, but he seemed preoccupied, as did Vivienne. Finral, on the other hand, peppered Jax and her companions with questions, ranging from Saphire's agricultural landscape to its culture and arts scene. His thirst for knowledge continued to impress her, and she couldn't help but think he'd be the ideal candidate for her leadership academy—if his interest weren't simply a stunt to win her favor.

"My, his enthusiasm knows no bounds," Uma muttered once the Savantians excused themselves from the table at around eight o'clock.

Jax giggled at her friend's assessment before taking a drink of water to quench her parched throat. She'd done more talking today than she had in months.

"Finral certainly did an admirable job trying to engage Miss Vivienne in the conversation," Perry pointed out. "I think he felt sorry for her."

Sabine snorted. "I think he feels a *lot* of things for her."

Perry tilted his head. "Care to explain?"

"Did you not see how tenderly he spoke about her mother's passing?" Uma raised an eyebrow toward him. "Governor Lothaine clearly knew it was a delicate subject and stepped in to help."

Sabine grimaced. "Yes, I feel rotten asking her about it."

"Don't worry, my dear. If you hadn't, I would've," Jax reassured her. "I wondered why Allard didn't assist us while trying to tame the blaze. Now, it makes sense."

Perry drummed his fingers against the tabletop. "Do you think the fire was set to throw him off-balance? A psychological attack?"

"It was the first thing that came to my mind after hearing how his wife died." A grim smile twitched on Jax's lips.

Uma's brow furrowed. "Such a feat would suggest that the Heartsworn lads are tangled up in this plot."

"Possibly." Jax absently twirled one of her loose ringlets as she pondered the scenario.

A look of bewilderment danced across Sabine's features. "Possibly? What would Dvorak or Vivienne gain by causing a mental blow to the Lion's Bane leader?"

"*That*, we don't have an answer to." Jax jabbed her finger in the air for effect. "And until we do, I don't think we can rule out any of our guests."

Perry cleared his throat. "Keep in mind, we still don't have confirmation that the fire was set deliberately, ladies." He gave them each a pleading stare as they all rose from the table to retire to their rooms for the night. "Let's not make villains out of everyone just yet."

Sabine and Uma chuckled lightly at Perry's remark, but as she strolled hand in hand with her husband, Jax couldn't silence the nagging seed of doubt taking root in her mind. She didn't think each of her guests a villain, but she feared one of them just might be.

Chapter Nineteen

As George's eyesight continued to adjust to the tent's dim interior, he took in Elias Pettraud's gaunt, sunken face. It had been months since George had last seen the man, and time had certainly taken its toll. He doubted he would recognize Elias in passing, save for the man's lavender eyes.

"T-thank goodness Percy has sent you to rescue me," the pitiful man whimpered as he struggled against his bonds.

Beside him, Serafina turned to George and raised a questioning eyebrow. He could tell she was confused as to why Elias said Percy rather than Perry. He simply gave her a reassuring nod. They didn't have time for George to explain how Perry's brothers had tormented him with the nickname his deceased mother used while she'd been alive.

Their attention was momentarily diverted by a loud crash outside the tent, along with the sounds of shuffling feet and murmured curses. Wondering if it had been caused by the rampaging horses, George stiffened in panic as he watched the tent flap flick open.

His shoulders soon relaxed as the moonlit silhouette of Emeraude's lithe, powerful frame filled the entryway before she whipped the tent flap shut behind her. In her left hand, she wielded a small, flickering torch, bathing the snug space in eerie light.

Elias shirked back from her as much as he could, still tied to the pole, his eyes blinking rapidly at the ever-changing light. "W-who is she? Is she with you?" He glanced toward George's direction. "Please, untie me and let's leave."

"Oh, I'm sorry." Emeraude stood above the man, a wide grin curling on her lips. She crouched down, and with her free hand, she grabbed a fistful of Elias's shaggy, oily hair. "But you're not going anywhere until we've had a nice heart-to-heart."

In all his years with the Ducal Guard, George had never heard such words spoken in a more terrifying manner. The Grandmaster of the Shadow Brethren's delivery chilled him to his soul, and his breath caught in the back of his throat. He hadn't even been the one she'd been speaking to.

Serafina's hand found his and gripped his fingers so tightly that pins of pain pricked at his eyes.

Emeraude's delivery made George realize that despite his grave distrust of her, her mercy was the reason he and Serafina were still alive. She could have easily ended them at any time yet had chosen to work with them instead.

Elias, for his part, had been scared into utter silence—tears leaked noiselessly from his eyes.

The effect she had on everyone drew an even more cunning grin across Emeraude's sharp face. She leaned closer to Elias so that she was within an inch of him. "Allow me to introduce myself, my dear lord," she purred in a condescending tone, "for I am the Shadow Brethren Grandmaster."

Elias's gaze widened and hope returned to his forlorn expression. "D-did my master send you?"

A sinking pit opened within George's stomach for the briefest instant before he noticed the hoof pick Emeraude had pressed under Elias's chin.

"No one *sends* the Grandmaster anywhere." Emeraude bared her teeth, the torch's shadows twisting her countenance into a terrifying devil.

George scoffed at her response. They didn't have time to play these word games. Who knew how long they had until the horses were wrangled and the guards came to check on Elias?

"Elias," he interjected softly, "we're here on behalf of both the Dark Magus *and* your brother." He gave the man a sympathetic smile, doing his best to sell the lie. "An alliance has been forged, and now we must ensure all parties deliver on their promise."

Elias's jaw dropped open. "Percy has allied with my master? Impossible!" He curled inward, disbelief in his frightened gaze. "Percy made it clear whose side he's on when he hid behind his wife's skirts."

And there we have it. George tried to keep his anger buried. Elias had inadvertently confirmed he was in league with the Dark Magus and that this Dark Magus character viewed Jax as his adversary.

"That's what your brother *wants* everyone to think." Emeraude twirled the gleaming hoof pick, catching on to George's scheme. "He commissioned me to broker a deal between himself and your Dark Magus friend."

Elias eyed George warily. "Then why are *you* here? You're Jacqueline's pet, aren't you?"

George bristled at the blatant offense but kept his voice measured. "I answer to the one with the deepest pockets. Lord Percival made me an offer I couldn't refuse."

"Who's she?" Elias nodded in Serafina's direction.

"She's a maid here at the camp," Emeraude answered in a bored tone. "She helped us gain access to you since we're holding her family hostage."

On cue, Serafina whimpered with her best Savantian accent, "Please, I did as you both asked. Please let them go."

"Hush, girl." Emeraude shoved the torch into Serafina's free hand, looking positively gleeful at their role-playing game. Her amusement caused George to question whether the woman was entirely sane. "Now, Elias," she cooed, stroking the prisoner's stringy, dank hair. "Tell us where the Favor is."

Elias struggled against his bonds. "All you have to do is untie me, and I'll take you to it. It's not far from here."

Emeraude drew back her hand as if she had been burned.

"What?" she hissed, seething with menace. "You don't have it on your person? How could you let the Dark Magus's prize out of your sight? What will he say when he learns of this betrayal?"

The prisoner's expression grew panicked. "Please, I know where it is. There's no need to tell my master such things. I-I had to leave it behind." Elias's explanation tumbled out. "Once I realized those blasted Dundainee merchants betrayed me, I knew I had to hide the relic. Otherwise, these mudpuddle dogs would have seized it from me."

"Leave it behind?" Fury danced in Emeraude's incredulous gaze. "How could you just leave the Dark Magus's prize behind for anyone to find?"

Elias sputtered. "Well, of course I buried it, Grandmaster. By the tree they kept me tied to. At the Dundainee camp. Covered it up exceptionally well, in fact. No one would think anything of it. It's safe, I swear. Once I got myself out of this mess, I was going to go back for it."

"And how were you planning to get yourself out of this mess?" George arched an eyebrow.

Elias's gaze darted down at his midsection. "I've stored ravenshade root inside the buckle of my belt. The guards sometimes take me for a walk through the camp, parading me around for their common-born filth to gawk at. The last time, they took me near the cooking fires. If I can get them to do it again, I was going to toss the ravenshade into a pot and let it wreak havoc on them."

George's blood ran cold at the dastardly plan. Elias's ravenshade root had nearly killed Verdine and Veritas Solis. If he tossed his whole stock into a cauldron, who knew how deadly the result could be? This man was willing to wipe out an entire battalion of soldiers without batting an eye. Maybe Emeraude wasn't the most ruthless among them.

"What about the other relics?" Emeraude's command was low and lethal. "Have you made any headway with them?"

Elias's face pinched with disappointment. "I-I have not. The master's instructions were only to secure the Solis relic." He glanced warily from Emeraude to George. "He wanted at least one Favor under his control before we launched our search for the others."

Emeraude pressed her lips together in a snarl. "You know nothing about where the others are?"

"Well, of course we know that the Kindheart is with that wretched archivist, but she went underground after Qylvard bungled the master's orders." Elias suddenly grew smug. "He never managed to get his hands on the medallion like *I* did with the sigil."

It took all George's strength not to glance over his shoulder at his beloved. It was evident that Elias didn't know about the Dark Magus using Emeraude to hunt down Serafina and the medallion; an encouraging sign that Elias was just a pawn in a larger game. Could the Dark Magus still be in the dark about Serafina's whereabouts, or had their brief encounter with Emeraude's nightmare stone revealed Serafina's location? He wished he knew what their enemy was truly capable of, but he couldn't ask Elias without the risk of destroying their ruse.

"The other relics, though, are a different story." Elias paled at the thought. "Master has yet to trace the family behind the Humblemind crest, and the Bravesoul pendant was lost long ago by some oaf whose family fell into the hands of the Shadow Brethren." He stilled and narrowed his gaze at Emeraude. "If anything, *you* should be able to track it down, Grandmaster. Don't your lot keep records of their spoils?"

Emeraude, however, didn't seem to hear his accusation. She sat back, and her gaze took on a faraway look. "The Bravesoul pendant, you say?"

George didn't have time to congratulate himself on being right about his deductions. He glared at the sniveling man. "You don't exactly have the sigil in hand right now."

Elias rolled his eyes, exasperated. "Well, untie me, and I'll take you to the Dundainee camp where I buried it."

"Under a tree inside the outpost walls?" Emeraude's question was soft, barely audible, but the coldness of it made George's hair stand on end.

"Yes, yes." Elias nodded hurriedly. "Untie me, and we'll—"

His head abruptly dropped to the side, his eyes frozen in

confused horror.

George blinked, attempting to comprehend Elias's strange behavior—as he scanned the man, he noted an alarming red liquid spreading across the collar of Elias's ragged tunic.

"What did you *do*?" George hissed as he turned to face Emeraude. The Grandmaster sat rocking on her heels, wiping the hoof pick clean of blood.

She leveled him with a chilling stare. "He told us where your relic has been hidden. What other purpose did he serve?"

Serafina scrambled to George's side, her eyes widening at Elias's lifeless form. "We could have asked him for more information about the Dark Magus!" She reached for Emeraude's wrist. "We could have figured out who we were up against."

"Please, this man was a pathetic puppet, nothing more. 'Master this' and 'my master that,'" Emeraude mimicked in a singsong sneer as she tugged herself free from Serafina's grip. "He knew nothing about the other Favors. He was merely an errand boy, sent to fetch the Intelligeye sigil. And besides, if we started asking questions about who the Dark Magus was, Elias would have known we weren't working for him."

While fury raged inside George over Emeraude acting so impulsively, he knew they didn't have time to waste. "We need to get out of this tent before the guards come to check on him."

Serafina glared at George, her nostrils flaring. He could tell she was upset at him for not being able to stop Emeraude from taking a life. He was angry at himself, too, but the Grandmaster's movements had been like a phantom's, utterly undetectable.

Emeraude rose from her crouched position and moved toward the tent opening, pressing her face against the slit in the fabric. "Come on. There's only one guard outside."

George wondered how she intended to sneak by the sentry, but his thoughts were interrupted by the jarring, clattering *crash* of wood snapping.

Without uttering a word, Emeraude knocked the torch from Serafina's hand and stamped it out, then grabbed the couple under their armpits and hoisted them to their feet in one smooth move. As if George, with his tall frame and honed muscle, weighed but a feather. She dragged them to the tent opening and pushed them outside into the chaos of the camp.

As George steadied himself, he spotted a tower of crates lying haphazardly across the ground near the tent. A stunned soldier struggled to climb out from under the rubble. Emeraude must have thrown something to topple the stacked boxes.

"Come on. Before he frees himself." Emeraude was behind them, propelling the dazed couple forward into the chaotic night. As the trio wove their way through the camp, drunken men stumbled by without a second glance, attempting to wrangle four remaining horses that still had not been caught.

The smoke from the campfires paired with the stagnant evening air made it difficult to breathe deeply as George, Serafina, and Emeraude hurried down a quiet aisle. It also helped them escape unnoticed.

None of them spoke until they were nearly halfway to the refugee settlement.

"You didn't have to *kill* him, Emeraude," George finally erupted on the assassin. "He had crimes to answer for. He had more answers to give us."

She halted her powerful strides, whirling on him. "There was no way we were getting him out of that tent. Even in the chaos, someone would have noticed a limping, bedraggled royal being led away by a soldier and two stable hands." Her hands went to her hips. "And we very well couldn't leave Pettraud with his captors. Who knows what intelligence he would have been willing to share with them? He could have offered Lion's Bane the Dark Magus's cooperation, whatever that might be."

"We could have learned more about his plans for the Favors." Serafina ran a hand through her auburn hair in exasperation.

"Why?" Emeraude cocked a challenging eyebrow. "He'll never get the Kindheart medallion from you, right? Why do you need to know his plans?" Her mouth twisted into a sly grin. "Unless *you* plan to unleash the power of the four Favors yourself."

Serafina stilled at the suggestion, and George knew the

Grandmaster had hit a nerve. Emeraude wasn't that far from the truth, after all. Serafina *did* want to collect all the Favors, but not for herself.

The haunting prophecy made by Ignatia Solaire, the first guardian of the Intelligeye sigil, floated through George's mind.

For an age, the Favors will slumber
until greed and darkness grow in number.
United, one crown seeks peace to restore.
To her, the Favors grant glory forevermore.

Both he and Serafina believed the era that the five-hundred-year-old prophecy referred to had finally come about. The Favors were in play, forced from the shadows of history by the Dark Magus's lust to possess them. Then there was the mention of the one crown, united, and the similarity between it and Jax's mission to bring equality and opportunity to the realm. What "glory" these Favors could grant his friend, he did not know. But he and Serafina intended to find out.

"There's another reason why I decided to silence Elias," Emeraude continued, lifting her chin in rebuke. "This Bravesoul pendant, the one my father lost to the Shadow Brethren, is *mine* by birthright. I will not allow you to take it from me."

George held up a hand. "We weren't going to—"

"Do you take me for a fool, Solomon?" Emeraude snapped at the interruption. "It's a tale as old as time. Now that the Solis family has forfeited their claim to the Intelligeye sigil to Serafina, she believes she's somehow been divinely selected to wield them *all* for herself."

Serafina took a step forward. "That's not true, Emeraude. If you found your family's relic and wanted to continue *protecting* it, I would not stop you."

Her words were careful and terse. George questioned whether Emeraude understood the cryptic threat at the heart of Serafina's pledge.

The Grandmaster held her fierce gaze for a long while. "I don't believe you," she finally said, turning her attention to the trail ahead. "Tomorrow, we'll leave for this Dundainee camp and retrieve the buried sigil. Once our contract is fulfilled, we'll part ways."

"And what will you do then?" Serafina pressed. "You have no idea where the Bravesoul pendant might be. Virtues, you didn't even know its name until Elias confirmed it. That's why you've stayed with us for as long as you have, am I right? Hoping you might pick up the faintest shred of a clue."

Emeraude's expression flashed with anger. "I am the Grandmaster of the Shadow Brethren. Nothing in this world is hidden from me."

"Oh, please." Serafina scoffed. "I saw your reaction when Elias mentioned the Shadow Brethren's records. You've already checked those, haven't you?"

"Yes, and they were of no help. The flame medal was sold off to some nameless fence, an untraceable figure." Emeraude's defiance melted. "To gain access to those records was the whole reason I became the guild's leader in the first place. What an utter waste." For the first time since they'd met, Emeraude sounded fearful and overwhelmed.

George folded his arms as he studied her in the bright moonlight. "No one in the guild could tell you about it?"

"The Brethren's treasury is managed by the Grandmaster. They are responsible for every transaction made," Emeraude explained. "During my ascension to the role, I invoked the True Answer to compel my predecessor to tell me whom he sold it to. Even under the compulsion, he couldn't give me a name."

"True Answer?" Serafina tilted her head in confusion.

Emeraude held out her forearm and pointed to her inky tattoo. "Another one of the guild's fail-safes to prevent corruption from within. Those marked with our seal cannot lie to another branded Brethren member when we invoke the True Answer. I asked him who my father's relic had been sold to, and he could tell me no more than what was written in our records."

Serafina's features grew slack with shock. "What happened to him?"

"My predecessor? He died shortly after our little chat." Emeraude tried to give an unaffected shrug, but George saw her struggling beneath the surface. "It's part of a Grandmaster's ascension rite to slay their forebearer."

George shuddered at the unnecessary violence this woman had grown up around.

"Our goal is to prevent the Dark Magus from gathering the Virtuous Favors for himself," Serafina said after a long minute. "If you are willing to work *with* us, Emeraude, I will help you find the Bravesoul pendant. It is my duty as one of the Favored Ones to aid my fellow relic bearers." She swelled with pride over the weighty new title she had bestowed upon herself and her mission. "And now that we have a name, perhaps we have a chance at locating it." She raised both her hands in a defensive stance. "I only ask that you leave the bloodshed behind you."

George gritted his teeth, wishing Serafina had not made such a bargain. But he reminded himself this was her personal undertaking, and she had told him more than once he could leave any time he wanted to. As much as he despised being in league with someone so villainous as Emeraude Odaire, he couldn't leave Serafina to her task alone. He couldn't abandon the woman he loved.

"You wish to forge a more extensive contract?" Emeraude's gaze traveled warily up and down Serafina's figure.

She shook her head in response. "No. Not a contract. A simple alliance. One forged on mutual respect for the other's position." Serafina held out her hand, her face a mask of resolve. "For you, too, will be a Favored One, should you accept your role as the Bravesoul pendant's guardian."

Emeraude studied the outstretched palm for what seemed like an eternity. Then, with two quick strides, she closed the distance between them and shook on the terms.

"I will help you keep the Favors from the Dark Magus," the Grandmaster pledged. "And I will not stop until the Bravesoul pendant is under *my* protection."

"The Virtues bind our covenant," Serafina added, the moonlight casting an ethereal glow around her as if in answer. "We, the Favored Ones, work together once more."

As the two women dropped their hands to their sides, George

awkwardly reached for the back of his neck, feeling tension build at its base.

"I will extend the same courtesy to you as I do to Lady Kindheart, George Solomon." Emeraude placed a hand on her heart and bowed her head. "Unless you should become a problem for her."

Serafina chuckled lightly as she threaded her arm through George's. "He has proven himself to me many times over. I trust him with my life and my secrets."

While the warmth of her against his body was slightly calming, George couldn't shake the growing sense of dread swirling within him. He'd been ready to cut Emeraude loose, but now, it seemed, their traveling duo had permanently become a trio.

"Let us return to the refugee camp for the night." Emeraude spun on her heel and resumed their trek through the forest. "We'll hunt down these Dundainee thugs in the morning," she called over her shoulder.

"Hunt?" George raised an eyebrow at her aggressive phrasing.

She shrugged, a devious grin on her lips. "Slip of the tongue. *Track.*"

He and Serafina kept a slower pace as they hiked through the moonlit forest, and Emeraude gradually pulled farther and farther ahead of them.

"I know you don't agree with our pact, George, but please, I'm asking you to trust me." Serafina's whisper barely reached his keen ears.

He glanced sideways at her. "Teaming up with the Grandmaster of the Shadow Brethren to find the other Favors? Was that really necessary?"

"You saw how swiftly she cut down Elias. How quickly she caused chaos at the war camp." Serafina's eyes glittered with unshed tears. "She scares the wits out of me, and I don't think we can risk having her as our opponent. I know you are one of the realm's best fighters—"

"But even I am no match for her." George knew it was a fact after witnessing Emeraude in action. He might be able to keep her at bay for a few minutes, but in the end, he would fall to her blade.

"She easily deduced my desires to find and obtain all the Favors. I'd prefer that she keep her Bravesoul pendant away from the Dark Magus than risk us losing our lives."

"What about the prophecy?" he challenged. "What about the one crown needing all the Favors to bring peace to the realm?"

She brushed a strand of loose hair away from her face. "What do we *really* know about the power of prophecy? They're just words on a page for now. I'd rather keep the Dark Magus from achieving his goal than traipse after some ambiguous fate."

"And you believe aligning ourselves with Emeraude is the only way to do that?"

"Maybe if it was just me, I might try to outwit her, but I cannot put you more in harm's way than I already have…" Serafina clumsily cupped his cheek in her palm as they walked. "As far as we know, Emeraude is unaware of the prophecies in play and that Jax may be the ruler fated to bring the Favors together. We just have to trust in ourselves and follow the path before us."

George clasped her hand and pressed her fingers against his rough lips. He longed for the day when he could hang up his weapons and just enjoy a simple life with her at his side. But until that day came, he would follow her to the ends of the realm.

"I trust you, Serafina. I'll play nicely with our newfound friend."

She let loose a bitter laugh. "As they say, keep your friends close and enemies closer, right?"

Chapter Twenty

"Duquessa."

Ziri's tense tone halted Jax and her companions at the foot of the foyer steps as they made their way toward their bedchambers in the west wing.

Sabine whirled at hearing her sweetheart, her face brimming with delight. "Finished for the night?"

Jax felt a surge of guilt over keeping the two apart, but Ziri's dedication to her role as archspymaster was not easily deterred, even by Sabine.

Ziri gave her a light kiss on the cheek in greeting. "Almost. I want to have a chat with Aizen first."

"Did you learn something while speaking with the staff?" Jax's words tumbled over one another. "What about the interior guards? Did anyone see anything?"

Ziri shook her head. "Nothing that struck them as overtly suspicious. The staff were engrossed with their duties preparing for dinner. The sentries reported nothing unusual, and no one used the manor entrances a good forty minutes or so prior to the fire." She paused. "I *did* find it curious that several of our guests were in and out of the kitchen right before the blaze broke out."

Jax recalled their vigorous game of badminton outside. She'd lost track of their guests' whereabouts shortly after joining her friends for the lawn game. "And?"

"It appears Lord General Allard tried his best to procure some wine from the staff. He got quite agitated with them, so much so that nearby guards were summoned."

Jax's eyes widened. "The Ducal Guard had to intervene?" Why was this the first she was hearing of such an altercation?

"Not exactly. Vivienne arrived around the same time, looking for her father, and was able to calm the Lord General's protests," Ziri reported. "Then, about ten minutes later, Yves stopped by to refill his water pitcher, and Dvorak and Lothaine asked our housemaids for new sets of towels."

Jax frowned. "Why weren't the staff already seeing to these needs?" Pitchers and towels should have been refreshed during the morning hours.

"Apparently, while working in his room, Yves knocked his water pitcher over and shattered it," Ziri explained. "In a panic to clean up the mess, he asked for assistance from his fellow guests. Both Lothaine and Dvorak offered their towels, and thus, there was a need for fresh ones."

Perry tilted his head. "Why not just call for aid from the staff?"

"This is purely speculation on the maids' part," Ziri hedged, "but Yves seemed quite panicked that he'd broken a priceless relic and feared the ire of his hostess, should you find out."

Jax couldn't imagine the cold man displaying such a reaction, but she then remembered the elaborate act he was putting on.

"I imagine his background fueled such a response." Uma folded her arms with a sigh. "Before you and Perry came to dinner last night, he mentioned that his family oversaw a textile mill owned by a cruel lord prior to the rebellion. He and his brothers were often whipped for the smallest infractions. I can't imagine what his punishment would have been for destroying something the lord owned."

"I see." At Uma's reasoning, Perry bowed his head in understanding. "I didn't consider the situation from his point of view." His cheeks colored with genuine regret. "Here I was, thinking it's only a silly water pitcher."

Jax, too, felt for Yves. Even though he was an honored guest in her home, his past traumas with nobility clearly still haunted him.

Sabine tapped her chin. "So, we have confirmation that Allard, Vivienne, Yves, Lothaine, and Dvorak were all notably moving about the manor around the time of the fire. I suppose any one of them could have slipped outside through a window to light the blaze."

"Especially during Allard's outburst in the kitchen," Jax mused. She flinched at the troubling scenario. It had been at *her* request that the Ducal Guard be positioned only at the manor doors rather than around the perimeter of the entire building. "If guards had to be summoned to deal with his demands, the nearest sentries would've been posted at the kitchen's service entrance."

"Does that mean Allard intentionally caused the distraction to draw them away from their posts?" Sabine suggested. "Or did someone see the opportunity Allard created and seize it?"

Jax considered several possibilities. "If it *was* intentional, that would mean Allard is working in cahoots with someone. Who? His daughter? Dvorak? If so, why set a fire that would trigger the trauma of losing his wife?"

No one had an answer for her.

"All these questions lead me to the reason I want to talk with Aizen." Ziri gnawed on her lower lip. "I want to pull back the extra men posted around the estate border and barracks and ensure our guests are properly watched tonight from *within* the manor."

Uma twisted her hands with concern. "You think whoever set the fire might try again?"

"I don't know what to think at the moment." Irritation danced in Ziri's bronze gaze. "I don't know our arsonist's motivation for setting the fire."

Perry tapped his foot on the floor. "What if there is no motivation, Ziri? Like I told the girls at dinner—" he motioned to Jax and her friends—"what if we're looking for trouble where there is none? What if it was just some random forest fire?"

"And what if it wasn't?" Ziri countered, her lips drawn in a grim line.

"I'm sure we'll learn more once the scene can be examined." Jax placed a reassuring palm on Perry's back. "But I would feel better having the guest wing under careful watch. Even if it means pulling some of the men from their posts near our suites."

"What if that's what the arsonist wants?" Sabine gripped Jax's forearm, her brow crinkled. "May I remind you that *you're* the most valuable thing in Glennfeld right now."

Jax wanted to roll her eyes at her friend's grandiose exaggeration, but now that Sabine had put the thought into her mind, she wondered if this was all some elaborate ploy to get to her.

"Sabine is right." Ziri rubbed her temples, exhaustion beginning to eat away at her. "Which is why I'm going to have Aizen pull men from the barracks and *not* from other areas of the manor. The Savantian guards are unarmed and lack the years of training our soldiers have under their belt. I don't consider them the threat that Aizen does. I'm more wary of the trusted delegates who can move freely through our halls."

Jax smiled her gratitude. "I defer to your expertise and ask that you convey my apologies to Aizen for teasing him about the seventy guards he brought. I now wish I had allowed more."

"Why not deliver that apology yourself?" The Captain's dry humor preceded his arrival in the foyer.

Before Jax could do so, Aizen explained his sudden appearance. "I just came from the veranda, ensuring we have four men stationed at every entrance." He stopped and assessed the worried group. "And I take it you now want our guests monitored more heavily?"

"Yes, Rami. Thank you." Jax glanced up the grand staircase, her gaze floating to the north wing.

"I've had someone patrolling the northern corridor since we thwarted the fire, but I'll send another man to assist." Aizen stroked the stubble on his square chin.

"Did you find anything noteworthy while out surveying the estate roads?" Jax asked, her voice inching upward with anticipation.

His displeasure deepened. "No. And, as expected, Yanis's team found no signs of an intruder anywhere along Glennfeld's border."

Jax felt the last of her dwindling hope extinguishing.

"I'm going to revisit the forest scene at first light," he added. "The ground will have cooled enough by then to allow for a more thorough inspection."

"I'll join you." Ziri's expression left no room for objection.

Aizen gave her a crooked smile. "I would be shocked if you didn't. Now, I'm needed back at the barracks for a briefing, and then I'll send as many men as I can spare to fortify the manor."

"I'll come with you," Ziri said. "I want to question the guards who were stationed at the kitchen service entrance this afternoon."

The two warriors bid the rest of the group goodnight and, after speaking with the sentries standing watch, departed through the front door.

Jax felt the tension in her shoulders begin to melt after hearing Aizen's reassurances that he would provide more interior guards, even if it meant pulling away the ones he'd reallocated to the estate border. It told her that he, too, suspected that the threat was coming from inside Glennfeld rather than outside.

But before she began questioning her suspects—her *guests*—she needed absolute proof of arson, so as not to entirely derail the peace talks.

As the Saphire group made their way back to their suites in the west wing of the house, Jax flinched at every shadow she encountered. With Sabine's theory that *she* might be the target of this bizarre attack curdling at the back of her mind, she prayed they all made it safely to the morning.

‡

Twisting, foreboding nightmares of thunderstorms and raging fires assaulted her dreams, and when she woke, Jax felt like she'd barely slept. She rubbed at her eyes, grimacing at the pinched pain that flared within her skull. "Not a good sign," she muttered to herself.

She climbed out of bed, letting Perry continue his unaffected slumber while she dressed herself for the day. While she sometimes still struggled with the numerous buttons her outfits boasted, Jax was happy that she no longer required Uma or Sabine's assistance for such matters. She'd rather her friends help her with the copious problems vexing the realm, not her appearance.

By the time she secured her golden crown in her hair, Perry stirred and yawned. "Donning your battle armor, my love?" His lavender gaze flicked to the glittering headpiece.

She laughed. "That's a good word for it. I hope it reminds Allard and Finral that they need to keep playing nicely with one another."

Jax appraised the clock on the fireplace mantle. "Would you like to join me for breakfast before the day's shenanigans begin?" She opted to keep her words lighthearted for fear that the weight of the realm would crush her if she dwelled on everything for too long. Despite her suspicions surrounding yesterday's fire, she *had* to help Savant reach a peace agreement.

"Of course." Perry tossed back the blankets and gingerly climbed out of bed. His movements were stiff but much less labored than they had been the previous evening. "Give me just a few minutes." He was even more adept than she without a valet to attend to him.

Perry ambled into the adjoining washroom, and Jax heard the splashing of a water basin as her husband readied himself. He returned a few heartbeats later with damp curls and a dewy glow on his face. He looked much more well-rested than her reflection conveyed.

As he pulled on a forest-green tunic, he noted her bemusement. "What?"

Jax came to his side and finished fastening the golden clasps for him. "I'm just fuming with jealousy that you can look so good at the drop of a hat, whereas I had to get up nearly an hour early to be presentable."

Perry chuckled, dropping his hands to her waist. "You could put on a burlap sack and be 'presentable,' my love."

Jax tapped the side of his temple. "Is your eyesight all right?"

He pulled her in for a deep, desperate kiss. "I know you're worried about the outcome of today, but if anyone can succeed in this, Jax, it's you."

"Thank you." She returned his kiss, wishing she could lose herself in his embrace and not have to worry about the security of the realm.

But alas, forgetting her duty was not who she was.

"Shall we?" She threaded her arm through his and led him away from their suite. Jax prayed that by the time she returned to their room tonight, Savant's future would be in stable hands.

Sabine, Yanis, and Uma were already seated in the banquet hall when they arrived. "Good morning, my dears." Jax smiled in greeting as she and Perry joined them at the table. "I hope you all slept better than I did."

"Not me. I jumped at every bump I heard in the night." Sabine did look quite pale in her mauve day gown.

Uma clicked her tongue in sympathy. "All seems quiet this morning. Which we can be grateful for."

Jax indicated to the empty seat next to Sabine. "I take it Ziri and Aizen are assessing the fire?"

Sabine responded with a grumpy nod.

As the dining hall attendants filled their glasses with freshly squeezed fruit juices, Yanis cleared his throat. "I stopped by to check on them during my morning run and asked if they wanted an additional set of eyes since they had a great deal of ground still to cover."

Jax winced at the thought of getting up and going for a run first thing in the morning—well, really, at the notion of going for a run at all.

Her disdain for the activity must have been evident on her face, for her friends giggled.

"Apologies for belittling your hobby, Yanis." Jax's cheeks grew warm. "Are you going out to help them?"

"No, ma'am. Aizen is worried too many boots will muck about the scene."

Jax's attention was momentarily diverted by the arrival of a glistening platter of sweet breakfast pastries overflowing with jelly, delivered by Madame Rosalyn. "Oh, my. The chef has outdone himself."

Everyone murmured their appreciation for the treats when the doors to the banquet hall burst open.

Dvorak flew into the room, his dark eyes wild with terror. "D-

Duchess Jacqueline, please send for help! It's Allard! He's...he's taken ill."

Jax was on her feet in an instant. "Send for Major Brennan," she told Yanis. While Glennfeld didn't have a healer in residence on the estate, Aizen had brought one of the Ducal Guard physicians, just in case.

Not wasting any time, Yanis tossed his napkin onto the table and darted out the doorway, making his way to the barracks.

To Sabine, Jax murmured, "Alert Aizen and Ziri. They're needed here immediately."

"Of course." Sabine scampered away without another word.

"Vice Lord Admiral, please calm yourself." Jax gathered her skirts and hurried to the trembling man's side. "Where is the Lord General?"

Dazed and shaken, Dvorak stared at her, his mouth bobbing open and closed before finally sputtering, "H-his room."

Jax sent a pleading look at Uma. "Help him to a seat, will you? He seems to be in shock." To Perry, she said, "Come with me," and grabbed his hand. "We're going to assist Allard."

As Uma nodded and draped her arm around Dvorak's heaving shoulders, Jax and Perry took off down the main corridor, running as quickly as Jax's billowing dress and Perry's sore muscles would allow.

Once they were in the main hall, Jax led the way to the north wing, her eyes open for signs of anything amiss. She found two sentries stationed at the entryway to the guest wing. "Soldiers, there's been a report that one of our guests has taken ill!" Incredulity and frustration further impassioned her heated tone. "What are you doing just standing here?"

The sentries straightened at her uncharacteristic rebuke, and the taller of the two asked, "Ill, Your Grace? We've heard nothing of the sort."

"Yes, all we've seen this morning is that short Savantian man hurrying off for breakfast," the other reported.

Jax and Perry exchanged confused looks. "Dvorak didn't tell you someone needed medical attention? Or request that you send for aid?"

"No, Your Grace." Both men's faces grew pale. "He just wanted to know the quickest way to the banquet hall."

Jax debated Dvorak's strange response for only an instant. "Could you please point the way to Corentin Allard's chambers?"

The taller guard stepped forward. "I'll take you there, Your Grace. Corporal Legue. Right this way." He nodded a wordless command to his partner before leading Jax and Perry down the dimly lit passage.

Sunlight had not yet made its way to this section of the manor, and chilling shadows carpeted the floor as they hurried in the corporal's wake.

"Here we are." Legue stopped in front of an ornately carved mahogany door. "Shall I?" he asked as he reached for the brass handle.

"Let me, Corporal." Jax took the lead and gripped the cool metal, somewhat surprised to find it unlocked. *I suppose since their apartments are adjoining, Dvorak must have used this door when exiting the suite rather than his own,* she surmised.

With a fortifying breath, she pushed the door inward and poked her head into the comfortably decorated sitting room. "Lord General? It's Jacqueline. Are you all right?"

Perry followed her inside, flanked by Legue. "Where is the old fellow? It doesn't look like he's here." Her husband studied the tidy room with growing concern.

Jax's practiced gaze examined the area with lightning speed. Where was Allard? She didn't hear sounds of anyone in distress, either.

She scurried toward the bedroom situated off the main sitting area. A quick look told her the Lion's Bane Lord General wasn't there.

"That leaves the washroom." Heart pounding, she darted toward the simple oak door standing slightly ajar on the opposite side of the suite.

Jax pressed her palm against the wood and pushed, the door resisting as if it were stuck or blocked. "Perry, can you…?"

He was immediately at her side, lending his strength, and soon, they'd inched the door open enough so she could slip inside.

As her eyes adjusted to the faint light, it became all too apparent what had been blockading the door—Corentin Allard's body.

"Oh, no." Jax's hand flew to her mouth to conceal the reflexive shriek that escaped her.

The Lord General sat propped against the large copper bathtub, his legs outstretched toward the entryway. His dark eyes were wide and glassy, and his neck was perched at an odd angle against his shoulder.

Perry joined her, his hand finding hers. "I think this poor chap's beyond saving." His pale skin lost its natural hue as he studied the deceased man.

Jax bobbed her head, trying her best to calm her fluttering stomach. There would be no need to search for a pulse. She'd encountered death enough times before to know what it looked like. Thank goodness she had not had time to eat any of the delicious breakfast pastries, or Jax might have gotten sick at the crime scene.

Hush, now, Jax, you're getting ahead of yourself, she reprimanded her morbid assumption. She had no idea if this was indeed a crime scene or a tragic accident. Yet.

Corporal Legue joined them in the tight quarters. "Virtues. What happened? Did the bloke slip or something while preparing for a bath?"

As Jax pushed her tumultuous feelings aside and beckoned her analytical mind forward, she studied the baffling display. Allard was fully clothed, and there was no water in the tub, which seemed to instantly disprove Legue's suggestion. She was certain no one among the trusted Glennfeld staff would empty a basin without alerting someone they'd found a dead body.

Her gaze dashed to the open door opposite where they stood. "That must lead to Dvorak's suite." A question continued to nag at her. If the Vice Lord Admiral had found Allard in their shared washroom, why hadn't he immediately informed the first person he came across that help was needed?

Perry confirmed her guess by sticking his head through the doorway. "Opens right into a sitting room."

Corporal Legue crouched beside Allard to do a closer examination. He touched two fingers to the man's neck and frowned. "Based on the temperature of his skin and the stiffness of the body," he said, giving a stomach-churning demonstration by trying to move Allard's arm, "I'd say he's been dead at least eight hours or more."

Jax did the math in her head. "That puts the time of death around midnight." Her brow furrowed. "What time did you come on shift, Corporal?"

"Nine, Your Grace." The guard straightened, his expression grim. "Captain Aizen pulled me from border patrol and assigned me to assist Hershall—the chap outside—given all the questions surrounding yesterday's fire. But by the time I joined him, all the guests had retired to their rooms for the evening. It was a quiet night. No one came out until this morning…the fellow we mentioned. Dvorak, was it?"

Jax pondered the scene, doing her best to assess Allard objectively. She'd think about the political ramifications later. Not to mention Vivienne losing a beloved father…

She shook her head free of her emotionally charged thoughts. A suspicious fire and now this? Were these events linked? If so, how?

"Well, if no one left their rooms after nine, then the only person who had access to Allard was Dvorak." Perry folded his arms as he came to her side. "There. We have our killer."

Jax smiled grimly at his apparent optimism.

"I-I don't think it's that simple, Lord Pettraud," Legue spoke up. "Allard doesn't show any signs of a fatal struggle. No blood, for one thing." He motioned to the relatively spotless washroom. "And there's no bruising to suggest a fight took place." The guard's gaze grew steely. "And neither myself nor Hershall heard anything resembling an attack."

"But would you, mate?" Perry challenged. His tone wasn't disrespectful, just one of genuine curiosity. "Aren't these walls thick enough to dull any noise coming from within the suites?"

"From the guest's chambers, yes, Your Highness. But each of the washrooms has a separate door leading to the hall for the servants to use." Legue strode toward a curtain hanging on the wall parallel to the outer corridor. He pulled it back, revealing a basic wood panel. "This door is very thin. We would have heard any strenuous activity through it."

"I see." Perry thanked the man for his explanation before turning to Jax and raising his eyebrows.

Jax could almost hear him saying, *I hope no one heard the "strenuous activity" taking place within* our *washroom after dinner last night.*

Her cheeks heated just picturing the intimate scene. What had started as a plan to help alleviate the lingering soreness in her husband's muscles had ended a bit more amorously than she'd intended. But Jax quickly pushed the sensual memory out of her mind. "If there are no signs of a struggle and Allard has no fatal wounds, could this be just a terrible accident?"

Maybe the poor man had died from a heart attack or something. Of course, paired with the shock of yesterday's fire, her mind jumped to sinister reasons, but perhaps she was putting the cart before the horse…again.

Legue clasped his hands behind his back. "I'm sure Major Brennan will be able to tell us with more certainty, Your Grace."

"Tell us what, Legue?" A tall, dark-skinned man entered the washroom clutching a medicinal satchel. He wore the armor of the Ducal Guard, although his breastplate was covered by a healer's tunic. He had to be Major Brennan, their physician.

"How a guest under my care and protection died." Jax couldn't stop her hands from wringing with worry.

Aizen and Ziri appeared in the washroom a heartbeat later, their soot-streaked faces etched with tension. "We'll get to the bottom of this, Duchess." Aizen dismissed Legue with a curt nod, as there wasn't much space for the six of them to remain. "I'll speak with you and Hershall momentarily. If our other guests begin to ask what is going on, please direct them to the banquet hall."

"Sabine filled you in?" Jax asked her two friends once Legue departed with a salute.

Ziri nodded. "Although she told us Allard had taken ill and needed aid."

"That's what Dvorak described when he blew into the banquet

hall," Perry explained. "How he could've been this mistaken, I don't know." He pointed, wincing at Allard's fallen form.

"Shock, I suppose." Jax leaned into her husband's chest. "As Vice Lord Admiral, Dvorak is Allard's strategic mind. He isn't normally on the battlefield, so I doubt he's seen much death."

While Brennan knelt beside Allard to examine him, Aizen continued his report. "Uma met us in the foyer to let us know Dvorak lost consciousness, but I figured Brennan was needed here more urgently. She and Sabine are tending to the Vice Lord Admiral in the banquet hall."

"Not sure much can be done to aid Allard now," Perry muttered.

Jax elbowed her husband lightly. "Finding out *why* he's dead would be a start."

Perry recoiled, abashed. "I apologize for my cavalier behavior. It's just…"

She knew what he was thinking. Was it really too much to ask the Virtues that they host one gathering without a dead body?

Silence settled over the room while Brennan continued his examination. From the reports Aizen had provided her about the men he'd selected for this mission, Jax knew Brennan had been with the Ducal Guard for nearly a decade. He'd trained under one of her own court physicians, Master Vyanti. He was someone whose judgment she could trust.

"I have good news and bad news, Your Grace," Brennan eventually said as he rose from his crouched position.

Jax sighed. "The good, please."

"I believe I have a cause of death for you." He began returning various medical instruments to his satchel. "It will require a bit more testing in the barracks' infirmary to confirm, but I'm fairly certain this man died from coming into contact with a plant called ardor root."

"Ardor root?" Jax wrinkled her nose. "I've never heard of such a thing before."

"You'd have little reason to." Brennan gave her a slight smile. "The plant is not native to Saphire. It's used most often in clothing dyes. Makes a beautiful shade of red, but it must be boiled down properly. Otherwise, contact with the skin can be fatal."

"Are you saying his *clothing* killed him?" Perry could not hold back a stunned snort.

Brennan grimaced. "No, Your Highness. I believe the victim ingested the root. He's got some unique discoloration under his tongue and inside his ear canals. It's indicative of ardor root poisoning."

Poisoning. Jax flinched. *So much for this being deemed a tragic accident.* "Any idea how Allard consumed this ardor root?"

"That's where the bad news comes into play," Brennan admitted. "I'll need to conduct an autopsy, Your Grace, but I have my suspicions."

Aizen nudged the physician in the arm. "You can speak freely in front of Duchess Jacqueline. She'll appreciate any theory at this point."

Jax nodded her agreement. "Yes, please."

Brennan sighed. "Well, I mentioned ardor root isn't native to Saphire. It thrives in humid, tropical environments…"

Oh, dear. She feared she knew where this was going.

"Mainly, from the northern grasslands of Savant."

Jax's fists balled at her sides. While she had her own suspicions about what had transpired, hearing it all but confirmed troubled her greatly. "So, this likely means one of our guests is a murderer."

Brennan's expression grew taut. "I know we're all here to champion peace, Your Grace, so I must ask you to hold off such accusations until I've verified my findings. I do apologize for requesting such a delay, but I'm sure you understand why."

"Of course, Major Brennan. Accusing one of our guests of murder would likely put a damper on our talks of peace." She managed a small grin to convey her sarcasm and considered the irony that she'd said the very same thing yesterday about arson.

The physician returned her smile. "I will send word as soon as I have concluded my tests. Until then," he said, shifting his focus to Aizen, "I would suggest feigning ignorance about this poisoning plot."

"Aye. We wouldn't want to spook our killer." Aizen stroked the stubble on his chin. "We'll announce that the Lord General passed away from an apparent heart attack."

Perry's eyebrows rose. "And let his assailant believe they've gotten away with murder?"

"For now." Jax placed her hands on her hips. "However, covering up such a crime will make it hard for us to interrogate suspects without them catching on."

"I'm sure you'll find a way, Duchess." Bemusement danced in Aizen's gaze. "Major Brennan and I will move Allard to the barracks' infirmary."

Jax began making a mental list of what needed to be done. "Can you have Legue wake our guests and send them to the banquet hall before moving the body? I'll make the announcement to them about Allard's passing. Except for Vivienne," she added hastily. "I'll break the news to her privately."

Aizen bowed his head, acknowledging her orders.

To Perry, she asked, "Would you find and discreetly inform our friends about what's happened? That way, as our guests gather, we all can be on watch for any telling signs of guilt."

Perry shot a hesitant glance toward Ziri.

"Hershall and I will stay with Jax while she speaks with Miss Vivienne," she answered his wordless question.

Jax kept her annoyance to herself. She didn't appreciate it when people spoke about her like she wasn't standing beside them, but she knew Perry was only concerned for her safety. And with a murderer on the loose at her peace summit, he had every right to be. Vivienne may have been Allard's daughter, but that didn't absolve her from suspicion.

Aizen then took a fortifying breath before surveying their anxious group. "Let's move."

Chapter Twenty-One

Jax hesitated a moment before rapping her knuckles against the polished wood door. "Vivienne? Are you awake? It's Jacqueline."

She shot Hershall, Legue, and Ziri a worried glance when only silence greeted them. As they stood in the shadowy hallway, her mind raced. She hadn't even considered the terrifying notion that some of her other guests might have been targeted by the poisoner, too.

Hershall's hand rested on his sword hilt. "Why not try again, Duchess?"

"She might just be sleeping," Legue offered, his wary tone not all too confident. Jax had asked Legue to hold off on waking the others until she was inside Vivienne's room.

Jax knocked harder this time. "Vivienne? I need to speak with you."

She finally heard rustling on the other side of the door. Very frantic rustling. "J-just a moment," a timid voice called out.

More than a minute passed by before Vivienne opened the door a crack. "Y-yes, Your Grace?"

Jax could barely see the young woman, but the skin on her face looked incredibly flushed. She shot an alarmed glance at Ziri and the sentries. Brennan had mentioned red spots being indicative of ardor root poisoning. Could the same be said of rosy skin?

"Are you feeling all right, my dear?" Jax pressed.

Vivienne drew the door open a bit more so that Jax could see her clad in a yellow nightgown. "I feel fine, Your Gra—Jacqueline." Her pert nose scrunched with confusion. "Is something wrong?"

Indeed, the flush that had been present seconds ago seemed to be receding. Jax cleared her throat. "I'd like a private word with you."

"Private?" Vivienne gulped, and she hesitantly welcomed Jax into the room. She grew even more uneasy when Hershall and Ziri followed behind.

Jax gave Legue a covert nod to see to the other guests, and then Hershall closed the suite door.

"What's this about?" Vivienne fidgeted with her nightgown as she sank into an armchair.

Jax took the seat opposite her, while her protectors remained near the entryway. "I'm so sorry to have to tell you this, but I'm afraid I have some shocking news. Your father passed away sometime during the night."

"W-what?" Vivienne's hands froze, and her eyes tripled in size. "No! That can't be."

"I'm afraid it's true." Jax reached out and patted her knee as the young woman began to sob.

"How is this possible?" Vivienne managed to choke out. "P-Papa was fine yesterday."

"The immediate guess is that he died of a heart attack, but my physician will provide an update after he completes a postmortem exam." Jax said a small prayer to the Virtues, asking for forgiveness over her necessary lie. She pulled out a white linen handkerchief she had tucked away in her pocket and handed it to the grief-stricken woman. "I'm so sorry."

Vivienne accepted the offered cloth and dropped her face into her open palms, her shoulders heaving with emotion. "I can't believe this. Oh, Papa. This is all my fault!"

Jax shared a wide-eyed look with Ziri and Hershall. Virtues, were they already getting a confession?

Vivienne continued to sob. "If only I hadn't given into his pleas for more wine. I knew it wasn't healthy for him, but I-I let him have it anyway."

Jax's racing heart began to slow. Vivienne evidently assumed her father's heart attack had been brought on by overindulging in alcohol. Which, given what Jax had learned about the man's drinking habits, seemed within reason.

"What happens now?" Vivienne looked up at her with a wobbling chin. "What happens to Lion's Bane? To this summit?"

Jax wished she had more comforting reassurances for the girl. She seemed genuinely distressed by her father's passing, and Jax wanted to believe in her innocence. But then Vivienne's stunning ballad from the first night echoed through her mind, and Jax realized that when it came to performers, one could never be certain.

"That remains to be seen," she answered with a measured gaze. "But you are welcome to stay here for as long as you need." Jax hoped her next question wouldn't seem too far out of line. She wanted to gauge Vivienne's movements prior to this morning. "Tell me, dear, when did you last speak with your father?"

Vivienne wiped her eyes with Jax's handkerchief. "Before I came down to dinner last night. So, around quarter to six?"

"Before dinner?" Jax repeated. "Not after?"

"N-no." Vivienne sniffled. "He'd told me not to disturb him, and I learned a long time ago not to disobey my father." She shuddered, and her palm touched her cheek as if reliving some phantom touch.

Jax debated how to proceed with her questioning. Anything more probing, and Vivienne might realize her father hadn't died from a simple heart attack.

"Do you know if any of the other guests spoke with your father after dinner?" She knew she was walking on thin ice. "I'm just trying to help my physician determine a more accurate time of death," Jax added in the hopes of explaining away her prying.

Vivienne's brow furrowed. "I'm afraid I don't know. I returned to my suite after dinner and haven't left it since."

Jax caught Hershall's gaze, and he gave a slight nod, confirming Vivienne's statement.

"And you heard nothing out of the ordinary during the nighttime?"

"No." The young woman chewed on her lower lip. "I was fast asleep."

Her curt response made Jax sit back a moment. Up until now, Vivienne had appeared forthright with her statements, but the way her gaze now darted to the floor gave Jax pause. "Asleep, you say? You went to bed right after dinner? You didn't socialize with any of the others?"

A traitorous, rosy flush returned to Vivienne's cheeks and spread down her neck. "I-uh, I went to bed."

Jax kept her expression neutral, but she noted Vivienne's fidgeting behavior with growing intrigue. "Is there some reason why you're lying to me?"

The embarrassed hue drained from Vivienne's face in an instant, and her brown eyes bulged in fear. "Oh, uh, well…"

"Because I asked her to, Jacqueline." Finral Lothaine's voice, initially muffled, startled Jax as the man himself stepped out from the large wardrobe in the corner of the suite.

Hershall took a defensive position between the disheveled man and Jax, but Ziri quickly placed a calming hand on his shoulder. "I don't think Governor Lothaine poses a threat," she murmured with a bemused smirk.

"Ah." Jax assessed the bedraggled couple, doing her best to keep her bubbling amusement buried. "I see I interrupted something this morning."

Both Finral's and Vivienne's faces resembled the insides of a freshly baked cherry tart.

"How long has this been going on?" Jax motioned between the two of them.

Vivienne looked to Finral, her teary gaze pleading. Before either answered, he rushed to her side and gathered her in his arms. She clung to him for dear life, sobbing quietly as he murmured words of comfort.

Jax would have found the whole situation rather moving, if the young woman's father hadn't just been found murdered.

"For nearly a decade now, Jacqueline," Finral admitted, still holding a crying Vivienne in his arms. "We met at the Library of Savant. I was a scribe in training, and Vivienne was doing her best to further her studies. Her father didn't believe she needed an education beyond what she'd received as a child, so she sought knowledge elsewhere." He paused and gazed down at her fondly. "The head scholar tasked my master with taking her under his wing, so he began tutoring the two of us."

Vivienne sniffed and looked up at Finral with a small smile, albeit a sad one. "We fell in love not long after, and when he received his certification a few years later, Fin asked my father for my hand in marriage."

"I could provide her with a good living." Finral swelled with pride. "Scribes are one of the most respectable positions a common-born can secure in Savant." His expression then clouded. "But Allard wanted something better for his daughter. He wanted her to marry a minor noble."

Jax couldn't resist a scoff. A leader of the citizens' rebellion had once wanted his daughter to marry into the very class he now wished to destroy?

"He tried finding me a husband but received no offers," Vivienne explained. "Several years passed. Prejudices between the common-born and nobility became deep, festering wounds inflamed by Duke Savant. I thought Fin might be able to try again, but by then, he'd been called to serve as an estate guard for the noble family who owned the earldom where he lived."

"Earl Bosquet didn't allow us to communicate with anyone, for fear it would *distract* us from our duties." Finral's expression hardened with rage. "I just wanted to serve my time and then return to Vivienne and my scribe work. I had only a few months left in my contract when Duke Savant was killed and our chance for a rebellion began. It didn't happen overnight, mind you. No, the fires of discontent had been burning for a long time. It was something we often talked about in the guard's quarters while being forced to serve the Earl. Savant's death gave us the perfect opportunity to finally step out into the sun."

"Fin was one of the best warriors among the estate guard, and they urged him to lead a group to the capital." Vivienne, through her tears, beamed proudly at her love. "I couldn't believe my eyes when I saw him across the battlefield one day. Strong, determined, and handsome as ever."

Finral pulled her closer. "I managed to get a message to her that same night, and we arranged to meet in secret." His fingers danced across the exposed skin of her neck.

"Did your father know you'd rekindled your romance?" Jax raised an eyebrow.

The couple shared a nervous look. "I don't believe so," Vivienne replied. "He knew we still cared for one another, but he was determined to keep us apart, especially once he learned Fin's rank within Heartsworn."

"I reached out to him many times with offers to form an alliance," Finral added. "I would've happily served alongside him as his second."

His gaze grew haunted. "But weeks into the rebellion, Allard's ideals took a dangerous turn, and I could no longer align myself with his views for Savant." He swallowed before asking, "And now you say he's dead?"

Vivienne covered her mouth, her sobs sputtering once more to the surface.

"I'm afraid so." While Jax saw Vivienne's raw pain on display, Finral kept his composure.

"That complicates things." His jaw set in a hard line.

Indeed. Aloud, she inquired, "Did you speak with him last night?"

Finral shifted uneasily on his feet. "No. I accompanied Dvorak and Vivienne back from the banquet hall, bid them goodnight, and retired to my suite."

Hershall cleared his throat. "I can verify his statement, Duchess. I saw all three return from dinner and enter their chambers around eight."

"Then how did Governor Lothaine end up in Vivienne's suite?" Ziri's sharp features tightened with murderous intent. She had taken the question right out of Jax's mouth. If Hershall hadn't noticed

Finral's movements, what else could he have missed before Legue came to assist him at nine? The thought was gravely troubling.

Finral cleared his throat. "Please don't direct your ire at your poor guard, Jacqueline. My appearance in Vivienne's room was a skilled act of deception that Yves assisted in. He…he helped me sneak into her room unnoticed." His cheeks darkened with embarrassment.

Hershall's bushy eyebrows drew together a moment before his mouth popped open. "You mean, his little mishap with the inkwell was all a distraction?"

"Mishap?" Ziri frowned.

Jax glanced at Finral for clarification. "Inkwell?"

He rubbed his shoulder sheepishly. "Yves spilled a bottle of ink all over himself and asked for this lad's help mopping it up."

Hershall spoke through gritted teeth, "To which I said I would send for one of the household staff to assist, as I could not leave my post. Instead, he just waved an ink-stained towel in front of my face and returned to his room in a huff."

"While Yves caused the scene, I snuck from my room into Vivienne's." Finral pointed to the front door. "I'm just across the hall from her."

Jax shook her head at the utter ridiculousness of the scheme. Vivienne and Finral certainly were the epitome of young and in love. "Forgive me, but I have a hard time picturing your ornery deputy as a willing matchmaker," she said dryly, pretending she hadn't overheard their cunning plans the other day.

At her mention of Yves, Finral suddenly grew uncomfortable. "He believes our relationship can be…of use to Heartsworn."

Vivienne patted him on the arm, her face one of understanding. "Something I am well aware of when it comes to Yves."

Not wishing to create undue tension between the couple, Jax asked, "What time did this whole charade transpire?"

Finral glanced down at his sweetheart. "Couldn't have been later than eight-thirty."

"It was eight twenty-two, Duchess," Hershall assured with authority. "I noted the event in my report for the evening as that was the last time any guest left their rooms until the morning."

Jax nodded her thanks, hoping her soft smile conveyed her apologies for initially assuming Hershall incompetent. He'd have no reason to think a man dealing with a spilled inkwell was a threat.

She turned her attention back to the couple. "So, did you two spend the whole night together?"

"I realized we deceived you and your sentries, Jacqueline, and for that, I apologize. But why all the questions?" Finral's tone became guarded. "I thought you said Vivienne's father died from a heart attack."

Jax inwardly cursed herself for being too invasive with her inquiries. "That's what my physician believes. I-I'm just trying to figure out if the Lord General may have cried out to anyone for help in the night."

"Oh," Vivienne whimpered, her watery eyes welling once more with tears. "I hope he didn't suffer."

Not wanting to lie any more than she already had, Jax decided it was time to take her leave. She didn't need an answer to know these two had spent a passionate night together.

"I'm certain Major Brennan will have more information for us soon." Jax smiled with strained reassurance. She had no idea how long it would take the physician to run whatever tests he needed to make his conclusions. "For now, I'm hoping you both might join me downstairs in the banquet hall. I know you might not feel like it," she murmured as her gaze met Vivienne's, "but you really should eat something to keep up your strength."

"I'll escort her down momentarily, Duchess." Finral's grip tightened around his beloved as she leaned into him.

Jax rose and departed to give the couple some privacy. As soon as she, Ziri, and Hershall stepped out into the hall, Legue appeared before them, winded and worried.

"Duchess, apologies. I've checked all the rooms twice now, and I cannot find the young Heartsworn leader anywhere." He glanced at his partner. "I need to alert Captain Aizen—"

"No need, Legue," Jax cut the distressed man off. "We found him. With Miss Vivienne."

Legue's eyes widened. "But how? No one left their rooms last night."

"Lothaine had his deputy distract me while I was on patrol alone," Hershall explained, his annoyance over the matter returning. "Remember what I told you about that bloke looking like he doused himself with ink? Turns out, his mate slipped across the hall while that Yves fellow kept waving a stained towel in my face."

As the two men spoke, Jax and Ziri wandered to the end of the corridor to assess the wing from a different vantage point.

Ziri's lips pressed together as she stood where Hershall had kept watch all night. "While I would like to find fault, I cannot blame him for his mistake, Duquessa."

Jax nodded her agreement. "It was quite the coordinated attack on Yves and Finral's part." She folded her arms and squinted down the long hall. Given that the Ducal Guard were stationed at the north wing's entrance to give their guests some sense of privacy, Jax could see how poor Hershall's focus had been distracted enough to miss Finral darting across the narrow passage.

"Blimey." Legue ran a hand through his tousled hair as Jax and Ziri rejoined the two sentries. "I'm relieved he's not missing, but Virtues, we've disgraced the name of the Ducal Guard."

"I wouldn't say that, Corporal." Jax patted the golden pauldrons on his shoulder. "Hershall was deliberately preyed upon by our visitors. However, I must ask," she said, turning her amethyst gaze on the sentry in question, "were there *any* other distractions like this at any time during the night? Even the smallest disturbance could prove crucial."

Hershall shook his head. "No, Your Grace. Not on my watch. I swear on my life. After the inkwell incident, Yves returned to his room, and no one came out until Dvorak did this morning."

Legue clapped his compatriot on the back. "I will swear to that, too, Duchess. There was no movement from the time I came on shift at nine until morning."

Jax tapped her chin as she considered the timeline. "Walk me through everything that happened last night."

"Well," Hershall began, "I arrived in the wing a few minutes before eight, and the day shift gave me a status report. 'Course, that was a bit chaotic, given the turmoil the fire caused. Only one man was assigned to the wing in the hours following the blaze, due to the others being needed elsewhere on the estate. But that guard hadn't run into issues with the guests, other than Allard's drunken antics." Hershall scratched at his wispy hair.

"What do you mean, his antics?" Jax asked.

Hershall shrugged. "I guess the fella reacted poorly to the fire and eventually convinced his daughter to let him have a few drinks to calm his nerves. The alcohol ended up making the Lord General more volatile as the evening wore on, according to the sentry I relieved. Allard kept coming out of his room, barking orders and demanding more liquor. The old man even stumbled into the wrong suite at one point."

Jax frowned at the unflattering description of the Lord General's behavior. How had Allard become so intoxicated if all he'd had to drink was Vivienne's wine? Could his drunkenness have been a side effect of ardor root poisoning?

"The sentry debated sending for Major Brennan," Hershall continued, "but Allard finally calmed down and settled into his suite around seven-thirty. I took up my post at eight, and the Vice Lord Admiral, Governor Lothaine, and Miss Vivienne soon returned from the banquet hall." He pointed to the large open archway near the entrance of the wing. "They were all in their rooms by eight ten, at the latest. Then Yves came out at eight twenty-two covered in ink and waving a mucky towel around."

Hershall's cheeks flushed crimson. "I should've realized something was amiss, but given what the daytime sentry told me, Yves seemed like he might be a bit of a klutz."

Jax held up her hand in pause. "What did the officer tell you that makes you say that?"

Hershall folded his arms. "Oh, something about Yves accidentally knocking his water pitcher to the floor and causing a fuss while Lothaine and Dvorak helped him clean the mess up."

Ziri nudged Jax in the side with her elbow. "That aligns with what the kitchen staff told me yesterday," she muttered.

"You're right." Jax snapped her fingers as the memory burst to life. "Yves needed a new pitcher, and Dvorak and Finral requested towels." While she was glad to have confirmation regarding some of her guests' movements, she wasn't sure what it amounted to just yet. "Anything else, gentlemen?" she asked the sentries.

"No, Your Grace. Legue came on shift at nine, and all was quiet until Dvorak came barreling down the hall this morning." Hershall frowned. "I still find it odd he didn't mention his man needing a doctor to us."

Legue scoffed. "Maybe he thought we couldn't leave our posts?"

Another lingering question popped into Jax's mind. "Did you see which room he came out of?"

Legue's brow furrowed. "Well, at the time, we were both facing away from the suite doors, surveying the hall ahead." He pointed in the southern direction of the manor. "But we both whirled when we heard a door open."

"Dvorak was already in the hall at that point, and where his suite is right beside Allard's..." Hershall trailed off with a wince. "I suppose we cannot be certain, Duchess."

Jax tapped her chin. If she remembered the room assignments correctly, the guest suites with adjoined washrooms belonged to Allard, Dvorak, Finral, and Yves. Only Vivienne had her own private bath. That meant that Dvorak was the one person with unfettered access to Allard during the night and, to raise suspicions even more, he'd also been the one who discovered the body. Jax mulled over the perplexing puzzle pieces. Anyone with half a brain could see means and opportunity stacking up against Dvorak, indicating either he was an incredibly foolish killer... or an innocent man being framed.

She cast a desperate glance at the nearby clock on a mantle. *I do hope Brennan is quick with his tests.* She wanted to ask the delegates more pointed questions to begin narrowing down a suspect. But until they knew for certain Allard had been murdered, Jax would need to hold her tongue to keep the peace.

"Thank you, gentlemen." She nodded her appreciation for Legue's and Hershall's assistance. "I suppose it's time to see to my guests."

Chapter Twenty-Two

George bolted upright from his dreams, his foggy mind clearing as pleading cries echoed from outside.

"But we need those, Lieutenant. We've got mouths to feed, too."

George recognized the stress in Marie's voice. What was going on?

He gently nudged Serafina from sleep. "Something's up. I'm going outside to investigate."

She nodded as she yawned, blinking several times as she acclimated to the new day. "I'll follow shortly."

George hurriedly tugged on a fresh tunic and pants before scrambling out of the tent. He shielded his eyes against the bright morning sun as he scanned for signs of Marie.

The matron stood at the entrance to a nearby storehouse, barring the way of the imposing lieutenant George had seen stop by the blacksmith's forge at the war camp. The soldier was accompanied by several men. With determined strides, George set off toward the group.

"Apologies, Miss Marie, but I'm afraid feeding our army takes precedence at this time." The lieutenant roughly pushed her aside, sending Marie stumbling, and George arrived on the scene just in time to catch her from falling to the ground.

"What's the meaning of this?" George growled in his best Savantian accent.

The lieutenant barely gave him a second glance, so his speech couldn't have been that bad. "I don't answer to you." He pushed his way into the storehouse, followed by his men.

George released a shaken Marie and lunged forward to follow, but she grabbed his sleeve to prevent him from going further. "Let it go, lad. It will do no good."

As much as he yearned to teach the lieutenant a lesson about respecting civilians, George heeded Marie's advice. "What's going on?"

"That brute says Commander Crowe is claiming our food stores in the name of the Lion's Bane army." Marie spat out her nephew's title and shook with visible rage. "Apparently, several crates of rations were destroyed last night at the war camp due to some runaway horses, and he believes it is his right to take ours."

A guilty storm raged within George's stomach. *Virtues, this is our fault.* He surveyed the refugee settlement, his shame doubling with each hungry gaze he met. He hadn't given a second thought as to how their plan to reach Elias might affect the innocents around them. And now, these poor people who had already suffered so much would have to survive on even less food.

"Where's the nearest market? Perhaps we can assemble a group and set out to buy supplies?"

Marie's eyebrow arched at his offer. "With what funds, may I ask?"

George swallowed. He and Serafina had rationed their gold reasonably well during their travels. He was sure once she learned of the predicament they'd caused, Serafina would agree with the offer on the tip of his tongue. "My wife and I have money saved."

"The settlement wouldn't be able to pay you back."

"I know," he assured the matron. "But you've already been kind enough to take us in and feed us. It's the least we could do."

Marie debated his offer before sticking out her hand. "I shall accept your generosity to fund such an endeavor. I'll send Gunther and his lads to South Haven, since they know the area better." They shook on their deal, and then Marie whispered, "But let's wait until our lieutenant friend departs. He doesn't need to know our stores will soon be replenished."

By the time the officer and his men emerged from the storehouse with their arms full of grain, Serafina had joined them.

"What's happening?" She brushed her auburn hair out of her face, her expression troubled.

George explained in low tones the reason for Lion's Banes' visit, as well as his solution to the problem.

The corner of her lip curled as Serafina's prismatic eyes sparkled. "Ever the hero." She kissed his cheek as a show of her approval. "I'll retrieve our purse."

George wordlessly thanked her and waited beside Marie to ensure the Lion's Bane soldiers left without causing further trouble.

Once the lieutenant and his men departed, Serafina discreetly dropped ten gold coins into Marie's palm.

The matron's eyes doubled in size. "Virtues, I-I can't accept this much. Why, this is nearly half a year's work!"

George's heart clenched at her reaction. If these people had known the fair wages that Jax had issued across her holdings, perhaps they would have revolted against the Savantian establishment sooner.

"We insist." Serafina squeezed the matron's forearm.

Marie still looked stricken. "I'd feel much better about this if I could offer you something in return."

Serafina's features grew sharp with intensity. "Well, we are in search of some…information."

Marie visibly stiffened at the drawn-out remark. "What kind of information?" She eyed them with simmering suspicion.

George took a breath. "Could you tell us where the Dundainee make camp?"

"What would a nice couple like you want with those thugs?" Marie did her best to sound unaffected, but her eyes belayed her fear.

Serafina debated her answer. "They've taken something of ours, and we'd like to get it back."

Marie's gaze flicked to the pile of gold in her palm, and chilling understanding seemed to dawn over her that she wasn't dealing with an ordinary husband and wife. "W-we can't afford to deal with their kind of trouble," she whispered.

George rested a hand on her shoulder. "I assure you," he said, dropping his accent, "we have no intentions of coming back here, or indicating to the Dundainee that this camp had any involvement in our dealings."

Marie staggered back, clutching the gold to her chest. "Who *are* you?"

"It's better if you don't know." Serafina gave the woman a sad smile, her Beautraudian lilt a quiet fluttering on the morning breeze.

George watched the matron grapple silently with their request. He hoped they hadn't played their hand too early in an effort to try and gain her trust.

"The Dundainee took over an old outpost about two leagues due north from here," Marie finally muttered out of the side of her mouth. "When they're all in residence, there are about forty of them." While her face was a mask of indifference, her eyes shimmered with warning.

"Noted." Serafina reached into her coin purse and dropped three more gold pieces into Marie's trembling hand. "With that, we'll collect our things and be on our way."

As George and Serafina turned to head toward their tent, Marie burst out, "Stop by Samuel near the cooking spits. Tell him Marie said you were owed a travel pack. Should keep you fed and watered for a few days, at least."

George dipped his chin in thanks. "Take care of yourself, Marie. May the Virtues watch over you."

‡

The couple rushed to their tent to pack, finding Emeraude already waiting for them, ready to go. She wore dark traveling garb and a thin forest-green cloak with her hair tied back from her face. While she didn't look very threatening, George caught the glint of daggers strapped to the thighs of her pants from under her cloak.

"We have our course," George said in greeting before diving inside the tent to gather their bags and weapons. It didn't take him long to secure his pack and sword underneath his own cloak. Serafina moved equally as swift, hooking her crossbow to her belt.

"Where?" Emeraude asked as soon as they stepped out of the tent. She tapped her foot impatiently, and it was clear from her annoyed expression she was ready to be away from here.

George nodded over his shoulder. "Two leagues due north. If the terrain is level, the horses will have no issue getting us there within the hour." He was compensating for the fact that Emeraude didn't have a Crepstian mount. They would be forced to travel at her horse's slower pace.

"Let's get moving then." She turned on her heel and headed toward the stables.

They collected the animals and stopped to speak with Samuel, per Marie's instructions. The man didn't blink twice at their request and soon provided them with generous saddlebags filled with dried meats, fruits, and water.

As Serafina strapped everything to Emma's saddle, she murmured to George, who stood with his back to her, doing the same with Merida's tack, "If all goes according to plan, we could make for the northern border tonight."

George considered the possibility while desperately trying to tamp down his hopes. If they were successful in retrieving the Intelligeye sigil, what did that mean for them next? Now that they had formed this new alliance with Emeraude Odaire, what challenges lay ahead? How were they supposed to locate the other missing relics?

He tried imagining returning to Jax's court while Serafina scoured the Saphirian ducal archives for any mention of the Virtuous Favors. He knew Jax would welcome him back and allow him to resume his duties as Captain, but how could he serve her in good faith if he knew the Grandmaster of the Shadow Brethren was within the walls of the city, researching the Favors alongside his beloved?

Serafina's cool touch pressed against his neck as she snaked an arm around him. "One day at a time, George Solomon." She kissed his temple.

He smiled at her tenderness and at how observant she was—she'd clearly noticed his anxiety about what came next. "You know me. Thinking ten steps ahead."

"Let's focus on getting the sigil back." She patted his cheek and then climbed atop Emma.

She was right. Their mission was to retrieve the sigil and return to Saphire with news of Elias. His questions about the future would be adventures for another day.

George hoisted himself into Merida's saddle, and soon, Emeraude joined them atop a black stallion that reminded him of Jax's beautiful steed, Mortimer.

"Ready?" The Grandmaster raised her eyebrow, her gaze cocky and challenging.

In answer, George nudged Merida into a canter and led their merry band toward their next foe—the Dundainee.

Chapter Twenty-Three

"What do you make of our lovebirds, Duquessa?"

Ziri's question drew Jax out of her muddled thoughts as they arrived outside the banquet hall doors. "That remains to be seen. Vivienne's anguish over her father's death seemed genuine enough, but…"

Ziri raised an eyebrow, urging Jax to continue.

"But his death certainly removes some hurdles regarding her relationship with Finral." Jax hated thinking so poorly of the couple, but throughout her many investigations, she'd learned love was just as strong a motive as gold and power.

Ziri bobbed her head. "Indeed. When it comes to motives, our pool of suspects isn't lacking."

"You're absolutely right." Jax frowned. "Everyone gains something from Allard's death. Dvorak takes over his mantle. Vivienne gets to be with the man she loves. Finral and Yves deal a blow to Lion's Bane's very heart." She counted them off one by one on her fingers. "Now to figure out who had means and opportunity."

Together, the two took a steeling breath, and Ziri pushed the doors inward. Jax tried concealing a wince as curious gazes landed on her.

Here we go.

Holding her head high, she glided into the tense room and took stock of the scene.

Uma and Perry quietly consoled a red-faced Dvorak while Yves glared at the man, his expression annoyed. Sabine sat beside him, looking like she'd given up trying to make conversation with the cantankerous Heartsworn deputy.

"Is it true what Dvorak says, Your Grace?" Yves drawled, sounding almost bored. "The Lord General has taken ill?"

She didn't speak until she reached the head of the banquet table. "I'm afraid it's much more serious than that." Jax clasped her hands in front of her. "Corentin Allard passed away during the night."

"What?" Dvorak squeaked out. "Dead? That's not possible!"

Yves snorted. "Come now, are you surprised, man? Sounds like the old bloke's drinking finally caught up with him."

Jax held up a hand, silencing Yves's rude reply. "My physician is examining the Lord General as we speak. I hope to have more answers for you soon."

Dvorak twisted his napkin, his expression drawn. "Has Miss Vivienne been told?"

Jax nodded. "I delivered the news myself."

"That was kind of you, Duchess." He glanced warily across the table at the empty chair next to Yves. "And where is Governor Lothaine? Has anyone made him aware?"

"Haven't seen him." Yves shrugged.

Dvorak swallowed and opened his mouth to speak when the banquet door groaned, revealing Vivienne's presence in the doorway. She'd changed from her nightgown into a dark maroon dress. Probably the closest thing to mourning black she'd brought with her.

"My dear!" Dvorak rose from his chair and raced toward her, arms outstretched. "I'm so sorry about this terrible development."

Vivienne closed the distance between them and hugged the man tightly. "Oh, Uncle Nanteuil. I simply cannot believe it!"

"There, there," he patted the top of her head. "Surely, Duchess, Miss Vivienne should be allowed to remain in her room—"

"She needs food to keep her strength up," Finral announced as he stepped into the light of the banquet hall. "And she wanted to be among friends."

Dvorak blinked several times at the Heartsworn leader, as if he couldn't quite figure out why Finral was speaking about his political opponent's best interests. "I-I see." He released Vivienne and held her at arm's length. "How are you feeling, my dear?"

"Overwhelmed." She managed a sad smile through her tears. "What are we going to do, Uncle?"

"In due time, my dear. In due time." He patted her hand.

Yves scoffed. "Time is one thing we do not have. Or have you forgotten we're in the middle of a war?"

"Hush, mate. She's just lost her father."

Yves stilled at Finral's hissing reprimand, and for a moment, Jax saw the caddish façade he'd donned for the summit slip. So, there *was* a heart underneath Yves's prickly exterior after all.

"No, your deputy is right, Governor Lothaine." Vivienne straightened her shoulders, her reddened eyes glowing with determination. "My father's passing is a personal blow, but we cannot allow his death to derail the possibility of peace throughout Savant." She wiped away her remaining tears with a dark blue handkerchief before tucking it into her dress pocket.

Jax admired the young woman's dedication and had to admit she was surprised by it. "While I am eager to see peace restored, I see no harm in postponing until Dvorak has had time to process his new position within Lion's Bane."

"My new position, Your Grace?" Dvorak's head tilted in obvious confusion.

"As its leader...?" Jax struggled to keep the question out of her voice and failed miserably.

The Vice Lord Admiral twiddled with the buttons of his suit jacket. "Oh, uh, Your Grace, that honor does not fall to me."

Jax frowned. "Then who—"

Vivienne stepped forward. "I am the one my father's mantle passes to, Duchess. I am the new Lord General of the Lion's Bane army."

Jax hoped she contained her astonishment better than the others gathered around the dining table. Perry and Uma shared stunned looks. Sabine clasped a hand over her mouth, and both Yves and Finral stared slack-jawed at Vivienne. Jax noted, in particular, the hurt in Finral's dark eyes. Was he acting, or had Vivienne kept this from him?

"I apologize for my uninformed assumption, Miss—Madame Vivienne." Jax bowed her head in concession. "I didn't realize Lion's Bane would not pass to its Vice Lord Admiral."

Despite Vivienne's distress, her smile had a calculated gleam to it. "I doubt anyone outside our circle of advisors did, Your Grace. It was my father's suggestion to protect the Lion's Bane leadership and to secure our victory."

"*Recent* suggestion?" Finral stared down his lady love.

Vivienne didn't quite meet his gaze. "I have been my father's successor since we launched our campaign."

Yves's brow furrowed with anger as he and Finral shared a wordless glance.

The wounded governor spoke no more, but his curled shoulders conveyed his inner turmoil.

His sullen attitude struck Jax as exceedingly curious. Did Finral not see the bigger picture here? With Vivienne now in charge of Lion's Bane, the two sweethearts could unite and govern Savant as they saw fit. Unless…unless Finral feared Vivienne would not so easily surrender her father's more aggressive ideals.

"Well, we've all had a shock this morning, and I'd like to give you all time to grieve," Jax said kindly, taking control of the strange situation. "I suggest we reconvene our peace talks later this afternoon. But right now, I think everyone could use some sustenance." She hurriedly waved to Madame Rosalyn, who had been standing watch from the corner. The estate manager sprang into action and ushered attendants forward with fresh trays of pastries, juices, and hot tea.

As everyone reclaimed their seating assignments from the first night, Jax kept careful watch over her guests. Allard's former spot sat glaringly empty, and it seemed Vivienne and the Heartsworn lads purposefully kept their gazes from resting on it. Only Dvorak stared forlornly at the vacant chair.

It was then Jax realized her earlier claim about motive needed revision. Dvorak didn't gain the leadership of Lion's Bane with Allard's death, and he was well aware of such a fact before the man's demise. So, what motive could he have to want Allard dead, if any?

Vivienne, on the other hand, now had two marks against her. Not only was she free to pursue the man she loved, but she also had the power of a rebellion behind her. Jax remembered the young woman saying she'd given her father a bottle of wine last night. Had it been laced with poison?

Jax tapped her foot as she tore a honey-soaked pastry into bite-sized pieces. *I hope Major Brennan returns soon with answers.* She wanted to ask everyone about their interactions with Allard without causing suspicions to arise.

And then, there is the matter of the fire, she mused while she chewed on the gooey, sweet bite. *It has to be connected to Allard's death, but how?* She thought back to Vivienne mentioning her father's fear of flames. Had someone set the fire to frighten Allard into retreating to his rooms, like a pig sent for slaughter? Could the poison have been lying in wait there? If that were the case, Vivienne's wine may not necessarily have been the murder weapon.

Jax rubbed her temples as theories swirled rapidly. *Calm yourself. It would be wise to wait for Brennan's report before barreling too far ahead.*

Perry cleared his throat and raised his glass, drawing everyone's focus. "Might I offer a toast to the late Lord General? May the Virtues guide him safely into the next life."

Jax smiled at her husband's thoughtfulness, and as everyone murmured a half-hearted "hear, hear," she seized the moment to question her suspects. "Did Allard mention feeling unwell after our session ended yesterday? I am aware that the fire left him out of sorts."

"You think the stress of the fire could have caused this?" Finral didn't look convinced.

Jax shrugged. "Any stressor can trigger a heart attack, I suppose."

Dvorak sniffed loudly and dabbed at his eyes with a napkin, then winced once he realized he'd captured everyone's attention. "Sorry."

Jax shook her head sympathetically. "There's no need for apologies, sir." Indeed, he appeared the only person distraught by the man's death. It was too bad she didn't have another spare handkerchief on her person, for he seemed to need one.

Vivienne showed none of the despair she'd revealed upstairs. In fact, her face was a cool mask of indifference. "He was shaken by the fire, but he didn't mention any physical discomfort."

"He looked fine when we crossed paths with him," Yves mentioned, and Finral nodded.

Perry took a sip of juice before asking, "When was this?"

Yves stroked his chin. "Governor Lothaine and I had just returned from a walk around the pond, so it had to be three-thirty or nearly four. He was in the foyer when we came inside."

Finral nodded. "He even said hello to us. Imagine my surprise." He let loose a light snort, but quieted once his gaze flicked to the empty chair across from him.

Jax did some quick calculations in her head. The fire had broken out around quarter past four, and she recalled the kitchen staff mentioning odd encounters with her guests in the time leading up to its discovery. Allard must have met Lothaine and Yves in the foyer on his way to try and procure some liquor from her stores. He'd walked away from the kitchen staff empty-handed then, but Jax realized in a heart-stopping moment that Allard had opted to have dinner in his room. Had his meal been poisoned? Her gaze darted anxiously to the dedicated Madame Rosalyn. Could she—no, Brennan had said that ardor root was native to Savant. It had to have been brought here by one of her guests...right?

Jax hated suspecting one of her own of the crime, but she realized she couldn't entirely rule out the staff's involvement until she knew more.

"How did he seem when you delivered his dinner, Madame Rosalyn?" Jax kept her voice light as she slipped on her unreadable Duchess façade.

The estate manager poured Sabine another cup of tea before replying, "I'm afraid I cannot say, Your Grace. He turned away the tray I offered. He was rather adamant that he only wished for a *liquid* diet." She pursed her lips in disdain.

While her statement brought momentary relief to Jax, it was fleeting. The avenues with which Allard could have been poisoned were drying up. Her contemplative gaze landed on a stone-faced Vivienne. Jax remembered the bottle of wine she'd given her father to soothe his anxious nerves. Had Vivienne really poisoned him?

A creaking moan came from the banquet doorway, and Jax's attention flew to Major Brennan standing at the threshold.

Not wanting her guests to be aware of their ongoing investigation, she rose before anyone could ask Brennan to introduce himself. "Excuse me, everyone. My…er…realmmaster is here for my daily briefing."

Perry and her friends did a double-take. *Realmmaster?* Jax could practically see the question dancing in their bemused expressions. She hid her small smile of satisfaction. The made-up title did have a nice ring to it.

"I shall escort you, Duquessa." Ziri was already on her feet and moving toward the door.

Perry, too, pushed himself away from the table. "While you're attending to matters of state, I shall see to some business of my own."

Jax nodded her acquiescence. She would be glad to have her husband and Ziri at her side to hear Major Brennan's report.

Uma and Sabine seemed to catch on as well. "We'll take our guests out to the gardens once everyone has had their fill of breakfast foods." A demure smile stretched across Uma's lips. "The fresh air will do us all good, given the sad events of the morning."

Jax sent a covert wink to her ever-astute shieldmaidens. *They always know just how to help me.* Depending on Brennan's findings, it would help to have the Savantians outside in case their rooms needed to be searched.

Jax didn't give her guests the chance to ask questions of their own. She gathered her skirts and hurried toward the exit, Perry and Ziri in her wake.

"Realmmaster?" Major Brennan raised a teasing eyebrow once the banquet hall doors were closed.

"Don't let it go to your head," Jax said with a wry smile. She cupped the man's elbow and led him to a private sitting area at the opposite end of the long hall. She wanted to ensure no one overheard their conversation.

They took their seats in the inviting armchairs situated in the center of the room, and Jax clasped her hands on her lap. "Please tell us what you've determined, Major."

The warrior physician bowed his head. "It was as I suspected, Your Grace. Allard died from ardor root exposure. I found remnants of its leaves in the man's stomach."

Jax shuddered at the gruesome image, suddenly wishing she hadn't eaten two sugary pastries.

Ziri's fists clenched at the news. "Can you tell how he ingested the ardor root? Through food or—"

"He didn't eat it, that's for sure." Major Brennan stroked his chin. "From what I can tell, the only other contents within the man's stomach were copious amounts of wine." His gaze grew steely. "If the ardor root didn't kill him, the disease rotting his liver would have taken him in mere weeks."

Jax and Perry exchanged shocked looks. "Neither Dvorak nor Vivienne gave any indication he was *that* ill." Jax twisted the fabric of her dress, her guilt over providing the man alcohol returning.

Major Brennan shook his head. "I doubt they knew the severity of the damage. It's impossible to know the extent to which alcohol affects the body until it is examined postmortem."

Jax made a mental note to curb her drinking habits even more than she already did. "So, you're all but certain his wine was laced? What about water?" She recalled the pitcher Yves had fetched in the moments before the fire.

Brennan gave a soft snort. "From my initial examination, it appears Master Allard favored only one source of 'hydration.' The wine in his stomach hadn't been diluted much, if at all."

"Virtues." Jax chewed on her lower lip. "I'm afraid this mystery has only one solution, then." Her forehead wrinkled at the notion. Could the answer really be that simple?

Perry ran a hand through his dark curls. "Vivienne told us herself she gave her father a bottle of wine before she came to dinner last night. She must be our poisoner."

"She kills her father and inherits his mantle." Ziri drummed her fingers on the arm of her chair. "It seems fairly straightforward."

"Except for the fact that Vivienne *told* us she was the one who gave Allard more wine to settle his nerves." Jax folded her arms in a huff. "Why would she freely admit such a thing if she intended to kill her father with the wine? Our guests know I have a habit of getting involved when dead bodies turn up."

Perry nodded. "Especially one under your own roof."

"Indeed, and where Vivienne seems like an intelligent, cunning mind…" Jax steepled her fingers together. "Wouldn't she realize we'd figure out the cause of her father's death?"

"You're giving her a great deal of credit, Jax," Ziri challenged. "Not to be disrespectful, although I suppose I'm the only common-born here…"

Jax and Perry both winced at Ziri labeling herself as such.

"…but would someone of Vivienne's standing really *know* the true extent of your exploits?"

Jax frowned at the uncharacteristic condescension in Ziri's barbed remark. It wasn't like her to judge others based on their background.

"We have proof that she does," Perry pointed out. "Vivienne made comments about Jax's mystery-solving capabilities when we dined with her last night. Sure, she was talking about the fire, but still…"

A long moment of silence passed before Ziri smiled with a coy shrug. "I see."

For some reason, Jax felt like her archspymaster had been testing them, but before she could question her friend's motives, Ziri's expression hardened.

"Then I think there's more to this mystery than meets the eye."

Chapter Twenty-Four

"I agree." Jax tapped her chin as she considered Ziri's weighted words. "Something quite foul is afoot."

"So, how shall we proceed?" Perry turned to his vexed wife for instruction.

Jax hugged herself as she paced around the private sitting room. "Let's begin by reexamining Allard's chambers. If no one visited him in the nighttime, the vessel containing the poison might still be there."

"I'll accompany you, Duchess." Major Brennan rose from his seat. "The ardor root will have left behind a bright, reddish film in whatever transported it."

Trying to tamp down her growing excitement over a mystery, Jax asked, "Has Aizen been brought up to speed?" She was somewhat surprised her Captain hadn't joined them for Brennan's briefing.

The physician nodded. "He's returned to assess the fire, looking for any clues as to how it started."

"Let's hope there's something left to find." Perry stroked his pale cheeks with a grim expression. "The fire's role in all this is still an unknown."

While Jax believed the fire had been lit to unsettle Allard into drinking, she couldn't simply assume. Confirmation was required.

"Ziri, will you assist Aizen? Two heads are better than one."

Her friend dipped her chin in understanding, although Ziri looked slightly disappointed to miss out on inspecting Allard's suite more thoroughly. "I'll report anything we find."

With their plan of attack in place, Jax, Perry, and Brennan headed upstairs to the guest wing after bidding Ziri goodbye in the foyer.

Two new guards stood watch at the guest entrance, looking alert and refreshed for the shift ahead.

"Your Grace, Your Highness." They bowed to Jax and Perry as the trio approached. "Major." They followed with a salute.

"Russell, Hennley," Brennan said, the exchange serving as a curt introduction. "Any activity up here?"

"No, sir." Russell shook his head. "We haven't even allowed the staff to ready the rooms, as instructed."

"Thank you, gentlemen." Jax smiled with relief over all the guest rooms being left untouched. It also meant Uma and Sabine had successfully corralled everyone into the gardens following breakfast. "We'd like to examine our victim's quarters."

Hennley stepped aside with a sweeping arm. "Please let us know if you need further assistance."

Thirty paces later, Jax, Perry, and Brennan arrived at Allard's door.

"Remember," Brennan murmured as Jax clasped the brass handle, "we're looking for a bottle or container with bright red film inside. But please refrain from touching it. Ardor root's potency is extreme."

Husband and wife bobbed their heads, not needing to be told twice.

"The poison is also moderately fast-acting," Brennan continued to explain. "Allard would have been dead within three, four hours—at most—after ingesting it."

Jax flinched. "During our initial examination of the body, Legue theorized Allard died around midnight. What did your postmortem show?"

"Legue has a sharp eye. I believe the Lord General died sometime between eleven and twelve."

Jax and Perry shared a perplexed look. "Vivienne gave her father wine *before* coming to dinner," Perry emphasized. "The timing doesn't exactly align with the crime."

"No, it does not." Jax inched the door open and stepped inside the guest chamber. As it had this morning, the sitting room showed little sign of disturbance other than what one would typically expect of lived-in quarters.

Perry followed behind her and made his way toward the connecting washroom door. "No bottles in here," he announced after he stuck his head in through the doorway.

Jax and Brennan took opposite sides of the sitting area. Jax's practiced gaze swept over the space, and she even knelt on the floor to look under the furniture. "Nothing here, either." She sat back on her heels with a frown.

Brennan selected a silver cup next to the water pitcher. "No red residue." He placed the cup back on the end table.

"That leaves the bedchamber." Perry's remark came out more like a question as he helped Jax to her feet.

Unless someone managed to trick our guards a second time…

Jax was glad she kept the critical comment to herself. As soon as they entered the bedroom, she realized they had their work cut out for them.

She counted five bottles littered around the room—one perched on a nightstand and four on the fireplace mantle.

"Oh my." Nervous laughter escaped Perry's lips. "I guess Allard didn't have as strong of a grasp on his drinking as poor Dvorak believed."

Jax grimaced as she immediately recognized the familiar label sitting atop the nearest bedside table. "This is from Glennfeld's wine cellar. It must be the bottle Vivienne gave her father because Dvorak confiscated the one I originally gifted Allard."

Brennan hurried over, a white handkerchief in his hand. Using the fabric as a layer of protection, he lifted the bottle, peered inside the neck, and sniffed the opening. His furrowed brow grew deeper.

"This shows no signs of ardor root exposure, Your Grace."

His words hung in the air.

"Are you sure?" Perry stared uneasily at the Saphirian wine.

Brennan set the bottle back on the nightstand. "Yes. Allard didn't die from drinking this."

Jax was already moving toward the fireplace mantle, skimming the labels of the four remaining containers. Given what Brennan had told them about Allard's time of death and the potent nature of ardor root, this news didn't entirely surprise her. "So, our suspicions that Vivienne poisoned her father or at least *gave* him the poison were completely misguided."

Brennan and Perry flanked her on either side as they studied the remaining bottles. "These three are the same label." Jax pointed to the different-sized spirits from the same distillery. "Troissaint Liquors." The name tickled the back of her memory. Where had she heard it before?

It took a minute for the knowledge to come to her. "Troissaint—this is an estate in Savant." She recalled the noble household coming up during a previous investigation dealing with old Savantian documents and treasures.

Although Perry hadn't exactly been in his right mind during the case, he readily accepted Jax's recollection as if it were his own. "So, do we think Allard smuggled these in with him?"

"Our guards wouldn't have given liquor bottles a second glance during their inspection of the guests' belongings," Brennan explained as he surveyed the Troissaint label. "They were only looking for weapons, not personal vices."

With his handkerchief, he lifted the lone bottle bearing a different label from the mantle. He sniffed, and his instant wince gave Jax and Perry their answer.

"This," Brennan coughed through watery eyes, "is our murder weapon."

It took all of Jax's willpower not to reach out and grab the bottle to examine it herself. Instead, she memorized every detail about the coppery label. "Faire l'Orange."

The name of the winery stirred no whisperings of recognition within her mind. It certainly hadn't come from her stores.

"Faire l'Orange?" Perry mused. "Sounds quite refined, but I've never heard of such an establishment before."

"Me neither," Jax admitted.

Brennan chuckled. "I'm afraid I know less than you both combined." He took out another handkerchief and carefully wrapped the bottle. "I'll bring this back to the infirmary for safekeeping. Should someone mishandle this, the consequences could be just as deadly as they were for poor Master Allard."

Jax shivered at the notion. "Thank you, Major. Please do be careful." She eyed Brennan worriedly as he cradled the bottle.

He smiled in reassurance before asking, "What are your orders, Duchess?"

Jax placed a palm on his forearm. "I'll task you with guarding the murder weapon, as well as the body."

Perry cleared his throat. "Do you think any of the men who inspected the Savantians' luggage might remember seeing this Faire l'Orange bottle?"

"I can ask, of course, but as I said before," Brennan replied doubtfully, "our men were focused on weapons, not vices."

"It can't hurt." Jax agreed with her husband's suggestion. "As for us, Perry and I will track down the source of this Faire l'Orange winery. See if we can determine who among our guests had access to their wines and how this bottle came to be in Allard's possession."

"And how exactly do we plan to do that, darling?" Perry raised a tentative eyebrow.

Her grin widened. "Some good old-fashioned sleuthing."

‡

Neither Ziri nor Aizen looked thrilled by her appeal. "We'll be back in time for lunch," Jax added as if the frivolous detail might sway them.

She and Perry had spent the last hour combing through their guests' rooms, looking for any evidence linking someone to the incriminating wine bottle. However, their search came up woefully empty. The only item of note found were love letters written by Vivienne that Finral kept under his pillow. While the correspondence markedly failed to mention that Vivienne would inherit her father's mantle, they didn't contain any information regarding a plot to poison the Lord General, either.

With no evidence of the bottle's origin, Jax suggested she and Perry dig up more intelligence on the winery itself. Perhaps they might be able to connect it to one of their guests. But the only way to learn more about Faire l'Orange was by leaving Glennfeld.

Aizen rubbed his chin, inadvertently smearing soot across his face. "You can't just go riding off to Grovershire, Jax. There are protocols and security measures that need following."

"What if we disguised ourselves?" Perry suggested, coming to his wife's rescue. "You know, as traveling scholars and the like."

Ziri considered his words. "May I remind you of your eyes?" She tapped the side of her temple for emphasis. "We don't have any of Master Charles's serum to mask their color."

"We'll keep our eyes down and hoods up." Jax seized the opening Perry had given her. "If *you* come with us, Ziri, you can speak on our behalf. We'll act as your assistants."

Ziri shot a skeptical glance toward Aizen.

He sighed. "I can finish up here." He motioned to the charred forest behind them. "Given that we've uncovered nothing useful among the ash thus far, finding out where the laced wine came from seems like a more fruitful course of action."

Her shoulders drooping in defeat, Ziri turned to Jax and Perry. "You're sure the Grovershire library will have the records you seek?"

Jax nodded eagerly. "Every major library throughout the continent maintains a current registry of established businesses. If this Faire l'Orange winery exists, it will be in the trade archives."

Ziri pinched the bridge of her nose. "All right. I'll saddle our best horses. Meet me outside the barracks in twenty minutes." Without another word, she took off at a run toward the southern border of the estate.

"What about your guests?" Aizen raised an eyebrow, studying the couple. "Wouldn't it be more fitting to simply ask them about the winery? To see who recognizes it?"

Jax pursed her lips. "I'd rather speak with them once I've

collected all the information I can about how the crime occurred." She fanned herself in the rising midmorning heat. "Besides, I doubt our killer will reveal themselves so readily."

"Very well." Aizen released a grumbled sigh. "I'm sure Madame Rosalyn can arrange for some more understated attire for you, befitting a scholar."

As Jax and Perry quickened their steps toward the manor, they giggled conspiratorially. Aizen called out, "And don't worry about me mucking through this burnt rubble all by myself."

"He's really grown on me." Perry's lavender eyes twinkled. "Aizen seems to finally understand there's no stopping you when a mystery is involved."

While Jax grinned at her husband's remark, a bittersweet melancholy rippled through her. Yes, Aizen had come around to her strange, stubborn ways rather quickly, and for that she was grateful. However, it also brought George and Serafina to mind as well as how dearly she missed them. With no recent news from the couple, she prayed they were doing all right.

As they reached the manor's front steps, Jax spied colorful kites floating in the sky above the east garden. "I see Uma and Sabine are keeping our suspects—*guests*—occupied."

The corners of Perry's lips dipped downward. "They'll start asking questions, Jax. A man is found dead, and the renowned crime-solving Duchess suddenly deserts her guests? They'll surely begin to sense something's up."

"I know." The knots in her stomach tightened. "As soon as that happens, our killer will realize they've been found out." Gathering her skirts, she darted up the marble stairs toward the entryway, eager to make haste.

The sentries welcomed them inside, and within a few minutes, Madame Rosalyn had a change of clothing for them both. The estate manager didn't ask any questions, either. Jax praised the Virtues that she had such devoted and accommodating staff to support her.

Ziri stood waiting with three bay mares by the time the disguised couple arrived at the barracks. Her unimpressed expression became clearer every step they got closer.

"What's wrong?" Jax asked once they arrived at her side.

Ziri sighed. "I thought your disguises would be a little more…disguising."

Jax glanced at her simple beige day gown and then at the white tunic and brown pants Perry adorned. "What more would you have us do?" She tugged on the hood of her elbow-length lightweight traveling cloak. "Better?"

"No. Here, I grabbed these." Ziri tossed them each a long, thick midnight-blue sash. "Gather your hair under this and tie it back."

Perry held the sash at arm's length, waving it in the wind. "Aren't these decorative leg wraps for the carriage horses?"

Ziri's stone-faced response silenced any further comment.

Jax and Perry did their best to hide their hair under the makeshift headwrappings. "Better?" Jax asked once they were done.

Ziri nodded. "You're both too well groomed. Your hair would draw as much attention as your eyes," was her explanation for the last-minute accessory.

Jax doubted as much, for Grovershire was a prosperous Saphirian city, its inhabitants well-cared for, but she let Ziri have her way. Anything to make her archspymaster feel more comfortable letting her sovereign walk through the streets of a major port city with only her for an armed escort.

The trio mounted their horses, and once the Ducal Guard opened the border gate, they were off, their pace a brisk canter along the dirt road.

"Anything we should know about Grovershire?" Perry called out to Jax over the pounding of hooves against packed earth.

She leaned forward, the leather reins rough against her palms, as she urged the mare onward. "While small in area, Grovershire is one of the more populated cities in the nation. It sits on the bank of the Augustine River—named after my ancestor's, Duke Allonious's, youngest child. It's one of Saphire's premier trade stops."

"So, we might even find someone selling Faire l'Orange wines on the street?" Perry beamed as his horse edged up alongside Jax.

She gritted her teeth as her horse jumped over a rut in the road. *That needs fixing.*

"Perhaps," she answered her husband.

They kept a steady pace, and the trio arrived at the city gates within thirty minutes. A massive sandstone wall surrounded tall buildings reaching toward the clouds, shielding Grovershire from any potential threat by land. By water was another matter. Jax knew from her maps that Grovershire's entire southern border abutted the Augustine River.

With their hoods up and eyes averted, Jax and Perry slipped off the backs of their horses, left the animals with the stablemaster, and followed Ziri as she led them through the bustling crowd.

Like many cities throughout the realm, members of the Ducal Guard stood watch at the entrance. However, due to the low threat against the nation, they allowed people to pass through the city gates freely during the day without requiring inspection. Once the sun dipped below the horizon, the gates closed, and anyone needing entry was vetted by the guards.

"Quite busy here today," Perry muttered, keeping their conversation private.

"Grovershire has a thriving market that supports much of the region," Jax whispered, doing her best to keep her gaze focused on the cobblestones beneath her feet. As much as she wanted to admire the city up close—for she had never actually been inside its walls— she knew she couldn't risk someone catching a glimpse of her telltale royal eye color.

Once inside the gates, Jax was momentarily overwhelmed by the cacophony of smells assailing her nose. Animals, food, humans, and river life alike mingled in the stale breeze, and she coughed as she adjusted to the potent aromas. Grovershire's imposing architecture was some of the tallest in Saphire, with stately buildings lining the main street.

"Any idea where the library is?" Ziri asked over her shoulder, her alert gaze never ceasing to assess the crowd around them for danger.

Jax closed her eyes, trying to recall if she'd ever seen a detailed map of the city's layout. "No, not really." She opened her eyes, her gaze settling on a disappointed Ziri. "I'd imagine it would have been built near the city square."

Ziri pressed her lips together. "All right. Stay close, you two. And keep your heads down."

Jax and Perry did as they were told and latched their attention onto the heels of Ziri's boots.

The trio trekked down the main street, passing block after block, when Ziri finally halted. "That must be it. Next to the water."

Jax risked lifting her head to peek, her heart racing with anticipation. The three-story limestone building had been constructed along the riverbank, its veranda the perfect place to read and watch the water flow along. "Answers lie within." She reached for Perry's arm and squeezed.

They navigated through the throng of people surging toward the lively marketplace situated in the city center. The tops of vendor tents peppered the scene, and Jax dearly wished she and Perry could leisurely stroll through the market, admiring its wares. *Another time, another life,* she mused with a heavy sigh.

Before long, they reached the riverbank, and Ziri bounded up the stone steps that led to the library's ornately carved oak door. She grabbed the brass handle, and the large slab of wood groaned as she pulled back and waved her charges inside.

Jax blinked as her eyes adjusted to the faint candlelight from wall sconces positioned strategically around the massive domed room. Rows and rows of shelves greeted them, stuffed with tomes and scrolls from all eras. The library hummed with gentle activity, with scholars and patrons milling about the main floor.

When no one came to greet them in the foyer, Ziri looked to Jax for instruction. "Let's see if we can find the trade archives ourselves," she suggested. As much as it would have been helpful to have a librarian or archivist guide them, the fewer people they had to engage with, the better.

The trio walked one by one along the aisle closest to the riverside. The people they passed paid them no mind, allowing Jax and Perry to lift their heads and assist Ziri with the search.

"Over there." With one hand, Perry reached for Jax's elbow, pointing toward the far corner with his other. "Might the information we're looking for be under 'economic archives'?" He squinted as he read the plaque hanging from an unobtrusive door.

Jax answered by gliding forward. "It's as good a place as any to start," she whispered to her companions.

When they arrived at the entrance, Ziri paused and scanned their surroundings before silently pressing the latch and pushing the door inward.

They slipped inside and found the archive to be much smaller than Jax had anticipated. It couldn't have been bigger than a staff washroom. Her heart fluttered with sudden panic, but she told herself the documents they needed had to be here somewhere.

"Cozy." Perry gave a sardonic smirk as he shuffled around Ziri to make some space between them.

Ziri's raptor-like gaze assessed the scene. "At least we will be able to make quick work here."

Jax nodded in agreement and pointed to the last shelf. "Let's each take an end and work our way toward the middle."

Ziri sprang into action while Perry gave her a playful salute. Jax smiled, wished them luck, and narrowed her focus on the task before her.

There was no clock in the small room, so Jax had no idea how much time had already escaped them when Perry gave a small clamor of triumph. "This looks promising. We're looking for a registry, right?" He held out a thick, bulging tome protected by a leather binding.

Jax accepted his offering, her spirits brightening as she skimmed the open page. Written on the yellowed parchment were the names of several Saphirian businesses Jax recognized, along with their year of incorporation and the name of the registrant.

"You've found it, Perry! Now, all we need to do is locate a record of Faire l'Orange." She flipped a mass of pages, beginning her search with the registered establishments in Savant.

Ziri joined them, and together, they hunched over the hefty book, making short work of the Savantian section without finding any mention of the winery in question.

Although disheartened, Jax wasn't ready to give up yet. "Savant's major trade partner for the last several years has been Zaltor." While

Saphire's political relationship had greatly soured with Savant in recent months, they'd never been strong allies, meaning Duke Savant had needed to look elsewhere for his imported goods.

She delicately thumbed through the pages, finding Zaltor businesses listed near the end of the registry.

"Here!" Perry, Jax, and Ziri all pointed to the same entry, their immediate cries of excitement echoing in the small chamber.

Ziri winced. "Let's hope no one heard that."

Barely bothered, Jax hungrily read the looping, inked entry they'd been searching for. "*Faire l'Orange Goods. Established 1208 under the management of Rohensio Gibran.*" Her nose scrunched at the surname. Gibran? "I don't recall any noble families by that name in Zaltor."

Ziri tapped her cheek as she studied the information. "What if this winery *wasn't* managed by a noble family, Duquessa?"

"You mean, this Rohensio may have been common-born? Well, that would be highly unusual for the time, but..." Now that her friend had put the idea in her head, Jax considered the possibility further.

Ziri cleared her throat. "The common-born, especially in the southern lands, would hardly have been able to afford the fine vintages on the market. But we know that has never stopped them from consuming wines and liquors."

Perry stroked his clean-shaven chin. "So, you think this Faire l'Orange brand was created...for the common-born by the common-born?" he asked, his voice trembling from his discomfort over the outdated and oppressive term.

Ziri nodded. "And it would make sense why our Savantian delegates would favor it over more high-class vineyards."

"I see your point," Jax admitted with a frown, "but Allard brought his own spirits from the Troissaint estate, which was managed for generations by a noble family before it became Crown property."

"Ah, yes." Ziri's lips twitched. "That's because Allard and his faction are backed by money. Who among our guests isn't so flush with gold?"

A sinking pit engulfed Jax's stomach. "Our gallant friends from Heartsworn."

Perry's expression darkened. "Both Finral and Yves knew of Allard's drinking problem. It wouldn't be farfetched to believe that they hatched this plot."

"I see what you're both saying." Jax's gaze dropped back to the incriminating entry. "It's just hard for me to picture Finral being involved. I was rooting for him. And Yves."

"Yves?" Perry's nose wrinkled as if he'd smelled something foul. "We've met some unpleasant people during our travels, Jax, and even then, he stands out."

Jax realized she'd never shared with her companions the rather brilliant political trap Finral and Yves had laid to convince Lion's Bane they were at odds. But before defending the deputy's surly behavior, she noted the final piece of information attached to the Faire l'Orange registry record.

Kutalé.

This name, she vaguely recognized. "Have either of you come across any maps of the realm in here?"

If her husband thought her request odd, he didn't show it. "Not in my area."

But Ziri darted to a lower shelf and extracted a long, rolled sheet of parchment. "Here, Duquessa." A small table was pushed against the back wall, upon which Ziri unfurled the scroll for them to view.

Jax's gaze flicked immediately to the border shared with Zaltor and Savant. The inked *Kutalé* bled into the paper, but it was still distinguishable enough. She pointed to the city name. "Our poisoned wine came from here."

Her keen gaze then moved to another unsettlingly familiar name etched in ink.

Ziri's eyes widened with the same realization Jax had come to. "And our Heartsworn delegates came from here." With her fingernail, she underlined *Bosquet.* The estate where Finral had worked and would eventually claim as Heartsworn's main war camp. On the map, they weren't even half an inch apart, meaning Bosquet was located only an hour or so on horseback from Kutalé.

"Making it very easy for our Heartsworn friends to obtain the wine and lace it."

Perry folded his arms. "Major Brennan said ardor root resides in the northern plains of Savant." He drew an invisible line from Bosquet to the aforementioned area. A very, very short line. "And is commonly used for dyeing fabrics red. Didn't Uma tell us that Yves's family operated a textile mill for some Savantian lord?"

Jax sighed as she rubbed her temples to alleviate the tension building behind her brow. "I think we have enough evidence with which to confront Finral and Yves."

Chapter Twenty-Five

George dropped from his saddle to the ground, a cloud of dust billowing out around his boots as he did so. "This area hasn't seen rain in a few days."

He studied their desolate surroundings. The Savantian landscape had changed drastically from the lush, vibrant jungle and fields that surrounded the refugee settlement. Tall, gangly trees arched toward the sky, their branches bare save for gnarled, thorny vines. The forest around them was filled with this strange species, with little else to carpet the rich soil, except for a small spring of fresh water, perfect for the horses.

"These are sécher trees. They are known to thrive in dry climates." Serafina pressed her palm against the brittle, prickly bark of a nearby trunk. "This small, arid pocket of Savant is affected by the Noirceur Mountains." She pointed to a peak in the distance that rose above the canopy.

An impressed grin stretched across George's lips, and Serafina blushed at the pride in his gaze. "Just something I remember from my time in the archives." She absently reached for her tunic, her fingers gripping the Kindheart medallion underneath the thin fabric.

Emeraude slipped off the back of her horse and dropped her reins to the ground, crouching to examine the dirt ahead of them. "Makes it easy to pick up a trail. We should be about a mile out from the Dundainee outpost." She tossed a glance over her shoulder, her gaze narrowing on George as he stroked Merida. "We'd best continue on foot."

He nodded his agreement. The horses would draw too much attention with their heavy gaits. "Our mounts are ground tied."

"As is mine." Emeraude rose and put her hands on her hips, her expression revealing minor offense that George might have thought otherwise.

Serafina cupped George's elbow with her free hand. "We should get going." In the other, she still clasped the Kindheart medallion hidden beneath her shirt.

He squinted at the bright sky, the sun almost at its peak. "We're taking a gamble that most of the outpost will be sleeping during the daytime. It might be wiser to wait for nightfall, even if the rogues are more active."

Emeraude unclasped her traveling cloak and stuffed it into one of her saddlebags. "We'll assess the situation once we have the camp in our sights and go from there." Her hands dropped to her thighs, where she stroked the hilts of the daggers strapped there.

Serafina and George also shed their outerwear. The summer heat had grown intense, and with the thorny vegetation all around them, they risked the fabric snagging. Yet, without the cloaks shielding their weapons, they would have a hard time convincing anyone they weren't a threat.

George gave Merida one last pat and took the lead through the strange, eerie forest. The absence of wildlife spooked him, and he wondered why the Dundainee had chosen such a remote location. At the sounds of his companions' footsteps, George realized the answer might lie right behind him.

"I'm surprised the Brethren allow for another criminal gang to roam these parts." He tossed a casual glance at Emeraude over his shoulder.

Her lip curled in a snarl. "Well, considering your Duchess made short work of our main enclave, the guild has been a bit distracted of late."

"You think these Dundainee are relatively new to the scene?" Serafina hastened her pace, so she was in step with the Grandmaster.

Emeraude gave a sharp nod. "Without the Brethren's strong hand to keep order, lawless rogues are springing up like weeds."

George scoffed at the ironic statement.

"You know, our dealings were always honorable, despite what you may think."

He could practically feel Emeraude's gaze burning into his back.

"There is no honor in killing on consignment," he grumbled.

Emeraude's gait now matched his own. "The contracts we take are carried out painlessly. Our targets do not suffer." Her tone was cool and measured. "They have already been marked for death by the commission giver. We merely ensure their passing is peaceful, rather than ugly."

George couldn't resist rolling his eyes at her delusions. "Is that how you justify what you've done? You truly believe the people you've *assassinated* would have been killed one way or another?"

"When you've seen what I've seen, yes." The haunted look returned to Emeraude's gaze. "It is an objective reality that good and evil exist. People like you and your Duchess are put on this realm to control the good. I am here to oversee the evil and make sure it is kept in check."

George's chest swelled as he tried summoning a retort, but he was stopped by Serafina's hand on his back. She hiked along on his other side and gave him a slight shake of her head. *It's no good.*

He realized she was right. Emeraude had been indoctrinated by the Brethren from an early, impressionable age. If she needed to see herself as some antihero, keeping evil in line with her deeds, then he saw no point in trying to dissuade her.

He continued eyeing Serafina curiously and noted her tight grip on the Kindheart medallion through the fabric of her tunic. "Everything all right?" She didn't normally draw attention to the relic, as she was eager to keep it hidden.

Serafina gnawed on her lower lip, not answering immediately. "Everything is fine."

Her hesitant response didn't convince him. "What's wrong?" He lowered his voice, although Emeraude was still within hearing range.

Wordlessly, she seized his hand and pressed it against her chest. Before he could question what she was doing, his palm felt a strange sensation against his skin. Heat. But not ordinary body heat. No. He quickly realized it was coming from the medallion. The Favor was radiating some kind of warmth.

He raised his brow at her, indicating he understood what troubled her, and silently asked, *What do you think it means?*

Her lips quivered with apprehension. "I think we're getting close," she said aloud, doing her best to sound unaffected.

George's eyes widened at her coded comment. Was the Kindheart medallion somehow reacting to the Intelligeye sigil being nearby? Could such a thing be possible?

It talks *to her, Solomon,* his inner self chastised. *Anything is possible.*

He swallowed his nerves and focused on the landscape ahead.

They trudged through the endless expanse of sécher trees, the sun climbing higher in the sky. The maze of roots bulging from the earth made the trek slow going, and it took them much longer than George anticipated to cover this final mile before the outpost.

"Look." Serafina grabbed his arm and pointed to a break in the overhead canopy.

He followed her command and saw the thinnest sliver of smoke rising above the trees. "Only one small fire," he murmured as he assessed the sky. "There can't be too much activity going on at the moment."

The signs of life reinvigorated them, and the trio hastened toward the smoke. It wasn't long before George caught sight of a wood barricade through the breaks in the trees.

He slowed his pace, Serafina and Emeraude immediately matching his stride. He darted behind a thick tree trunk and studied the shoddy ramparts. "Over a hundred feet long, I would guess?"

Emeraude nodded from behind a nearby tree. "I don't see anyone on patrol."

"It doesn't mean that they're not out there somewhere." Serafina craned her neck as if it would help her see more. "We should wait and see if someone is scouting the border." She tugged at the medallion, changing hands every so often.

George realized she was holding it away from her skin. Was it getting hotter?

Emeraude snorted. "You two can wait. I'm going in for a closer look."

George shook his head. "Waiting is the wisest option—"

She was already gone.

"Where'd she go?" Serafina crept over to his side, sharing his hiding spot. "How does she disappear so quickly?"

He shivered at Emeraude's skillset. "I'm not sure I want to know."

Serafina's fingers ran along his jawline, her touch making his chest ache with longing. "I know how difficult this is for you. Working alongside someone like her…it can't be easy for one with your noble soul."

As her fingertips flittered over his lips, he kissed her. "What frightens me most is that I *can* somewhat see her point. When the guild was at the height of its power, rogue gangs didn't roam the lands attacking innocents at will. Crime was organized, sophisticated, even." George reached for the tension building at the base of his neck. "Now…with these Dundainee fleecing anyone they can, it just seems lawless."

An impish grin blossomed on Serafina's face. "Well, I won't tell Emeraude your little secret."

"Thanks. Now, what's going on with the medallion?"

The delight on her face vanished. "I-I'm not sure. It's never reacted this intensely before." She pulled it free from under her tunic and let it rest atop the fabric.

"May I?" He brushed his fingers against the gold disc, surprised to find it even hotter. "Is it irritating your skin?"

"A little. But nothing I can't handle." Serafina shifted, the Kindheart medallion reflexively swinging back and forth. "The sigil *must* be inside that outpost."

He reached into his pack and pulled out a scrap of cloth. "Here. Wrap it up in this."

"Thank you." She wasted no time binding the medallion. "Always my hero."

He leaned over to kiss her when he caught movement out of the corner of his eye. "Down!" he hissed, pulling Serafina to the ground with him.

She wordlessly searched for the source of his panic, and her gaze widened as a large gate swung open in the center of the ramparts and out trotted thirty-some men on horseback.

George pressed his body into the dirt, willing himself to remain unseen as the horses carried their riders southwest of the camp. He strained his ears to hear the muffled commands being issued among the large group.

"—and with Montague in South Haven, that should cover it," a voice from the front of the pack called. "Remember, no one gets to the border guards without paying us a little crossing tax first."

The men raised their arms and bellowed various shouts of understanding.

"Now, get going, you crooks!" the deep voice ordered, and the round of laughter that followed was soon drowned out by the horses picking up speed as they rode away from the outpost.

Once the woods had quieted again, George and Serafina pushed themselves up from the ground and brushed their clothes free of dirt.

"If Marie's calculations were correct, there can't be that many people left inside the fort." Serafina studied the closed gate with shrewd determination. "Perhaps we should make our move now?"

"But how do we get in?" George balled his hand into a fist. "We can't very well knock on the front door."

"I think I have a way."

Emeraude's ghostly reappearance beside them sent both George and Serafina staggering back on their heels.

She smiled with evident satisfaction. "There's a tree on the northeast side of the outpost with a branch overhanging the barricade. We should be able to drop down onto the ramparts and go from there."

"Sturdy enough for us all?" George raised a dubious eyebrow. His muscular build was far heavier than Serafina's soft curves or

Emeraude's toned figure.

The Grandmaster didn't acknowledge his question. "It's the only way in."

"Will we be able to get back out?" Serafina asked, her expression hesitant.

At this, Emeraude shrugged and stroked the dagger at her side. "We will, one way or another."

George did not like the possibility of more bloodshed. The Dundainee may be gold-sucking leeches, but violence was his least favorite solution to any problem.

"I think this is our one chance." Serafina laid a tender palm on his forearm. She must have seen the indecision written all over his face.

He stared into her kind eyes, wishing to be far away from here, with her hidden and safe from the Dark Magus and his mysterious plans. "Fine." His focus switched to Emeraude. "Show us the way."

‡

George studied the ancient tree with uncertainty. "That branch doesn't even look like it can hold you, Odaire." No wonder she hadn't answered his earlier question.

Emeraude folded her arms. "This is the only branch close enough to the ramparts that allows us entry."

"Well, it doesn't take much to guess why." Serafina scoffed, sounding uncharacteristically perturbed. "It's hardly a security threat. A squirrel scampering atop it might snap it in two."

"If you're so scared," Emeraude said with a sly drawl, "you can wait here while I get inside and retrieve the sigil."

"No," George retorted. "We're coming with you."

"*Tsk tsk.*" The Grandmaster shook her head. "You still don't trust in the power of our contract." She stuck her lip out in a little pout.

Serafina gave her a hard glare. "The sigil is *mine* to protect. I will not leave it to others."

Something in Emeraude's gaze softened. "Now that, I understand."

George believed they were witnessing her unreadable mask slip for the briefest instant, revealing the true pain Emeraude felt over being parted from the Bravesoul pendant. He wondered, and not for the first time, if there was some mystical, divine connection between the Favored Ones and their assigned relic. It would explain why Emeraude felt this compulsion to locate the treasure her father had so desperately offered up his children for.

But how such a fantastical bond could exist, he did not know. Until he began traveling with Serafina, concepts such as magic and mysticism were the basis of children's bedtime stories. Yet, between Serafina's connection with the Kindheart medallion and the deadly bonds Emeraude spoke of, unexplained phenomena had permeated his reality.

Emeraude's evident sorrow was only on display for a fleeting moment. Her face soon turned stony and focused. "If we're going to make it inside, we'll have to move quickly. Lady Kindheart, you'll go first. Then Solomon, then me."

"What?" George balked at her plan. "I'm the heaviest here, so the branch has a higher chance of breaking under my weight. Shouldn't I go last?"

Emeraude rolled her eyes. "If you want to accompany us inside, you'll go after your lady love."

George felt his cheeks glow at her teasing and noted a pink hue spreading up Serafina's neck. "But what if the branch snaps? How will you get in?"

Emeraude laughed quietly at his question, shaking her head as if dealing with naive children. "The only reason we're using this branch as an entry point is for *your* benefit. There are at least ten different ways *I* can infiltrate this outpost."

Her arrogant confidence sent a spike of irritation down his spine, but he held his tongue, telling himself that he didn't really care if Emeraude made it inside the Dundainee's camp. He'd rather be done with her.

George held out a hand to Serafina, bending his knee to give her a boost up the tree. "Be careful." He kissed the underside of her wrist as she steadied her foot atop his thigh before pushing off.

With the grace of a skilled adventurer, Serafina propelled herself up the trunk, pausing momentarily to assess the situation as she reached the base of the sickly branch. George heard her sharp intake of breath before she darted forward, the branch moaning as she swung herself down onto the rampart and out of view.

While George watched the scene with cringing anticipation, Emeraude merely looked impressed. "I'd never have guessed she'd spent her adulthood as a scholar." The offhanded musing was more to herself than George.

They waited for what seemed like an eternity before the distinctive call of a meadowlark, Serafina's signal, reached their ears.

"All right, she's secure. You're up, Solomon." Emeraude gave him a pat on the back, almost as if he were a longtime comrade.

Rather than shooting her a look of daggers, George focused on the task before him. In order to preserve the integrity of the branch, he decided he would jump from its base onto the rampart's platform rather than scramble across it. He told himself he was doing it because he and Serafina needed an exit from the outpost, not because Emeraude needed an easy way in.

He rubbed his palms together and crouched in a sprinting position. Willing his adrenaline to kick in, George lunged forward, running at the trunk head-on. His left foot landed first on the bark and pushed his body upward. His right foot was able to take another step before he was forced to grab a lower branch and heave himself to the tree's next level. In a few breathless seconds, he was at the base of the sick limb, the tree already groaning under his more substantial weight.

Give it all you've got, Solomon. His inner voice spurred him onward, and with a low grunt, he vaulted from the tree onto the platform, curling his arms and legs as he rolled into the softest landing he could achieve. The *thump, thump, thump* of his muscular frame spinning to a stop was audible, but mostly absorbed by the wood planks.

Not giving himself any time to acknowledge the pain radiating through his body, George scrambled off the rampart. As soon as his feet hit the dirt, he dove into the nearest shadows. Only then did he take in the immediate environment around his hiding place.

The area was deserted, with several rundown structures parallel to the barricade creating a narrow alleyway. The buildings didn't boast many windows, so George guessed them to be storage units of some kind. Whatever they housed, it wasn't valuable enough to warrant sentries, for he spied no signs of human activity anywhere.

His relief, however, was short-lived. He caught sight of something moving out of the corner of his eye, and just as he was about to prepare himself for company, his vision adjusted to the shadows and he spotted a woman's hand waving him down. *Serafina.* She'd found herself a hiding spot behind some large barrels.

He'd regroup with her in a minute. For now, he pursed his lips together and pushed out a whistle mimicking the cry of a Savantian sunburst hawk. *There.* Now, Emeraude knew it was safe for her to follow.

His signal still echoed down the abandoned alley as George inched forward. He scanned the area one more time before making a mad dash for the barrels. Serafina scooted to the side, pressing herself against the wall of one of the storehouses to give him space to crouch next to her.

They didn't exchange words, only tender squeezes of reassurance as they waited for Emeraude to make her move. George strained to listen, but an intense wind swept through the alleyway, drowning out any indicative noises. While it kept him in the dark, it at least masked their movements from anyone inside the camp.

As they waited, his shoulders began to loosen, the anxiety over his own crossing beginning to wane. *She should almost be inside—*

CRACK!

The sound rattled like an explosion, and Serafina jolted beside him, her eyes doubling in size. George was already searching for its source when Emeraude appeared in front of the barrels.

"Branch snapped," she hissed. "We need to move before someone comes to investigate." Without another word, she took off down the alley, deeper into the belly of the outpost.

Cursing under his breath, George leapt to his feet and pulled Serafina along with him. He'd barely put any of his weight on the limb. How had it broken under Emeraude's crossing?

His cynical side had an immediate response. *She probably did it on purpose, so we'd have to fight our way out of here.*

"This complicates things," Serafina muttered quietly as they kept to the shadows and followed in the Grandmaster's wake. "Any sign of—ow!"

Before George could ask what had hurt her, he heard a shouted "Oy! Over here."

He yanked Serafina behind a pile of hay just as a tall man dressed in black stepped into view by the barrels they'd originally been hiding behind.

From their position, George could see the man examining the area but couldn't make out his expression. His face was shaded by a large-brimmed hat. His head moved side to side as he assessed the alley. George, too, followed his unseen gaze and was relieved to find that Emeraude had also concealed herself. *Only because her presence would reveal ours, too,* he told himself.

As the man in black glanced upward, another figure dressed in the very same attire burst onto the scene. "What caused that noise?"

"Looks like that sickly branch finally fell down." The first man pointed to the rampart platform where the broken limb had come to rest.

His companion visibly relaxed. "Thank the Virtues. Boss has been after me all week to get that dealt with. Looks like the wind did it for me."

"Indeed. Break it up, will you?" the first snapped with annoyance. "We can use it for kindling tonight."

"Y-yes, sir." The seemingly more junior of the two climbed up the rampart and pulled the jagged branch to the ground. Together, the two disappeared behind a building, their conversation lost to the changing weather.

George eyed the sky warily. Dark clouds hovered above them and the wind grew fiercer, ripping down the aisles of the outpost. While a storm would help mask their presence, it could also dull their own senses.

Serafina sagged in George's arms. "That was close. But with the branch gone, how are we going to get out of here?" she asked through gritted teeth.

George searched his mind for a solution. The outer wall was at least twenty feet high. It would be dangerously reckless to drop down from it. There was no guarantee one of them wouldn't sprain an ankle, twist a leg, or worse. "That remains to be seen," he admitted grimly. "Are you okay?"

"I'm fine." Serafina stepped back into the alley, brushing off bits of hay latched onto her tunic. "Where's Emeraude?" she asked as she shifted back and forth on the balls of her feet. She couldn't seem to stay still for long.

George joined her but kept his shoulders hunched—as if that made him any less visible. "Somewhere up ahead, perhaps?" He pointed to the long alleyway that ran the length of the outer wall.

As Serafina moved to follow in her phantom footsteps, George grabbed her elbow. At her questioning gaze, he reminded her, "We didn't come here for Emeraude. We came here for the sigil. Elias mentioned a tree he'd been tied to, right? It shouldn't be that hard to find a tree inside this camp."

Indecision flickered in Serafina's prismatic gaze before she nodded with firm resolution. Were his own eyes playing tricks on him, or did he spy pain mingled in her expression, too? "We should see if we can get some height." She tilted her head toward the darkening sky. "We'd get a better sense of the camp's layout that way."

George nodded his agreement when the melodic chirp of a nightlark pierced the rustling wind. His focus snapped to the sound's direction, where he spied Emeraude waving from a third-story window of a nearby storehouse.

One step ahead of you. George almost heard the patronizing sneer in her smirking expression.

Chapter Twenty-Six

"Elias said they kept him tied to a tree." Serafina shaded her brow as her pinched gaze traveled the rooftops that sprawled across the outpost. "But I don't see any within the walls of the camp."

George leaned closer to the third-story window. "You'd think it wouldn't be that hard to spot." A tree among the utilitarian structures would no doubt stand out.

Emeraude pointed to the largest building within the encampment, near the main gate. "Unless it's hidden behind there."

George studied the long, windowless complex. "A barn? Or a carriage house?" This had once been a functioning outpost before the Dundainee took control. An outpost would need a sizable space to house merchant wagons.

Serafina stuck her head out the window and glanced upward. "We could try the roof. We might have a better vantage point."

"I don't think that's a good idea. We'd be out in the open." While George hadn't spotted anyone patrolling the area, it didn't mean they weren't there.

But Emeraude had already hoisted her lithe frame onto the windowsill—in the blink of an eye, all he saw was her dangling feet as she rappelled the outer wall. A second later, those, too, had vanished.

His expression twisted with annoyance. "She doesn't bother consulting us, does she?"

Serafina chuckled lightly and patted his arm. "I, for one, appreciate leaving the physical exertion to her. Besides, if the remaining Dundainee are patrolling the outpost, Emeraude has a better chance of escaping detection than either of us."

George folded his arms with a huff. "Getting repeatedly shown up by that woman isn't great for my ego."

Serafina leaned in and kissed his cheek. "Look on the bright side. At least we have a moment alone."

Despite their predicament, her alluring words coaxed a smile from his lips, and he attempted to pull her close.

But Serafina resisted his advances, leaning her body away from his. He was about to ask what was wrong when he noticed the glittering gold of the Kindheart medallion. The scrap of cloth he'd given her to wrap the Favor looked to be singed and falling apart. He thought the burnt smells he'd caught whiffs of had been from the outpost fires. Not the medallion.

"It's getting hotter."

His simple statement brought tears to her eyes. "Yes." She glanced down at her chest, pointing to the faint outline burned into her tunic.

He ground his teeth at her clear discomfort. "Do you want me to wear it? Or I can put it in my pack?"

She shook her head. "No. We…we just need to focus on finding the sigil."

Before he could convince her otherwise, Emeraude's body came swinging through the window, and she landed with little noise on the floorboards. "Incoming," she mouthed as she pulled both George and Serafina down into a crouched position.

Hiding from the window's view, George soon heard approaching footsteps from the alley below.

"Blimey," came a rough voice. "Hard to believe the news about the war camp. Think they'll come to reclaim the silver they paid?"

Another man snorted. "If they do, they'll be met with much less generosity than last time. We sold that dumb bloke for a steal."

George shared a knowing look with his companions. These men must've been talking about selling Elias to Lion's Bane.

"Think it will set them back in the fight?" the first man asked.

"Who cares? The longer this war drags on, the more we profit." Greed dripped from the reply. "Yesterday alone, we took in nearly fifteen gold from poor sods fleeing to Hestes."

"The boss's idea for a crossing tax has been quite lucrative."

The conversation faded, indicating the men had vacated the area.

"A crossing tax, huh?" Emeraude's nostrils flared with indignation. "What scum."

George didn't bother commenting on her hypocrisy. Emeraude Odaire clearly lived by a different set of principles than he.

"Were you able to get a better vantage point from the roof?" Serafina whispered, returning to the situation at hand.

Emeraude nodded. "There's a dead banyan tree in the shadows of that large building. It's got to be the one Pettraud spoke of."

"A dead tree?" George shuddered at the imagery her words invoked in his mind. "Feels ominous."

"It's clear on the other side of the outpost." Emeraude ignored his remark. "And as you just heard, patrols are wandering these pathways, so we'll need to move carefully."

Serafina's jaw set in a grim line. "Understood."

"With any luck, this wind will bring some rain with it and mask our trail." Emeraude scooted back a few steps, still in her crouched position, and surveyed the loft they'd been hiding in. "Ah-ha." She shuffled over to a stack of moldy hay bales. "Here." She began tracing patterns on the dusty floorboards. "This is a rough layout of the outpost."

George and Serafina knelt beside her, taking in the many little squares and rectangles that made up the camp's interior. "You were only up there for a few minutes, yet you remember the layout this clearly?" Serafina studied the map.

Emeraude shrugged. "I have a good memory."

"Impressive." The corner of Serafina's lip curled upward.

The Grandmaster's cheeks darkened, and George suspected

Emeraude was pleased by Serafina's praise. "While this would be the fastest way," she continued as she pointed to a path cutting through the center, "I think this would be the safest." Her finger traveled over a longer route.

"Let's get moving, then." George helped both women to their feet. "Who knows when the rest of their crew will be back?"

‡

"Oy! You hear something?"

George uttered a silent curse as he pressed himself into the soft, muddy ground. He'd been inching his way along the short wall that separated them from their intended destination. Even though he couldn't see it from his current position, he knew the dead banyan tree loomed ahead. Its long shadows washed over the earth around them.

He wrinkled his nose, resisting the urge to cough at the rancid aroma assaulting his nostrils. He was sure there was more than mud mixed into the dark dirt, but he tried not to think about it since it had yet to rain.

"Nah." The responding voice sounded disgruntled. "You been at the brew already?"

"N-no! Of course not." Yet the answer did not sound genuine, and the sound of footsteps scurrying away gradually lessened the tension in George's shoulders.

He felt a nudge at his boot and glanced backward to find Emeraude's expression urging him onward. Nodding, he inched through the mud using his elbows, dragging the rest of his body noiselessly behind him. *Just a few more yards…*the end was in sight.

He stopped once he arrived at the edge of the barrier, determining his next move. The short wall had been the perfect cover to carry them across the open courtyard where the large barn waited on the opposite side. They'd only encountered two patrols as they wove through the outpost, and he prayed to the Virtues their luck would hold out with the weather.

Emeraude and Serafina crouched behind him.

"We're close," he heard Serafina mutter softly. He glanced her way. She'd rewrapped the medallion in thick burlap she'd found along their route. The pain in her eyes told him she still felt the strange heat emitting from it.

"We'll stand watch," he whispered to her.

Serafina nodded. With the inexplicable connection the Kindheart medallion had to its sister Favor, they hoped she could easily locate the buried sigil.

George watched her take a deep breath and dash from beyond the wall's shadows. As she sprinted toward the base of the banyan tree, he and Emeraude pulled free their weapons.

"I'll take the north." Emeraude's gaze landed on one of the courtyard's far entrances.

This left George to take the nearby southern opening. Based on the map Emeraude had drawn for them, this would be the path they'd need to take to make it toward the outpost's main gate. If the Virtues were on their side, they'd be able to slip out unnoticed. If the Virtues weren't…

Overhead, thunder rumbled.

We'll worry about that when the time comes. George willed himself to focus on his task, which meant keeping an eye out for any of the roaming Dundainee.

He adjusted the sword's hilt in his hands. It had been a while since he'd had reason to wield it. Before, his sword had always felt like an extension of his body, part of who he was, but now, as he clasped it, a cold detachment spread through him, and he couldn't grip it comfortably.

Get it together, Solomon. Now was not the time for existential reflection.

As he paced about the courtyard, the only sounds he detected came from Serafina. Dirt flew as she frantically dug beneath the base of the tree. He could sense her panic from here. She knew they needed to make quick work of this.

"Virtues, how deep was he able to bury this thing?" Serafina hissed.

George was about to ask whether she was digging in the right spot when the sound of steel clanking together filled the air.

He whipped around to face the north wall where Emeraude stood guard. His stomach dropped as he saw she had company.

A man already lay dead or dying at her feet, and she parried the blow of another with her daggers. Two others charged her way, their blades brandished, ready for a fight.

The second Dundainee was already on the ground by the time George sprang into action. Emeraude was pursuing the third Dundainee, and seeing he was soon to be outnumbered, the remaining man began to back away from the chaotic scene.

"Stop him!" came Emeraude's fervent command. "Before he raises the alarm!"

Sword at the ready, George burst forward, his boots driving into the soft ground as he lunged toward the fourth interloper. He closed the distance between them within a few breaths, his fingers reaching to grab hold of the man's cloak. Feeling the fabric against his palm, George yanked it toward him, sending the man flying backward with a strangled yelp. Since his right hand was holding the sword, George threw his left arm around the man's neck and covered his mouth with his forearm to silence his cries.

He managed to wrangle the man's arms behind him, locking him in a tight grip. George was a good half a foot taller than his captive and had at least thirty pounds of muscle on him. The lad had no chance and must have realized it, for he went limp with fear.

"Stay quiet. I won't kill you," George muttered the harsh reassurance as he dragged the man back toward the center of the courtyard.

His prey detained, George assessed the horrible scene at Emeraude's feet. She stood over the bodies of the three others, looking satisfied with herself.

"We said no unnecessary bloodshed!" George couldn't contain the rage boiling within him.

Emeraude was immediately at his side, her gaze hard and cold. If George hadn't had years with the Ducal Guard under his belt, she would have scared him senseless.

"I didn't *kill* them." Her dark gaze flickered with a bewildering emotion. Hurt?

"I just knocked them unconscious." In one swift move, her fingers reached for the neck of the man George held captive. The lad's eyes went wide before rolling back into his head. He slumped and became dead weight in George's arms.

"What did you do?" George asked in astonishment as he laid the man out on the ground.

Emeraude simply stared at the unconscious Dundainee. "Something I learned a long time ago when I first began working for the Brethren. I realized that those with higher body counts were revered within the guild. So, I padded my resume a bit."

He studied her, unsure whether she was telling him the truth or only what she thought he wanted to hear. "Why not offer Elias the same grace?"

She lanced him with a cool stare. "He was a threat. These men are not. Besides..." She broke away, and her gaze took on a far-off look. "I did you a favor, Solomon. Otherwise, Pettraud's blood would have been on *your* hands."

He swallowed as the truth wriggled within him. There was no way he would have been able to get Elias out of Savant, given their circumstances. Jax had tasked him with finding Elias and bringing him to justice. Whether that justice was delivered by George's hand or Saphirian trial, she cared not. His Duchess wanted the threat dealt with.

Yet Emeraude had understood his uneasiness over ending another person's life and had taken that burden upon herself. It was some twisted, warped form of kindness, he supposed.

"Thank you."

Her eyes widened. She clearly hadn't been expecting him to acknowledge her deed. But she quickly gained control of her emotions and plastered on an unreadable mask. "You're welcome."

"Where is it? Where is it?" Serafina's panicked mutterings pulled George's attention toward the banyan tree.

"Go help her." Emeraude nodded in Serafina's direction. "We

won't be alone for much longer."

George's gaze swept over the unconscious quad. "How long will they be out?"

"If no one comes to wake them beforehand, we have an hour at most." She gave an indifferent shrug.

George wanted to be out of there within the next five minutes. Sliding his sword into the sheath strapped to his back, he raced to Serafina's side.

She looked up at him, tears welling in her eyes. "It's so hot, George. The sigil has got to be here."

His concerned gaze traveled to her neck, and horror at what he saw punched him in the gut. The medallion's radiating heat had somehow seared through its burlap wrapping and her tunic, leaving behind a blistering red welt on the pale skin between her breasts.

He searched for the culprit and found the gold disc lying beside Serafina on a small rock. The aquamarine stone in the center shimmered violently in the faint sunlight that struggled behind the dark clouds overhead. The burlap swatch had been burned away, the Favor glowing molten red, and George wondered how the metal retained its shape.

"I-I couldn't hold it anymore." She held up her blistered palms. "I can't use its power to find the sigil."

He grasped her wounded hands, silently begging her to stop hurting herself. "Let me help."

She nodded, the hurried motion breaking the invisible dam that kept her tears from falling.

He knelt beside her, and as he surveyed the holes she'd dug, she sagged against him. "What if it's not here?" Her voice trembled.

George studied the trunk of the banyan tree. Serafina had already dug several holes at its base, only to find more earth and roots.

"He wouldn't have been able to dig very deep." He stroked the thickening beard growing on his chin. His seasoned gaze flicked back to the center of the courtyard. "Elias would have been monitored regularly, so he couldn't have taken too long to hide it."

He noted a metal ring sticking out from the tree trunk. "This must be where his chain was hooked." He stood and stepped back to assess the scene from a greater distance. As he did so, he saw a discarded rusty metal pail lying on its side only a yard or so from the tree.

Hmm.

Elias hadn't mentioned being kept anywhere else within the outpost, so this tree had served as his outdoor prison. He'd been kept under the Dundainee's watch for less than a day, but the man would have no doubt been given a place to relieve himself.

I wonder…

His heartbeat quickening, George rounded the other side of the banyan tree, which faced the outpost barricade. *A spot of privacy.* George knelt at the trunk, immediately finding a small circular outline where the metal pail had sat to serve as a latrine.

His gaze raked the soil around it, his hand reaching instinctively for a small mound of grass. He batted the dried greenery away, finding a patch of disturbed earth underneath. It only took a few sweeps of his palm before his fingers brushed against a heat so intense, he whipped his hand back with a foul curse.

"I think I've found it," he hissed around the front side of the tree. "But how in Virtues are we supposed to pick these things up?" He sucked the burned tops of his fingers to alleviate some of the pain.

Serafina was there at his side, her gaze locked on the shimmering gold peeking out from a layer of dirt. In her hand, she held the rock with the Kindheart medallion atop it, like a pillow carrying a crown.

"We've done it, George." Her eyes glimmered with hope. "We're so close. We can't give up." She turned around, searching for something. "Find a flat stone, will you? Maybe we can scoop it out of the ground."

As she shifted her crouched position again, her balance faltered, and her blistered hand holding the rock dipped forward.

George couldn't react fast enough and watched as the Kindheart medallion slid from its resting place, plummeting to the ground toward its sister relic.

An immense, forceful blast knocked George backward, his body flying as if it had been launched by a catapult. He collided with the outpost barricade, dropping nearly ten feet from the tree. Beside him, he heard a sickening *crunch* as Serafina landed in a crumpled heap.

Chapter Twenty-Seven

Georg realized he couldn't hear himself screaming as he called Serafina's name. An aching, piercing horn bashed his eardrums, drowning out all other sounds in the world. Or something that sounded like a horn. In his dazed and terrified state, he couldn't quite tell.

"-fina! -rafina! *Serafina!*" George finally heard his own hoarse voice as he grabbed her by the shoulders and pushed her hair away from her bruised face.

Oh, Virtues, no. Please...

She coughed and groaned, her eyes fluttering open. "George? Are you all right? What happened?"

Tears leaked down his cheeks as relief left him momentarily speechless.

With him being no help for answers, Serafina pushed herself up using her elbows and gingerly moved her head back and forth. "What was that? An explosion?"

As George tried to process what had just happened to them, he saw Emeraude limping toward them across the courtyard. Her jaw was gritted tight with pain, and she clutched the side of her abdomen. "Can you both walk? We need to get out of here."

For the first time since meeting her, she sounded worried.

Although his joints ached in protest, George was able to ease himself upward using the outpost barrier for support. Serafina did the same, and as she stood, her injuries became all too apparent.

"Your leg!" His battlefield training kicked in, and George ripped a section of his tunic shirt to wrap around her right leg. Her trousers from the knee down were soaked dark with blood.

Emeraude handed him one of her daggers to cut away the pants' fabric. With a nod of thanks, George made quick work, the material dropping away to reveal the extent of Serafina's wound.

A huge gash ran nearly the entire length of her calf. George cursed that he had nothing to cleanse it with, but he had to stop the bleeding. Taking the cleanest part of his tunic, he pressed it gently against her tender skin and began wrapping it tight to close the wound.

Serafina did her best not to cry out from the pain, and only her muted whimpers reached his ears while he worked. He'd seen the injury countless times while with the Ducal Guard, but his men had been tended to with clean bandages and sterile tools. "You need a healer."

He left the rest unspoken. She'd lose her leg if they didn't find her help soon.

Serafina nodded, her face having lost all its natural color.

"What we need is to get out of here. *Now.*" Emeraude hoisted Serafina's arm over her shoulder to lend her support. "That blast, whatever it was, damn near blew through the entire outpost. The Dundainee will be searching for its origin."

George's gaze darted to the banyan tree. Or what was left of it. The force had snapped it in two, with its top splayed out across the courtyard. How he and Serafina were still alive…

Did the Virtues protect us?

"We…can't leave…without the Favors." Serafina's breathing was becoming labored, and it looked like she was doing everything in her power to remain conscious.

It physically pained him to see her suffering so greatly, but George knew she wouldn't abandon her mission. Even if it killed her.

"Start heading toward the main gate," he instructed Emeraude.

She raised an eyebrow but nodded her understanding a heartbeat later.

As Emeraude began to drag her away, Serafina struggled against her grip. "I need...to get...the...Favors."

"You're in no condition to do anything," Emeraude snapped, giving George an exasperated look.

He knew they needed to move quickly. He could already hear raised voices in the distance.

A crack of thunder roared across the compound, and the dark skies finally released their impending assault. Rain pelted the ground, turning the hard dirt into slick mud within seconds.

Great.

As fast as his sore muscles would take him, George stumbled over to the banyan tree trunk, its bark strewn across the ground. He kicked away bits of splintered wood, and even in the downpour, the glittering Kindheart medallion gleamed up at him from the shallow hole it had fallen into. George removed what remained of his tunic, hoping to wrap the relics and carry them out before they burned through the linen. But to his surprise, he felt no heat as he reached for the gold trinket.

"It's completely cool." In perplexed amazement, he snatched the medallion off the ground without issue. Realizing he didn't have time to figure out why, he brushed away the remaining layer of dirt, revealing the Intelligeye sigil in all its glory.

Just as Corporal Lunara's drawing depicted, the Favor had been molded into the shape of an eight-pointed star. A beautiful amethyst gem had been inserted within the piece, and even though it was flecked by muddy dirt, it still radiated refined elegance.

He could have admired the relic for much longer, but time was against him. George scooped it from its hiding hole, relieved that it, too, was cool to the touch. He draped the medallion over his neck and slid the sigil into his front pocket.

"Check the wagon house! It sounded like that blast came from there."

The remaining Dundainee were closing in—or perhaps even the

men Emeraude had put to sleep had been woken by…whatever they'd just witnessed.

Regardless, he needed to get his companions out of there.

It didn't take George long to catch up with Serafina and Emeraude. His beau was barely conscious, and he doubted she even knew he'd returned to her side. Emeraude, however, was alert and on edge, though her feet dragged sluggishly over the ground.

He noticed how she still clutched her side, and to his concern, Emeraude's shirt had become stained with red. She, too, must have been hit by the blast. "I've got her." He hoisted Serafina into his arms, pressing her against his chest to protect her as much as possible from the rain. "Patch yourself up."

"There's no time." Emeraude seethed through bared teeth. "I'll do it once we're clear of here." She limped forward, able to move quicker now that Serafina was no longer her burden. "We may be in luck. Let's hope that explosion pulled the outpost patrols inward. The entry gate might be unmanned for a brief window."

"So we're going with 'explosion'?" George raised an eyebrow, trying to bring some levity to the situation.

Emeraude didn't take the bait. "I don't know how else to explain what we saw. Or didn't see." Her words turned into a strangled whisper. "It was like some invisible force erupted right before us."

Loud shouts carried on the wings of the storm, spurring George forward. Emeraude, to her credit, managed to keep in step with him despite her injury. As they scurried down vacant alleys, hiding among dark shadows, George kept his gaze focused on the looming outpost gate peeking out from the rooftops.

Serafina's delusional murmurs had quieted, her heartbeat fluttering against George's chest. He mentally clocked its rhythm, encouraged by its returning strength. His haphazard bandaging had done its job to stop the bleeding, allowing Serafina to maintain dominion over her precious lifeblood.

Emeraude, however, left a deadly trail behind her as they hobbled through the encampment. She needed to tend to her wounds, or she wouldn't remain upright much longer.

They paused at the corner of a small storage shed, their options for cover beginning to run out. "The gate is just beyond that next building." Emeraude's remark came low and laboriously.

George shifted Serafina's body so that she lay on his back along with his sword. He would need greater use of his arms if they were going to spring themselves from this self-imposed prison.

"Come on." He grabbed Emeraude's arm and hooked it over his neck. She didn't protest his aid, which told him she must feel even worse than she looked.

Summoning all his strength, George launched himself and his comrades out of the shadows and onto the main path that ran through the outpost. The gate stood only twenty feet or so ahead of them—a beacon of hope and a seal of condemnation. A massive wood log barred the gate shut, a security measure that would require at least three able-bodied people to move.

Curses whistled through George's mind as he frantically scanned the massive gate and wiped the rain from his eyes. It was only a matter of time before the sentries returned to their post. *How in the Virtues do we get out now?*

A storm cloud shifted overhead, and the sun's struggling rays slipped through momentarily. The light glistened against the sheets of rain, creating a stunning rainbow before them. The mesmerizing sight reminded him of Serafina's eyes. But as beautiful as it was, the sudden emergence of the sun banished the shadows that had so helpfully concealed George and his companions from view.

Yet, to his amazement, the sun also brought their salvation, for the shimmering rainbow illuminated a small side door next to the gatehouse only a few yards in front of them. With pain and panic clouding his judgment, George hadn't remembered outposts were built with secret gatehouse exits only accessible from the inside.

His pulse racing, he staggered toward their chance for escape, Emeraude doing her best to shuffle beside him. But her bulk against him grew heavier and heavier with each step, and by the time they reached the hidden door, she was all but dead weight.

The gruff calls of angry men tickled his ears as George heard armor clanging down the aisles behind them. The sentries were returning to their abandoned posts. He couldn't tell how many of them were coming—their pounding footsteps were too jumbled against the drumming of the rain. He could perhaps take two or three on his own, but that meant leaving Serafina and Emeraude open to potential attack. *It can't end here.*

He silenced all his senses but sight, choosing to focus solely on making it out the side gatehouse door and into the sanctuary of the forest.

George fumbled with the small bar latching the exit and ducked through the low threshold, tumbling free from the outpost's confinements. He slammed the door shut behind him as he fled with his companions, knowing the discarded bar would reveal to the Dundainee that someone had escaped their grasp, but it couldn't be helped.

He didn't stop his pitiful attempts at a full-out run until the outpost was but a smear against the forest backdrop. His chest burning from the exertion, he collapsed as gently to the wet ground as he could so as not to injure Serafina or Emeraude any further.

"W-well done, Solomon," Emeraude murmured as he propped her against the trunk of a jungle oak. Her eyes were closed, and her ordinarily rich skin had lost its luster.

He then lay Serafina across the ground, placing her head on a patch of soft moss. Her nose wrinkled slightly, but other than her shallow breathing, she showed no sign of waking.

George rubbed the fear, frustration, and rain away from his eyes. Thankfully, the storm was beginning to die down. But that was only one obstacle. He needed to get Emeraude patched up so they could make their way back to the refugee camp to find a healer.

"Let me see." In his crouch, he propelled himself to face Emeraude and found her tugging up her shirt, her rusty skin slashed open just beneath her ribcage.

She squirmed as she tried to assess her wound. "Damn," she wheezed. She lifted her left arm and averted her gaze from his. "I have a small pack strapped under my shirt. Can you please unclasp it for me?"

George did as he was told, his hand snaking gingerly up her tunic. Her flesh gave way to the feeling of leather, and he deftly unhooked the belt that kept the pack plastered to her body. There wasn't time for him to be embarrassed over touching her feminine curves—to him, he was just tending to another wounded soldier.

Once the small bag was free from its hiding place, he dropped it into Emeraude's outstretched palm. She flipped back the flap and dumped the contents into her lap. George spotted a needle, thread, some gauze, and three miniature glass vials. He waited patiently for his next instructions, but they weren't what he expected.

"Pour…the vial with the yellow wax seal…on Serafina's leg." Emeraude reached for the needle and thread. "It should…help sterilize it for now."

He nodded and carefully selected the tiny container from her lap. A red-tinged liquid sloshed inside, but it couldn't be more than a few drops. Afraid the tiny vial would shatter in his grip, George carried it with the reverence of the Crown Jewels as he shuffled back to Serafina's bruised form. Setting the vial on a nearby piece of moss, he went to work undoing the bandage he had haphazardly tied, relieved to find that it had hardened slightly. *Good, at least she's stopped bleeding.*

He pulled back the stained fabric, his stomach twisting at the sight of her calf. Not wanting to waste any more time, he pinched the vial between two fingers and peeled away the wax seal. As deftly as he could manage, he emptied its contents into the gash, each drop landing with a slight hiss.

"Arghhh!" Serafina's cries startled him, and he teetered before falling on his backside.

His shock wearing off, a grin broke out across his face to see her awake—complaining, but awake.

"Virtues, what in the realm is that?" Serafina cursed loudly as she writhed with obvious pain, her expression morphing with affronted anger when she noted George smiling. "It's not funny!"

He laughed, his relief making him giddy. "Yes, it is." He rocked himself forward, his lips meeting hers in celebration.

"My leg is on fire." Serafina raged against him, although she paused to kiss him back.

"That means the laudaetum is working."

George broke away from his patient and turned his attention to Emeraude. "What is laud—" He broke off his question as his brain registered what was happening before him.

Emeraude, with a branch between her teeth, was busy stitching up her side as if it were the latest summer fashion.

"Virtues, Em, don't you want some help?" Serafina gasped at the startling sight.

Emeraude paused her work, and despite the incredible pain she must have been in, the corner of her lip twitched with a smile. "I'm fine. I've suffered far worse than this while on a contract."

George shook his head, vexed once again by the cunning, enigmatic woman.

"Laudaetum is a strong antiseptic we favor in the Brethren," she finally answered his lingering question. "I never go anywhere without a few vials on my person."

For once, George was grateful for her habits.

"We still need to get you to a healer," Emeraude added, nodding toward Serafina's leg, "but you won't lose it."

"Lose it? Virtues, George!" Serafina grabbed his arm, her grip surprisingly strong for her precarious state. "The Favors. Did we—" But she answered her question as her eyes landed on the gold piece hanging against his bare chest.

Her hand immediately flew to the Kindheart medallion, her fingers tracing a circle on his skin. "And the sigil?"

He slid his hand into his pocket and tugged free the eight-pointed star they'd searched an entire nation for. As he placed it in Serafina's open palms, he treasured the absolute delight that ignited across her face.

"Are they…hot to the touch?" Emeraude's words were somewhat strangled as she operated on herself. "I…saw you struggling to hold the Kindheart medallion earlier."

Serafina turned the Intelligeye sigil over in her hands. "No. The burning sensation is gone."

George pulled the medallion's chain from over his head and held it out for her to reclaim. "Whatever that explosion was, it seemed to terminate the source of the heat."

"An explosion?" Serafina's gaze pinched with mild confusion before her eyes widened. "That's right. The medallion fell into the hole where the sigil was buried and…"

"*Boom*," Emeraude grunted as she tied off her stitches.

"Boom." The word trailed off on Serafina's chapped lips, her expression dazed.

Something white filled his vision of her, and George realized he was staring at a handful of gauze Emeraude held in front of him. She'd somehow already managed to get herself back onto her feet.

"Wrap her leg in this. We need to keep moving. The Dundainee will probably send a patrol to scout the area now that the rain is letting up. Those men we incapacitated know we're out here." She scanned the forest. "We'd better find our horses and make haste."

George accepted the gauze and lifted Serafina's leg off the ground. She hissed in pain but didn't comment further as he wrapped the wound. "There." He gave a satisfactory nod at his work. "That'll keep for a bit, but we need to find a healer."

"Our best bet is to return to the refugee camp." Emeraude leaned against a tree as she kept watch on the forest around them. "We know for certain we'll find help there."

As George aided Serafina to her feet, he winced at the thought of involving Marie and her people any further in their schemes. He'd already promised her they wouldn't return and bring trouble. If the Dundainee suspected them to be hiding amongst the refugees, how would they retaliate?

But Serafina's quivering figure made him silence his qualms. She may be conscious, but she'd lost a great deal of blood. Even if Emeraude's laudaetum prevented infection, there were still a hundred ways she could take a turn for the worse. "We'll need to cover the tracks our horses leave. We don't need the Dundainee showing up at the settlement and wreaking havoc."

"I wouldn't be so sure we'll be welcomed back." Serafina gave an awkward chuckle. "We make for a rather frightening crew."

He forced a smile of calm reassurance across his lips. "Marie will help us."

George kept a darker thought to himself. *I won't allow her to refuse.*

Chapter Twenty-Eight

"Who would you like to speak with first, Duquessa?"

Jax drummed her fingers atop the arm of her chair as her gaze skimmed the shelves lining the elegant Glennfeld study. "Whoever you can find, Ziri. Send both Finral and Yves here."

Acknowledging her directive with a salute, Ziri darted from the room, leaving Perry and Jax alone for the first time since returning from their adventure at the Grovershire library.

"How do you plan to ferret out the truth?" Perry questioned. "Do you really think either man will admit so readily to the plot?" He sat opposite her in a plush chair by the fireplace, his hand absently massaging his abdomen. Jax suspected his muscles had grown sore from their expeditious return ride.

A wry chuckle escaped her. "I doubt it will be that simple." She considered her plan of action before sharing, "What if we told Finral we suspect Vivienne of poisoning her father? Convince him we're going to prosecute her to the highest extent of the law?"

Perry's brow furrowed. "You think his guilt will betray him into confessing?"

"It's worth a try."

"But what if Yves is the only one behind the plot?" he countered.

Jax leaned against the chair's welcoming headrest. "We approach it the very same way but swap out our suspect. If Yves is as committed to his governor as I believe him to be, he won't let Finral be framed for a crime he didn't commit." During their trip back to the manor, Jax had finally been able to share the Heartsworn scheme she'd overheard and how truly united the two men were in their cause.

"What if Yves sacrifices himself to protect Finral? Moreover, what if Finral sacrifices himself believing he is protecting Vivienne?"

The potential outcomes Perry raised made her head spin. If their loyalties ran deep, her suspects could very well try and take the fall for each other. "Let's just see what they have to say."

A knock drew their attention to the door, and Yves stepped hesitantly into the grand study. He admired the high walls stacked with books and scrolls before settling a bewildered gaze on his hosts. "General Axesinger said you wished to speak with me?"

Jax wordlessly beckoned the deputy governor to take the other open seat opposite her. She and Perry had purposely positioned themselves so they could assess their quarries from every angle, looking for cracks in the killer's façade.

"Thank you for coming." Jax clasped her hands on her lap, her unreadable Duchess mask slipping into place.

Yves shifted on the cushion, and then realizing he couldn't look Jax and Perry in the eye simultaneously, rested his trepid gaze on her. "How can I be of help, Your Grace?"

"We've learned some disturbing news regarding the Lord General's passing." She kept her tone measured and calm, hoping to put him at ease.

Yves cocked his head to the side. "Disturbing? How so?"

"Our physician has completed his postmortem exam and found evidence that Allard was poisoned." Jax let the condemning words linger in the air.

Yves's eyes bulged as he went rigid with shock. "Poisoned? You mean to tell me the man was murdered?"

"I'm afraid so." Jax nodded with dismay.

"How could this happen? Under *your* watch?" He jabbed an

accusatory finger her way.

"That's what I intend to find out." Her expression hardened.

Yves's jaw dropped as realization dawned in his eyes. "You suspect me?"

"We'd be foolish not to." Jax lifted her chin. "Allard was the final hurdle between Heartsworn and a new era for Savant. With him gone, Heartsworn's victory is all but secured."

Yves narrowed his gaze. "It seems you don't have a very high opinion of Vivienne's ability to lead Lion's Bane in this continuing battle."

"That couldn't be further from the truth." Jax shrugged. "We already know that she and Governor Lothaine are *intimately* involved with one another." She paused to let the knowledge sink in.

Yves's eyes doubled in size. Clearly, Finral had not told his friend that their affair had been found out.

"It only makes sense," Jax continued, "that Vivienne and Finral unite under one banner to lead Savant together."

Yves folded his arms. "From the picture you paint, Duchess, it sounds like the lovebirds have more reason to want Allard dead than me."

"Ah, yes, perhaps," Jax admitted.

His deflection is interesting, she mused to herself. She'd expected Yves to protest Lothaine's innocence, but instead, he appeared to be distancing himself from his comrade.

Perry leaned forward, the movement seeming to remind Yves he was in the room. "Are you familiar with Faire l'Orange?"

Yves eyed Perry with distrust. "The Zaltorian winery? Of course. What common-born isn't?" He huffed. "It's one of the few luxuries in life we've been permitted by your lot. Although after drinking the wine you gifted us," he added, his gaze returning to Jax, "I realize it wasn't much of a luxury to begin with."

She allowed a sympathetic frown to grace her lips to show her disdain for the circumstances Yves and his people had endured at the hands of Qylvard Savant. "Have you ever heard of ardor root?"

The color drained from his face. "Why do you ask?"

Jax arched an eyebrow. "From your response, I take that as a yes."

"Well, of course. My family has worked in textiles for decades." A scowl grew across his face. "My grandfather died from shoddily processed ard—" He cut himself off, his face going pale. "Are you saying Allard was killed with ardor root?"

He pieced together that puzzle quickly.

"Yes," Jax replied matter-of-factly. "We found a bottle of Faire l'Orange wine laced with it."

"Faire l'Orange? But that would mean…" Yves stared into the fireplace, his brow wrinkling with confusion.

"Mean what?" Jax egged him on.

He shook his head. "I have nothing but my word, Duchess, yet I promise you I had no hand in this plot."

"Does that mean you think Finral did?"

Yves grew even more troubled by Perry's probing question. "I-I don't want to believe such a thing."

"But you suspect him capable?"

His eyes watered as he answered her. "Finral has long worried Lion's Bane would seize power and set Savant back with Allard's equally oppressive ideals." Yves ran a hand through his wispy hair. "He also desperately wanted Vivienne to be free of her father's clutches. But to resort to something so dastardly…he's better than that. *Smarter* than that."

From her assessment of Finral, Jax had once believed so, too. Now, she wasn't sure. As she considered the pieces in play, a wary notion entered her mind. Who else knew Yves's history with ardor root? Did Finral? Had he used ardor root specifically because of his deputy's connection to the poisonous plant to point the finger at Yves, rather than himself?

Or, on the contrary, was Yves trying to direct her away from him using her own logic against her? Her head spun with questions.

"Master Yves, could you recount for us your movements yesterday afternoon?" Jax requested, forging ahead with the interrogation. She knew Yves certainly had motive and means to kill Allard, but did he have opportunity? How had the poisoned wine come to be in Allard's possession? He'd said at dinner their first night that he wasn't desperate enough to accept a drink from the enemy, so how had the poisoned wine fallen into his hands?

"Yesterday?" Yves rubbed his temples as if to jar his memory. "Well, once your summit session concluded, Finral and I took a walk around the property to discuss matters of state. When we came back inside—where we briefly ran into Allard in the foyer—I returned to my suite to make a written record of our time here. But I didn't get very far with my notes, you see, for I accidentally knocked over a pitcher of water. Dvorak was out in the hall at the time and heard the glass shatter. He quickly came to my aid and Finral soon joined, having heard the commotion from our shared washroom."

Yves's cheeks reddened. "They helped me clean up the mess, and we then went down to the kitchen to request a new pitcher and towels. I returned to my room but was interrupted by shouting coming from downstairs. Finral and I both went to investigate, and we saw the whole household in a clamor over the news of a fire. I filed out with Finral to assist however I could."

Jax remembered Yves and Finral arriving together at the scene of the blaze. Dvorak had arrived shortly after them, followed by Vivienne and her father.

But the latter half of Yves's statement also triggered another realization. Since all hands had been needed, the sentries guarding the north wing would have been pulled away from their posts, leaving the guests' rooms temporarily unattended. The perfect distraction. Had someone used the fire's chaos to leave the poisoned wine in Allard's chamber?

"And once the fire had been tamed?" Jax pressed.

Yves shrugged. "I returned to my suite for the night. I bathed and had dinner brought up by Madame Rosalyn. I planned to spend the evening writing letters home to our comrades, but I ended up spilling my inkwell over myself." His nose wrinkled at the memory.

"You seem to be prone to spills, my good sir." Perry raised an eyebrow.

Yves's expression turned somewhat bashful. "Indeed. When your sentry offered to send for a staff member, I insisted I didn't want to trouble anyone, returned to my room, cleaned up my mess, and retired to bed."

His story aligned with what Hershall had shared about the night's happenings. "Finral and Vivienne gave us the impression that your inkwell mishap was intentional."

He fidgeted under Jax's gaze. "I told them I'd create a distraction so Finral could sneak into Vivienne's chamber. However, I was merely going to strike up a conversation with the guard." He rolled his eyes. "My clumsiness happened to have a different plan in mind."

Jax gave an absent nod as she replayed his comments. The distraction hadn't been much, just enough to allow Finral to dart across the hall into Vivienne's suite. Certainly, he wouldn't have had time to deliver the poisoned wine in that window. No, she reckoned it had to have been placed in Allard's room during the fire. The Ducal Guard had been forced to abandon their posts, so no one would have been monitoring the guest wing.

But Allard had been the *last* person to arrive outside during the fire. Who else would have had access to his room but Allard?

A light knock interrupted her thoughts, and Ziri appeared in the study's entrance. "Governor Lothaine, as requested, Duquessa."

She stepped into the room, and Finral appeared behind her, looking solemn. When his gaze landed on Yves, his shoulders straightened.

"What are you doing here, mate?" he asked with warm camaraderie.

Yves, however, regarded him with a wary expression, and Jax wished she knew what the deputy was thinking. "It's probably best for Duchess Jacqueline to explain."

Finral faltered a step at his friend's cool, cryptic response. "What's going on here?"

She waited until he took a seat in the last empty chair by the fireplace. "There's been a development concerning Lord General Allard."

"Development?" Finral's gaze swept over everyone before resting again on Jax.

"Did you kill him, Fin?" The accusation that flew out of Yves's mouth seemed to stun him almost as much as it did Finral.

The Heartsworn leader did a double take. "What are you on

about? *Kill* him?"

So much for letting me explain, Jax said to herself with an inward sigh.

"I'm afraid Allard's death was not the tragic heart attack we originally believed"—*or told you about,* she thought—"but rather the result of poison."

Finral gripped the arms of his chair. "What in the Virtues...does Vivienne know about this?"

"No. Not yet." Jax shook her head. "I planned to share the news with her once we had more...answers."

"Answers?" Finral parroted before glancing toward his deputy.

Yves didn't meet his gaze.

"Wait. Do you think *I* had something to do with this?" Finral jumped up from his seat, only to find Ziri's restraining hand on his shoulder.

As she forced him back into the chair, he rebuffed, "Is this how you treat dignitaries, Duchess? By labeling them murderers without reason?"

To Jax's surprise, Yves cleared his throat. "They've got evidence, Fin. Damning evidence."

"How could they? I didn't *do* anything—"

In an instant, Yves burst toward Finral, grabbing the man by his collar. "How could you? We were so close. We had them right where we wanted—why throw it all away? For her? For Vivienne?"

Finral twisted out of Yves's grip and smacked his hands away. "What's wrong with you, mate? I had nothing to do with this!"

Yves stared at the Heartsworn leader with tears in his eyes. "I want to believe you, but I can't..." He shielded his face with his hands and sank helplessly into his chair.

Finral stared slack-jawed at his weeping deputy before turning to Jax. "Just *what* is this evidence you have that has turned my closest confidante against me?"

Jax studied him. If she didn't think him a killer, she would have admired his composure, because she saw the heartbreak in his eyes. "Please, sit down, Governor Lothaine."

He did as he was told, and she laid out the facts thus far. "Allard died due to ardor root poisoning. We found a wine bottle laced with the plant in his chamber."

"Ardor root?" Finral's eyes widened, and his gaze flicked to Yves.

Jax dipped her chin. "Yes. My physician confirmed it. You may not be aware, but ardor root is not native to Saphire, so its presence here is most strange."

"I'm familiar with ardor root." Finral swallowed. "In Savant, we learn as kids to stay away from it." He again glanced at his deputy. "Poor Yves lost his grandfather to ardor root poisoning."

"Well, Allard lost his life to it after drinking from a bottle of Faire l'Orange someone left for him —"

"Faire l'Orange?" Finral's nose scrunched.

Jax couldn't quite understand the confusion on his face. "You're familiar with it, are you not?"

"Well, of course I am." He reached for the back of his neck. "It's a favorite drink of the common-born back home. I thought that was why you gifted us a bottle of it."

Now it was Jax's turn to feel confused. "I gifted you wine from a *Saphirian* winery."

"Yes, on our first night." Finral waved away her comment. "I'm talking about the bottle left in my chamber yesterday afternoon."

Jax, Perry, and Ziri all shared concerned glances. "What bottle?"

Finral stared at her like she'd sprouted another head. "Don't you remember? I found it in my room as I was readying for dinner. I even thanked you for it."

Jax searched her memories, and Finral's gratitude suddenly came to the forefront. *"I haven't gotten the chance to properly thank you, Jacqueline, for the hospitality you've continued to show us all. Your taste in wine is really quite surprising."*

At the time, she thought he'd simply been referring to the gift she'd had Madame Rosalyn place prior to their arrival. But now...

"I'll admit, when I saw it, I was a bit amazed that the realm's most prominent ruler even knew of Faire l'Orange. That you went out of your way to procure it for us was —"

Jax held up her hand. "Finral, *I* didn't gift you a bottle of Faire l'Orange." Her heartbeat began to quicken. "Where did you put this wine? Did you drink it?"

He shook his head. "I-I left it on the table where I found it."

Jax was already on her feet, signaling everyone to follow her and for Perry and Ziri to keep an eye on their guests. "Show me, Finral, if you will."

Now looking even more unnerved than he had when being accused of murder, the young man nodded and led the way to the north wing, everyone else in tow.

They wordlessly marched past the sentries manning the wing's entrance, and before long, they stood in Finral's suite.

"It's right over—" He stopped short in the middle of his sitting room. "Wait. Where is it?" He frantically ran to a side table piled with books and papers. Finral scattered the items before getting on his knees and looking underneath the surrounding furniture. "It's—it's not here. But I swear it was."

Something about his panicked demeanor seemed genuine. "When do you recall last seeing it, Finral?" Jax inquired.

"Well, I noticed the bottle as I was getting ready for dinner." He scratched at his dark hair. "I thought your staff might have placed it while I was washing up after the fire…or maybe it was even here when I returned from our session, and I just didn't realize. As to when I last remember seeing it…I'm not sure. I guess before I left for dinner?"

"Not when you returned?" Jax pressed.

Finral shrugged. "I…I had other things on my mind by that time." His cheeks grew traitorously pink.

Perry arched an eyebrow in suggestion. "Plotting your rendezvous with Vivienne?"

The lad nodded.

Jax paced around the suite, her mind whirling at this new revelation and what it meant for the investigation. If it had not been for Finral's remark at dinner last night, she might have thought the Heartsworn governor was skillfully covering his tracks. But she very clearly remembered him commenting about her *surprising* taste in wine. At the time, she hadn't thought much about the adjective he'd chosen, but knowing what they knew now, it made complete sense.

A Saphirian Duchess serving Faire l'Orange would have been out of the ordinary for a Savantian with his background.

She mentally sifted through their evidence, her gaze trailing out into the hall, as they'd left Finral's suite door open. While Vivienne's room was directly opposite his, her father's was just one door over.

Wait…hadn't one of the Ducal Guard sentries mentioned something about Allard leaving his room to beg for more alcohol from the day shift? She quickly resurfaced Hershall's account in her memory. *"Allard kept coming out of his room, barking orders and demanding more liquor. The old man even stumbled into the wrong suite at one point."*

"Virtues," she hissed as startling awareness dawned over her. She hadn't given Allard's actions much thought at the time because his drunkenness wasn't entirely noteworthy, but now, it painted everything in a new light.

Jax gripped Finral's arm, seizing the young man's attention with her next words. "I don't believe Allard was meant to die during this summit. *You* were."

Chapter Twenty-Nine

Her declaration was met with stunned silence.

"We need to speak with the daytime guard on duty yesterday afternoon *before* Hershall took over." Jax was already gathering her skirts and heading for the suite door. "You two, please stay here and lock the door behind us. For your safety," she instructed the bewildered Heartsworn duo.

Ziri caught up to her out in the hallway, with Perry not far behind. "What have you figured out, Duquessa?" Ziri kept her voice low as they hurried toward the second-story landing.

"Something Hershall said while giving his report yesterday has me rethinking this whole calamity." Jax's fists balled at her side as her long, determined strides carried her forward. "He said that in the wake of the fire, the day guard didn't report anything out of the ordinary other than Allard stumbling around drunkenly, asking for more liquor to be sent to his room. Hershall commented that Allard apparently went into the wrong room before realizing his error and returning to his suite. At the time, I dismissed the action, chalking it up to simple intoxicated behavior."

Perry sucked in a breath as he fell in step with her. "You think Allard may have pilfered the poisoned wine from whatever room he stumbled into?"

She gave a curt nod of her head. "Exactly. I want to know whether that room was Finral's."

"Crowley was on duty after the fire," Ziri spoke up. "His lungs are a bit sensitive, so Aizen had him pulled from outside patrol and sent to watch the north wing once everything calmed down. I believe he'll be stationed in the west wing today. We rotate postings so our guards' alertness isn't dulled by the repetitive mundane."

Jax corrected her course and set off toward the area of the manor she and her companions resided in.

"Jax! There you all are." Uma's breathy exclamation halted their footsteps just as they reached the west wing entrance.

She turned to find Uma and Sabine hurrying toward them, expressions of concern etched deeply into their faces.

"We're trying to find Governor Lothaine," Sabine clarified as the two women met up with them. "He excused himself from our croquet game earlier, and Vivienne has been asking after him. We arranged for her and Dvorak to take tea in the conservatory while we tracked him down."

"We just ordered him and Yves to lock themselves in Finral's suite," Jax hurriedly reassured her.

Uma's brow furrowed at her wording. "Has something happened with the case?"

With an anxious nod, Jax beckoned her friends to accompany them. "The whole investigation has been turned on its head." While she didn't have time to bring them up to speed, she did explain their intended destination. "I have a few questions for one of our sentries."

They found Crowley standing guard near their rooms. The stout lad grew tense as they approached him. "Your Grace? General Axesinger?" His gaze pinched with confusion.

"Officer Crowley," Jax began, "I understand you oversaw the goings-on in the north wing yesterday after the fire was under control."

He nodded in confirmation. "That's correct, ma'am. Captain Aizen personally made the assignment."

"When you arrived, you didn't relieve anyone, did you?"

"No, ma'am. Everyone had been pulled from their post to deal with the fire." He straightened his shoulders even more. "I was the first person to arrive on the floor. I did a sweep of each room to verify nothing was amiss and then kept watch while the guests returned to their suites."

Jax smiled to let him know he'd done well, given the circumstances. "Do you remember the order of their arrival?"

He closed his eyes as he recalled, "The lady—Miss Vivienne, came back first, her clothes a bit disheveled. She was followed by the two Heartsworn lads. Then Masters Dvorak and Allard returned." Crowley opened his eyes. "The older man, Allard. He was in a right state, he was. From the mutterings I overheard between him and Dvorak, it seemed the fire had triggered some type of manic episode."

"What happened after the guests returned to their rooms?" Jax pressed.

"Well, I'd say about a half hour later, Dvorak appeared and knocked on Miss Vivienne's door. They spoke, about what I can't be entirely certain, but the young lady grew awfully concerned by the end. Once Dvorak returned to his room, Miss Vivienne visited with her father."

Jax recalled Vivienne's earlier comments about trying to quell her father's agitated state. "Did you see her carrying anything into his room?"

Crowley thought for a moment. "Why, yes. I do believe she had a wine bottle tucked under the arm facing my direction." He pointed down the hall to recreate the vantage point he would have had on the other side of the manor.

This aligned with Vivienne's story about giving her father her bottle of Saphirian wine, which they had found in Allard's chamber. "Only one bottle, yes?"

"From what I could see," Crowley replied. "She was only holding one."

Jax tapped her chin as she considered her next question. "How long did their exchange last? What happened after?"

"She didn't visit with him for more than ten minutes." Crowley scratched at his hay-colored hair. "In fact, when she came out, she approached me. Miss Vivienne asked that if her father demanded any additional alcohol that evening, I disregard his request however I saw fit. I didn't bother telling her Madame Rosalyn had already sent a missive detailing the same instructions to everyone within the household at *your* command."

Jax bobbed her head as the beginnings of a theory stirred.

"Miss Vivienne returned to her room, and then shortly after, both Masters Lothaine and Dvorak came out inquiring about dinner. While I said I'd be happy to send for their food, they both begged off and ventured downstairs." He pointed toward the second-floor landing, which also would have been in his view from the north wing.

"Miss Vivienne did the same not fifteen minutes later. Madame Rosalyn came up at six-thirty with a tray, which she first offered to Master Yves. He came to his door, accepted it, and took it into his chambers." Crowley paused to stroke his beard. "When Madame Rosalyn returned with a tray for Lord General Allard, things…got a little heated. He nearly flipped the tray in her face, asking her to bring him more wine, not food. When she declined and took her leave, he followed her down the hall. I had to step in and request that he return to his chambers."

Jax's heart quickened. They'd finally reached the pivotal point of the story. She noted her companions all listened with rapt attention, despite the fact Sabine and Uma still didn't even know what they were looking to uncover.

"The drunken mess that he was, Allard entered one of the rooms opposite his suite. The one belonging to Governor Lothaine." Crowley suddenly looked uncomfortable.

"Normally, I would have run to stop him, but since I was the only person on duty, I didn't want to risk leaving my post over such a trivial matter. Instead, I merely called out his name to let him know his error. He couldn't have been in there for more than thirty seconds before he came staggering back out into the hall. Poor chap practically fell headfirst into his room."

Jax winced at the image. "When he came out from Lothaine's

suite, did you notice him holding anything?"

"Not from where I was standing, Your Grace, no." Crowley's cheeks paled. "Has something gone missing from the governor's room?"

She nodded. "A bottle of Savantian wine. We suspect Allard might have taken it." Thirty seconds may not seem like a lot, but it was certainly long enough for Allard to enter Lothaine's room, see the bottle of Faire l'Orange on the side table in the sitting room, and possibly abscond with it tucked under his tunic.

"I see." Crowley gulped, clearly upset by this development. "If that's the case, please see that the price of the wine is taken from my wages, Duchess, for it is my fault for allowing Allard to commit such a crime."

Ziri placed a hand on the sentry's arm. "There is no need to shoulder such blame, Crowley."

Indeed, if Crowley had left his post and searched Allard, he would have confiscated the stolen wine and merely placed the poisoned bottle back in Finral's chambers. The whole scenario made Jax wonder if the Virtues had somehow intervened to spare the young governor from such a deadly fate.

Crowley acknowledged Ziri's remarks with a smile that came across more like a grimace. "I appreciate that, General, but I have still sullied the name of the Ducal Guard."

"By not leaving your post—as directed—you have been able to provide a valuable account of the evening." Jax offered her own heartening reassurances. "Your pay will not be docked for such actions, officer. You said so yourself, if you had been paired with another guard, you would have had the freedom to go to Allard's aid rather than simply call out to him. It is *my* fault that we didn't have more guards attending this summit, so it is I who will bear the blame."

Crowley's jaw dropped, and Jax realized her words of encouragement had had the opposite effect. The poor man looked horrified. "Duchess, I cannot ask you to—"

"You ask nothing of me. I only state the truth of the matter." She gave him a tight smile before adding, "Please continue to watch our quarters in such a diligent manner."

He saluted, and Jax waved her companions back toward the landing.

"Well, that all but confirms it," she whispered once they were out of earshot. "Allard encountered the Faire l'Orange wine when he stumbled into Finral's room. It would have been easy for him to slip it under his shirt, hiding it from Crowley's view when he staggered back into his own suite."

Uma and Sabine shared spooked looks. "This is the wine that you've determined killed him?" Uma asked, clearly putting the missing pieces of information together.

Jax hurriedly explained everything Major Brennan had shared about ardor root, Faire l'Orange, and its close ties to the Heartsworn delegates.

Sabine's nose wrinkled. "It's almost *too* closely linked to Heartsworn, if you think about it."

"How so?" Perry tilted his head.

Sabine began counting her fingers. "Well, for one, ardor root is found in northern Savant, near their base. The wine used to carry the poison also neighbored the area. Then there's Yves's history with ardor root, given that's how his grandfather died…"

Jax's stomach flipped. "It's almost as if everything has been purposely pointing to Heartsworn."

Perry snapped his fingers, his eyes wide. "And if *Finral* was the intended target, who better to suspect than his irritable deputy, who's displayed nothing but open animosity toward him."

It all made terrifying sense. "Our killer tried to deliver us the solution *they* wanted us to believe." Jax's lips set in a grim line. "Yves takes the fall for Finral's demise, effectively crippling Heartsworn from the inside out."

Uma shuddered. "And who would benefit most from such an implosion?"

Ziri answered her rhetorical question. "Our dead man."

"But he wouldn't *be* dead if he knew about the poison, so that leaves us with Dvorak and—" Jax stopped midsentence when she spotted a familiar figure rush into the foyer below. "Aizen!" She waved, catching the disheveled Captain's attention as he scanned the room.

He spotted their group on the landing and took the stairs two at a time. Based on his ragged appearance, he must have just come from the scene of the fire.

"I finally found something amongst the debris." He held out a soot-covered palm. "What do you make of it?"

Jax leaned closer to examine his find. It looked like a scrap of charred, dark blue fabric with a looping design stitched with golden thread. "How did this survive the blaze?"

"I found it pinned under a rock." Aizen stifled a cough. "I think it belonged to a larger piece, but the rest burned away, save for this little corner preserved under the stone."

With a fingernail, Jax gently flipped the swatch over, fearful it would disintegrate if she touched it any more forcefully. "Oh my."

On this side, the golden thread didn't form a looping design, but rather three letters.

VLA.

Sabine frowned. "Do we know those initials?"

"We do. VLA…Vivienne *Lark* Allard," Jax breathed with dismay as she recalled the Lord General's pet name for his daughter. This, paired with the color of the fabric, triggered another memory. "She used a similar handkerchief in the banquet hall this morning. Right after we informed the others of Allard's passing."

Aizen held the fabric closer to her face. "What does this smell like to you, Duchess?"

Jax eyed him before taking a slight whiff. Expecting only smoke and soot, she was surprised when a harsher scent floated through her nostrils. "This smells like lamp oil!"

"Oil?" Perry echoed, and in turn, everyone confirmed for themselves.

"I think *this* was used to start the fire." Aizen pointed to the scrap of cloth. "From what I can tell, the fire burned the hottest where I found this. Even the rock it was pinned under showed signs of heat distress. It wouldn't be out of the realm of possibility for someone to light a homemade fuse—a piece of twine or ribbon—which would burn slowly before reaching the oil-soaked fabric."

Jax folded her arms. "We suspected the fire and poisoning were tied together. At first, I thought it had to do with tormenting Allard, but now, I think Vivienne used the fire to create chaos, giving herself the chance to slip into Finral's room unnoticed and leave the laced wine."

Perry wrung his hands. "It's hard to believe her capable of such a thing, but given her intimate ties with Finral and Heartsworn, she would know just how she could frame Yves for her lover's death."

"You said you left her with Dvorak in the conservatory?" Jax looked at Sabine and Uma.

When they both nodded, Jax held her head high with determination. "Then let's go confront our killer."

Chapter Thirty

Vivienne sipped her tea with a melancholy expression while basking in the sunlight streaming through the conservatory's windows. As Jax glided into the room and assessed the young woman's appearance, she realized that Vivienne was still blissfully unaware that her father had been poisoned by her own hand. It was time for Jax to carry out her plan.

"I'm glad I found you both." Jax plastered on a sympathetic expression. "I have some news regarding Lord General Allard's passing."

Vivienne's eyes watered at the mention of her father. "I still can't believe he's gone. I'm trying s-so hard to keep my emotions in check, like he taught me a good leader should..." She swallowed. "But it's difficult."

Jax reflected on Vivienne's cold, calculated demeanor earlier, when they'd all been together in the banquet hall. Had she merely been wearing an unaffected mask, as Jax often had to? Or was her ruthlessness simply beginning to show?

Dvorak patted her hand. "Your father would be very proud of how you've handled yourself in the wake of his death, my dear." A tender smile stretched across his own tear-stained cheeks. "A true leader."

Vivienne straightened her shoulders. "What news do you bring, Jacqueline?" She motioned to the empty settee across from her.

Jax clasped her hands together and chose to remain standing, as did all her companions. While Perry remained in her shadow, the others fanned out around the room should Vivienne try to make a break for the exit.

Jax took a fortifying breath before addressing her suspect. "Your father's cause of death. I'm afraid it may shock you."

"Shock me?" Vivienne squinted her teary eyes, confused.

Jax dipped her chin. "Lord General Allard was murdered."

"What?" Both Vivienne and Dvorak stared at her, mouths agape. "How? Who?" Vivienne cried.

"The who will become all too apparent once you learn the how." Jax motioned Aizen forward. "But first, does this look familiar to either of you?"

On cue, Aizen presented the charred piece of fabric for the duo to inspect, making sure the initials were on full display.

"No—why should it?" Vivienne's nostrils flared with sudden anger. "What does this have to do with my father's murder?"

"Vivienne, please," Dvorak murmured, doing his best to soothe the obviously agitated woman. His gaze flicked nervously to the handkerchief, and Jax wondered if he recognized Vivienne's initials.

Aizen shielded his palm with his other hand to protect the scrap of evidence. "We believe this was used to ignite yesterday's blaze."

"As I said, what does that have to do with my father's murder?" Vivienne snapped.

"Everything." Jax stepped forward. "For while the estate was thrown into chaos to contain the flames, your father's killer made their move."

Vivienne's anger seemed to have been replaced by sudden fear. "What do you mean?" Her hissing tone had lost its biting edge.

Jax chose her words carefully. "A bottle of poisoned wine was left lying in wait."

"You're saying someone *poisoned* my father?" Vivienne's expression grew more troubled.

"Not intentionally," Jax admitted. "But rather, your father encountered a deadly drink meant for another."

"You're speaking in riddles, Jacqueline," Vivienne huffed, throwing her arms up. "What are you trying to say?"

"That your father died by drinking a bottle of Faire l'Orange wine laced with ardor root intended for *your* political opponent." Jax's tone matched the young woman's with equal fierceness.

As her heated words sank in, Vivienne's eyes widened. "Wait. My political opponent? You mean, Finral?"

Jax gave a somber nod and noted how Dvorak no longer patted Vivienne's back with fatherly kindness. In fact, he had inched away from her altogether.

He's put it together.

Vivienne also must have noticed Dvorak was no longer at her side to comfort her. "So, Father is dead because he drank poisoned wine meant for Fin?" She glanced back at Jax, her manner somewhat frantic.

"Yes. I suspect our culprit selected both the wine and the poison to frame Master Yves for the crime." She paused as a grim smile graced her lips. "I doubt they expected us to find such a telling clue among the fiery rubble." She pointed to the embroidered handkerchief in Aizen's hand. "Those are *your* initials, are they not?"

"Well, yes, but I swear, I've never seen that piece of fabric in my life."

Her panicked protest troubled Jax. There was a strange ring of truth to her cries. Jax shook the doubt from her mind. "We know whoever set the fire did so to draw everyone outside the manor while they placed the poisoned wine in Governor Lothaine's quarters. That you and your father were the last to join the firefighting efforts narrows our scope dramatically. And since your father wouldn't knowingly have ingested poisoned wine—"

"That, Duchess, is where I'm afraid you are wrong."

Dvorak's quiet remark cut through her like a dagger. "Excuse me?"

The pensive man stared at his hands as if bracing himself before raising his head. "I told Allard it would be too risky to carry out such a deadly scheme under your watchful eye. But there was no stopping him when he got something in his head."

"Uncle Nanteuil, what are you saying?" Vivienne choked out.

He rubbed his temples, aging right before their eyes. "That I'm the reason your father died, my dear. Although that was never my intention...*our* intention."

Newly ignited rage boiled within Jax. "You and Allard planned to poison Finral and set up Yves to take the fall? At *my* peace summit?"

He met her glare with equal determination. "This is *war*, Duchess. From your faraway gilded castle, it may not seem so dire, but to us, *everything* is on the line. Our lives, our hopes, our futures...Allard and I had a plan to rebuild Savant, and Heartsworn was the only thing left in our way."

"And you thought *killing* me was the answer?"

Finral's harsh rebuke came from the conservatory doorway. He and Yves stood there, ashen-faced, having apparently disregarded Jax's earlier command to lock themselves in Finral's suite.

"I came here in good faith, hoping to reason with Allard." Tears glimmered in Finral's brown eyes as he strode closer to Dvorak's cowering figure. "There was no need for us to work against one another. We could have found common ground and moved forward together to bring Savant the bright future she deserves."

"Common ground?" Dvorak spat out the words. "You, who would live happily alongside nobles as if they'd never robbed you of your dignity and freedoms? Allard would never agree to such a thing. Savant belongs to those who broke their backs building it. The nobles don't deserve such grace. They've infested our lands for too long. An extermination needs to be carried out to begin anew."

Jax shuddered at his hateful vision.

"And to do so," Dvorak continued, "Lion's Bane needed to take control. Allard and I feared we would be outmaneuvered at this summit, given how the Duchess's ideals mirrored Heartsworn's so greatly. We knew she'd be sympathetic to your cause, not ours."

Jax held her tongue. It was clear that Allard and Dvorak had never truly believed her to be a mediator. With their innate distrust of nobles and royals, they didn't think her capable of adhering to her commitment to let the Savantians decide their own fate.

"Since our covert attack against Heathcliff's group went so smoothly, we figured we could do it again."

Jax's brow furrowed at the vaguely familiar name. Hadn't he been mentioned at dinner during their first night here?

"Heathcliff's group?" Yves came to stand beside Finral, his expression murderous. "So, you *were* responsible for the death of his councilors?"

Dvorak dipped his chin. "In these desperate times, the call of the bottle is strong. All we had to do was ask our spies to skillfully place a poisoned barrel in the officers' tent." He sighed. "It was a shame Heathcliff didn't partake in the merriment that fateful night, but he still came around to our side in the end."

He glanced at the two Heartsworn lads. "Allard knew that we wouldn't get so lucky with you. If we took out Lothaine, Yves would carry on in his wake. Oh, yes, we knew how deep your loyalties ran, even if you pretended to not get along around your adversaries. So, we had to figure out a way to get rid of both of you." His lips drew into a thin line. "To do so under the watchful care of the renowned Duchess Jacqueline seemed nearly impossible. How could we take out our enemies without the finger of blame being pointed at us?"

"By making it look like *I* killed Finral." Yves growled. "That's why you used a wine you knew we common-born drank and had access to. A poison you somehow learned *I* had a history with."

"Indeed. My spies are the reason I've always been so valuable to Allard. It's how we also knew the public 'tension' between you was all a pathetic power game." A slight smirk curled on Dvorak's lips. "We figured we could place the poisoned wine in Lothaine's tent or something, although we had to adjust our plan once we learned we'd be staying inside the manor for the duration of the summit. We didn't expect such niceties from one with royal blood." He sneered at Jax.

"But we quickly adapted. It helped you were so trusting of your guests, Duchess, posting only a handful of men within the manor's interior. All we needed was something to draw them outside. It was Allard's idea, the fire. Perhaps I should have protested more."

His gaze took on a haunted look. "Given the Ducal Guard were posted at the manor doors, I managed to sneak out of a first-floor window without being noticed. I then headed for the woods, where I used some spare bowstring and a handkerchief to rig up a fuse and set it alight."

"Bowstring?" Jax then remembered Aizen's report and how Dvorak had surrendered his longbow to the Ducal Guard upon his arrival. Apparently, the weapon wasn't as lethal as the parts used to make it. "How clever of you." Her remark wasn't a compliment.

Dvorak shrugged. "It's a stalling tactic our men have used many a time in battle. It only made sense to implement it here. While I was in the forest, Allard was tasked with causing a scene in the kitchens so I could sneak back into the manor." He motioned to his soft frame. "I didn't trust that I'd be able to climb inside a window without calling attention to myself. The fuse allowed enough of a delay that I could be seen moving about the manor in the time leading up to the fire's outbreak."

Yves snapped, "That's why you were out in the hall when I smashed my water pitcher. You'd returned from playing arsonist and were hoping to be seen."

"Yes. Your clumsiness helped provide me with an alibi." Dvorak leered at him. "Once the blaze was noticed and everyone began dashing madly about to put it out, I placed the poison in Lothaine's chambers. Simple, really. But as with well-laid plans, the Virtues had other ideas in mind." He pointed a finger at Jax. "And I blame you, Duchess."

Jax held her head high in defiance. "Your reasoning for such an accusation?"

"Your little 'gift,'" he snapped. "Your *generosity* doomed Allard the moment he stepped into his suite. He'd been sober for so long. But the night of our arrival here, that all ended. He couldn't get enough."

Jax flinched at the memory of Allard's drunken state, trying to tamp down her guilt. But she then remembered the Troissaint bottles they'd found in Allard's room and realized that Allard's sobriety was all an illusion, a secret he'd kept even from his comrade.

"I told him the next day, right after your first session, that we needed to call the plan off." Dvorak began to wring his hands. "He wasn't fit to carry it out effectively. But he was worried, given how the summit was progressing. He felt that Lothaine had outmaneuvered him and that we needed to act fast. So, we set our plan into motion."

"Why use a handkerchief with Vivienne's initials?" Jax pressed. "Were you planning to frame her, should things not work out with Yves?"

Dvorak reached into his jacket and extracted a dark blue linen square. "That was not my intention whatsoever. VLA are *my* initials. Vice Lord Admiral."

Jax narrowed her gaze. "But I saw Vivienne use a similar handkerchief this morning."

"Because I lent her mine when she arrived in the banquet hall."

Jax shot a questioning glance at Vivienne, searching for confirmation. The stunned woman managed a slight nod. "He did give me one, but I honestly cannot recall what it looked like." Her chin quivered with sincerity.

A flicker of regret crossed Dvorak's face. "Vivienne was never meant to be involved with any of this. She was our great hope for Savant's future."

He continued with a sigh, "When we heard the shouts calling for everyone to assist with the blaze, we acted immediately. Lothaine and Yves dashed out like heroic loons, allowing me to place the poisoned wine I'd secured. Allard was meant to keep Vivienne occupied with a feigned fit over the fire so that I wouldn't be the noticeably last person to leave the guest wing."

Vivienne's face contorted with anger. "You mean, his outburst was all an act?"

"It was meant to be, my child. However..." Genuine trouble etched into Dvorak's features. "I believe this is where things went truly wrong. Whether his mind was still in a weakened state from the night's drinking or what...the harsh reality of the fire awakened something traumatic within your father and set him off. Even after the fire was doused, his panic couldn't be contained. I feared something had broken within him." Tears leaked from his face. "I hoped a good night's sleep would do Allard good. I visited with him, using our adjoined washroom to move between our suites, and gave him a sleeping draft. I then went across the hall to ask Vivienne if she would sing him a calming song."

Jax sucked in a breath. A sleeping draft?

Dvorak noticed her reaction. "Yes. Had I known Vivienne would instead supply him with more wine, I would have acted differently."

At the confused expressions in the room, Jax explained, "It is not recommended to mix the two. Depending on the individual, the mixture of such a tincture and alcohol can cause everything from hallucinations to an even more inebriated state."

It explained why Allard had been so intoxicated when he'd only had access to Vivienne's half-drunken bottle of wine. Why he'd been staggering about the wing, in search of more to satiate his addiction.

"Between the fire, the sleeping draft, and the desperate need for alcohol—" she counted off all the offending circumstances—"poor Allard lost control of his senses. He wasn't in the frame of mind to realize the Faire l'Orange bottle he found while stumbling about the guest quarters was the one he'd ordered to be poisoned."

Dvorak nodded at her assessment of the sad situation. "When I saw him lying on the washroom floor this morning, I merely thought his drinking had finally caught up with him. I had no idea that our plans to end Heartsworn had all gone so horribly wrong." His gaze dropped to his lap, and he finally slumped with defeat.

"That must have changed when I waltzed into the banquet hall this morning." Finral's voice held no sympathy.

Dvorak shook his head. "I merely assumed you hadn't cracked open the bottle yet, Lothaine."

"And yet, you said nothing. You didn't rethink your plans, even with your leader dead." A lethal cold emanated from the Heartsworn governor. "You didn't stop to think that I might uncork my special gift and share it with Yves, killing us both. Or bring it with me while I visited Vivienne in her chambers."

Dvorak's eyes widened as he looked at the woman who called him uncle. "What? That nonsense is still going on? Vivienne, you said you put an end to it!" He reached for her arm, but she snatched it away.

Shaking with a storm of emotions, Vivienne rose from the settee and glided to Finral's side. "You and Papa obviously had your secrets. I have mine, too. While I may have kept my role in Lion's Bane from Finral, it wasn't because I ever meant to betray him."

Her gaze turned pleading as she locked eyes with her beloved. "It was because I intended to join him. I knew Papa wasn't in good health and that my eventual ascension as Lion's Bane's leader was only a matter of months, if weeks away. I wished for us to join forces with Heartsworn and put aside our differences to rebuild Savant. But I feared that if Papa got wind of my intentions, he'd remove me as his successor. To protect the future I so desperately wanted, I couldn't risk telling anyone. Even you, my love." She cupped Finral's cheek in her palm before turning to Dvorak, her devotion now turned to steely resolve.

"So, yes. We both had our secrets. But here is where we differ, Uncle. I knew the dangers of my plan, whereas you were so consumed by your need to win that you failed to see the countless ways you stood to lose by carrying out such an ill-conceived plot."

Finral wrapped an arm around his beloved, but his gaze never left Dvorak. "You should have heeded your own misgivings, Vice Lord Admiral. Trying to murder your foe under the nose of Jacqueline Xavier? It's like you were asking to get caught."

Aizen hoisted Dvorak up by the arm, looking to Jax for orders. "What would you like done with him?"

"I leave his fate to our Savantian friends." She gestured to a drained Finral, Vivienne, and Yves. "For as I have said since the start of this summit, I am merely here to mediate."

Finral spoke wordlessly with his deputy, and Vivienne gave him an encouraging squeeze. "We'll take him back with us to Savant to stand proper trial, Jacqueline. Until then, please do us a favor by allowing him to wait in your dungeons."

She let loose a light chuckle. "I'm afraid I have no dungeons to offer here at Glennfeld, but Captain Aizen will isolate him in the estate barracks until your departure." She raised a searching eyebrow. "Any idea about when that might be?"

"Soon, I hope." Finral threaded his fingers through Vivienne's. "But I believe we have a peace agreement to settle first."

Chapter Thirty-One

Serafina's low murmurs jolted George awake.

"Her fever is finally breaking." Emeraude dabbed at Serafina's forehead, which glistened in the dim light of the camp infirmary. "She's beginning to stir."

George cursed himself for falling asleep at Serafina's bedside. "How long was I out?" He rubbed his eyes, still feeling the burn of exhaustion.

"Not nearly as long as you need." Emeraude assessed him with a stern glare. "You took quite a beating from that blast. You really should let the camp's healer take a look at that nasty bruise on your back."

He shrugged off her concern, trying to ignore how stiff his lower back muscles had become. "It's just a bump."

She didn't press him further on the matter. "Marie brought some porridge for dinner." She pointed to three bowls sitting on the small end table beside Serafina's cot in the makeshift infirmary.

George stared at the warm meal, his stomach wriggling with guilt. "We really need to leave in case the Dundainee catch wind of our trail. We cannot let this camp suffer for our offenses." He and Emeraude had tried their best to cover their tracks on their ride back here, but the rain and mud had made such an attempt tricky.

The Shadow Brethren Grandmaster waved away his concern. "This camp won't be their focus."

"How can you be so sure?" he challenged.

"Because I dropped a Lion's Bane patch on the ground in the outpost courtyard. I grabbed it while working at the war camp yesterday. If anything, the Dundainee will believe Commander Crowe is at fault and give *him* something to worry about," she scoffed.

Surprised by her oddly thoughtful actions to spare the refugees trouble, George studied her. "You have a really strange sense of justice, Odaire. I can't quite figure it out."

She scowled at him. "I learned a long time ago I could only rely on myself to right the wrongs around me." She tore her gaze away from him, but not before he caught the haunted look in her dark eyes. "I don't relish taking lives. But I *will* do whatever I must to fulfill the oaths I've made."

Something within him stirred. Recognition...and sympathy. "I suppose I understand that."

"You do?" Her expression revealed sincere surprise.

He nodded. "I've had to take many a life in the line of duty to satisfy the pledge I made to the Ducal Guard. Not once was it ever something I enjoyed." He reached out toward Serafina and brushed away a strand of auburn hair that had fallen across her cheek. "Their faces used to come to me in the night. Those slain by my blade."

"Used to?" Emeraude's question was quiet. "Do they not now?"

"No." He smiled warmly at the reason. "My heart isn't as bruised and tortured as it once was."

Serafina stirred against his hand, and her bright eyes fluttered open. "Where are we?" she murmured. Instinctively, she reached for the medallion hanging from her neck as she struggled to sit up. "What time is it?"

George eased her back onto the pillow. "We're in the infirmary tent at the refugee camp. It's nearly sundown. But everything is all right."

"Both Favors are safe," Emeraude added for good measure.

Serafina visibly relaxed at the news. "Thank the Virtues. I thought we were done for."

"*You* almost were." George brought her hand to his lips. "Please, don't scare me like that again."

Her lips curled into an apologetic smile. "Who would have thought hanging out with me would bring you more danger than being Captain of the Ducal Guard?"

"It is danger I will willingly face if it means staying by your side."

Her prismatic eyes watered at his heartfelt words.

Emeraude cleared her throat. "So, you have retrieved the Intelligeye sigil and dealt with Elias Pettraud. What next?"

What next, indeed? The mission he and Serafina had come to Savant for was complete. They could leave whenever Serafina was strong enough to journey back to Saphire. Yet, it wasn't as if he had a position in the Ducal Guard to return to once they arrived home. Sure, Jax would welcome him back among the ranks, but…

George dug the star-shaped relic from his pocket, admiring the sparkling amethyst once more. They'd suffered so much hardship to find this small golden sigil. Questions about prophecies and the true nature of magic swirled in his head. A few months ago, such thoughts would never have entered his mind. The Favors had opened his eyes to so many unknowns across the realm. What were the Virtuous Favors, truly? What did the Dark Magus want with them? Did the man have some way to harness the tremendous power that caused the explosion back at the outpost?

"We find the Bravesoul pendant, right?" Serafina tilted her head, almost confused by Emeraude's question.

The Grandmaster's eyebrows rose. "You truly mean to keep to our agreement?"

"Of course." Serafina looked offended. "Besides, won't our covenant *kill* me if I don't?"

"The covenant only applies to that of the Shadow Brethren," Emeraude murmured, her gaze dropping to the floor. "Not to the client."

"Well, either way, I said I'd help you find your father's treasure." Serafina reached for Emeraude's forearm and clasped it. "I intend to do so. We have a higher calling, Em—beyond the Shadow Brethren and my archives. We are Favored Ones. And we have a duty to fulfill."

Some emotion glimmered in Emeraude's eyes. What it was, George wasn't exactly sure.

"What about you, Solomon?" She turned to him suddenly, her words barbed. "Are you going to run back to your Duchess and turn me in?"

"My place is with her." George threaded his fingers through Serafina's. He still had so many questions about the Favors and their strange powers. But there was one thing in his life that was certain and true. He belonged with Serafina Braeknoch. "As for Jax…" His voice trailed off.

"We need to inform her of what's transpired," Serafina asserted. "We owe her that much. And that includes telling her about *your* involvement, Emeraude."

"I don't see that going well for me."

George chuckled at the Grandmaster's dry delivery. "If you are willing to align yourself with us against the Dark Magus, I'm sure a truce can be reached. Jax understands the threat he poses, even if it is an unknown one for now." He took a fortifying breath. "But you must do so as Emeraude Odaire, not the Grandmaster of the Shadow Brethren."

Her face became an unreadable mask. "I cannot abandon who I am, and I *am* the Shadow Brethren." Her steely tone softened. "But I *can* change my ways."

Emeraude held a hand to her heart. "I swear on my honor that I will not take a life on this mission unless it is absolutely the last resort."

Her pledge resonated with him. She valued honor, even if they had different ways of claiming it. George remembered that she had merely incapacitated the Dundainee guards back at the outpost rather than killed them. She was capable of mercy. In fact, she seemed to prefer it.

George held out his hand. "I shall hold you to your promise."

She shook it, her grip as firm as her determined gaze. "What awaits us in Saphire?"

"Answers, hopefully." George reached for the back of his neck. "Saphire is the center of the realm's trade. Perhaps we might find some merchant or antiquities dealer who has heard tales of a flame-shaped pendant."

Serafina gingerly propped herself into a sitting position on her bed. "We may be able to convince Jax to allow us access to the ducal archives. *Sanctioned* access," she cut off Emeraude from suggesting anything else. "With all we know now, perhaps we might also find a clue regarding the Humblemind crest. There's a chance its protector might know more than us about the whereabouts of the Bravesoul pendant."

"But first, *you* must rest," George reminded her. "You need to stay off your leg for at least three days to allow it time to heal."

Serafina frowned. "But if we delay here too long…" She began counting on her fingers.

"What?" Emeraude glanced back and forth between the two of them. "What happens?"

Serafina stuck out her lower lip. "We'll miss Carriena and Bernard's wedding."

This appeared to be the last thing Emeraude expected. Her jaw dropped open, and genuine bafflement enveloped her face. "A *wedding*? You're going back for a wedding?"

"Don't worry." George smirked. "We'll get you an invite, too."

Emeraude crossed her arms with a roll of her eyes.

"I know you are just as eager to pursue the Favors as I am, Em." Serafina rested her head against the pillow once more. "But this life has taught me to revel in the happy moments we're given. Let's not allow fear and angst to overshadow that."

The Grandmaster merely harrumphed in response.

She'll come around. George mused as he assessed Emeraude's half-hearted scowl. He then turned to Serafina and kissed her temple. "Rest up, my love. We have more adventure ahead of us."

Chapter Thirty-Two

"Are you sure it's a good idea to let Finral, Vivienne, and Yves discuss things alone?" Perry murmured in her ear.

Jax tugged herself away from admiring the beautiful sunset stretching across Glennfeld's grounds and kissed her husband's cheek. "I've always believed the people of Savant capable of charting their own future. I'm confident our remaining delegates will reach a satisfactory resolution."

Uma set the book she'd been reading on the patio table. "Do you think Vivienne will stand by her father's beliefs? Or does she really have her own ideals?" Concern pinched her gaze.

Sabine absently played with the end of her plaited hair. "After everything we've heard today, I'd hate to think she'd choose Allard's intolerant and violent path."

"Indeed." Ziri reached for Sabine's hand and stroked it tenderly. "Hasn't this realm suffered enough death?"

With her head resting on Perry's shoulder, Jax admired the peaceful calm that had descended over the estate. "We certainly have seen enough of it, haven't we?"

Memories fluttered to the surface of her mind, and she remembered the first time she had been truly touched by death with the murder of her dear parents. How she had assumed the throne in the wake of such tragedy — an act that would ultimately come to alter the very fate of the realm.

Her parents weren't the only people she mourned. Over the years and throughout her adventures, she had lost many treasured allies. Names and faces appeared as she remembered such friends fondly. Henrick, Cornelius, Ezarath, Persephone, and so many others.

As if he sensed her melancholy thoughts, Perry hugged her close. "But we've also seen the wondrous side of the human spirit and how good is destined to slay evil."

His optimism banished the dark shadows clawing at her heart. Yes, she had lost a great deal, but she had gained so much more. Peace throughout her lands. Bonds mended between family. Friends who would follow her anywhere. A husband she truly and deeply loved. She had so much to celebrate. So much to hope for. "Thank the Virtues."

"I think we have *you* to thank, Jax." Perry tipped her chin up with his finger so their gazes locked. "You have been the beacon to light the way."

She appraised his handsome face. "You flatter me. I never would have been able to achieve half of it without you. *All* of you." She pulled away from Perry, making sure she had the attention of her dear companions. "Together, we have helped guide the realm to a better future. All because you have never left my side even during the most trying times."

Uma wiped away a stray tear, and Sabine's cheeks grew rosy.

"And until you send us away, we never will." Ziri's oath drew murmurs of agreement from the others.

"Even if you *did* try to send us away, we wouldn't listen." Uma chuckled.

Jax's throat tightened with emotion, but she was prevented from answering by the arrival of three somber figures joining them on the veranda.

"Jacqueline," Finral acknowledged her with a deep bow. "I know we have asked much of you already, but I'm afraid we have one more favor to request."

Beside him, Vivienne and Yves nodded their solemn agreement.

Jax steeled herself for their decision. "What service may I be?"

Vivienne glanced at her companions before clearing her throat. "We'd like you to instruct us how to roll out democratic elections across Savant."

"After talking things through," Yves began, "we realized the heart of our goals has always been the same—to give our people power to determine their own futures."

Finral held his head high. "It's time we end the fighting and allow just for that. As of this moment, Heartsworn and Lion's Bane are no more. By whom Savant will be ruled is for the people to choose." He took a deep breath. "I know it will not be easy to implement, but we hope that by joining the Unified Duchies, we may rely on your grace and assistance as we bring structure to our nation."

Jax wasn't sure she'd heard him correctly. "What was that? You wish to join the Unified Duchies?"

Finral nodded. "If our time with you has shown us anything, it is that you care about the realm more ardently than anyone we've ever met. We've seen the respect with which you treat others, the passion you feel toward justice, and the autonomy you give without question to those with a good heart." He reached for Vivienne's hand. "While Duke Savant sullied our nation, we must own up to ravaging her as well. We need help if we are to rebuild, and under your shepherding wing, we truly believe we can achieve a future where every Savantian thrives."

"You've helped us so much already." Vivienne looked at Jax earnestly. "I hope we can continue to rely on you as we navigate these challenges."

Jax studied the trio, almost afraid to believe them. Echoes of Finral and Yves's whispered conversation about war games haunted her memory. "Is this something you *all* want?" She stared pointedly at the Heartsworn deputy.

Yves cleared his throat, looking sheepish. "Indeed, Your Grace. I must confess I haven't been the most gracious guest to you, and for that, I apologize. I didn't always believe that democracy was the way, but I trusted Fin's instincts when we founded Heartsworn. As always, he proved to be right."

"I—I don't know what to say." Jax felt her heart fluttering beneath her palm. "Except that I will gladly welcome you to this new world we are building. Together, we will accomplish the future you envision."

Proud tears pricked at Jax's eyes as her hands took on a life of their own and applauded the revolutionary trio before her. Perry and her friends soon joined her, their cheers heralding a new, glorious era.

‡

Three weeks later

"May the Virtues bless your union."

Jax rose to her feet as the moving ceremony concluded, her palms aching from clapping so hard. Beside her, Perry whistled, and as Carriena and Bernard glided down the aisle, guests tossed white rose petals, showering them with love and affection.

"A beautiful service," Perry murmured in her ear.

Jax wiped the happy tears from her eyes. "And Carriena looks so stunning." She admired her longtime friend's shimmering ivory gown handstitched by the Saphirian royal tailor. Sabine and Uma had also outdone themselves with Carriena's sweeping updo and makeup, but the blissful expression on Carriena's face was the loveliest element of all.

As Jax and Perry followed the wedding procession leading from the palace throne room into the grand ballroom, they waved to all their dear friends and family who had traveled across the realm to attend the joyous event. With peace restored to all corners of the continent, the atmosphere radiated with promise, hope, and delight.

Music from a small orchestra swelled as the guests flooded the glittering hall, ready to dance the night away. While part of Jax yearned to dash right out onto the dance floor and wrap Carriena in a tight hug, she would visit with her dear friend once the initial swarm of well-wishers had subsided.

"Jacqueline!" her grandfather, Duke Mensina, boomed as she and Perry made their way toward his group. "You've pulled out all the stops for this event." He scooped her into a crushing embrace.

"Dearest Grand-Père, it's been too long." She kissed him tenderly on the cheek, ever so grateful that they had put aside their political differences long ago. "But you seem to be aging backward."

Her grandfather swatted away her compliment. "Now that the village premiers and Governor Rodanthe have taken over most of my workload, I find myself able to enjoy life much more."

Heartened to hear Mensina was thriving under its new democratic system, Jax greeted each of her aunts with a kiss. "I'm so happy you all could attend."

Seeing Amia, Adella, Adelaide, and Annette, her mother's four sisters, filled her with bittersweet joy. How she wished her parents were here in this moment, too. Although, as she glanced skyward, she suspected they were.

Annette, the oldest, cupped Jax's cheek in her palm. "I'm thrilled such an occasion brought us together." She leaned in closer, her smile beaming with pride. "Darian will be back soon. He went off in search of pickled eggs."

"Pickled eggs?" Jax's nose wrinkled just thinking about the pungent smell.

Annette giggled. "It's all I'm craving these days." She rested her hands on her growing belly. "I'm looking forward to your little cousin's arrival so I can eat normal foods again."

Jax and Perry shared knowing looks with one another and laughed. "I imagine so."

They chatted with the Mensina group but were soon pulled away to greet the other delegations in attendance. Duke Tsade Tandora, Duke Arthrinius Beautraud, and Duchess Rianne Zaltor enveloped the couple in warm hugs, as did Duke Langdon of Lysandeir.

"Have you seen my sister yet?" Langdon asked once he released Jax. "She's positively glowing."

An envious lump formed in Jax's throat, but she swallowed it.

"Are you and Lawrence prepared to be uncles?" She raised a teasing eyebrow as she studied the red-haired Duke.

Langdon's cheeks turned the color of his wild tresses. "As ready as one can be."

"Lysette will be a wonderful mother." Jax had learned the couple's happy news upon their return from Cetachi. She scanned the crowd for them now and found Jaquobie fawning over his pregnant wife.

Perry must have followed her gaze. "Although, if fatherhood mellows Jaquobie any more than being a husband has, he may very well melt onto the floor."

They spoke with Langdon a few minutes more before he excused himself to find his brother.

"I believe I see him by the beverages with his lovely fiancée." Jax pointed toward the couple. She was encouraged to see that Lawrence's engagement to Genevea Bahadur had not been thwarted by tragic events involving the young woman's disgraced mother.

As Langdon bid them goodbye, Jax spotted the Montivarius siblings, Charles and Giovanna, chatting with Hendrie and his date, Hilde. Giovanna, an acclaimed performer, would soon be singing a selection of songs Carriena had requested for the wedding reception. Charles, ever the doting brother and dedicated physician, handed her a glass of pale-yellow liquid while they chatted with Perry's private secretary and Uma's future sister-in-law. Whether the tonic was meant to calm Giovanna's nerves or help soothe her voice, Jax did not know. She only knew guests were in for a thrilling performance.

She and Perry waved at the happy group, and as Jax's hand came back down to her side, her stomach rumbled.

"Shall we find some refreshments?" Perry motioned with a chuckle, having somehow heard her yowling hunger over the din of the crowd.

They strolled along the perimeter of the dance area, smiling at their many friends floating gracefully across the floor. Sabine and Ziri captivated onlookers as the exquisite couple twirled around, although Jax found Uma and Yanis just as mesmerizing. Carriena's colleagues from the Academy were also among the dancers, with

Headmaster Daghir in his husband Casimeer's arms, looking more content than Jax had ever seen him. Her old friends, High Priestess Edrice and her husband, Ammon, beamed as they waltzed by. Jax looked forward to catching up with the couple and seeing how Edrice's sister Hazel was faring, as the Ancient Faith leader could not leave her Zaltorian temple to make the journey.

"Jax! Can you believe it? I'm married!"

Bounding out from the crowd, Carriena pounced on her, delight sparkling in her lilac eyes.

Jax giggled as she held her friend's hands. "How often did we talk about this day while attending school?"

Carriena's smile widened. "It's much different than we'd planned, though. I never thought I'd get to marry for love." Her gaze found her husband, Bernard, talking animatedly with her father, Thanasis Brunovaris.

Indeed, Carriena had been the Crown Princess of Isla DeLacqua before a change in circumstances had made Jax its sovereign.

"I'm so happy life turned out this way." She pulled Jax into a tight embrace. "Thank you, my dear sister."

Tears spilled from the corners of Jax's eyes at Carriena's moving remark. At the time, she had not relished upending her friend's destined path, but it brought joy to her heart to know Carriena had only love for her.

The beaming bride was soon pulled away by other guests, allowing Jax and Perry to resume their stroll around the room.

Near the refreshment table, they came upon Isaiah, Kaul, and Galahad Pettraud debating with which drink to begin the celebrations.

"This party is set to last into the wee hours of the morning," Perry reminded his three older brothers with a pleading look. "Please don't overindulge and embarrass me."

"We would never," Galahad guffawed, clapping Perry on the back while grabbing a glass of thick mead with his other hand. With a wink, he sauntered over to a group of single women who all eyed him appreciatively.

Isaiah shook his head in resignation at their elder brother's caddish behavior. "He'll now take that as a challenge."

Jax half-listened to the Pettraud brothers' conversation, content to let Perry enjoy this time with his siblings. She was beyond grateful they had remained close and hadn't been ripped apart by Elias's vicious actions. Instead, her gaze continued to take in the grand scene, her heart bursting at the sight of so many treasured companions.

For much of her childhood and early adult life, Jax had spent her time alone, sequestered away from the world with only the people assigned to her for company. Yet, since taking the throne, the walls around her heart had crumbled, and her world had grown tenfold, all thanks to her dearest confidantes who had stayed by her side through it all.

Her throat momentarily tightened as she realized one important person missing from the sea of faces. *I suppose I was asking too much of the Virtues for him to make it.*

As her amethyst gaze came to rest in the far corner of the ballroom, familiar, warm chocolate eyes locked on hers. Jax smiled, believing she had concocted the image of her oldest friend among the celebrants, but when the vision waved her over, she felt her jaw go slack with astonishment.

"Perry," she interrupted his conversation apologetically, "am I seeing things?" She indicated to the corner.

"Well, I'll be!" A wide smile broke out across Perry's face. "They made it!"

Leaving the Pettraud brothers confused in their wake, Jax and Perry dashed through the crowd as quickly as the partygoers would allow. Jax felt like her heart might burst, and only when George and Serafina stood several feet from them did her chest flood with relief.

"I can barely believe my eyes." Jax threw her arms around the couple, burying her tears in George's shoulder.

She felt warm hands on her back as he and Serafina both embraced her. "More like we're a sight for sore eyes." George chuckled as they parted.

Serafina tucked a strand of her auburn hair behind an ear, her cheeks pink. "I told George we should wash up and change before coming, but he worried we would miss the toast."

Jax only now registered that her friends stood before her in worn and ragged traveling clothes. "Giovanna is just getting ready to perform. Dinner won't be served for another hour or so. If you'd like to take some time to rest, please do." She assessed them with growing concern.

They had both lost a great deal of weight since she'd last seen them, and from the haunted looks in their eyes, they'd experienced their fair share of horror along the way. But she also noted how George's arm wrapped protectively around Serafina's waist and how her fingers absently stroked the back of his hand as if by habit. The telltale displays of their love for one another brought Jax such a deep, overwhelming happiness that she didn't quite have the proper words to describe it.

George glanced at Serafina. "If you haven't heard Giovanna Montivarius sing before, we really can't afford to miss it."

"But we look…" She motioned to their dirtied garb.

"Just one song. Then we'll change." He hugged her close.

Not wanting to sully their tender moment, Jax held her tongue, although her insides writhed with questions.

Perry, though, didn't hesitate. "We'll have plenty of time to discuss your adventures in the coming days, but please, I must know. Is Elias…?" His question hung uncomfortably in the air.

"His schemes will no longer hurt you, Perry." George's shoulders sagged with heavy regret. "Of that, you can be assured."

Jax stifled her shock. She had hoped they would be able to bring the traitor back alive to stand trial for his crimes. She regretted that her friends had been forced to deal with him themselves.

Serafina must have noted her concern. "His life was not taken by our hands, although we were present for his departure from this world." She shot a wary glance at George.

"I apologize we could not deliver him as requested," George spoke more to Perry than to Jax.

Jax slipped her hand into Perry's and lent her husband her silent support.

Perry's chin quivered, but he swallowed and bowed his head. "I understand. I am relieved he will trouble us no more."

Jax didn't quite believe him, and from their saddened looks, neither did George nor Serafina. But Perry straightened his shoulders and plastered on a cheerful expression. "With that nastiness out of the way, might I bring you both a platter of nibbles? You must be famished."

George and Serafina's immediate response was to protest, but Perry waved away their comments. "Allow me." As he ambled toward one of the banquet tables, Jax realized her husband likely needed a moment alone to compose himself over the news about his deceased brother.

To her friends, she shifted to a happier subject. "I can't tell you how good it is to see you." Jax grasped their hands, hoping to convey her sincerity.

George grimaced, and when Jax released him, he reached for the back of his neck. "You may regret that statement when you see who we've brought back with us."

At her puzzled expression, George motioned for Jax to follow them out into the shadows of the quiet hallway. Once they were situated in a private nook, he sighed. "I believe you've already met."

Jax opened her mouth to ask what in the Virtues he was talking about when a lithe figure stepped into view from behind a stone pillar. As recognition ignited within her, Jax gasped.

"Emeraude!" she sputtered, not quite believing who stood inside her castle. To George, she hissed, "What is *she* doing here?"

A sheepish look enveloped his face. "It's a long story."

"She comes in peace, Jax. You have my word." Serafina jumped to his rescue. She shot Emeraude an unreadable glance before adding, "She's a descendant of one of Allonious's comrades. She's pledged to help us protect the Favors."

Jax stilled at the mention of her ancestor. "You're one of the Forgotten Ones?" she asked, remembering the ominous title Serafina had been given by her father.

"*Favored* Ones," Serafina interjected with an enigmatic smile. "I think it fits our quest better."

Jax considered her companions, these mythical guardians of

strange relics.

"Might we speak somewhere a little more private?" Emeraude's lilting voice had a hard edge to it. "Who knows who may be watching?"

Although the hallway was empty except for the patrolling guards, Jax agreed. "We can use my study." As much as she wanted to encourage George and Serafina to rest and change, she needed to understand why the Grandmaster of the Shadow Brethren stood before her.

"What about Perry?" George tilted his head.

"I'll find him and be along shortly," she replied, giving him wordless instruction to escort the others to her study.

Jax hurried back into the ballroom in search of her husband. She tried to cement a happy, unaffected smile on her face so her friends and guests wouldn't worry.

Where are you, Perry?

She found him standing at one of the banquet tables heaped with food, only his plate was empty. He just stared at it, seemingly a million miles away.

"Darling?" She tenderly touched his elbow.

He shook himself from his stupor. "Sorry about that. I—I guess Elias's death hit me harder than I imagined."

"You have nothing to apologize for." She rubbed his back in reassurance. "Despite everything, he was your brother. I'm the one who's sorry it ended as it did."

He kissed her hand, his eyes glistening with gratitude. "Did George and Serafina head to their rooms to rest?" He glanced around, looking for their friends.

"Not exactly." She tugged him away from the food. "Come with me."

He wordlessly obeyed, and soon, they stepped inside the security of their shared study.

"So, what's going—Virtues!" Perry stopped short at the sight of Emeraude Odaire sitting casually in an armchair. He held his arm out, as if to shield Jax. "What is she doing here?" he snapped accusingly at George and Serafina.

"We can explain." Serafina rose from the sofa cushion, holding her hands up in a conciliatory manner.

Jax assessed the odd trio. "Please do."

Taking turns, Serafina and George shared the story of their incredible Savantian adventure, beginning with their visit to the Solis estate and ending with their escape from the Dundainee outpost.

"Emeraude is committed to helping us protect the Favors from the Dark Magus." Serafina's hand pressed against her chest, and Jax suspected the Kindheart medallion rested beneath her ragged tunic. "In return, we have offered to help her find the Bravesoul pendant."

"How can you trust her?" Perry ran an exasperated hand through his dark curls. "She's the Shadow Brethren!"

Serafina winced at the anger lacing his words.

"My word is my honor, Lord Pettraud," Emeraude murmured as she stretched her long limbs. "And the Bravesoul pendant is *mine*. I will not allow it to fall into the hands of this Dark Magus. Of that, you can be assured."

"Forgive me for *not* being assured," Perry grunted with a huff.

Jax stepped in to alleviate the tension. "Darling, these artifacts are not *our* concern. If Serafina and George are content with this partnership, then who are we to stop them?"

Perry looked at her, aghast. "You're the Duchess of nearly the entire bloody continent! Shouldn't you be concerned?"

She chuckled at his incredulous reaction. "From the way I see it, these Favors are relics of the past. My gaze is to the future." She paused and offered an apologetic smile to Serafina and George. "You have my support, always, but I don't feel it my place to involve myself in your affairs unless my aid is requested. I am not a Favored One, after all."

Serafina bowed her head. "Your understanding continually amazes me, Jax." When she lifted her gaze, her diamond-like eyes glimmered with emotion. "We know you have more pressing matters to attend to, given the encouraging news we've heard about Savant."

Jax smiled. "Yes, there is much to do in the realm." Her expression cooled. "But I cannot deny that this Dark Magus character worries me. What trouble might he bring if he fails in his quest to find these treasures?"

"Whatever trouble it may be, we can handle it," George pledged. "It's what happens if he *succeeds* that worries me."

"So, I take it you intend to scour the realm for the remaining two Favors?" Jax raised an intrigued eyebrow.

Serafina and Emeraude both nodded without hesitance. After a long moment, George did, too. "We plan to rest for a time," he admitted, "but then, yes, I suppose a new adventure will begin for us."

Jax detected something in her old friend's gaze, something that left her slightly unsettled. He wasn't telling her the entire truth. That much she knew. She had initially presumed this when he and Serafina mentioned old documents the Solis twins had shared with them. What was in those old documents, they hadn't revealed, but Jax got the feeling their contents greatly affected her companions and their choices.

However, George was allowed to keep his secrets, and she trusted him to do what was right. Jax knew he would never do anything to jeopardize her safety or the realm's…other than bringing her face-to-face with the Grandmaster of the Shadow Brethren, that is.

"Then you shall have access to whatever resources Saphire has at her disposal." Jax pocketed her concerns for now. Whatever they were hiding, George and Serafina had earned her trust many times over. When they wanted to tell her the full truth, they would.

At her generous offer, Serafina sagged with visible relief. "Thank you, Jax. Your support means a great deal." She gnawed nervously on her lip before asking, "I hope we aren't testing your good nature by asking to review the ducal archives?"

Jax had certainly not expected so bold of a request.

"We'd like to see everything we can about Allonious Xavier," George hurriedly explained. "Knowing what we know now, perhaps there's something among his personal records that might aid us."

Jax frowned. "The ducal archives…" A few years ago, she would have laughed at the thought of someone other than one of royal bloodline being allowed access to her family's private documents. However, times had changed, as had she. "As long as you're careful with the material, I see no issue granting such a request."

A smile broke out across Serafina's face, and she reached for George's hand. "Then our quest continues."

He stared down at her, his devotion evident in every inch of his face. "Our quest continues."

Emeraude yawned. "I was promised a bath, a good meal, and a warm bed." She eyed them with an annoyed glare. "Our quest can wait until then."

Jax couldn't believe that her former Captain of the Ducal Guard laughed at the Shadow Brethren Grandmaster's comment. *What strange fate the Virtues weave.*

"Why don't you two head to my suite?" George suggested as he placed a guiding hand on the small of Serafina's back. "I'll be along shortly."

Emeraude gave Jax a flourishing, if albeit mocking, bow before heading toward the doorway.

"Thank you, Jax." Serafina threw her arms around her in a grateful embrace before ushering Emeraude to follow her.

When the door snapped shut behind them, George sighed. "I know you have a million more questions, my friends. And I hope to be able to share the answers in time."

Perry met George's sincere gaze. "We will be here waiting."

Jax nodded, suddenly overwhelmed by a feeling of loss. George and Serafina had only just returned from their journey, yet it felt like she was bidding farewell to them rather than hello.

"Y-yes," she finally choked out. "For no matter where this new adventure takes you, you will always have a home with us here in Saphire. My dear, dear friend." She closed the distance between them, wrapping George tightly in her arms. "It's time to follow your heart," she whispered so that only he could hear.

She felt hot tears on the shoulder of her gown, and when she pulled away, George rubbed hastily at his eyes. "I don't know what I'm getting so emotional for. It's not like we'll be leaving today."

She laughed and helped wipe his rough cheeks. "No, but in pursuit of these Favors, you *are* leaving behind the life you once knew." She motioned absently to the regal study that surrounded them. "Closing one book and beginning another."

George held her gaze for a long moment. "I will be forever grateful to the Virtues to have met you, Jax. Both of you." He glanced meaningfully at Perry.

"It was all *your* doing, George Solomon, not the Virtues." Jax smiled. "Now, go wash yourself up. Carriena will have all our heads if you come to her wedding dinner looking like death warmed over."

George snorted and dipped his chin in teasing acquiescence. "Whatever you command, oh great illustrious Duchess."

Jax giggled at their longtime joke as he departed the study.

Perry came up behind her, pulling her back against his chest as he wrapped his arms around her. "The Grandmaster of the Shadow Brethren, partnered up with our dear Captain on some wild treasure hunt? You're really not going to insert yourself into *that* mystery?" His warm breath tickled her ear.

She leaned her head against him, nestling herself in the nook of his neck. "I won't deny I'm intrigued by these Virtuous Favors, but I meant what I said. They are a link to the realm's past. My sights are set on the future."

Her hands dropped to her belly, where new life, new hope, now grew. Master Vyanti had confirmed it for them only this morning. She and Perry had yet to share their long-awaited joyous news with everyone. There would be time for that later. For now, this precious little beginning was theirs to cherish.

"And what a future it will be." Perry kissed her temple and held her close, his hands resting atop hers. "Although if Carriena discovers we're missing out on her party, our future won't be a long one."

Laughing, Duchess Jacqueline Arienta Xavier and her husband strolled hand in hand toward the lively ballroom, sounds of the joyful celebration guiding their way. As she savored the happy moment, Jax welcomed the trials they would surely face as she and her beloved companions worked to make the realm a better place. No matter the uncertainties or challenges they might meet along the way, they would face them as they always did.

Together.

The End

While Duchess Jacqueline's story has drawn to a close,
more mystery and adventure await in

The Favored Ones

a new series coming to the Realm of Virtues

Until then, may the Virtues watch over you.

Acknowledgments

It's extraordinarily humbling to pen the final acknowledgments for the Court of Mystery series. So many people have influenced the life of Duchess Jacqueline's story that it's hard to narrow this dedication to a select few.

First, I must thank Sarah Wu for her editing expertise. She came into this series at *Innocence Imprisoned* and jumped wholeheartedly into the Realm of Virtues. I am so grateful to have found her, and I look forward to collaborating with her on future writing projects.

I never would have gotten this far without the guidance of Bettye Underwood. Bettye helped shape Jax's voice for much of this series, and I will cherish the wisdom and knowledge she shared with me.

Graphic designer Mihail Uvarov has been with the Duchess since the beginning. I am still astounded that this brave man asked to design the original cover for *Eternal Empire* while his homeland of Ukraine was under attack. His dedication to his craft and his country is truly inspiring, and he is continually in my thoughts.

I can't imagine where Jax and her friends would be without Melissa Green. Readers might be stunned to learn that Melissa is the reason several main characters made it to the conclusion of this series. That's right. Some of Jax's companions were not destined to survive or even exist. However, Melissa's breathtaking audiobook performances made me realize that I could not do away with them.

Thus, storylines had to be rewritten, and new characters introduced. Without Melissa giving life to this world, I would never have arrived at the plotline for **The Favored Ones**, either. Her influence has been truly that monumental.

I must thank my dedicated support system of readers who have taken this journey with me. I write these stories for you, and I hope Jax's tale leaves you filled with hope for a brighter future and content in the knowledge that good always triumphs over evil.

Finally, thank you to my husband, my parents, friends, and extended family, who have supported this dream throughout the years. I hope you are proud.

Author's Note

Writing "The End" hits differently this time around. After fourteen books, Duchess Jacqueline's time adventuring around the Realm of Virtues has drawn to a close. When Jax first walked into my life in 2017, I never dreamed this was where our path together would lead. I honestly thought *The Ducal Detective* novella would be a one-off experiment where I tested the waters of my story-telling abilities. Wow, I couldn't have been more wrong, could I? I am so incredibly grateful that readers pushed me for more. I'm grateful they wanted me to expand the Realm of Virtues, visit more duchies, meet new friends, and solve more mysteries. As much as I'm sad to write about Jax's final adventure, I'm overjoyed that my dear friend has found happiness and peace in her life. Virtues, she deserves a bit of rest. And she's definitely earned a reprieve from murder and mayhem, allowing her to focus on getting the realm in order.

Although *Eternal Empire* marks the conclusion of Duchess Jacqueline's crime-fighting exploits, I'm thrilled to reveal that it's not the end of our adventures within the Realm of Virtues. There's a whole continent to explore, after all, and readers will get the chance to return to Saphire in the future. George and Serafina have a challenging mission ahead of them, and in time, their story will be shared in a brand-new series called **The Favored Ones**. And as much as I would love to deliver this new adventure to you right now, I do need to take some time away from the Realm of Virtues and tackle other writing projects. For this series to be as enchanting as the Court of Mystery, I need to give myself some space to begin anew, and I hope you'll stay connected with me to keep apprised of future updates.

If you enjoyed *Eternal Empire*, please let me know on your favorite book review platform. Your comments and ratings make a world of difference. Thank you for all the kindness you've shown me so far. I appreciate it more than you could possibly know.

If you're eager for more adventures with Duchess Jacqueline, sign up for my **newsletter** at **www.saraheburr.com**. As a newsletter subscriber, you'll get immediate and exclusive access to my Realm of Virtues stories featuring fan-favorite characters. There's more of the Realm of Virtues to explore while waiting for George and Serafina's next adventure to take flight.

Again, thank you for joining Duchess Jacqueline and me on this unforgettable journey. Until we meet again, may the Virtues watch over you.

Sarah E. Burr Books

Glenmyre Whim Mysteries

You Can't Candle the Truth
Too Much to Candle
Flying Off the Candle

Book Blogger Mysteries

Over My Dead Blog
Dearly Deleted
Fatal Sign-Off

Trending Topic Mysteries

#FollowMe for Murder
#TagMe for Murder
DM Me for Murder
#Throwback for Murder

Court of Mystery

The Ducal Detective
A Feast Most Foul
A Voyage of Vengeance
A Summit in Shadow
Throne of Threats
Paradise Plagued
Burdened Bloodline
Sovereign Sieged
Crown of Chaos
Harrowed Heir
Ravaged Reign
Innocence Imprisoned
Ardent Ascension
Eternal Empire

www.saraheburr.com

About the Author

Sarah E. Burr has been dreaming of being Nancy Drew since her small-town days in Appleton, Maine—but when corporate America didn't deliver any mysteries, she started writing her own! Now an award-winning author, Sarah pens the Book Blogger Mysteries, Court of Mystery series, and the fan-favorite Trending Topic Mysteries and Glenmyre Whim Mysteries. Her cozy crafting caper, *You Can't Candle the Truth,* was a 2022 finalist for both the NGIBA and Silver Falchion awards, while *#TagMe for Murder* was a 2024 NGIBA finalist for Best Click Lit Fiction.

A proud Sisters in Crime member, Sarah also runs BookstaBundles, a content creation service for authors. She co-hosts *It's Bookish Time TV*, a cozy web channel full of fun author interviews, and blogs for *Writers Who Kill*.

When not plotting her next whodunit, Sarah sings show tunes, plays video games with her husband, and takes long walks with her adorable pup, Eevee. Want free short stories and exclusive updates? Join her newsletter here: https://bit.ly/saraheburrbookssignup.

9 798227 474957